# In the Shadows of Fate

## Rick Jurewicz

**DIRE HAND
PUBLISHING**

PO Box 2144, Indian River, Michigan 49749

Copyright © 2017 Rick Jurewicz
Cover Design Copyright © 2017 Rick Jurewicz

All rights reserved. This book or any portion thereof
may not be reproduced or used in any manner whatsoever
without the express written permission of the publisher
except for the use of brief quotations in a book review.

This is a work of fiction. Names, characters, businesses, places, events and
incidents are either the products of the author's imagination or used in a
fictitious manner. Any resemblance to actual persons, living or dead, or
actual events is purely coincidental.

ISBN: 0692938842
ISBN-13: 978-0692938843

For Mom,
Always encouraging my
wild imagination. My
true angel.

For my family,
with love
always.

# In the Shadows of Fate

A NOVEL

Rick Jurewicz

## PROLOGUE

The leaves cast their shadows dancing upon the grounds of the old Victorian style home, only minutes beyond the midnight hour. Radiant moonlight washed across the expanse of sky, exposing details in the darkness oft not seen by the wandering eye at that late hour of the evening. A subtle breeze snaked across the dense forest landscape. The incessant chirping of crickets, and the rattling of the still emerging foliage of the north wood trees, were the only sounds that could be heard in an otherwise serene late-spring night.

The month of June had already been unseasonably warm in the northern woodlands of Michigan, but the nights brought a chill that reminded you of where you were in the world. There were still a long many weeks out into the coming summer months to get the real sustaining heat that the season can bring, even to the often cooler Upper Peninsula area of the state.

A soft wind carried the scent of the estate gardens from the rear of the house up the hillside to the nostrils of the man sitting in the darkness, hiding away from the moon's brilliant sheen, as he looked down upon the once proud home not far away. He closed his eyes and breathed it in, only for a moment. The sweet aroma that so much time and work had been put into nurturing, year after year, by hardened hands. A labor of love and beauty, carried on for decades, since long before he had ever even set a foot on the property.

The grizzled man, who now looked well beyond his age of almost 50, thought it odd that the garden fragrance had found his nose over the far less pleasant stench of the gasoline that had been poured in abundance around the base of the old home down the hill. Two five-gallon cans, emptied and discarded near the front and back entrances of the house, and a third can that he had dragged along with him away from the house.

A trail of gas had been left behind on the rocky path the man had climbed up the hill. He was only a few feet from where the can had dropped its last drops, and for the past 20 minutes he sat in silence, his eyes lost in the entrancing sway of the shadows.

He smelled as if he hadn't bathed in quite some time, despite those kind folks that had offered him opportunities to do so in the good, little northern town. The residents had felt sorry for the man, but for the most part, he chose to keep to himself and not to cause a bother to anyone. Old man Sherman had offered him a bunk in a back room behind his farm and grain store, but instead the man would often find shelter from the elements in the pole building where Sherman kept his tractor and supplies. It was from the pole building that the man had taken the gasoline, over a three night period. He hauled each full can by hand to the dense brush up the hill from the home he now gazed down upon.

The man had tightly tied strong ropes from the handles

of the two main entrance doors of the home to the railings of the large porch that stretched across the entire length of the front and rear of the house. He knew that the fire would burn the ropes eventually, but hoped they would hold tight, for just long enough.

The pain echoed in his head every single night. He had to make it stop. He knew he could not take another night of it; the dreams, the voices that whispered through his every last thought. There was no distinction now between waking and sleeping. There was only the torment he carried that clawed at his heart and burned in his mind, a mind which grew more fragile with every minute that passed.

*It was right, this thing he must do. Yes...it has to be*, he would tell himself. This act of cleansing would free his soul from the pain and the anguish that ate at him from his insides. There was no other way.

His hand trembled as he raised a cigarette to his dry lips. His face had not been touched by a razor in years, but occasionally it occurred to him to trim down his unkempt beard, now looking as if it had only been a few weeks since his last shave. He flipped a scratched up old Zippo lighter open with his thumb and dragged the wheel down against the flint, sparking the flame that reddened the tip of the cigarette. He then flipped the lid back over the flame and put the lighter away in his pocket.

There was no doubt in his mind that he would be found, and he toyed with the thought of letting the flames take him away as well. But the courage to do so was not in the broken man. It may seem a cowardly thing, this thing that he must do, but it was a necessary one. He had kept telling himself this, and he believed it, although he did not know why he believed it. He had either gone mad, or he had been *chosen* to do this thing which he was about to do. Whichever it may be, in the end, fate would have its way with Daryl Grimes.

Grimes' hand, shaking with every drag of the Marlboro Red, found itself steady for the final draw of nicotine on that cool June night. The red tip glowed to reveal the reds and grays in his beard, and then with a sharp flick, he sent the still hot cigarette butt into the gasoline trail, instantly igniting the fumes. The flames blazed down to the front porch where the trail had started, and quickly spread around the entire bottom floor of the house. The weathered old wood of the home took to flame fast, and the chipping and flaking paint offered almost no protection from the fire.

Grimes picked up the last gas can and started walking on further up the hill into the forest lands. The winds began to pick up, accelerating the spread of the fire up the outside walls, and engulfing a large portion of the ground floor. But those winds also carried something that Grimes had not anticipated. He could hear, even from his far distance and over the crackling hiss and roar of the flames, the cries of a small child coming from the upper level of the home. He stopped, and his heart began to pound harder in his chest. His lips quivered and his hands began to shake.

Daryl Grimes dropped to his knees, letting the gas can fall to his side. With his hands to his face, he began to sob harder than any other time he had cried in his life before now. He lied down in a fetal position, slowly writhing and convulsing as the tears streamed across his face. With quivering lips he muttered, in almost no more than a whisper, the same desperate plea over and over, until he would speak words no more...

"Please my God, forgive me."

# CHAPTER ONE
*Nineteen Years Later*

Miranda woke up screaming, her dark blue t-shirt soaked in a cold sweat. She could feel her breathing beginning to labor as the hyperventilation set in. Clenching her fists in the sheets, she tried in vain to get a grip, but the pounding in her chest made it hard for her to give her breathing the concentration that was needed to slow herself down.

In the darkness, Miranda's door flew open to the silhouette of a young woman in a long t-shirt standing in the doorway.

"Miranda!" cried the voice from the doorway, and the figure quickly moved to the bed and held a hand on both of Miranda's shoulders, moving her face in close to Miranda's.

"Sweetie, you need to breathe. Come on. Short, deep breaths, just like before."

The girl moved her hands gently to Miranda's face, and started breathing the short breaths with her as she tried to calm her friend. Miranda started to get a hold of herself again, her face a mix of sweat and tears.

"That's it…you're doing fine," said the girl to Miranda as her breathing returned to a much calmer, steadier pace.

"Lydia," Miranda whispered.

"That's right...I'm here. You're okay. Just keep breathing," Lydia answered.

Miranda put her face into her hands for a moment, and tried to wipe the wetness from her cheeks. "What the hell is happening to me?"

"Another nightmare?" Lydia asked, already knowing the answer.

"It was the same nightmare...the same one from when I was a little girl... I keep having it over and over again..."

Lydia sat silently for a moment, giving Miranda a chance to compose herself a little bit more. Her concerns had been growing for some time now over the sudden and startling upheavals in the nights over the past several weeks. Each one seemed to intensify and were becoming far more frequent.

"Was it always like this when you were having them before...when you were a kid?" asked Lydia.

Miranda swung her legs out from under the sheets and put her feet on the floor. For that moment she seemed to be somewhere else, lost in the dark shadows of her subconscious. She was thinking about the dream again. She thought about how she had had it so many times when she was very young. The dream had always been the same. But now, there was something different.

She would always remember seeing herself in a large room of a very beautiful house. Solid oak walls with paintings of landscapes depicting gorgeous autumn scenes and rocky cliffs with spectacular waterfalls. The floor was the most memorable part of the room; white, pearlescent marble tiles stretching far across the entire span of the room. Then of course, there was the man playing at the large, white piano. At first, Miranda could not see his face, just as she hadn't been able to when she was younger. She walked slowly, closer and closer to the man who was always wearing an all white suit and had blonde hair that went just beyond his shoulders. With every step she took, and the closer she got, the man played faster and faster until finally she was upon him, standing by his side. Sitting atop the piano was a wooden box, intricately carved with designs that may have resembled small flowers, and it was about twice the size of an ordinary cigar box. She could never help but notice the box for only a moment in the dream. Her eyes would quickly move to the man's face as she stood there by his side, looking down upon him. She could see his side profile clearly; his face looked young and smooth, and his jaw was strong, yet it was what she could only describe as sympathetic. His eyes stayed shut as he played his fiery notes. As soon as her eyes met his face, his playing would stop with a final and furious slam upon the keys with his long, pale fingers.

Then, he would open his eyes. When Miranda was a child, the dream would end just before this part. But not any longer, which made all the difference in how the dream seemed to affect her so drastically now. When the man in white opened his eyes, there was only blackness. Deep, endless blackness. The man would then turn his emotionless and expressionless face towards Miranda, and she could feel the blackness of those dark eyes pierce her very soul, bringing on waves of helplessness and terror like nothing Miranda had ever felt.

That is when the episodes like tonight had started. The sweating. The screams. The humiliation of feeling helpless and scared in front of others. Miranda hated feeling weak in front of others. She hated feeling weak at all. It had been more than 10 years since she last had these dreams, but they were nothing like they were now. At first she thought it was the stress of everything that had been going on in her life lately. Holding down two jobs plus a full class load. Everything seemed to be finally catching up with her.

Miranda had taken on harder things than being a full-time student on a shoestring budget. She made the decision a long time ago that she needed to leave home and do things her own way. Now she was 22, more than four hours and hundreds of miles away from the small town where she had grown up, and she was doing exactly what she wanted to. She was making it on her own.

There had been bumps along the way, and more than a few changes to her college major and her overall curriculum over the last few years, but she was now well on her way to a sociology degree with a minor in journalism. Those who knew her thought that a sociology major was an odd and interesting choice for a girl like Miranda. Although she found the study of societies and culture exceptionally interesting, she herself was not always what one might say the most socially interactive of people. That wasn't to say that she was anti-social. She had friends and would go out for the occasional night on the town and attend all sorts of events around the city. Art shows were often a favorite of Miranda's, as well as public music performances, whether they be in the local parks or the late night clubs.

Much of the time though, Miranda would find herself either going alone to these kinds of events, or perhaps Lydia would go along with her. She was always very focused and serious about the things that she immersed herself in. There were times when people would just assume that she had a snobby side, which although was not the case, suited Miranda just fine. She was just as well off to do without people that were prepared to judge others without trying to really get to know what they were about, although she was well aware that she didn't often make that easy for people in the case of herself.

Lydia Snow was not the type of person to pass quick judgment on others, always choosing to be open to all of the unique differences that make up who people truly are. Miranda could tell this from the moment they met, and that was one of the reasons the two of them got along so well. This seemed to surprise others though, being that they came from very different backgrounds and had a very different sense of style and personality.

Lydia grew up in Cincinnati, raised in a well-to-do family of some stature in the circles that they ran in. But things like social status and wealth didn't matter to Lydia. She was a bookworm, always reading a textbook for her classes, or diving head first into whatever the latest popular novel series was; she admitted only to a few close friends her guilty pleasure of reading the latest undead romance series of the moment. But her truly greatest guilty pleasure, which was a significant clash to the things in Miranda's world that she had passion for, was her love of sports. She loved them all, watching and sometimes participating. She knew everything that was going on in college football at any particular moment. Lydia was a cute blonde girl with her hair almost always in a ponytail, slim and athletic, and she loved having on sweats and a t-shirt more than anything else over wearing frilly dresses or the latest fashions. She was, in appearance, a contrast in almost every way to Miranda.

Miranda's hair was naturally jet black and had some curl in it, which quite often would leave it wild and untamed looking when Miranda was in a hurry on her way out the door and had barely run a brush through it. She often preferred to wear slim-fitting faded denim pants and was herself on more casual days, a plain t-shirt girl. She would often be seen wearing band shirts of obscure music groups from the 1970s through the 1990s.

Joy Division, The Cure, Concrete Blonde and Jane's Addiction were some of her favorites. In her left ear, she wore a small Eye of Horus silver earring, and a black, pearl-like stud in the upper part of her ear. In her right ear were three small silver hoops. She wore little makeup most of the time, but she had a natural glow about her face that didn't require a lot of work, which secretly made Lydia crazy at times. Even though Lydia had no problem stepping out in her sweats to run errands, she always had to put some sort of a face on first.

Miranda's favorite accessory was her leather motorcycle jacket. It had been a gift from a former boyfriend back in high school, and through the years of beatings it had taken back in her wilder days, it well earned the worn and weathered character it now had. Although it was a men's leather jacket, it had been small on her boyfriend, but even running a little large for her small frame, it looked great on her.

Despite the differences in style, background and attitude between Miranda and Lydia, the one thing that helped create a deep respect and appreciation for one another was their common determination to go out into the world and make it on their own. Lydia *could* have help from her parents at any time, but chose to do things her way, and was willing to work hard to make it happen. She would still receive cards with cash from time to time from home; much of that was put into donation jars at soup kitchens and other various charities. She appreciated what they were trying to do for her, but she felt that if she was willing to work hard to take care of herself, she liked to consider those who couldn't work and could really use a little extra help.

"Miranda?" Lydia said softly, as Miranda finally shook off her momentary lapse of awareness of the world around her.

"I'm sorry. I don't know where I was. I think I am

finally going off the deep end," said Miranda.

Lydia smiled and put an arm around Miranda's shoulders.

"Hey. Welcome to the rest of the world. You're gonna be all right. Everybody has shit get to them every once in a while. Maybe going home and getting some down time is what you need," said Lydia.

Miranda put a hand to her forehead when Lydia said the word.

"Home," she said quietly to herself, seeming to again forget Lydia was right there listening.

"You make it sound like you are going to serve a prison sentence. I've met your parents, and they seem like nice enough people. It's not my business or anything, but did something bad happen between you guys?" asked Lydia.

"No. No, it's nothing like that. I just…I don't know. I feel like an alien or something when I am with them the last few years. They always mean well, and I know that. I just feel so out of place when I am there anymore," said Miranda.

"That's just how it feels when you've been gone for so long," said Lydia. "You are your own person, making your own way in the world. Going home again is never an easy thing."

Miranda let out a little laugh and a smile. "Yeah. Especially to Native Springs, Michigan! Population…I don't even know. It's small though, that's for sure. Maybe they've got a good coffee shop with Wi-Fi by now. At least there I could feel a little more at home."

"Native Springs," Lydia smiled. "Every time I hear that town's name I start to think you lived in a giant bottle of water."

"I know, right!" laughed Miranda.

There was an awkward pause between the two of them

after the short moment of laughter.

Lydia broke the silence.

"I think this might be good for you. You need to talk to someone and get this stuff with the nightmares figured out. There has to be something…this kind of stuff can make people go crazy."

"That's reassuring," Miranda responded.

"I'm not saying I think you'll go crazy or anything," said Lydia. "I'm just saying that I care about you, and that I am really hoping that whatever is happening with you, you can maybe take a few steps back and see whatever you need to see to help you figure this out."

Miranda sat stoically, and then looked up at Lydia. "Thank you, really. I think you are the only real friend that I have sometimes."

"It might seem like we may be from two different planets," Lydia said, "But I think we share a moon or two!"

"Does that even make any sense?" asked Miranda, smiling.

Lydia laughed. "I am gonna head back to bed. I've got a *Modern Perspectives of Ancient Religious Practices* test that I will probably bomb anyway, but I will at least give it a try. It's early, so I will probably be gone before you get up, so give me one more hug before you go."

Miranda got up and they gave each other their goodbye hug.

"You know," Miranda said, "If you need to find another roommate, I understand. It's going to be tight without my half of the rent."

"Bullshit," blurted Lydia. "This room will be waiting for you when you decide you are ready to come home. If I have to actually keep some of that cash mom and dad send my way, then that is what I will do. Just worry about yourself right now."

Miranda felt a little warmth wash over her when Lydia called this her home. It made her feel like even though she had to leave for a while, there was still a place of her own to come back to.

"Thanks, Lyd," Miranda said.

"Anytime, Miri," Lydia said with a smile. "Night."

"Hey," Miranda interrupted as Lydia was about to close the door behind her. "Leave the door open, okay?"

"Sure," said Lydia. "No problem. I'll leave mine open too."

Miranda got back into bed and pulled her sheets over her once more. She didn't think that she would get anymore sleep that night, but she had to try. She had a four hour drive ahead of her in the morning, and she hadn't packed anything yet. Not that it was going to be hard to pack. Most of everything she had could be packed into a large trunk that she lived out of the first year and three apartments that she had when she first came to town. She liked to keep things light and simple. At least that was one simple part of her life. She couldn't tell what she had more apprehension about at that point, just before she slipped back into sleep's grasp. Was it the fear of the nightmare returning again in that same night? Or, was it simply the thought of going home? 'Just try to sleep,' she told herself. Tomorrow, like many other long days and longer nights, coffee would be her best friend once more.

Interstate 75 was relatively barren in the northbound lanes that Thursday morning. Miranda had some help from Michael, the neighbor who lived in the apartment below her and Lydia, with loading her large trunk into the cargo area of her 2009 Pontiac Vibe. The car was a gift from her parents last year after the junker '89 Buick she had been driving for some time rolled its last miles before the engine seized beyond repair. At the time, her options were very limited. She did need a vehicle, and she thought that it would allow her parents the chance to feel like they were helping (which they really were of course), being that she was always so determined to go it all on her own.

She made a quick stop at *Feast'n'Baristas*, her favorite coffee shop just off campus, to get some of the best caffeinated fuel around before she headed up the road. Donatello, a six-foot-four-inch Jamaican barista, who Miranda had gotten to know quite well over the last several months, was working at the counter.

"ME-ran-dah! Looking beautiful as always this fine morning!" Donatello started, as he always did, with his own special brand of charm. He set one of the house latte mugs on the counter. "Double shot espresso café mocha, no whipped cream?"

"To go, today, Donny. I am going to be out of town for a while," Miranda said with disappointment in her tone.

"Well, then this one is on me. No charge. You just make sure to not be gone too long. This place needs your smile!" Donatello said to her with his large, toothy grin.

Miranda smiled back. "You know that I don't like to smile."

"Oh, I know. But when you do, it makes the rest of us feel like anything is possible!" he said with a sarcastic, yet playfully friendly retort.

Miranda gave him a quick hug across the counter, took her café mocha and headed down the road.

In mid-October in Michigan, the weather can be almost

anything. Miranda had driven through snow storms in a few rare occasions that time of year with her parents when she was younger, and more recently had been riding around in a t-shirt with the windows all the way down. Luckily, today was in between those two extremes, but leaning more towards the warmer side. The windows stayed up, but it was bright, sunny and dry, with few rogue clouds in the sky.

    The coffee had been gone for an hour now, and she was dreading having to stop and get gas station coffee or machine mixed cappuccino. Miranda's iPod was on top of her leather jacket in the passenger seat. She had been listening to the soundtrack to the Rocky Horror Picture Show, which she always had fun listening to, especially this time of year. She had actually gone to see both a live performance of the show as well as the movie during one of the interactive shadow cast shows with her friends Crystal and Ryan. Miranda didn't get into dressing for those occasions, but those two almost always went as Magenta and Riff Raff. It was probably their favorite thing in the world to do.

    The *Time Warp* started to play through the speakers, which was ironic because she had just seen a bright green sign on the side of the road with the words "NATIVE SPRINGS - 52" on it. She sometimes felt like heading back home meant traveling backwards in time to a place that somehow got left 15-20 years behind the rest of the world. The town had only gotten its first fast food restaurants in the last 12 years. That may have been a step towards a more modern feel, but to Miranda, it didn't do anything to help its overall identity. Native Springs for years and years still carried a small town rustic appeal. The lakes surrounding it are very beautiful and draw every sort of sportsman, from fishermen to swimmers, boaters and skiers.

Outside of the town itself are miles and miles of state managed forests for hunters, hikers, and wildlife enthusiasts. But these days, even with the vast natural resources, the advent of fast food and the struggle to put sewers in the town as ways to both protect the watershed and promote economic growth had tainted, in Miranda's eyes, the quaint, small town feel. Even though she felt she had to escape to a larger, more steel and concrete based environment in the world, she had a special place in her heart for the cozy comfort of the town she knew as a young child. Now, it was a place trapped between two distant worlds, as it was destined to be eventually, being right off the main interstate going straight through the middle of Michigan's northern Lower Peninsula.

There was nothing overly exciting about the last several miles before her freeway exit. The colors of the trees farther south off the interstate were far more vivid and lustrous than they were around this area. Some golden browns and yellows, with a few occasional oranges and reds were all that was left to see, while many trees had already lost most of their leaves. This far north, there had already been a couple hard frost mornings, and usually on a day after an evening hard frost, you can sit quietly under the trees in your yard and watch a steady stream of leaves fall from the trees for hours. That was one of the things that Miranda would think about sometimes when things seemed to pile up too high on her plate in the big city. She would sometimes just sit quietly in her room and close her eyes and try to imagine sitting in her family's yard as the leaves slowly fell from above and landed around her and upon her. She could almost see herself running around in the backyard under the tall oak and maple trees, trying to catch the leaves as they fell.

She found herself daydreaming, and almost missing her

exit ramp. Another unsettling feeling that brought her back to reality was the fact that she wasn't returning to her childhood home. Her parents had closed on the sale of the home back in early June, and they moved five miles to the other side of town. The two story home they had for years was more room than they needed and getting very expensive to heat in the recent harsh winters, so they bought a few acres outside of town in a smaller subdivision and put a modular home on a full basement. Her dad said it would be cheaper to heat, and he could build a workshop and hobby room down in the basement over time, which Miranda quickly caught on to the idea that this was going to be a long work in progress.

Miranda's return home proved to be a logistical problem as well. While her parents didn't necessarily need as much space, and could easily accommodate the rare visit home from the prodigal daughter, they weren't quite prepared for what possibly could be a longer term stay. The upstairs had three bedrooms; one occupied by Miranda's parents, another by her 17-year-old brother Steven- who was not about to share a room with his older sister- and the third being used as both an office for her father and a craft room for her mother. The basement was one large, open room full of boxed things that, several months after being moved into the house, still needed to be gone through, put away or thrown away.

Miranda volunteered to take the basement without a second thought. All she needed was a little space; maybe throw up a few sheets as walls and a cot or mattress for a bed. It would be perfect for now, and even better, it would give her a little more of a space barrier between her and her family. She loved her family, but she had been in her own space for so long now that she needed a place of refuge, especially in this new and unfamiliar dwelling.

It didn't take long to find the new house. In a small town like this, you are familiar with almost all of the layout of the land, and Miranda had had friends that used to live in the Sherwood Trail subdivision. It was about a one mile loop off the main highway that still had many undeveloped land parcels. She drove along until she saw the sign hanging in front of the blue modular home.

The sign read "Stratton" in large letters on top. In small letters below the larger name it read "Robert, Lorri, Miranda & Steven".

The driveway was still only gravel. Miranda thought she remembered her father saying that a garage and paved driveway would come next year. That prompted her to think that the basement was going to be filled even more with miscellaneous junk than she originally anticipated. But it was okay. As long as she got her personal space, she was fine with it. She pulled into the drive, and already saw her mother's silhouette through the larger front window looking out into the yard.

The front door opened, and Steven was the first out to greet his sister as she stepped out of the car. His brown hair was much lighter than hers, but longer now than the last time she had seen him back around Christmas when she came home for a short two day visit.

"Sissy!" Steven said with a silly tone in his voice. He had always called her 'Sissy' when they were younger.

"Oh, my bouncing, baby brother!" she said back, as she hugged him, and didn't notice until that moment that her 'little' brother was now a few inches taller than she was. She wasn't short at all, being five-foot-nine, but he had to be at least six-foot-one or even taller now. Her mother came to the door, and Miranda could see, even through her smile, the concern in her eyes.

Miranda walked up to her mother as Steven proceeded to grab the trunk out of the back of her car.

"Hey mom," she said, trying to keep a smile on her face.

Her mother came down off the porch and put her arms around her daughter.

"I've missed you, baby girl," Lorri Stratton said to her daughter. "I'm so glad you're home."

"I've missed you too," she told her mother, feeling a little guilty. It was true that even though she had missed her mother, she didn't think that this was going to feel like her idea of home.

"Steven can give you the tour of the house. I would, but I want to get dinner finished before your father gets home from work. We've got something set up for you in the basement. Your brother can help you take your trunk downstairs."

Lorri retreated back into her kitchen, and Steven led Miranda to the stairs descending into the basement.

Miranda could smell sawdust as she followed Steven down the stairs. She could feel her anxiety jump up a few notches as she stepped downward into the unknown.

"It sucks you have to stay down here. Dad installed a de-humidifier just the other day," said Steven. "Not that it was all that bad to begin with, but he didn't want to take any chances with dampness or mold or anything."

Mold. Great.

She soon saw what the sawdust was all about, and against her will, a little smile did come to her lips.

In the far corner of the basement, there was a room. It was a room with real walls; not curtains or old sheets.

Steven caught a glimpse of her momentary grin. "Dad

had me down here the last three days working on this with him. He said he didn't want you to feel any less at home than the rest of us. It's only temporary, until he finishes the basement, but…"

"But it's yours for as long as you need it to be." The voice from behind startled Steven, but Miranda only felt warmth in the sound of her father's voice. They had not heard him come down the stairs, but even the tough girl in Miranda had a soft spot for the sight and sound of her father. Her mother had always been the nurturing parent, the one who would mostly take care of feeding them, getting them ready for school, and making sure they did their homework. But as she got older, it was her father that was the encouraging one. It was him that first told her she could do anything in this world; she just had to believe in herself. It was also her father that told her that if she felt she needed to go far away from this place, then that is exactly what she should do, much to the chagrin of her mother.

Miranda walked over to her dad and gave him a big, long hug. "Thank you Dad. It's perfect."

"Did you check it out inside yet?" her father asked.

"She didn't get that far yet," said Steven. His grin widened.

"Well, it's not much," Robert said. "But I think you of all people will make it work for you."

Miranda stepped into the room that she would be staying in for an undetermined duration. Although there was no door on it yet, there was a thick curtain over the door opening, which was fine considering that she had expected the walls to be made of similar material. Inside the room was a twin bed to the left, with an end table next to the bed and a large, old antique lamp lit up on top of the end table. There was also a small desk and chair, and a short dresser that she could use for both storage and place her trunk upon if she chose to. It was only then that she noticed the walls of this little makeshift room had been wallpapered with all of the posters that she had left up in her room from the old house. Nine Inch Nails, Soul Asylum…much of it she didn't listen to so often anymore, but it didn't matter. This really was starting to feel like a home away from home.

Robert broke the silence. "We're gonna let you get settled in. Come up for dinner whenever you are ready. Your mom has lasagna waiting for you. Welcome home, Miranda."

Sleep never seemed to come easy for Miranda anymore, and the mornings always came far too soon. She felt that she hadn't slept any better, or any worse, than she slept in her bed back at her apartment with Lydia. Steven had left for school, and her father was up far before anyone else had awakened to head to his auto body shop, but Miranda had not noticed either one leave. It wasn't until her mother called down the stairs to let her know that she had some errands to run that Miranda, in a half daze, realized she was alone in the house.

In only her black tank top and underwear, Miranda climbed up the stairs in search of morning nourishment. The cupboards were full of sugary cereals only; she had hoped, although knew it would most likely be in vain, for shredded wheat or maybe some oatmeal. She opted for a bagel with cream cheese. The coffee pot was still on, and even though it wasn't the deliciousness of the coffee from the café back home, she did appreciate the fresh ground blends her mother would find at the local grocery store.

All that was left to do this morning was ponder and shower. Shower was easy, and badly needed, but the pondering came with a little more thought and complication. All her parents really knew about her coming home was that she was starting to fall behind in some of her school responsibilities. She didn't tell them about the nightmares. She remembered telling them about the first dream when she was a little girl, but only in passing, as it didn't seem like such a big deal at the time. They didn't come with the newfound intensity that they brought with them now. A realization came to her that she really didn't have much of a plan at all in what she was going to do when she got here. All she knew for sure was she felt that something inside was telling her she needed to come home. And now, all she could do was to take it one step at a time. Maybe she would look up some old friends and see if they were still in town?

Right. That didn't seem likely at all, she thought. It wasn't like she even really wanted to be here, and seeking "old friends" to her somehow seemed like adding insult to injury. Return home with your tail tucked between your legs in defeat, and then parade yourself around in front of everyone you snubbed your nose at just a few short years before. No, Miranda decided to stick with the original plan, as loose as it may be; one step at a time.

The shower felt good, but like her sleep, was unexpectedly cut short. She heard a banging at the front door, and thought perhaps it was her mother with an arm full of groceries waiting for her to hurry up and open the door for her. She quickly dried her hair and wrapped a towel around herself as the banging came again.

"I'll be right there Mom!" Miranda yelled, and hurried to the door. As she opened the door wide, a man in a blue uniform stood in the doorway in front of her, and at that moment both of their eyes widened in surprise. Miranda closed the door halfway as to not feel so exposed in front of the stranger, who she at first had not even noticed was holding a box in both of his hands.

"Uh…good morning," said the man, with an awkward pause. "Sorry if I caught you at a bad time. I just needed a signature. I couldn't just leave it on the front step without a signature."

"It's fine. I can sign for it."

The man handed her the box and she placed it on the chair beside the front door, and turned back to him to sign her name on the electronic tablet that he had strapped to his leg.

"Thank you! You have a wonderful day!" he said with a huge smile, and she knew full well that she had probably just made his whole day.

She closed the door and started back to the bathroom before she was struck with a sense of curiosity as to what someone may have had delivered. Was Mom playing the Home Shopping Network game again, or perhaps ordering new quilting materials from eBay? New video games for Steven? She peeked at the label and was immediately shocked as to what the address read:

Miranda Stratton
4319 Sherwood Trail
Native Springs, Michigan


Miranda picked up the box once more and took it to the dining room table. There was a lot of tape on the box, so she found the junk drawer in the kitchen and pulled out a pair of orange handled office scissors. Her only guess was that maybe she had left something important behind that Lydia had overnighted to her, but there was no return address on the package label. Cutting away the packaging tape she pulled the flaps open, and with what she saw that moment she was overtaken by a feeling as if all of her breath had just left her body at once. Her hand came to her mouth as her sharp blue eyes kept their gaze on the object sitting in the box in front of her.

      Inside of the cardboard packaging box was another box, slightly smaller in size than the one it was shipped in. Made of dark wood and intricately carved with small, flower like designs throughout, it was roughly the size of a small attaché case or an oversized cigar box. Miranda sat slowly down into the chair by her side as her mind began to focus and comprehend the fact that the same box that she had been dreaming about for nearly 18 years was sitting before her, delivered right to her very hands.

## CHAPTER TWO

Miranda sat for several minutes in the kitchen just staring at the box. The sound of a car pulling into the driveway snapped her out of the dreamlike daze she had fallen into. She took the box inside its packaging and went downstairs into her room in the basement, broke down the cardboard box, and placed the wooden box beneath her duffel bag from inside of the trunk.

"Miranda, could you give me a hand?" Lorri's voice called out from upstairs.

"Just a second mom, I am getting dressed!" Miranda called back to her.

"No wonder you're slipping behind in classes if you are sleeping in this late!" Lorri called back, trying and failing in an attempt at humor.

Miranda came up in jeans and a t-shirt and took the two grocery bags her mother had in her arms from her second trip through the door from the car. She placed them on the table, and picked up the scissors that she had left out and put them back in the drawer as her mother went out to get the last bag of groceries.

"You don't have to try and figure out where everything

goes just yet," said Lorri on her way back inside. "I am still trying to figure out what works best where."

"I put the cold stuff away already," Miranda responded, trying not to show her anxiousness. "I am going to go and lie down for a little while. I have a headache...I don't know if it's from the drive yesterday, or just not getting enough sleep."

Lorri sighed and pursed her lips. "I was hoping we would get a chance to sit down and catch up a bit. I'm worried about you, Miranda. I know how hard this is for you. Coming home like this. Ever since you were very young you seemed like you were like a little bird in a cage, waiting for that door to open so you could fly out and never look back. When you did, I was sad. But I have always been so proud of you. I would just like the chance to get to know you again."

"I know, mom," she said, relieving herself of some of the tension she was feeling. "I just need some time to catch up with myself here. We can talk later this afternoon."

"Alright. You take your time. Whatever you need. I'm always here for you."

Lorri kissed her daughter on the forehead, and Miranda went back down the stairs and into her room. She drew the curtain closed, and pulled the box back out from under her suitcase.

Holding the box in her hands seemed surreal to her. It almost felt as if the immaterial had just become material, which didn't seem rational to Miranda. She prided herself in her sense of rational thought, especially when it came to trying to understand the unknown, mysterious or even supernatural. She kept an open mind to all things, but chose to look at things with keen scrutiny. This, holding this box in her hands at that moment, didn't feel rational on several levels.

The box was heavy for its size, but she didn't know yet

if it was just the weight of the box itself, or of the contents inside. She lifted the lid, and the box was lined with a deep hunter green felt, both in the compartment of the box and the underside of the lid. The only thing that sat inside the box was a VHS-C videocassette. Miranda recognized the type of tape it was because her parents had a video camera like that when she was a child. Many home movies had been made with that handy little camera. There was a plain label on the tape with the handwritten words "M. GALE – 3 years".

Miranda crossed the basement and stopped near the bottom of the stairs to turn the basement lights on. She listened for a moment to her mother busily moving about in the kitchen, probably still trying to arrange the groceries in a way that pleased her. She was very particular about her sense of order, and Miranda had no doubt that even after a few months, she still wasn't completely satisfied with the new kitchen.

The boxes were everywhere in the basement, many stacked against the walls, some in seemingly random piles around the room. But she knew that the things her mother deemed more important, such as personal keepsakes, family photo albums and home movies, would be kept in a place on top of other things for their safety, and most likely close to the stairs to be arranged at a later time. These are what Miranda was looking for, and surprisingly, they were easier to find than Miranda had anticipated. Three boxes sitting on top of milk crates just beneath the stairs.

The top box was all photo albums and scrapbooks her mother had made over the years of Miranda and Steven growing up. She found herself distracted for just a moment looking at the scrapbook pictures of the day they had brought Steven home from the hospital; his big sister holding him while sitting in a large recliner in the old house. She put it aside, and moved on to the next box.

This box had several VHS and VHS-C tapes of old home movies, "Miranda's 5th birthday", "Stevie's First Christmas", and so on. Packed alongside of the tapes was the old nylon video camera case. Miranda took the case from the box, turned the lights back off in the basement, and returned to her room. These cameras were some of the first to have a flip out screen to view and review what you filmed, so even though she didn't have a television to watch in her room, she could watch the tape right on the camera screen to see what was on it.

The camera battery was dead, but luckily all of the original components were still with the camera, including the wall plug in power cord. She slipped the tape into the camera, and carefully pressed play.

At first, only blue popped up on the screen, which made Miranda feel a slight jolt of panic that she would find nothing on the tape. Then, a date popped up in the lower right corner that read "6/12/1993". On the screen she saw a dark haired toddler wearing a white dress, and a woman with equally dark hair holding the hands of the little girl overtop of her head as she walked towards the camera. Miranda realized that the volume was turned down, and quickly turned it up. A woman's voice came from behind the camera.

"Hey there little girl! Are you dancing with your mommy?" said the voice.

"Yes she certainly is," said the child's mother as she held the young girls hands, moving steadily closer to the camera now.

Miranda could hear piano music in the background. She watched the little girl's face light up when she looked up at her mother, whose face could not clearly be seen on the tape because the long and dark curls of her hair obscured the view.

# In the Shadows of Fate

The woman was always looking down at her daughter.

Then a realization occurred to Miranda that there was something familiar to her about what she was seeing. She backed up the tape to the beginning and watched it again, and then again.

The video itself was short, but its content spoke volumes. The room that this little girl was walking in towards the camera, with its white marble tiles and oak trim along the background walls, was definitely the room that was in her dream, just as the box the tape had arrived in was certainly the same one from the dream. Miranda was seeing this film from the opposite direction that she saw it in the dream. But what shook her far more was the fact that she somehow knew that *she* was the little girl on the tape. The woman that had been called the girls mother on the tape did not look anything like the mother she knew moving about upstairs in the rooms above.

She went back across the basement and brought the box of photo albums to her room. As she dug through the pictures for the next hour, she realized that she could not find any pictures of her before she was four years old. No baby pictures. No scrapbook of her coming home from the hospital. After age 4, there were tons of pictures from every year, up through high school graduation and the day she left Native Springs for college. 'Miranda – First Day of Kindergarten'. 'Miranda – Fourth Grade Camping Trip'.

She replaced the albums and photos in the box and returned the boxes to their place under the stairs, and spent the next couple of hours lying in her bed staring at the ceiling, which was basically the exposed floor joists of the main level of the house.

If she thought she was coming home to get her head

back in the game, and to find some peace of mind, this wasn't nearly what she thought would get her to that place. There were a few things that had become clear to her, even without talking to her parents. First, although the people that she had always loved and looked up to that had raised her and cared for her, her parents in the truest sense of the word, were not where she originally came from. And even though her rational mind fought against this thinking, she felt that the arrival of this box and tape the day after she had come home from being away from Native Springs for almost a year was no coincidence. Whatever it was that was haunting her mind and manifesting in her dreams was somehow connected to the arrival of this new revelation, and even if these dreams were somehow repressed memories related to something from her past, this was something that she still could not just let go of. She needed answers as to why these dreams have started again, and suddenly intensified, and those answers may lie only in a place that existed before her earliest memories. Where was this place on the tape and in her dreams? Who sent her these things and knew when she would be coming home? The only clue she had as to where to begin was written on the label of the tape. "M. Gale – 3 years".

Miranda's head was swimming with thoughts and questions. Had there been some reason why her parents had never told her that she had been adopted? For a moment, the thought had crossed her mind that there may have been something shady or deceitful about how she came to be with her parents, and maybe that was why it was never revealed, but she quickly dismissed this thought. Her parents were as straight-laced as they come, and she knew there was no way they could involve themselves in something like that.

After considering the whole of the situation, Miranda felt it best at this point to keep everything to herself for the time being. Not knowing the truth had not made any difference in her life, at least until now, and they must have had their reasons for never revealing it to her. But she also knew that they wouldn't understand what to make of the dreams and the mysterious arrival of the box, not to mention the timing involved with both. She needed to slip out of the house to both clear her head and start digging to see what she could come up with on her own.

Lorri was watering plants in the living room when Miranda came upstairs with a messenger bag slung over her shoulder.

"I'm going to go into town and see if anything has changed since the last time I was here," Miranda told her mother.

"Did you want me to come along? Not that much changes around here very fast, anyhow," said Lorri.

"No, it's alright. I shouldn't be too long. I'll be back before dinner," she said.

Lorri was anxious to sit and talk to her daughter. Her worry had been evident in her face since Miranda arrived home the day before. But she knew Miranda was an independent spirit and moved at her own speed, so she didn't want to put too much pressure on her to talk, fearing that it might push her away. Lorri just forced a smile instead of saying too much.

"Okay. Well, have fun. I did forget to pick up coffee creamer at the store, so if you remember, could you stop and pick up a bottle?" Lorri asked.

"Yeah, I will," said Miranda, as she moved her way through the front door. "Is there anywhere in town that has free Wi-Fi?"

"I think the restaurant down by the river has it. I forget what the place is called now. It's changed hands so many times in the last few years. I think it might be called the Creek Ridge Tavern and Restaurant now, or something like that. And, of course, there's Burger King."

"I'll try the restaurant. The child play areas in fast food places frighten me!" said Miranda.

Out the door she went, and just over five minutes later she was in the parking lot of the Creek Ridge Tavern. The place was a very casual, family oriented eatery on one side. A separate room definitely had a bar's appeal, with beer mirrors, a pool table, gaming pull tab lottery machines and a large screen television on the wall, which no doubt was either always tuned to whatever the sporting event of the moment was, or CNN the rest of the time.

The smell of fresh, home cooked breakfast was still in the air, but it started to mingle with the smell of burgers on the grill. She had come in just before the lunch rush started, and found herself a table in a far corner of the main family dining room near a large stone fireplace. The atmosphere here was pleasant and rustic, with large dark stained log beams high above, braced beneath a vaulted ceiling. The walls were all log sided, with framed prints of deer, bear, and waterfowl scenes - all creatures native to the northern parts of Michigan. She had been here before when it was a pizza place in years past with her family, but it was nowhere near as nice looking as it was now.

She placed her laptop on the table as the waitress brought her a cup of fresh brewed hot coffee that she had just ordered.

"Be anything else?" asked the young girl, notepad in hand, pager clipped to her waist alongside the pale blue Creek

Ridge Tavern t-shirt, worn by all of the floor staff members.

"No, thank you. I'm fine."

"Just coffee then? I'll bring you a carafe."

"Thank you. That would be great."

The girl nodded and walked out of the dining room through a set of swinging doors that looked like extra wide wooden window shutters.

The Wi-Fi connected and she was surprised how fast it was. Her first search attempt in Google started simply with the word "Gale", which brought many results as she expected, but nothing that immediately gave her any help in what she was looking for. That is, as far as she knew what she was looking for. She was going in blind, looking for any clues as to the tape's origin, so really any shot in the dark that brought back results would be a good thing. Next, she tried "M.Gale", with still no apparent relevant results. She browsed a few sights that she hoped would spark something in her mind and memory, but still there was nothing.

Finally, the thought occurred to her that perhaps the combination of the name on the tape and the date on the recording had some significance. She was running out of options, she typed in "M.Gale 06/12/1993".

The result came back at the top of the screen, "Did you mean 'Gale – June 13, 1993?'" A number of results came back suddenly, so Miranda clicked on the top result, an archived article from the online version of the *Upper Peninsula Herald Times*:

Tragedy Strikes Prominent U.P. Family
GALESTONE, Michigan – June 14, 1993

Surviving members of a beloved Upper Peninsula family, as

well as friends and the townspeople of Galestone, are still reeling today from the loss of several members of the Gale family in a house fire in the early morning hours Friday. At this point, the exact cause of the fire is still unknown, but sources close to the Michigan State Police have informed us that the fire is being handled as suspicious, and are not ruling out foul play.

The Gale family has lived in the home since they first came to the area in the late 1930s. Francis Gale first brought his family from the UK to the United States with dreams of investing family money in the prosperous Michigan iron mining business, and helped develop mining operations in the area of Pointe Ridge, Michigan, which brought several people and jobs to the small town. As the town quickly grew and business was strong, the people of Pointe Ridge in the late 1940s changed the town's name to Galestone, after the family that breathed life into a once sparse and depressed area.

When the mines became too dangerous to dig any longer in the mid-1970s, they had to be sealed for the safety of the community. No longer producing, many of the townspeople whose families had been there for decades had to leave Galestone, leaving only a fraction of the population. The Gale family stayed, living off the remaining fortune that had grown during the mine's glory days, but in recent years it had been rumored that much of the old wealth had dried up. The overall appearance of the once beautiful Gale Homestead had increasingly looked in decay in the past several years, and much of the house staff had been cut back to a mere handful of people. The Gale's tended to stay to themselves in the recent months, rarely being seen in the community, which has caused even more speculation as to what may have happened in this once peaceful and prosperous home.

Reports have come in that the victims of this tragic fire are family patriarch and son of Francis Gale, Thomas Gale, 55; Thomas's younger brother, Edward Gale, 50; and Edward's 16-year-old daughter, Cobie. Also lost in the blaze was Suzanne Gale, 22, daughter of Thomas Gale. Escaping the flames were Victoria Gale, wife of Thomas Gale, and the 16-year-old son of Thomas and Victoria, David Gale, as well as Suzanne Gale's three-year-old toddler, whose name had not been released at press time. Also, a nanny is said to have escaped the burning home as well.

Francis Gale passed away of natural causes in December of 1988 at the age of 89.

The survivors had been treated for minor smoke inhalation at a local medical facility, and released Friday evening.

The incident remains under investigation.

Miranda bookmarked the story, and typed in the search bar "Gale Fire Investigation Michigan". The next item she found had the headline "Suspect Arrested in Galestone Fire Death Investigation".

GALESTONE, Michigan – June 16, 1993

An arrest has been made in the arson investigation in the Upper Peninsula that claimed the lives of four members of the once prominent Gale family of Galestone, Michigan.

Michigan State Police, in cooperation with local sheriff's department officials, announced Thursday that they have taken into custody 49-year-old Daryl Grimes, a local homeless man that once worked for the Gale Mining Company. Police believe that Grimes may have had a grudge against the

Gale family, blaming them for the loss of his job years ago. After the mine closed, Grimes was hired by the Gales to do handiwork and gardening around the Gale Homestead after the former gardener moved on, but Grimes was also cut from his job with the Gales once more when costs no longer permitted Grimes' further employment. Gasoline was found as an accelerant at the scene, and police dogs had been called in to search the surrounding area, which led them to Grimes hiding in the forest less than a quarter mile from the Gale home. He was found with an empty gas can in his possession, and immediately taken in for questioning and later charged the same day.

Police and the prosecutor's office say the evidence is substantial, but have stated that Grimes has not uttered one word since he was taken into custody. Grimes will be undergoing psychological evaluation in as early as the next few days.

Miranda sat back in her chair as she studied a picture of the Gale home after the fire. There had been significant damage to one corner section of the house, and more extensive damage to the floors above. Much of the external structure of the house stood intact but was badly burned. She was trying to remember any fragment of a memory she had of the house, but nothing came to her. She started to wonder on a conscious level if she was letting her imagination run away with itself in all of this, but her gut told her something different. She had noticed that the child's name was still not mentioned in the second article, as well as any of the other survivors or victims. Finally, she did a search for "Daryl Grimes", and found an article on the trial and verdict:

# In the Shadows of Fate

Guilty Verdict Found in Gale Murder and Arson Trial
April 5, 1994

A unanimous guilty verdict was returned yesterday on all counts for Daryl Grimes, 50, the man charged in the deaths of four members of the Gale family of Galestone last year.

The verdict brings to a close the long and difficult ordeal that Victoria Gale and her 17-year-old son, David, the only surviving members of the Gale family, have been going through since the terrible tragedy that occurred in June of last year.

Grimes has not spoken since he was taken into custody just a few days after he started the fire that killed Thomas Gale, Edward Gale, Suzanne Gale and Cobie Gale. He was found competent to stand trial last July, despite efforts from the court appointed defense to prove otherwise. The guilty verdict calls for a mandatory life sentence without the possibility of parole.

Mrs. Gale and her son have been making preparations for months to move to Great Britain at the conclusion of the trial.

"We have endured a tremendous loss to our family. As much as we appreciate all the love and support that we have received from the incredible people of Galestone, my son and I feel there is nothing left for us here. It is time for us to move back to my husband's family roots, and try to find peace in what this world still has left to offer our family. We thank you all from the bottoms of our hearts," Victoria Gale said in a statement.

Miranda looked at the photograph on the screen of Victoria Gale and her son David. Victoria was a beautiful woman, especially for her age, dressed in a long black dress and wide brimmed, velvet hat. David, standing beside her, had a stern and sullen look on his face. He had short, dark brown hair, with eyes that were a soft, pale blue. Miranda felt sad at that moment, not being able to imagine what the two of them had gone through. But that moment seemed suddenly overshadowed by the fact that there was no mention of the granddaughter once more. Had the press just forgotten about her? Miranda was puzzled by this. If this woman in the picture was the little girl's biological grandmother, whose only daughter was lost in this horrible fire, then why would she have given up her daughter's only child?

"Miranda?" said a man's voice beside her.

Miranda looked up and saw the man, in his early 20s with piercing blue eyes and thick, medium length dark brown hair standing beside her. He was wearing blue jeans and a brown leather jacket, with a black motorcycle helmet in hand. She quickly closed down the screen on her computer and stood up from her table.

"Jake," Miranda said his name as she rose from her seat. A slow grin came to Jake's face, giving Miranda a slight touch of relief in the awkwardness of the moment. She dug deep and pulled out a smile of her own.

"Oh my God! It's...it's good to see you," Miranda said with a hug, not sure if the words fully matched the true sentiment she was feeling in that moment.

"What are you doing here? I thought you were living far, far away from little Native Springs," said Jake, with a mildly sarcastic tone.

"I am. I just...I came home for a few days. My parents wanted me to check out the new house, and I had some time off from classes, so I thought I'd come up and visit for a few days," Miranda lied. Her reasons she came home, she felt, were best left kept to herself.

"Ah...I see," said Jake. "So you visit your parents after not seeing them for almost a year by hanging out alone in a local restaurant playing around on your computer?" he said with a half grin on his face.

"I guess that's it then," Miranda shot back, with a cool smile. She wasn't surprised Jake Neilson was giving her grief for anything or even everything. He had good reason to. For one thing, it was because he could see right through her, even after not seeing her for almost four years now.

Jake and Miranda had been together on and off for most of their high school years. When Miranda had let loose a wilder side of herself years back, she and Jake were a hot and heavy item. The partying, the drinking, the all night rides on Jake's Harley Davidson. Jake and Miranda were two white-hot souls burning hot and fast through their teenage years. Of course with that kind of relationship comes the more volatile side as well; the fighting, the screaming, the breaking up just to get back together again a few days later. It was this that brought about the other reason she expected static from Jake. She broke off their relationship the day of their high school graduation. He wanted to talk...he begged her to talk, or even to scream at him and tell him why, but she wouldn't fight with him. Without tears, and without any apparent regret, she told him that she was sorry. She told him to never look back. Miranda felt she had her reasons, but they were her reasons, and that was all she felt she could offer him then, hoping one day he might understand.

And now here he was, with every reason possible to hate her. He stood in front of her, post-hug, with that smart-ass grin on his face, giving her a hard time like it was the day before graduation. A day when Jake still believed they were about to face a new and uncertain world beyond high school beside one another.

"Yeah," he said after a long pause, his eyes locked with Miranda's. "I guess it is." His eyes glanced down to her beat up leather jacket, the one he had given her years before.

"I hope you're taking care of that," he said, nodding down to the jacket. "It's a classic…just like you."

"I take care of it just fine, thank you. It means a lot to me…whether you believe it or not," said Miranda.

"Jake! Your order's up!" a voice called from the bar side of the restaurant.

Jake looked away across the room for only a moment, then fixed his eyes on Miranda's face, which made her feel a little uneasy, not knowing why.

"Well…you take care of yourself. Maybe I'll see you around before you take off again," he said with that same smirk he'd been holding for almost the entire time since the moment he first spotted Miranda in the tavern.

Miranda didn't say anything to this. She returned the same grin to him, and gave a slight nod of her head as he turned to walk away. Jake took one more quick glance over his shoulder at her as he crossed the room. He took his order and walked out the door. She could hear the Harley's engine fire up outside, and slowly fade into the distance. She sat back down, and tried to shift her focus back on what she would do next.

With the Gales moved back to Europe so many years ago, and the fact that it seemed obvious that she was something they no longer wanted in their lives, she felt that tracking them down via the Internet to try and get answers might not be the most successful way to go. But the town of Galestone was still there and within reach, just a six hour trip up the roads in the wilds of the Upper Peninsula. Perhaps a ride north would do her some good, and maybe even provide her with a little illumination as to what might have happened in the Gale house that still haunts her dreams today. Maybe it was nothing. But with all that she had found out today alone, she was driven to find out as much as she could about where she had come from. Who were the Gales behind closed doors? What might the locals still know, about both the Gale family and the man that tried and almost succeeded in killing an entire family? And why did her grandmother give her up? What secrets were still held in the town of Galestone?

She knew that her parents, especially her mother, would not be crazy about her running off so soon after her arrival home. And they would especially not be comfortable with her real reasoning as to where she was going and what she was doing.

She decided she would go home for the night and put what she had discovered that day, as hard as it may be, out of her mind and concentrate on being the good daughter and enjoy some quality time with the family. That would also offer the opportunity for her to come up with something to tell her parents as to why she was leaving for a couple of days. After she finds what she needs, she can take the time to explain everything when she returns home.

Rick Jurewicz

## CHAPTER THREE

"I don't understand why you are running off so soon after you just got here," said Lorri, as Miranda brought a small suitcase borrowed from her parents up the stairs from the basement, along with her messenger bag and computer slung over the other arm. Her father grabbed the suitcase from her to help her out to her car.

"Thanks, Dad," she said with a smile. "It's only going to be a couple of days, Mom. I promise."

"But you just got home yesterday," her mother said. "Can't you at least wait a couple more days to get a little more settled in?"

"I've been home for two days already, Mom. My friend Tammy from school is staying with her parents at their cabin in the U.P. She has gone on and on about the place. She found out from Lydia that I was home, and invited me up for a few days. They are only going to be there for the next couple of days, and if I don't see the place for myself, when I get back to school I will never hear the end of 'how great it is' and 'you should have really come up,'" said Miranda.

"It'll be fine, Lorri," said Robert. "She will have plenty of time to catch up more when she gets back, and I can't think of a much better place to decompress for a few days than in the middle of nowhere, which is pretty much anywhere in the U.P. And it's not like she will be alone. She will be with her friend and her family. She'll be fine."

Lorri hugged Miranda. "I know she will be fine! Alright. Have a good time then. Drive safe. Call us when you get up there, okay?"

Robert walked his daughter out to the car. "See you, sweetie," he said, giving Miranda a quick kiss to her forehead.

"I'll see you in a couple days," Miranda said back to him. The two smiled at each other, and she waved as she went back down the road.

Miranda was only about 20 minutes up the road when she got a text from her father. It read "Check glovebox – just in case. Have fun. Dad." She opened the glovebox, and inside on top of a small leather booklet in which she kept repair invoices, registration and proof of insurance, was her father's credit card and two $50 bills.

"Dad," she said to herself with a little shake of her head. She took the card and money out and put it in her jacket pocket. She planned on paying it back to him regardless if she decided to use it to stay any longer than she anticipated. As far as her parents knew, she had a place to stay rent free while she visited the Upper Peninsula, so she assumed he wanted to help his cash strapped daughter with some gas money for the trip up. It was sweet, but it wasn't necessary. It was true that she was currently without a job, and a full-time student on leave for a while, but she was also very smart with her money and had been saving for quite a while. She had student loans out, and had already been paying them back for some time. Not having to do a ton of driving and not having a car payment, along with sharing the apartment rent with Lydia, actually gave her some room to breathe, financially speaking. She didn't even need both jobs that she had been working. But they were easy jobs, and being that she didn't burden herself with an over active social life allowed her the time to have both of them. One of the jobs was working for a company that did retail product shelf resets in a variety of different stores. The work times were flexible, and most of them came late at night, offering her anywhere from 10 to 20 hours a week. The other job was working in the campus library, which was another 15 plus hours a week. Miranda did prefer the library job. She loved books, and found quite a bit of time to read when she didn't have to be actively helping students find periodicals or help return books to the shelves that had been checked out.

The hum of the Pontiac crossing the grating of the Mackinaw Bridge can be unnerving to some, but it didn't really bother Miranda too much. It had been years since she crossed the bridge for any reason, rarely having a need to travel to the north side. The five mile span of the bridge crossed the Straits of Mackinaw, and connected Michigan's Upper and Lower Peninsulas. It was once the world's longest suspension bridge, and drew people from all over the world to either see it or just to say that they crossed it. Many locals took its majesty for granted, just looking at it as a way to get from point "a" to point "b", whether it be traveling to work, or as a means to get between northern Michigan's "Indian Casinos" that seemed to be popping up in more and more places in these regions of the state. But the bridge truly was an engineering marvel, built with blood, sweat and tears.

She paid her toll at the tollbooth, and exited I-75 heading west on US-2. The road was a busy one that many people seemed to forget was not an expressway. She kept up with traffic, but the farther out she got from the bridge, the busyness of the road seemed to slow somewhat. It was about another two hours before she came upon the road heading northward once more that would take her to the town of Galestone. She still had somewhere between another hour and a half to two hours before she would reach the three mile turnoff to the town.

    The entirety of the trip took about five and a half hours. For many people, it would have been a full 6-hour trip, but Miranda had a tendency to have a heavy foot on the gas pedal. The road in from the main highway was paved but broken and worn down. It was wide for all of the iron ore trucks that used to traverse it on a regular basis, but she had a feeling that there was not an awful lot of traffic traveling this road these days. About the only draw in the town anymore was the scenic wilderness areas, but these areas were not easy to explore due to the rocky and rough terrain that was part of the natural landscape of the Upper Peninsula. These hiking trails catered more to experienced hikers and rock climbers, although others did come to the town just for the seclusion.

    It was truly a beautiful place, but didn't have the scenic lure of the Pictured Rocks area of the Lake Superior shoreline in Munising, or the historical significance of Marquette, both within a couple hours drive. Galestone, however, had its own quiet serenity, but that was barely enough to keep it going on its own. Miranda passed the Buckshot Tavern, the only year-round local eatery in town, and turned into the driveway of the Wellman House Bed & Breakfast.

    The bed and breakfast had actually only been there for about six years now. Owned by Beverly and Tom Wellman, the house had originally been the home of John Pittman, a foreman at the Gale mines who had worked for Francis Gale for many years. After the mine closed, John and his family moved on and had to leave the house behind. The house eventually went back to the bank, and had been for sale up until the day the Wellman's bought it for less than $20,000 six years back. It was an absolute steal for what the structure was, on the 4 1/2 acres of property that it had been built on. It needed a lot of work for it to be what they wanted it to be, but Bev and Tom retired in their fifties from one of the big Detroit auto companies and were looking for an investment, as well as the peace and quiet of being as far away from the big city as they could afford to get. Now they had a beautiful, Victorian style white painted bed and breakfast in some of the most glorious wild country Michigan had to offer.

Miranda had found the Wellman House on the Internet when she was looking to find somewhere to stay once she got to Galestone. For a room during the week in the off-season, Bev told her on the phone they would only charge her $35 a night for a small single room with a single bed. It wasn't even one of the rooms that they normally rented unless they had an overflow of guests, but Miranda readily accepted whatever they could offer for that price.

She walked up to the steps of the main porch when a man quickly came out of the front door to help her with her bags.

"Well hello there," said the tall, thin man. He was dressed in casual blue jeans and a flannel shirt with a black turtle neck beneath it, and had a friendly and upbeat tone in his voice.

"Hello," she said back. "I'm Miranda Stratton…I called about a room yesterday and spoke to Bev."

"Ah yes. That's my wife," he said, extending his free hand to her. "I'm Tom Wellman, owner, operator, and occasional entertainer of sorts. Well, I own it with my wife of course. She's the one that really makes the place run along smoothly."

Tom led her inside and Bev stepped out from another room; a beautiful woman, thin like her husband, with graying hair and a soft smile.

"You must be Miranda," said Bev, with her hands clasped in front of her. "Tom can take you up to your room. If you need anything at all, or have any questions, please feel free to come down and find us. If we aren't around, just ring the bell once. That's usually enough for us to hear it."

"Thank you," said Miranda. "And thank you for the deal you gave me on the room. I really appreciate it."

"Oh, don't mention it, dear," said Bev. "It's nice to see new faces out here. Not to mention we love having people tell others about our little town. Always a chance it'll bring more back."

Tom led her to her room, and even though it was small, it still had the homey appeal the rest of the house had. Tom placed her bags on a small dresser, and left her to settle in. She decided to get in a quick nap before she started exploring the town. It was just after 2 p.m. when she fell asleep, and she woke up around 5:45 p.m. She had slept longer than she had planned. Miranda got herself cleaned up and realized she needed to get something to eat.

It was a short walk to the Buckshot. She did not notice Tom and Bev on the way out, and had just assumed that they may be out eating dinner themselves. The tavern was a dark stained log building, which at first reminded her of the Creek Ridge back in Native Springs. But that changed after she got inside. After pulling open the door using the deer antler door handle, she stepped into a building with what had to be hundreds of antlers hanging on every wall, as well as several on the ceiling. There was an old Bob Seger song on the jukebox, and a couple of guys were playing at a pool table. There were maybe a dozen actual patrons in the place at that time, and almost all of them stopped for a moment to glance at the newcomer walking through the door. Most of them quickly went back about their business, but Miranda noticed that the glare of one of the two men playing pool lingered a little longer than she felt comfortable with. He was tall, with a light brown beard and a trucker cap on his head, in khaki colored heavy work pants and a red flannel shirt. She looked away, deciding to ignore the man, finding a seat on the side of the tavern farthest away from him.

A waitress came up to her with a menu and sat it down in front of her on the table.

"Can I get you anything to drink, sweetheart?" said the waitress, whose nametag had the name 'Mary Ann' printed across it.

"Can I get a Diet Pepsi?" asked Miranda.

"Sure can," said Mary Ann. "I'll go and get that for you and be right back to get your order."

She was dressed casually, and Miranda wondered if perhaps she might be the only person working at the time. She couldn't imagine a place like this needing a lot of employees, especially this time of year. Galestone was only about 16 miles south on the main highway from Arlo, which was considerably larger than Galestone. It was probably the closest place for full-time residents of the town to get the basic necessities and groceries that couldn't be found in Galestone. There was a gas station just up the road that may have had some convenience items, but that is all that she had seen coming into town.

When Mary Ann returned to the table, Miranda decided to keep things simple and ordered a grilled chicken breast sandwich from the menu, no mayo.

"Lettuce and tomato okay on that?"

"Yes, please. Thank you." Miranda responded.

Out of the corner of her eye, Miranda noticed the man at the pool table looking at her again. She continued to try and ignore him, and thought that maybe it would help to engage Mary Ann in a little more conversation to perhaps get the man to stop looking in her direction.

"Here you go. One chicken breast sandwich, no mayo," said Mary Ann, returning with the order. "Anything else I can get you?"

"Maybe you can help me," said Miranda, keeping a friendly smile on her face. "I am in Galestone working on an article for my journalism class. I go to a university in southern Michigan, and a large portion of my grade is based on the article I am working on about Michigan's iron ore mining history."

Mary Ann had a skeptical look in her eyes. Miranda wasn't sure if it was because she wasn't interested in helping, or if it could be that Mary Ann had no idea what she was talking about.

"Well, how can I help you?" asked Mary Ann.

"The part of the story that I am working on now involved Galestone's part in the mining history. Do you know much about the Gale family?"

"Well sure, I would guess. The town is named after them and all. It's been ages since the Gales have been around this area. Almost 20 years, I think," said Mary Ann.

"Did you know any of them personally?" asked Miranda.

"I've been in this town for almost my whole life. That family was a huge part of this town. They did some pretty

wonderful things to make this town what it once was. When the mines closed down, so did pretty much the rest of the town. They were the lifeblood of Galestone. After that, the Gales kept to themselves pretty much. I would see the two girls and the young boy from time to time, more so than the parents," said Mary Ann. "Shouldn't you be taking notes or something? Isn't that what you writer types do?"

"I have a very good memory," said Miranda with a quick smile. "I understand that there was a fire at the Gale home not long before they left the area. What do you remember about that?"

"Oh, the fire was a terrible thing. A sad day for the town. That night was a nightmare for everyone. I remember Sam Hesselburg banging on the door in the middle of the night for my husband Ken. That's Ken over there behind the bar cleaning up." Mary Ann pointed to a robust looking man in his mid-fifties with salt and pepper hair and a thick mustache. He had a serious look about him, yet still looked as if he could be warm and welcoming.

"He's a good looking man. You must be very proud," said Miranda, carefully trying to gain more of Mary Ann's favor. "So what happened then?"

"Ken ran outside and I followed. You could see from here the bright glow up the hill road through the trees. The place was in a rage of a fire. Since there hadn't been enough people living in the town anymore to be able to afford a fire department, the firefighters from Arlo had been called, but they were still 15 minutes out. So, as many of the men and women still living here in town grabbed whatever they could carry water with and rushed to the house," she said. Leaning in closer, she whispered, "I suppose it made them feel like they were actually doing something to help, God bless them. But so much of that house was in flames, there really wasn't anything anyone could do. It's a miracle that Mrs. Gale and her son and granddaughter survived at all."

"That is such a horrible thing," Miranda said, her eyelids half-closed looking down at the table.

"It was that, yes. I remember young Suzanne – that was Mr. and Mrs. Gale's daughter - coming into town pushing a stroller with that sweet little girl inside. She was like an angel, with the darkest hair and the brightest blue eyes. And Suzanne was such a vibrant and beautiful girl herself. A real sweetheart of a person. It is such a shame that little girl of hers didn't get the chance to grow up knowing her mother," said Mary Ann.

Miranda sat silently for a moment as if she was lost in thought, and then regained her composure and looked again at Mary Ann, who seemed as if she was waiting for Miranda to answer a question.

"I'm sorry. I can't imagine how it must be like, never knowing who your parents were," Miranda responded.

"Well, I can't say I ever knew for certain who the father was. You know how small towns are though. There were rumors," she said.

"What rumors? If you don't mind me asking. I won't use them in the story, I am just curious, now that you brought it up," said Miranda.

"Well, there was this handyman sort that worked for the Gales. What was his name?" She tapped her chin as she thought for a moment. "Gabe. That was it. I'm surprised that I actually remembered it after all these years. Well, sort of surprised, I suppose. He was quite a handsome man. Hard to forget. I never heard his last name though. He lived right there on the grounds in a guest house, and not long after Suzanne became pregnant, he just vanished," said Mary Ann.

"Vanished?" asked Miranda.

"Vanished. Poof. Gone!" said Mary Ann. "Some people thought that maybe Tom Gale paid him off to leave town. Some others thought it might be something more. You know..." Mary Ann leaned forward and made a slow slashing gesture across her throat.

"Really?" said Miranda, looking more intrigued by the sudden theatric notion. "What do you think happened?"

Mary Ann let out a short burst of laughter. "I don't believe the Gales were like that. I think he just up and left. I think he's a fool if he did, leaving behind those two beautiful girls. You never know. Maybe if he had stayed, what happened to Suzanne could have gone a totally different way. Who can tell…only God knows for sure," said Mary Ann. "Hey, that sandwich is gonna get cold sitting on that plate. My cooking is too good to get cold and go to waste!" she blurted out. Mary Ann prided herself in her homestyle cooking, and it was praised by almost all who found their way through the town of Galestone.

"I'm sure it is. I just got too caught up in your story. You have been very helpful to my article," said Miranda. "Do you think it's possible for me to actually visit the Gale house?"

"The grounds and property are gated up, and there really isn't much left to see at the house. It was pretty badly burned. The papers from back then really under reported the extent of the damage, anyhow, there isn't much to see," said Mary Ann.

"I've come so far to work on this story. It almost would seem shameful to not visit and take a few pictures of the remains of the home for the article. Is there any way I could get in there that you know of?" she asked.

Mary Ann thought for a moment, and held up a finger

as if to tell her to wait, and walked to the bar and spoke to her husband. Miranda watched as the man glanced over towards her, and then looked at his wife and shook his head in apparent disagreement. She held her hands out as if she was pleading with him, and he raised both hands and came out from around the bar, and both approached her table.

"My wife here says you are writing a story on the Gales?" said Ken in a deep, powerful voice.

"Yes, that's right," Miranda said, getting up from her chair to reach out and shake Ken's hand, which caught him slightly off guard. "I'm Miranda Stratton."

Ken shook her hand in return, and then continued. "She also told you there really isn't much to see up there?"

"Yes. I understand. But it would mean a lot to me if I could get a look at the place. It helps writers like myself to get a feel for the people that she is writing about. To touch where and how people lived…" she said.

"And where people died," he said, almost cutting her off.

"Yes. That's true. And how they died. I can assure you, I am not trying to exploit a tragedy. I am trying to share more of what they did for Galestone and its people," said Miranda. She watched Ken's eyes narrow, as Mary Ann looked up at him.

"Well, I personally don't think that it's a good idea, but unfortunately you have my wife convinced, and when she has something made up in her mind, it's a mind hard to change. Harry Thornton is a lawyer that lives over in Arlo. He oversees the properties that the Gales once owned. I will give him a call in the morning. You give Mary Ann your phone number, and if he can come down and meet with you, then maybe he can give you the quick tour. But no guarantees."

"Thank you. That's all I can ask. I really appreciate it," Miranda told him.

Ken nodded his head, and Mary Ann smiled again at Miranda. Miranda took a white paper napkin from the table and wrote her cell phone number on it, and handed it to Mary Ann.

"Thank you for everything," she told Mary Ann once more. Mary Ann smiled and sat by as Miranda had finished eating her now cold sandwich.

"That was the best chicken sandwich I think I have ever tasted."

"Well thank you, sweetie!" said Mary Ann, as Miranda paid her bill and left a tip almost as much as the price of the entire meal.

Miranda left the Buckshot, and started back up to the Wellman House. It had gotten dark quick, and the night was quiet except for the sounds of crickets in the bushes and the occasional whippoorwill call from somewhere out in the darkness. She picked up the pace and saw the light from the porch of the bed and breakfast. There were no other lights on the road, and Miranda noticed a silhouette of something in the road ahead of her. She slowed down a bit, and tried to squint her eyes and get a better look at whatever it was in the darkness. She stopped then completely as she noticed the shape moving closer to her, until finally the lights from the tavern behind her reflected in two eyes looking in her direction.

She thought it was a dog, and then she heard the low growl as the creature took a few more steps closer to her. Miranda froze in fear as she realized that this was much larger than a dog. She had never seen a wolf before, in captivity or any other way except on TV, but she was fairly certain that at that moment she was face to face with one. She had no idea what to do. Should she run? Stay still? Play dead? She wasn't sure she could even move. Her heart was racing.

As the creature came closer, she could make out its form and face more clearly; its white teeth fully visible now, a low snarl breaking through the silence in the darkness. She stared forward; her eyes met the wolf's eyes directly on. In that moment as the gaze of the animal met her gaze, it immediately dropped its head and Miranda could hear the whimpering sound coming from the beast.

From behind Miranda there came a thunderous bang, and the wolf dropped the rest of the way to the ground, laying motionless. Miranda whipped herself around, startled by the loud noise that was now ringing in her ears. Standing in front of her was the man from the tavern that had been watching her. He stood several feet away, and lowered the pistol in his hand while several other people from the tavern, including Mary Ann and Ken, with a shotgun in hand, came running out to see what the gun shot was about.

"What the hell's going on, Dean?" yelled Ken.

"God damn wolves are coming right into town now," said the man, whom Miranda now knew was named Dean.

Ken looked and saw the corpse of the wolf. "Jesus Christ! That's the biggest wolf I've even seen near town! What do you suppose brought it up here?"

Mary Ann broke in, speaking to Miranda. "Are you all right, honey?"

Miranda still looked a little shaken. "Yes. I'm okay. I guess your friend Dean here just saved my life." She looked at Dean suspiciously, not completely convinced that the fact that he had been there in the darkness so near to her had been for her benefit at all.

"Are you staying at the Wellman House?" Mary Ann asked Miranda.

"Yes. It's not that much further. I'll be alright," she said.

"I'm sure you would be, but you're not gonna take any chances. Ken, walk this girl the rest of the way, would you?" said Mary Ann.

Ken nodded, and Miranda thanked him. He walked her down the road the rest of the way to the Wellman House, while Dean pulled the wolf corpse off the main roadway. Miranda walked into the house and made her way up to the room, still a little unnerved by what had just happened. She kept thinking about the eyes of the wolf as it looked at her. She knew what had just happened, but she didn't know why. It made no sense to her.

The moment just before the shot rang out, when the large wolf lowered its head and broke its gaze from her, it froze in terror of the girl standing only a few yards away...and Miranda knew its fear.

Dawn seemed to come quickly after the events from the night before. Miranda was awakened by the ring of her cell phone, and at first couldn't remember where she had left it. She hadn't even undressed fully to sleep, just pulling off her jeans and crawling into the bed. The ringing was coming from her back pants pocket, and she scrambled over and retrieved it.

"Hello?" she answered, hoping she didn't sound like a zombie on the phone.

"Miss Stratton?" asked the voice on the phone. It was a man's voice, with a very businesslike tone to it.

"Yes, this is," she responded.

"Harry Thornton. I received a call from Ken Carlson over at the Buckshot Tavern. He said you were interested in visiting the Gale property?" asked Harry.

She sat up quickly, trying to get her composure.

"Yes, yes. That's right. I am doing a writing project for a class, and it would be a great help if I could visit the house and the grounds. I'm trying to get a feel for the history of the area and its part in the early mining days of Michigan," she told Thornton.

"Ken didn't say too much about it really. But, I would suppose you are in luck. It's in the contract that my firm has with the current owners of the property to pay a monthly visit. It's a few days early, but my schedule was clear today, and after Ken called I figured that I could come up this morning," he told Miranda.

"That would be great. Thank you so much," she said.

"I am actually on my way there now. Do you think you could meet me at the main gate to the home in about 20 minutes?" asked Harry.

"I can be there, yes. Do I just follow the main road in and it will take me there?" she asked.

"All the way to the end. I will see you shortly," said Harry.

"Alright, thank you again. I'll see you soon," she said.

"Okay. Buh-bye."

Miranda went to the bathroom sink to throw some water on her face and wake herself up. She wasn't prepared for the call so early, and now she could feel the anxiety building inside of herself. The feeling made her very unsteady. There was no real reason for the tension she was feeling, she thought, except for the fact that she was walking into a place of great sadness and tragedy. But this tragedy was connected to things about herself that were just beginning to come to light. That was enough in itself to feel tension about. She grabbed her jacket and headed downstairs.

Although she had a fondness for the Wellmans at the bed and breakfast, she had preferred to avoid them that morning. They reminded her a lot of her own parents, but she didn't have time for the small talk this morning. She hopped in her car and headed up the road. The carcass of the wolf was gone from the spot where Dean had dragged it, although the blood trail from where it was moved could still be seen somewhat on the road. Following the road straight through town, she noticed several buildings that looked like they had been closed or abandoned for several years. Galestone was as close as it comes to being a ghost town without it crossing that line completely.

When the buildings in town came to an end, the road narrowed somewhat and she followed it another quarter-mile to a large, wrought iron gate. The gate was tightly clasped in the middle of two large, swinging 10-foot-high doors. The chains were padlocked onto the gate door near where the clasp held it firm. When the two gate doors were joined, as they were now, a large letter 'G' was formed, written in a sort of fancy calligraphic script.

Looking up at the large black fence, Miranda found herself once again searching for some fragment of a memory that might put down any doubt that she may have had that this wasn't all some wild goose chase brought to life by a crazy dream. Although the memory did not come, at this point she knew better than to have such thoughts. Even without knowing for sure, the feeling that she had inside was telling her that something beyond her had led her to this place.

The sound of a vehicle came from up the road, and Miranda got out of her car and waited for it to come fully into view. A black Cadillac Escalade pulled up beside her car, which seemed tiny beside the Caddy. A man that Miranda guessed was in his sixties, with thinning grayish-brown hair wearing a grey sports coat and black trousers stepped out of the Escalade, and walked around the vehicle to greet Miranda, stretching out his hand to her.

"Miranda? Harry Thornton," Harry introduced himself.

"Hi. Nice to meet you," Miranda responded. "I just want to thank you again for allowing me to do this."

"Well, it is kind of an unorthodox thing, and to be honest, I hadn't decided to allow it until I saw you. There are a lot of people that like to pull stunts for all the wrong reasons. People get strange kicks about visiting places looking for ghosts or who knows what. A few years back a bunch of kids from Arlo drove down here and busted through the old lock and chains I had on here. Someone from town saw the cars drive on through up towards the house later in the evening, and thought it seemed suspicious. Turned out the kids were up there drinking, smoking dope and playing with Ouija boards. The police came and cleared them all out of there, and I bought bigger chains. You don't have any intentions of that sort here, do you Miss Stratton?" asked Harry, his face crooked with an impish grin.

"I can assure you that I don't. I'm hoping just to get a chance to look around, maybe take a few pictures…all to use in my article," said Miranda.

Harry paused and eyed Miranda curiously for a moment. "Well then, I can take you up to the house. You can wait in my vehicle while I unlock the gates."

As a habit, Miranda didn't get into a stranger's car, but she didn't feel she had any reason to fear Harry. He seemed like a man that took himself and his job seriously, so she actually felt lucky that he was allowing her the opportunity to see the house at all. Harry got back into the Caddy after the gates were secured open, and pulled on up the driveway. It was long and twisty, so Harry proceeded slowly.

Harry reached into his coat pocket and removed his cell phone.

"Reception is very spotty out here with all the rocks and valleys. Excuse me while I check my voicemails, if I can actually get a good enough signal," he said. He held the phone up to his right ear for a few moments, and put it back away in his pocket.

"I figured as much. Most likely I'll have better luck at the house. It's more open up there," he said.

Miranda said nothing. Her mind was somewhere else entirely. She looked ahead as they climbed up the final incline of the driveway. The driveway opened up into a large circle that rounded in front of the Gale house. In the center circle of the driveway was a stone fountain, about 14 feet across with a statue in its center of a man with enormous feathered wings on his back, which Miranda took to be an angel of some sort overgrown with vines and weeds. The statue had its right knee brought up to rest on the rocks beneath its foot, and the angel leaned its right arm down upon the knee with its head tilted towards the ground, as if it were in mourning or deep in thought.

The house was, or at least had been in all its glory, a beautiful Victorian style home, no doubt inspired by the family's early European history. It appeared to be built entirely out of wood instead of using local stone or brick, three stories high with a large covered porch that spanned the entire front of the main structure of the house. Windows had lined the front of the lower and middle levels, with two dormers at the third floor that had arched windows in each. Most of the windows had been broken out, no doubt due to the fire, and some probably over the years by vandals that had made their way past Harry's security efforts.

The sun had risen behind them in the east over the trees now, and as it illuminated the front of the house, much of the extent of the damage could be seen just from the front of the house alone. It was amazing that any of the house had survived such a blaze. The rear sections of the house, especially the upper levels, were almost completely gone. Harry and Miranda exited the car and stood looking up at the shell of the formerly majestic dwelling.

"Quite a shame, isn't it?" said Harry, looking on at the house.

"It looked like it had been a beautiful place to live once," Miranda said pensively.

"Oh, this house was a masterpiece. Francis Gale had a hand in every step of the design and building of this place. He was more than just a smart businessman, you know. He had a keen eye for art and design. Many of the paintings that hung in this house were painted by Francis himself years ago. Beautiful, beautiful paintings of the landscapes around this area and on the Lake Superior shoreline," said Harry.

"You've seen the paintings yourself?" asked Miranda.

"I did indeed. I had been to this house several times before the fire. I handled some legal affairs for Tom and Victoria from a few years before the fire up until the surviving family left the area. Mostly just a few trust issues and such, and a few lawsuits from people who thought they had more coming to them than they did after the mines closed. No one who worked for the Gales. Just some of the connected industries, the trucking companies and such. None of it really amounted to anything. After most of the fortune was gone, and then with Thomas Gale gone, in light of the scope of the deaths and the trial that followed…well, no one wanted to push things any more after that."

"Who owns the property now?" asked Miranda.

"Specifically, it's hard to say. Our firm gets a check every six months from an LLC owned by a larger corporation, just to oversee the property and make sure people are not abusing the lands and resources. It happens like that a lot. Land speculators buy up all sorts of land under one company name or another, trying to throw snoops off who might be trying to gauge the true value of land and not jack up the prices if they think one person is after it all. All we do is receive a check and do our monthly runs. It's actually really easy money for us!"

Miranda pulled her camera from her inside coat pocket and stepped towards the house. She stopped a few feet away from where she started and looked back at Harry.

"Do you think it would be alright if I took a look inside the house? Just inside the door. Maybe get a few shots," she asked.

Harry looked apprehensive about this request.

"I'm not sure it's a good idea. The remains of the home were not considered structurally sound after the fire, and I am sure after all these years it's far worse for wear," he told her.

"I promise I will watch myself and be careful. I won't venture too far inside," she told Harry. "You can come and be my chaperone if you'd like," Miranda said playfully, trying to lighten up the situation.

"Alright. You go on ahead and just be careful. My firm would probably have my hide if they knew I let you in there, so you can just keep it between us," Harry said with a sharp wink. "I am going to try and check my messages again. Don't go too far inside. If you were to get hurt, I would have hell to pay. And by the way, anything you use in your article, I know *nothing* about. How you got here, how you got in. It's all on you. Do we have an agreement?"

"Of course. And I will be careful, I promise. Thank you," she said to Harry, smiling.

Miranda started off to the door, while Harry watched her carefully as she moved closer to the house and farther out of earshot. The look on his face became more serious now, as he moved around the other side of his vehicle, still keeping an eye on Miranda the whole time as she moved in through where the front door once was, now gone from its hinges.

Harry dialed his phone, now with almost full reception. It was the same reception that he had had when he pretended to check his messages on the way to the house. After a few short rings, the call was answered.

"Yes?" said the cool, even toned voice at the other end of the line.

"There has been a development," said Harry into the phone.

"What sort of development?" asked the voice.

"I am sending you a photo I took a short time ago," said Harry. His voice sounded anxious and serious.

"Of?" asked the voice, with a hint of annoyance at Harry's vagueness.

"It regards what you have really been paying me for all these years," Harry replied.

Harry sent the picture he secretly took of Miranda in the Escalade with his cell phone camera to the faceless voice across the airwaves, and waited for some time before he was spoken to again.

"What is her name?" asked the voice, whose words seemed to slow and deepen in tone. This was unnerving to Harry.

"Miranda Stratton. She came to Galestone telling people she is working on an article about Michigan mining history. What do you think?" asked Harry.

"It's her."

"How can you be sure of it?'

"I KNOW it is her," stated the voice, now sounding icy and almost frightening. Harry felt a chill come over him from the sudden change.

"What do you want me to do?" asked Harry.

"She could be lying about her name. At least *part* of it. I want you to stay on her. Follow her. Are you in Galestone now?" asked the voice.

"Yes. We are at the Gale house," Harry said.

"I am sending a couple associates to meet with you. In the mean time, find out everything you can about her through your resources. EVERYTHING. Where she lives, who her friends are; I need everything. Do you understand me?" asked the voice.

"I understand. I will stay on her," Harry assured.

"I want to know what she has discovered already. How did she find out about the Gales? And who else might know," said the voice. "Everything hinges on this girl."

"I will find out everything that I can, I assure you," Harry said, trying to mask some of the apprehension he was feeling from the call. The line disconnected before Harry could say any more.

Miranda stepped inside the doorway of the Gale house. It was mostly dark, although the ceiling of the first floor was very high, allowing more light into the rooms. She glanced back again at Harry before taking a few more steps inside and proceeded down a hall to the right side of the building. She stepped slowly. Debris was everywhere over the floors, and much of the surfaces inside of the house, protected from most of the wind and the rain, still had a film of old ash glazing them. Large sections of wall and ceiling had been burned through on the lower levels, but something seemed to have caused most of the destruction to be contained in the upper levels. It was as if the fire climbed the walls like a slithering predator, attacking the sleeping family in the top floors of the house.

There were two doors that Miranda first came to in the hall. To the right was a door that was open, and the room appeared to be some sort of a study or office. It was the open doorway to the left that drew Miranda's attention the most.

She stepped into a large room, and immediately she felt a chill up her spine. With all of the debris covering the floor, it wasn't until she ran her foot along the surface of the floor to push some broken wood and ash aside did the color of the once brilliant marble floor break through the years of being hidden from the world. Her eyes darted around the room, and she could see the spaces where the paintings had once lined the walls. She knew what every one of them had looked like, because she remembered everything from her dream. Stepping further into the room, she could see across the way a large section of ceiling that had fallen from the floor above, now laying atop an object ahead. Fear crept in the back door of her subconscious. For an instant she felt frozen where she was, not sure if she could continue moving forward. It was like walking into a dream or a nightmare, but one that fear itself was the only true thing to be afraid of. But there was also a fear of the unknown; a fear of finding answers that quite possibly should not be found.

She finally moved closer to the area where the ceiling

had fallen from above. She put her hand on it to try to move it aside. It moved far easier than she had anticipated. When it shifted, a raccoon hissed at her from underneath where it had been hiding. She let out a short scream, quickly trying to muffle it with her hand and not attract the attention of Harry outside. The raccoon darted in the opposite direction, far more afraid of her than she was of it, although she couldn't have been convinced of that in the moment. In the spot where the second floor had fallen laid the remnants of the white piano that she had dreamed of so many times over the years. She half expected the man playing it to be there as well. Perhaps some charred skeletal remains that had been missed or left behind, but there was no one else there with her.

Atop the piano there was a rectangular spot roughly the size of the box she had received in the mail. The space looked as if it had not been touched by ash and had sat empty for a very long time, now thick with dust and droppings from mice. Miranda stared at the empty spot for several seconds and found herself feeling empty in that moment. She had come full circle, and she had nothing else to go on. She knew that the box came from this place. She knew that she had been here as a young child, although she still had no memory of it. The box and the tape had found their way to her, but she still didn't know how or why.

There was a hallway leading out of the room down to where what once was a large glass double doorway leading to the backyard gardens of the estate house. The doors had either been knocked away or removed after they had been badly damaged from the fire, leaving the way clear to see into the rear garden area behind the main house. All that Miranda could see from this distance out the doorway was overgrown and unkempt hedges, and part of what looked liked a large, round stone fountain, dry and covered with what looked like bird droppings. The grass around the fountain was long and intermixed with all sorts of weeds, and it had looked as if there once had been flowers growing about in beds that were now dead and weed ridden as well.

Miranda looked about the debris of the room. At first, there was almost nothing that seemed discernable or whole until she saw the corner of a piece of paper sticking out from beneath an overturned end table. She moved the table to find that the page was almost completely intact, save for one corner that was singed by the fire. Beyond that it was a full sized 8 1/2 x 11-inch sheet of paper with a small amount of water damage. She picked it up and turned it over to see if there was anything on it worth seeing. As it turned out, it was that and more.

Miranda fixed her eyes on what was a crayon drawing of a little stick girl in a blue dress. The little girl in the picture was drawn with black hair, and held the hand of a taller girl with blonde hair, also drawn as a stick figure. Both were smiling, and overhead in the sky shone a bright, large yellow sun. Then, for the first time, something of a memory started to come back to her.

She could remember fragments. She could see herself sitting on the floor with her crayons coloring this very picture. Looking up from her crayons and paper, Miranda watched the blonde girl come over to her and kneel down beside her.

"*What are you coloring, Miranda?*" asked the girl, smiling brightly down to her.

"*It's you and me. You're taking me for a walk.*"

"*That is such a beautiful picture! You are such a wonderful artist,*" said the girl. "*Would you like me to put your name on your picture?*"

"*Put your name on it, too! Because it's you!*" said Miranda

*excitedly, pointing to the blonde girl in the picture.*
"Okay! I will put both our names on it!" said the girl.

Miranda stood looking at the names beneath the drawn characters on the paper. Beneath the little girl with the black hair was her name, Miranda. And the name beneath the stick picture of the blonde girl was 'Aimsley'.

A noise came from the hallway behind her, and she quickly folded the drawing and shoved it into her jacket pocket. Harry appeared in the doorway, stepping cautiously all the way.

"Everything all right in here? I heard some noises, and thought maybe the roof was coming down again," he said.

"Just a renegade raccoon. Spooked me a little, but I'm fine," said Miranda.

"Well, this is a little farther inside than I am comfortable with. I think it's about time that we get moving along. Did you get everything that you needed?" asked Harry.

"I think I did," she replied.

"Okay. Well, then I guess it's mission accomplished," he said.

Harry turned and started back in the other direction, and Miranda followed behind him. They said very little to each other on the way back to the main gate. Harry once again secured the large iron gate, and Miranda thanked him once more for allowing her the chance to see the house.

"Will you be staying here in Galestone much longer?" asked Harry.

"I haven't decided yet if I will stay one more night or leave today still," she told Harry.

"Well, if there is anything else I can help you with, you have my number on your phone, so you can give me a buzz," said Harry.

"Thank you, again," said Miranda. She paused for a second, and then turned to Harry again. "Have you spoken to anyone from the Gale family since they left here?"

"No, I'm afraid I haven't. Once they left, I believe they'd just as soon put this place behind them and leave it there. I can't say that I blame them," he said.

"Thanks," she told him once more, and got into her car and drove down the road, back to the Wellman House.

Tom was sweeping the front porch of the house when Miranda returned just before he took his lunch break.

"Well, someone was up bright and early this morning. You missed a great breakfast Bev cooked up. You're more than welcome to join. After all, that is what we do, bed AND breakfast," Tom said, trying for some humorous small talk. It was well meant, but his delivery needed some work. Miranda just smiled and acted as if she hadn't realized there was a breakfast that came with her room, and told him how great she thought that was. He nodded, and kept on sweeping up, so she headed up to her room and closed and locked the door behind her.

She pulled the picture out of her jacket again, and looked at the name, Aimsley. She knew that there hadn't been an Aimsley mentioned in the articles that she had read online. Was there another relative not mentioned? While she pondered this, it came to her that perhaps Mary Ann at the tavern might know who this Aimsley was. Mary Ann seemed to be eager to help her out, so maybe she or her husband might be able to help her with one last thing.

Miranda decided to stay one more night, if Tom and Bev allowed it, and head back to the Buckshot for another meal that night and hopefully get some insight as to who Aimsley may have been to the Gale family. She was anxious, but knew that she had to be patient and not too pushy with the townspeople. They were helpful and friendly, but she knew all too well how small town people had a tendency to be suspicious of strangers asking a lot of questions. So for the time being until dinner, she decided to lay low in her room. She decided to send a short text message to Lydia to see how things went on her class test yesterday. She wasn't sure if she was ready to share any of what had transpired in the last few days with anyone quite yet, but when she was, Lydia would most likely be the first person she knew she could talk with.

Miranda entered the Buckshot around 6:30 that evening. She had decided she would drive down to the tavern rather than walk this time. No more uncomfortable beastly encounters, with either a lone wolf or Dean lurking in the shadows with some unsavory appetite of his own. She did not notice the black Escalade parked up the road from the tavern, with Harry waiting nervously inside, watching Miranda's every move since she left the Wellman House.

As soon as she was inside the door, Harry stepped out of the SUV and took a quick glance around. There was no one in sight, so he moved around the corner of the tavern and reached into his jacket pocket while standing near Miranda's car. Harry pulled out a black object from his pocket that looked similar to a small flash drive. He knelt to the ground, slid a button forward on the object, and reached up under the front wheel well of the car. With a magnet that was built into the device, Harry secured it to the frame of the car. He stood back up, and after another quick glance around, hurried back to the Escalade. Harry then pulled his cell phone from the console of the Escalade and activated an application he had installed on the phone. The screen prompted for an access code, for which he typed six numbers onto the screen. A map appeared on the screen, then zoomed in to a smaller area, and then another even smaller area. Soon, it was identifying a location within 2.5 meters of the device on Miranda's car.

Harry smiled with a sense of self satisfaction. The investigator that worked for Harry's law firm had done a splendid job of acquiring the device and the information about Miranda so quickly. Harry had done exactly what he was instructed to do and stayed close to Miranda without her catching his scent through the whole day, working from the Escalade like a mobile office, on the phone and on the computer. A background check on Miranda, records of employment and address changes, and even transcripts from her classes returned unremarkable findings. She had had a few minor brushes with the law back in high school, but that wasn't exciting either. The firm's primary investigator, Clarence Stockman, had ways and methods of getting information that go far above and beyond what was generally considered public information, and he did it with much speed and efficiency. He didn't ask questions about why the firm wanted specific information, and the firm didn't ask how he acquired it. It was a working relationship that worked well. But even upon compiling everything he could come up with that afternoon, there was nothing in any of it that indicated she was anything more than a college journalism student and regular 22-year-old girl. Perhaps he had jumped the gun in contacting anyone about her arrival in Galestone? The voice on the phone didn't seem to think that was the case. Not one little bit, actually. It mattered little to Harry. He had a job to do, and he was being paid well for the job. So much so that he paid Clarence $200 extra to bring him the GPS tracking device down from Arlo that he placed on the underside of Miranda's car. He would stay on Miranda's trail personally until the associates that his *other* employer was sending made contact with him. For the time being, it was just sitting and waiting.

Mary Ann waved and said hello across the dining room when Miranda entered the tavern. Miranda smiled and waved back at her, while Ken briefly glanced up from drying glasses behind the bar, only raising his eyes enough to see it was her and continuing like he hadn't noticed she was even there. There were a few more people in the dining room that night, as well as Dean and another man, a different one from the night before, playing at the pool table once again. Dean paid no attention to her this time, which relieved her a bit. She crossed the dining room and took the seat near the corner where she sat the night before. Mary Ann came out and brought her a Diet Pepsi, and took a moment to sit down and visit with her. There was another younger girl helping out that night, which gave some relief to Mary Ann.

"Did you get everything that you needed today? Harry stopped in earlier and said that he took you down to the house this morning. He's such a sweet old guy, at least until you get Ken and him together with a few beers talking about the good old days. Get a few beers in that man, he can become an obnoxious and arrogant S-O-B, if you know what I mean," said Mary Ann.

"He was very nice," said Miranda. "It was a huge help to me and my story. I just wanted to come in and thank you and Ken again for contacting him for me."

"It was our pleasure, sweetie. I just hope to get a chance to read your story when you are all through with it. Maybe you could mail us a copy when you are done with it?"

"I will, definitely. You know, I was wondering if there was one more thing that I could bother you with?" asked Miranda.

"Well sure, I can try," Mary Ann told her, smiling. Miranda noticed that she was wearing far more make up than she had the night before, and wondered if it had anything to do with Harry's arrival in town that day.

"When I was at the house, I came across a name on a piece of paper. It was a drawing, and it had the name Aimsley on it, along with the name of the little Gale girl. Do you know who Aimsley might be?" asked Miranda, carefully watching Mary Ann's expression.

Mary Ann looked on like she was trying to recall something. "Aimsley. Yes…it would be Aimsley Carter. That was the little girl's nanny. How could I forget that brave young girl? Aimsley was the one that saved the little girl's life. That house was in flames, smoke coming from every window. Mrs. Gale and her son made it out the front door on their own, but it was Aimsley that got the little girl out."

Miranda's eyes widened at this revelation. She felt her heart drop for this person whom she had no memory of whatsoever, and felt a small amount of guilt for not remembering.

"Do you know what happened to her?" asked Miranda.

"You know, I was up in Arlo about six months ago, and I stopped by this bookstore in the old part of town. I'd never stopped there before, and I was curious what they might have for a good cookbook - I am always looking to try and cook up a new dish for the guys that come in all the time - and I would swear that the woman working at the store reminded me a lot of that girl. I think at one time I might have heard that she came from Arlo before she came to live with the Gales. She even looked at me like she might have recognized me, but it's been so many years now, neither one of us said anything to each other besides talking about the books I was buying," said Mary Ann.

Miranda sat silently for a couple moments, and then noticed that Mary Ann was looking at her differently than she had seen her look at her before. The smile that had been on her face slipped slowly into a flat, emotionless stare, and Mary Ann slowly slid her hands, which had been outstretched farther upon the table, back to the edge of the table. An unsettling feeling gripped Miranda, but she didn't know why, or what had come over Mary Ann so suddenly. She looked at Mary Ann with concern, not knowing what she should say, wondering if she was alright. Mary Ann looked intently at her, and finally spoke, her voice lower and slower than it had been before.

"I remember that beautiful little girl…seeing her when her mother and Aimsley would bring her into town. Always dressed in the cutest little dresses, little bows in that jet black curly hair. She had hair like her mother," said Mary Ann.

Miranda relaxed her shoulders some, not realizing how tense and twisted she had become. She waited for Mary Ann to continue.

"Aimsley came into town one day, pushing a stroller with the little girl in it. I had been on a walk up through town when I came upon them. I stopped, said hello, leaned down and smiled at the happy, beaming little angel. And when I said hello, Aimsley said to the little girl, 'Miranda…can you tell the nice lady hello?'" Mary Ann said, now almost in a whisper.

Miranda wasn't sure what to say to her. It wasn't really a feeling of shame that possessed her at that point. She felt like the deception that she had been playing at had just been revealed, and she did not know what was going on behind Mary

Ann's eyes now as they looked upon her.

"I'm sorry," Miranda told her, as softly as Mary Ann had just spoken.

"It is you," said Mary Ann. "You're little Miranda, aren't you?"

"I think so. This is all something I am trying to put together," Miranda told her. "I am sorry that I didn't say more to you before now. I needed to see the house to know for sure if it was true. Please forgive me."

"You need to leave," Mary Ann suddenly told her, in a low whisper. "Tonight."

Miranda was taken aback by this. "I am really sorry. I will leave if you want me too…"

Mary Ann cut her short. "No, you don't understand. You need to get away from this town and never come back…and never look back!"

"What are you talking about?" asked Miranda, puzzled by Mary Ann's sudden change in presence. She seemed so much more serious and determined, a side that wasn't at all apparent in the sweet, down to earth tavern hostess she met the day before.

"This town…that family…there is something just not right about things having to do with the Gales. It was the best thing your grandmother could do for you, getting you away from it all," said Mary Ann.

"What do you mean? I thought the Gales were benefactors to the town? That they are the ones that breathed new life into it? The 'lifeblood' of the town. Isn't that what you said?' asked Miranda, more startled by the turn.

"They may have given this town business and prosperity for many years, but there were other things about that family. Strange things happened in and around those people and that house. The night of the fire…my God, please forgive me…when the town found out about the fire…we all didn't run rushing to help. Not at first. Nobody said it, but we all knew everyone was thinking it. Let it burn…" she said, her eyes starting to tear with the shame of what she was saying.

"What could they have done that was so horrible that you would let an entire family die?" Miranda demanded, feeling the anger begin to reel within her.

"No one knew! I know that sounds horrible, but people would hear things…we could just feel there was something wrong with that family. Something *dark*," Mary Ann said, hiding her eyes. Miranda looked around the room, but no one had noticed yet that their conversation took an unexpectedly ugly turn.

"So what was it then? What changed everyone's mind into trying to save them?" asked Miranda bitterly. She felt deep contempt for this woman that she had seen so kindly and teeming with hospitality when she had met her the day before.

"I did. I pleaded to everyone that there were innocent people in that house. That there was a little girl that had never done anything to anyone, and that it wasn't her fault who her family was. That she and her mother were good people and didn't deserve to die," Mary Ann told her through tears streaming down her cheeks. "Everyone seemed to snap out of whatever had come over them, and almost everyone in town marched out to the house to do whatever they could to help."

"And maybe if everyone had acted a little sooner, my mother might still be alive!" Miranda said, her voice even louder now. The exchange between Mary Ann and Miranda had escalated to a minor commotion that had attracted the attention of Mary Ann's husband Ken, standing alongside the bar. He came right over to the two of them and saw his wife in an inconsolable state, her head down on the table, sobbing.

"What the hell is going on over here?" Ken asked in his deep voice loud enough to catch the attention of the men playing pool across the room. Dean looked up from the shot he was about to take; his opponent looked over as well, a younger man swigging from his beer bottle as he peered across the room.

"I was just leaving," stated Miranda. "I won't be any more trouble." She stood up and started to move past Ken toward the door.

"Not before you tell me what is going on here!" he said to her sternly.

He reached out and grabbed Miranda by the shoulder. His intent was to slow her down, still demanding an answer. Miranda turned her head towards him; her eyes pierced through him like daggers of ice. In that second it seemed that Ken's hand was overtaken by a painful cramping, contorting his fingers and causing him to release her immediately. Miranda seemed not to even take notice of the pain he was in, only the fact that he had released her. She kept on for the door, looking back one last time at Ken consoling his wife at the table where she left them. She got into her car, and drove back to the Wellman House.

She felt herself calm more once she was away from the tavern. She couldn't quite understand how that all came over her so quickly, and how the anger had such a hold on her. There was a lot of different emotions going on inside of her. Confusion, frustration, anger, resentment…sadness for those she never even got the chance to know.

First thing in the morning, she was leaving Galestone. She needed answers now more than ever, and she needed to know what would cause a whole town to almost allow an entire family to burn to death in their home; especially a family that brought prosperity to a dead little corner of the world. Hopefully, the answers would come with Aimsley Carter.

Rick Jurewicz

# CHAPTER FOUR

Shortly after midnight that night, a twin engine Learjet 60 touched down at the Chippewa County International Airport. The airport was a small airfield converted from a closed United States Air Force base, with miniscule use compared to the mammoth metropolitan international airports in cities around the world. A skeleton staff worked the terminal at that hour, near the town of Kincheloe, whose population was primarily staff and guards from the three prisons in town, as well as relatives of several of the prisoners housed within the prison walls.

Besides the pilot and two crewmembers, the aircraft had only two passengers. As the door opened, a man stepped into sight wearing a dark colored suit jacket and dark trousers, with a white dress shirt and no tie. Standing about six-foot-two at about 230 pounds with a shaven head, he seemed an ominous presence. The only luggage he had were two black briefcases, one held in each hand. This man was followed by a slightly smaller, less intimidating figure of a man in his early thirties, wearing blue jeans and a light-gray colored sports jacket, again without a tie, with short light-brown hair and rectangular framed glasses. The second man carried a charcoal gray messenger bag over his shoulder, with leather trim on the cover flap.

As the two men set foot on the concrete landing strip, a waiting car approached the aircraft. The driver exited the car, a silver late model sedan, and approached the men as the sounds of the aircraft drifted slowly into the background.

"Which one of you would be Mr. Skye?" asked the driver of the vehicle, a short man with dark, curly hair and a nose too large for his face.

The man with the shaved head spoke without movement or expression, save for his thin, stern lips.

"I am Mr. Skye," he said.

The little man shuttered for a moment in the baleful presence of Mr. Skye.

"I...um. Yes, sorry. Were you requiring a driver, or will you be taking the car on your own. Everything has already been taken care of..."

"Yes, thank you," said the man with the glasses. "You'll have to excuse the shortness of my friend here. It's been a long flight, and he is not a fan of turbulence. It makes him very irritable."

The little man nodded, with a try for a smile at Mr. Skye, who still stood without expression, staring at the little man. The smile on the little man's face disappeared as quickly as it came. He looked back to the man with glasses.

The man with the glasses extended his hand to the little man, who noticed the silver ring on his right middle finger. Even in the darkness the ring glistened, catching any and all light that it could, accenting the inscription of an almost circular crescent moon with points that meet at a single star. In the center of the circular moon was a single point that looked as if it may have been encrusted with a small diamond.

The little man reached out to the hand of the man with glasses slowly to shake it, but before the hands met he was cut off by the man.

"The keys. I will take them," said the man.

The little man backed his hand away slowly without saying a word, and reached into his pocket and handed the man with glasses the keys to the sedan.

"Thank you," said the man with glasses. "I am Mr. Cain. We won't be needing a driver. We like to take in the sights as we go along. Please, thank your supervisors for us in providing accommodation on such short notice."

"I will, certainly," said the little man, nervously. "Anything else you need?"

"No," said Skye abruptly.

The little man nodded, and turned back towards the terminal walking rather quickly. The two men watched as he walked away, turning only once to look over his shoulder as if to make sure the men were not right behind him as if they were going to jump out and frighten him. Mr. Cain turned towards his associate.

"Charming as always," said Cain to Mr. Skye. Skye only grunted in response. "If you cannot be somewhat amicable, then perhaps you shouldn't say anything at all. You're a professional. Try and blend in a bit, will you?"

Skye said nothing, just a slight nod. He was a man of few words, speaking more with his actions, and in his line of work, his actions spoke volumes, mostly to individuals who either wouldn't dare breathe a word to anyone about anything he instructed them not to speak of…or of those who would never speak or be heard from again.

The men got into the car, Mr. Skye now behind the wheel. Mr. Cain pulled out his cell phone and pulled up the messaging screen.

TO: ENOCH
We have landed. Instructions?

TO: CAIN
Head to Arlo. Meet with Thornton – I will send you contact information. Collect all data. He has tracking information. Take care of details.

TO: ENOCH
And the girl?

TO: CAIN
Follow her for now. Keep me informed as to her movements and those she makes contact with.

The next message was Harry Thornton's cell number. Cain dialed the number and waited through a few rings.
"Hello?" Harry answered, groggily.
"Is this Mr. Thornton?" asked Cain.
"Yes? Who the hell is this at this hour?" Harry demanded.
"This is a gentleman whom you were told would be contacting you regarding Miss Stratton. Are you awake and paying attention now, Mr. Thornton?"
Suddenly Harry seemed awake and attentive to the man on the phone.
"Yes. I'm sorry. What can I do for you?" asked Harry, apologetically.
"Are you still keeping a close eye on the girl now?" asked Cain.

"She headed into the place where she is staying hours ago. It's called the Wellman House, a bed and breakfast here in Galestone," said Harry. "I would imagine that she is asleep."

"Good," said Cain. "And do you have any idea of where she may be headed when she leaves this place she is staying?" asked Cain.

"After she went into the Wellman House, and it looked as if she might be in for the night, I stopped to speak to my friends at the Buckshot Tavern. She was inside for only about 10 or 15 minutes, not really enough time for a meal, so I went in later to see if I could find out what she was there for. Mary Ann Carlson, one of the owners, spoke to the girl and said she asked about the nanny that lived with the Gales at the time of the fire, Aimsley Carter. She lives in Arlo now; I looked into her from here, and she owns a bookstore called 'The Book Stops Here!' Cute name. I drive past the place almost every day, but I've never really paid much attention to it. I'm not really a big reader. Anyway, I'm a betting man, and I would bet for sure that if she is looking for answers, that's the next place she will go."

"You have the GPS tracker in place?" asked Cain.

"Yes, I do. Do you want the app access code?" asked Harry.

"Not over the phone. In person. We also need everything else you have gathered," said Cain.

"But I could just send you everything that I have through an e-mail..." said Harry.

"Our employer *insists* that we meet and do the exchange face to face. No electronic transfers. Besides, how else will you get your money?" stated Cain. "Do you have a private place that we can meet?"

Harry hesitated at this. He knew who he was working

for, and that alone caused him great trepidation. However, he did not know these men. But he also was well aware that $250,000 was a lot of money, and being the betting man that he was, he needed the money to pay off other scary men that he owed a portion to. Those men had already implied threats against his family, so Harry wanted to put all of that behind him and move on.

"I…have a hunting cabin on Bear Lake. It's a large lake, just southeast of Arlo. It's a five acre piece of property, heavily wooded so it's very private. 1439 Bear Lake Road. We can meet there whenever you'd like," said Harry.

Mr. Cain entered the address into his cell phone's GPS and quickly found its location off of the main highway to Arlo.

"Is it empty?" asked Cain.

"Yes, why do you ask?" Harry asked, nervously.

"My associate and I have had a long night. We are still about 2 ½ hours from Arlo by car, and we're looking to find a place to stay for the night. Somewhere we can remain relatively unnoticed. I am sure your cabin will do nicely. You stay where you are and make sure your guess is correct as to which direction the girl will be traveling in the morning. Follow her from a distance, and if she is truly going to Arlo, we know where she will be going, so let her go and you go to your cabin. We will meet you there in the morning, if all goes as assumed," said Cain.

"That is kind of irregular…I'm not sure I am comfortable…"

"Mr. Thornton, this is not a request. Do not confuse this with the idea that there are options involved here for you. If you want your money, you will do as you're told. I won't even go into what could happen if you interfere and try and warn the girl of the *interest* in her," said Cain, his voice firm and direct.

Harry frowned. "I'm sorry. That'll be fine. There is a key underneath the left side of the front porch on a nail, near the house."

"Thank you. We'll see you in the morning, Mr. Thornton. You have our number. Call us immediately if anything changes," said Cain. The line disconnected.

Harry felt a pain in his stomach. He was starting to feel as if this may have been a huge mistake on his part, allowing these people to know of Miranda's coming to Galestone. But all he was seeing were dollar signs, and focused on a quick fix to the problems that he had gotten himself – and his family – into. He reached into the glove box and grabbed a bottle of antacid tablets, knocking back three or four to ease the burning sensation inside. It helped only a little. He wanted this over with as soon as possible, and tried to keep his eyes open and on the Wellman House and Miranda's car. But soon, he was asleep again, dreaming about back room poker games that he actually was winning for a change. Harry continued to win, if only in his dreams, until the sun rose at dawn.

Miranda awoke even earlier than she had planned, around 5:45 a.m. It was just as well though, she thought. She wanted to get on the road to Arlo early, and depending how things went today, she considered heading home and coming clean with her parents as to what she had actually been doing the last couple of days. It had crossed her mind that if she had gotten a start later than expected, she might stop by and apologize to Mary Ann for the way she had reacted the night before. Mary Ann only seemed to have her well-being in mind, even though the thought of the people of Galestone almost letting everyone in that house burn appalled her to no end.

Now, it was a matter of why such a thing could have happened. Also, she felt that someone wanted her to find these things out, but she still didn't have a real clue as to who that may have been, or why now after all these years.

The shower felt good, and helped her to relax. She tried to imagine what it might have been like growing up in a family like that, especially here in the middle of nowhere. Living in Native Springs itself had always made Miranda feel somewhat out of touch with the rest of the world, and Galestone was that much further off the beaten path. There was also the fact that the Gales lived a closely guarded life, and kept much to themselves, especially after the mines had closed. Thinking about that struck a chord in Miranda's mind, being that she herself kept things guarded, letting only a few close people really get to know her. The Gales, she was sure, had their own reasons for this, given their position in the town. But perhaps there was more? This thought was beginning to seem more and more evident the further she went down this road in search of who she was and where she had come from. Even with the love of her parents back home, she had found herself for years struggling with a sense of personal identity. There was a part of her that simply wrote it off to being quirky and marching to the beat of her own drum. But at the same time, even when she was very young, she always felt there was something – something deep and inherently important – that was missing from her life.

At around the time she was nine-years-old, she had started reading some of her father's old superhero comic books she had found in the basement of the home she had grown up in. Miranda almost expected that one day her parents were going to come to her and tell her that they had found her in a cornfield in a crash landed rocket ship, and that she was from a far away planet, destined to be a great and powerful hero. Obviously, that had never happened, but now instead of a distant planet, she had found a forgotten little all-too-human part of the world that had been touched by something dark and mysterious.

Miranda packed her things and was heading out the front door by 6:30 a.m. Bev and Tom had not yet awakened, so she left them a little note of thanks for their hospitality, and promised to let others know back home what a beautiful place they had. That was what they had hoped for the most, and she was more than happy to oblige in whatever way she could. There was always the possibility that this whole adventure could become a story someday, especially with the twists and turns she had experienced already. She decided not to have high hopes for her meeting with Aimsley. If this turned out as nothing, she would stop trying to dig into her past and put it behind her. She would come clean with Robert and Lorri, and she would agree to speak to a therapist about her nightmares.

When she came to the end of the road leaving Galestone, she stopped for a moment and turned on her blinker to head south, the direction that would take her home to Native Springs. After a moment of hesitation, she switched the direction of the turn signal to the north, and turned up the road to Arlo. She did not notice the Escalade in the distance behind her. Harry was being as careful as possible not to be too obvious. He turned to follow her up the road, staying a fair distance behind her to try and not attract her attention.

Harry continued to follow the car for about 10 miles until he reached the turnoff onto Bear Lake Road. He made a right turn, and followed it past the first two-track driveway a quarter of a mile down the road, and then made a left turn into the drive that led to his cabin. The property was heavily wooded and secluded, and he began to feel a bit jittery as he approached the cabin.

Harry noticed the silver sedan in front of the cabin and parked the Escalade along side of it. He walked to the front door and tried the knob. It was unlocked, so he quietly proceeded into the cabin. As soon as he stepped into the cabin he was grabbed and pushed face down into a couch in the cabin's front room. He turned over quickly, scared out of his mind, which hit an even higher note of fear when he saw the barrel of a gun pointed directly at his face, only inches from his nose.

"Don't shoot, don't shoot!" Harry cried, throwing his hands up as he laid back onto the couch. "I'm Harry…Harry Thornton! I talked to you last night…please…"

Mr. Skye held the gun steady at Harry's face. Mr. Cain walked out from the bathroom, pants on and shirtless, with a towel around the back of his neck hanging over his shoulders.

"Mr. Skye, I don't believe that is necessary right now," said Cain, calmly. "Mr. Thornton, it might have been more appropriate to *knock* before entering, don't you think?"

"But…it's my cabin," said Harry, his eyes quickly shifting back and forth between the two men. Mr. Cain raised his eyebrows at this, and gave a quick glance at Mr. Skye, who did not respond to Mr. Cain's glance.

"Well, anyhow, please, sit down and have some coffee. I am sure we all have lots of things that we would like to be doing today. No time to be lying around on the couch all day. Allow me a moment or two to finish getting dressed. I am sure Mr. Skye and you will find lots to talk about while I am finishing up," said Mr. Cain.

Harry slowly got up from the couch and walked around the opposite side of it to the round table in the small dining room of the cabin. He didn't take his eyes off of Mr. Skye any more than Mr. Skye took his eyes off of him. Harry sat down at the table, and Mr. Skye brought a cup of black coffee and set it down on the table before Harry.

"Th...thank you," said Harry. Mr. Skye only nodded, which was more than Harry had expected at that point. He had still not heard the man say a single word since he had entered the cabin and Mr. Skye threw him down onto his couch. He thought of how undignified that was for a moment, only to remember that it could have gone a lot worse than it did.

Mr. Cain walked down from the short hallway to the bathroom again, fully dressed as he was the night before. He reached out his hand and shook Harry's.

"Now," said Mr. Cain. "My name is Mr. Cain, and this is my associate, Mr. Skye. I am the one you spoke to last night."

"Yes..." said Harry. "Hi..."

"Yes, I think we are passed that now," said Mr. Cain. He then nodded to Mr. Skye, who retrieved from the kitchen counter one of the two briefcases he had in his hands when he left the plane. He placed it on the counter and rotated it in the direction where it could be opened up to Harry. Mr. Skye reached around it and clicked both locks open on the case, and revealed the contents to Harry. The briefcase was full of fifties, twenties, and ten dollar bills. A huge smile came to Harry's face and his hands reached out to touch the cash. But just before his fingers could reach the case, the lid slammed shut in front of him. He jerked his fingers back, and for an instant scowled at Mr. Skye, only to wipe the scowl from his face just as fast when he glimpsed the menace in Mr. Skye's eyes.

"I assure you that this briefcase contains the $250,000 that you were promised for your services," said Mr. Cain. "However, your services are not yet complete. Do you have the information that we requested?'

"Yes, I do," said Harry. He reached into his pocket and retrieved a flash drive and handed it to Mr. Cain. Mr. Cain retrieved his own laptop from the messenger bag he carried and loaded the contents of the flash drive onto the computer. He reviewed the information from the drive, and then closed the lid shut on the computer.

"The access code for the tracking app is 881956," said Harry.

"The information you retrieved for us. Where did it come from?" asked Mr. Cain.

"The law firm I work for has a man we pay to look into these things. He doesn't ask questions, he just gets results," said Harry.

Mr. Cain smiled at this. "Sounds like my kind of guy. And the computer that you have with you. Is there a copy of the information on it now?"

"Yes…it was e-mailed to me, and I put it on the flash drive for you," said Harry.

"It is in your vehicle?" asked Mr. Cain.

"Yes, why?" asked Harry, feeling agitated again.

Cain nodded to Skye, and Skye went out to the Escalade and retrieved the computer as Harry just sat by and watched. Mr. Skye brought it back into the cabin, and set it on the table near Harry.

"Now, just one last thing and we will be on our way," said Mr. Cain. "Is there any other information we need to know that you haven't shared with us?"

"No…no…you have everything now," said Harry.

"Thank you, Mr. Thornton. You have been a splendid help to us. Our employer will be most pleased," said Mr. Cain enthusiastically.

"You're welcome," said Harry with a small smile, placing his hands on the briefcase in front of him, "and thank you."

"Oh, it's been our pleasure," said Mr. Cain, turning around with a pistol in hand with a long silencer barrel. He turned the gun towards Harry's chest just as Harry looked up. The look on Harry's face turned to shock as Mr. Cain fired two shots at close range into the center of Harry's chest. The shots knocked Harry in his chair back against the wall behind him. His head was still up as he gasped for breath. Mr. Skye reached quickly into his jacket and pulled out the gun that he had originally trained on Harry, and put one more bullet into Harry's forehead, finishing him. Harry slumped forward onto his precious briefcase in front of him.

Mr. Skye gave a sharp look to Mr. Cain.

"You don't always get to have all the fun," said Cain. Mr. Skye frowned and put his weapon away. Cain entered the code Harry had given him into his phone, and it began tracking, pinpointing a location in Arlo.

"Well, for the time being, it looks like the fun will have to wait," said Cain. "It's time to go to Arlo. We will leave things here as they are. It will be a day or two before anything should be found."

"What about the money?" asked Mr. Skye.

"I was told we were to leave it. It's what he was to receive, even though it cost him far more than it was worth. I still don't know whether he is the lucky one who got out easy when all is said and done. Right now, our focus is the girl and that is all."

Miranda pulled up to the bookstore around 7 a.m. that morning. She parked on the curb and looked at the sign on the door that told her the store would not be open until 8 a.m. There was, however, a small bakery right across the street from the bookstore, so she decided she would go and see if she could get a half-decent cup of coffee and maybe, if fate was on her side that morning, a delicious blueberry muffin.

The bakery was small, and she was not surprised to see a police officer, a county sheriff's deputy to be precise, sitting at the counter next to a man in blue overalls who looked remarkably like Dean back in Galestone, although a little shorter, she thought. A grey-haired woman that looked too young to have grey hair was the only person working behind the counter.

"What can I get you dear?" asked the woman.

"Do you have blueberry muffins?" asked Miranda, sporting the perkiest smile she could muster that morning.

"Yes we certainly do, and they're the best in town! Isn't that right, Ernie?" she said, speaking to the officer across the way.

"Damn straight, Caroline," replied the officer, not even bothering to look up from his newspaper. The woman grabbed a fresh muffin from the glass case at the end of the counter and brought it to Miranda. "Anything else I can get you?"

"Just a black coffee if it isn't too much trouble," said Miranda.

She poured Miranda a cup of fresh brewed coffee and returned to her work behind the counter. The muffin was probably the best blueberry muffin that Miranda had ever tasted. And the coffee was, although not that wonderful roasted blend of paradise that she knew back home, a pretty decent cup of coffee, which was all that she had hoped for.

Arlo was larger than she imagined it would be. It was at least twice as large as Native Springs. There were two fast food restaurants that she passed on her way into town, and she was sure that she had seen a sign that told her a Wal-Mart was less than a half-mile away. This part of the town was considered more the "old town" district, once the main street through town, now a quieter and more down to earth remnant of the town in its early days. This part of town reminded her of what Native Springs once had been, while the rest of the town was what she feared her home town would eventually become if those who owned the greatest percentage of property in Native Springs have their way.

"Damn greedy bastards!" the man in the overalls blurted out. "There's not gonna be any kind of hockey season at all this year if those assholes don't stop carrying on about their $20 million salaries! Doesn't anyone remember what the game is about? Why they love to play to begin with?"

"You got that right," said Caroline, pulling a tray of freshly baked loaves of 8-grain bread out of the huge oven, and placing each loaf on a metal cooling rack. "It's like that in almost all those sports now. It's no good for 'em anyway. Look what all that money did to Tiger Woods!"

"Screw Tiger Woods! That's not even a real sport, golf! Now hockey – that's a man's game. Racing across the ice…firing the puck at the opposing goalie…I would give my left nut to play on one of those teams, for even one game. And they wouldn't even have to pay me! It's all about the love of the game. The glory. That is what it should be about!" said the man in overalls.

"I thought you already gave your left nut to Ernie here to not haul your ass off to the county lockup last week when you ran your pickup off the road leaving Bob's Saloon?" said Caroline. The man only grunted and went back to his newspaper, while Ernie sipped his coffee and pretended like he hadn't heard a thing.

    Miranda had one-and-a-half more cups of coffee before she finally noticed a car pull off into the alley behind the bookstore. She watched for a few more minutes until she could see a woman unlock the front door of the store and turn the sign on the door from "Sorry, We're Closed" to "Welcome! We're OPEN!" She laid $15 on the counter, covering the cost of the muffin and coffee with a few extra dollars for a tip, and walked out the front door of the bakery.

    As she crossed the street, Miranda noticed the silver sedan parked just up the block about a hundred feet away. There were not many other cars parked on the streets of old town Arlo at that time of the morning. She could make out that there were two figures sitting in the car, but she had no reason to feel concern, giving it little thought with everything else that she already had on her mind.

    Miranda walked up to her own reflection in the glass front door of the bookstore, and paused with her eyes upon the face in front of her. She had never given much thought to her reflection before, not being a vain person in the least. Now it seemed that even though she was very comfortable in her own skin, the reflection before her held a sort of mystery that she had never had cause to notice before. For a moment she recalled the curls of black hair hanging down from Suzanne's head that she had seen in the videotape. She wondered what else there might be within her that she will find in the search for her birth family?

    All she could see from outside the door were rows and rows of books, many looked like new releases on one wall, and there were several other shelves that looked like they held many used volumes, mostly paperback, and some older hard-covered books with tattered jacket liners. She pulled the door open, which caused a little bell at the top of the door to jingle as she walked into the store. The store smelled like a combination of old paper and newer carpeting, mixed with a scent that probably came from a vanilla scented air freshener. There is not much that can stifle the odor of old paperbacks, but the vanilla did try and temper the musty aroma.

The woman who had opened up the store that morning was standing behind the counter, looking down at something behind the counter, most likely counting her cash register's start-up money for the day. She had long blond hair that was pulled back into a thick ponytail, and was wearing eyeglasses on her face that seemed to sit closer to the end of her nose as she counted the dollars down below, and sorted them into the proper slots in the cash drawer. She dressed very conservatively, wearing a blue full-length dress with white accenting on the sleeves and around the waist.

"I'll be right with you in just a second," said the woman, her voice soft and friendly, still not looking up as Miranda slowly stepped forward. Miranda reached into her jacket pocket and held the drawing from the Gale house in her hand. She felt a wave of nervous energy rush over her again, which made her feel slightly awkward, but she moved closer to the counter and the woman finally finished with the money and placed the drawer in the register, and tightly pushed the register closed. She looked up at Miranda, face to face, with only a few feet between them.

"Now, what can I help you with this morning?" asked the woman with a smile. Miranda just stood looking into her eyes for a moment, trying to make out flashes of memory rattling around inside her brain. The woman just looked back at Miranda, without much response, waiting for Miranda to tell her what she was looking for in her store on that bright and sunny October day.

Miranda found herself momentarily without words. She placed her hand with the drawing on the counter, and the woman glanced down at it as it was placed in front of her. The woman took it in her hand and looked at it for a moment with a hint of confusion on her face, which Miranda could then tell had turned to another feeling entirely, as she could see the woman sink down as if her legs had failed her for a brief moment. She put her free hand on the counter to steady herself, as Miranda looked on at her reaction to the drawing in her hand. The woman looked to Miranda again, finally, and tried to form a word with her mouth, but nothing came out at first. Miranda could see her eyes begin to redden and glass up.

"Miranda?" said the woman, almost whispering her name. "Oh my God..."

"Yes...my name is Miranda Stratton," said Miranda, with a comforting smile on her face. "You are Aimsley Carter?"

"Yes," said Aimsley. Aimsley walked around the counter past Miranda to the door, turning the lock and flipping the sign to the "CLOSED" side. She turned back around, and walked to Miranda. She stopped short, looking at her, and then without warning wrapped her arms around Miranda and broke down sobbing, burying her head in Miranda's shoulder. Miranda wasn't comfortable much of the time even with people that she knew well in situations like this, but she could feel the depth of raw emotion that Aimsley was letting out, and she could feel her pain and her fear...the profound sadness pouring out from within. She put her arms around Aimsley and held her until the tears finally subsided.

# CHAPTER FIVE

The Book Stops Here bookstore, owned by Aimsley Carter, was larger inside than it originally appeared to Miranda from the outside. The store that had been next door had been a Celtic gift shop for a period of time, which in the middle of the Upper Peninsula of Michigan never really stood a chance of surviving. After that, it had been a head shop for a short period, selling hand blown glass pipes and various other smoking supplies. Hookahs, rolling machines, clothing and t-shirts with marijuana leaves on them had lined the many racks throughout the store, as well as art inspired by many rock bands and musicians of the 1960's and '70's. It did surprisingly well for a time, which had drawn some unsavory customers at times into the bookstore. Finally, the store was closed permanently after the two men who ran the shop were arrested for selling large amounts of marijuana out of the back room of the store. All of the equipment and merchandise was seized as evidence, and the building remained empty until the owner of the vacant establishment offered it to Aimsley very cheap, allowing her to expand on more books, and to create an area for people to come in and sit and relax as they browsed the different volumes and periodicals the store offered. There was a long, four-seat couch and two easy chairs, all situated around a coffee table with several different magazine titles neatly displayed upon it. It was from this area that the smell from the new carpeting had come from. Aimsley spent months working on the new addition to the store, and what she had come up with was a very homey, comfortable and cozy place for people to spend time enjoying both new books that they had purchased, or books they wanted to check out the first chapter of to see if it was something that they wanted to continue with. Aimsley loved everything about books, although she had not yet gotten around to writing the one great novel that she had always wanted to write of her own.

Miranda had seated herself on one end of the couch, and Aimsley sat on the edge of one of the easy chairs. Aimsley had gotten herself a cup of tea, and offered some to Miranda, but she politely declined, having her fill of coffee for the time being at the bakery just a short time before. Neither woman said much at first, still both feeling out of sorts from when Miranda had revealed herself to Aimsley. Finally, it was Aimsley that spoke first.

"I'm not sure where to begin," she said, her fingers tightly clasped together placed on her lap. "For a moment after I saw the picture, I thought I might be looking at a ghost. You look so much like your mother."

Aimsley said those words with a smile, but her eyes held so much sadness in them. Miranda let a hint of a smile come to her own face.

"I would guess that you have a lot of questions, Miranda," said Aimsley.

"Did you send me the video tape?" asked Miranda directly, yet softly. She was trying not to come across too anxious.

Aimsley paused for a moment looking down, and then looked to Miranda once more.

"I did send it to you."

Aimsley stood up, and turned half away from Miranda, as if she was feeling some shame in her actions.

"I'm sorry. I had no business to cause any disruption in your life. I should have just destroyed that box and been done with it."

Miranda stood up and approached her. "It's not like that at all," she said. "I just want to know who I am."

"What's on that tape is a fragment of a chapter of your life that is tragic and heartbreaking, and it should have been left in the past," said Aimsley.

"Then...if you feel so strongly about it, why did you send it to me? How did you even find me, or know what my name was now?" asked Miranda.

Aimsley turned her back all the way to Miranda now. Her head was tilted towards the floor, and several seconds passed before she said another word.

"I suppose if you've made your way all the way here, then you must have been to Galestone?" asked Aimsley. She turned back around to face Miranda again, and she seemed more together and serious than Miranda had seen her yet. "That's where you found the drawing? You've been to the Gale house?"

"I have, yes," said Miranda.

There were suddenly several knocks on the front door of the store. Aimsley excused herself and went to the door. Miranda followed from a short distance away, and listened to Aimsley speak to the man that came to the door. Miranda could see that he was probably in his mid to late-fifties, thick grey hair a little longer in the back, with a thick grey mustache to match the hair. He wore a camouflage jacket that went down past his waist, with dark blue jeans, and had a large hunting knife strapped to his side.

"Hello, Kent," Aimsley said, warmly.

"Mornin' Aimsley," said Kent. "Not planning on opening till the big event?"

"I was just taking a few minutes to catch up with an old friend," Aimsley told Kent. Kent looked up and saw Miranda standing near the corner of the bookshelf nearest the counter looking on. Miranda smiled politely at him, and Kent nodded back, returning the smile.

"Miranda, this is Kent Parker," she introduced. "Kent is a retired conservation officer from Newberry. He just published his second book, stories of different things he's experienced during the years he was on patrol. We're doing a book signing today, from 11 until 3. Kent, would you mind giving me a few more minutes to speak with Miranda?"

"No, that's fine. I'm gonna head across the street for coffee and say hello to Caroline. I'll be about a half-hour, and then we can start getting set up," said Kent.

"Thanks, Kent. I'll see you in a few minutes," said Aimsley, as Kent gave another wave and was out the door.

Aimsley turned back to Miranda.

"I'm sorry Miranda, I would close the store right now and tell you everything that I can tell you about the things you want to know. You want answers, I understand. I will do whatever I can to help you. I owe it to you, and I owe it to your mother. She made me make a promise to her a long time ago, and even though I couldn't be there for you all those years ago, I am here for you now. But I have been promising Kent for months that he could have a signing. The only time he really sells any books is when he gets to be face to face with the people, and he has been putting up flyers and telling everyone he knows to come down and bring their friends. I think it's going to be a busy day here," said Aimsley.

"No, I understand," said Miranda. "It's not like I was expecting you to stop your life just because I walked through your door. You don't owe me anything really..."

"I do. You have no idea how much I do owe you," said Aimsley. She placed her hand on Miranda's shoulder. "You can stay here all day if you'd like. Or, I live about a mile up this road next to the store. You are welcome to go there and wait, watch some television, or even just get some rest if you'd like."

"I suppose I could use some. It's been an interesting couple of days," Miranda said to her.

"Yes. I would think so. Go up to the house," she told Miranda, pulling a key from her purse behind the counter.

"You don't know me from anyone," said Miranda. "How can you just hand me a key to your house? I could rob you blind and you wouldn't have a clue."

Aimsley let out a short laugh. "I know that your mother was one of the sweetest, kindest people that I have ever known, and if you have any of her at all in you, then I would trust you with my life. Take the key, go and get some rest."

Miranda reached out and took the key from Aimsley's hand.

"Fourteen twenty-nine Hemlock. Yellow house on the corner, just less than a mile down Eastway Avenue. If you're hungry, whatever you find you are welcome to. As soon as the signing is done, I am closing and I will be on my way home. We'll have the rest of the evening to talk, and I will tell you whatever you want to know. You're welcome to stay for tonight if you'd like. I have a pullout in the living room. The extra bedroom is just office space and storage unfortunately."

"Thank you. I'd hate to be any inconvenience," said Miranda.

"Miranda...you don't know what it means to be able to see the beautiful young woman you've grown into. I just wish your mother could see you," Aimsley told her.

Miranda smiled again at Aimsley as she walked out the door. Walking to her car, she could see Kent across the street in the bakery through the front window chatting with Caroline. She didn't take notice of the silver sedan when she was leaving the bookstore, as there were more cars on the street for it to blend in with. She got into her car, and pulled down Eastway Avenue towards Aimsley's house.

Just as Mr. Skye turned the key in the ignition, Mr. Cain's phone began to ring.

"Yes?" Cain answered the phone. Mr. Skye pulled into the road and began to follow Miranda from a distance just after she pulled down Eastway.

"Yes, it is," Cain said to the caller. "Yes. I understand. We'll leave immediately." He pressed the END button on the phone.

Mr. Skye looked curiously at Mr. Cain.

"What is going on?" asked Mr. Skye.

"We have a new assignment," said Mr. Cain.

"More important than keeping track of the girl?" asked Mr. Skye.

"When we're given instructions by our employer, it's best to just do and not ask questions. Besides, the GPS locater is working perfectly. She won't be hard to find again. Don't be so concerned, my friend. I think you will enjoy our next task," said Mr. Cain. "Turn the car around."

"Where are we headed?" asked Mr. Skye.

"I will explain on the way. Just drive," said Cain.

Mr. Skye frowned. He turned the car around and drove in the opposite direction that they had taken when they came into town. He knew Mr. Cain was right. He had worked for a great many individuals and organizations over the years, and had done a lot of nasty things to both good and bad people. But this employer was unlike any he'd had in the past. It was best not to ask questions if the answers were not immediately necessary. Mr. Skye kept quiet and drove on.

Miranda easily found Aimsley's home on Hemlock, just as she described it. It was a quaint little home with a main level and an upper floor, one bedroom downstairs, and a second one on the floor above. The bedroom upstairs had to be Aimsley's; the one on the main floor had a roll top desk and chair with an older desktop computer on it. The rest of the room was cluttered with boxes and papers and various other items. She noticed a couple of boxes that had the word 'DONATE' written on them in black marker ink.

The kitchen was fairly small, which must have suited Aimsley just fine, but the living room was much larger in size, with a bookshelf that took up most of the wall at the far end of the room. Across the living room on the opposite side was a small fireplace with a 'U' shaped metal rack beside it filled with firewood. Above the mantelpiece over the fireplace was the only other modern looking thing in the whole house besides the old desktop computer - a 46-inch Sony flat panel television.

Miranda felt the home had a cozy and welcoming feeling throughout it. There were many items around the house that looked like homemade craft items. She noticed several quilts in different areas around the living room, as well as a boxed up quilt rack in the office/bedroom that was filled with the donation boxes and clutter downstairs. There were dream catchers hung on either side of the fireplace, and even the bathroom had crocheted decorations of fish and nautical designs.

    She sat herself down on the couch and turned on the television, trying to pass the time until Aimsley came home from the bookstore. Aimsley had satellite TV service, which Miranda imagined that living up here, in what she considered close to the middle of no where, was probably the only way to have any TV stations at all. She flipped to the History Channel and came across a special on the history and origins of Halloween, which was coming up fast, and found herself engrossed in the documentary. Before long though, she could feel her eyelids getting heavier, and she drifted off.

    The noise of her cell phone's ringer woke her from her mid-day nap. She looked at the phone, and the time was a little after 3 p.m. She saw that it was her mother's cell number, and realized that she should have called her herself before now to check in. She may be a grown woman on her own now, but she was still her parent's child, and they were entitled to worry about her, especially given the circumstances of the last few weeks.

    "Hey Mom," she said to Lorri, trying not to sound as if she had just been asleep in the middle of the day. She was supposed to be with a friend having fun, not crashed out on a stranger's couch somewhere.

    "How is everything going up there? Have you been having a good time?" asked Lorri.

    "Yeah, super. There's like nothing up here, so you have to make your own fun," said Miranda.

    "Yeah, it can be like that up there," said Lorri. "And how is your friend? Tammy, is it?"

    "She's good. She is glad that I am here though. I guess

when she went on about this place to me before, she remembered there being more to do here when she was just a kid. We've been keeping busy exploring the town around here. I think it's good for me to be here, to help clear my head," said Miranda. She was almost scaring herself with the realization of how easy it was to lie to her mother. It wasn't entirely without guilt, but if anyone would have a hard time understanding what she was truly doing there, it would be her mother.

"You'll have to bring her by sometime for a visit. Maybe when they come back through on their way home she and her family can stop by and have dinner with us? As a thank you for having you come up and visit with them," said Lorri.

"That might be a nice idea, Mom. I will see if they will have time to do that when they head home," Miranda told her.

"Speaking of home, do you have any idea when you will be coming home?" asked Lorri.

"I will probably head back tomorrow...maybe even later tonight," she said.

"I don't want you driving at night if you don't have to. The deer are running here all over the place right now, and I would imagine it's even worse up there. If you were to get into an accident, there may not be anyone for miles, and the cell phone reception up there is really spotty," Lorri told Miranda.

Miranda heard a car outside the house, and looked out to see that Aimsley had pulled into the driveway.

"Mom, I have to go. I think we are going to head out to dinner. I will stay until morning, so you don't have to worry," said Miranda.

"That sounds good. And, I won't have to worry about you falling asleep at the wheel, either," said Lorri. "I have to go anyway honey. Looks like there is a man from the gas company at the door. We got a call earlier that apparently the meter hadn't been hooked up properly and we have been being overcharged since we moved in. I don't know why it has too be so hard getting things right moving to a new place," said Lorri. "At least we should be getting a big credit on the next bill."

"That's good Mom," said Miranda, as Aimsley stepped into the front door with an arm load of groceries. "Mom, I gotta go. I will see you tomorrow."

"Alright sweetie. Drive safe. Love you," said Lorri.

"Love you too, Mom," she said, and she hit the END button on her phone.

Miranda took one of the bags from Aimsley's arm, although Aimsley was pretty much already to her small kitchen table where she set the other bag down.

"Did you find everything that you needed here?" Aimsley asked, putting the cold items into the refrigerator.

"Yes. The TV, at least. I fell asleep watching it," she said.

"Do you like chicken? I picked up a rotisserie chicken and mashed potatoes at the grocery store. I'm afraid I don't really cook a lot. Most of my time is spent at the store, and I spend a lot of time going to craft shows. I tend to eat on the run," said Aimsley. She seemed to be trying extra hard to seem casual, although it was obvious she was far from a relaxed state of mind.

"Chicken is fine, thank you. I really appreciate everything. Really. And I think I will take you up on crashing here tonight, if the offer is still on the table," said Miranda.

"Yes, of course it is," said Aimsley with much enthusiasm. "If you don't mind that pullout couch. You are more than welcome."

Miranda gave Aimsley the space to get the kitchen in order so they could sit down and have their meal. Aimsley set out the dishes and sliced up the chicken, and the two of them sat across from each other at the table. Miranda watched as Aimsley started eating and noticed that, even though it was very subtle, her hands quivered as she held her dinner fork. Miranda tried not to appear as if she noticed it, until Aimsley dropped the fork onto the plate. The sound should have startled Miranda, but all she did was raise her eyes from her plate and looked across at Aimsley.

"Is something wrong?" asked Miranda, trying to ease Aimsley's obvious tension.

"I'm sorry," said Aimsley, her eyes beginning to tear up once again.

"How was the book signing?" asked Miranda, attempting to shift the odd mood in the room to something more casual and mundane.

"It was...sniff...it was good. There was a really good turnout, actually. Kent sold probably more than 100 books today. He was happy with it, and just getting people into the store is great for me. It's the only bookstore within 50 miles, but there are still some people around that don't even know it's there. So I sold more than just Kent's book today, and that was a good thing as well," said Aimsley, getting herself back together.

"Well that's fantastic. A hundred books, eh? That's gotta be great for him," said Miranda.

Aimsley didn't respond at first. Her eyes were looking down at her plate, and she set her fork down upon her napkin beside the plate.

"I appreciate what you are trying to do, Miranda. I am sorry I am so out of sorts. You're probably thinking to yourself, 'What kind of a crazy person is this?'" said Aimsley.

"No, not at all. Please, don't worry about that. I didn't

mean to barge into your life and make you upset..." said Miranda.

"You didn't. You didn't barge anywhere. I led you here, whether I intended to or not. And I am not upset to see you. Quite the opposite, actually. I am so happy that you cannot possibly know. It's just that...well, seeing you brings back a lot of memories. Some very good memories...and some, very dark," said Aimsley, looking out the kitchen window and staring into the now darkening grey sky.

Neither of the two of them were really all too hungry, or if they were, it wasn't occurring to them to eat any more. Miranda put her silverware down and sipped from a glass of water.

"Would you like for us to talk now?" asked Miranda.

Aimsley looked back to her, and nodded her head. Miranda stood up from her chair, as did Aimsley, and she followed Aimsley into the living room. Miranda had left the television on from when Aimsley had gotten home. She turned the power off while Aimsley started a small fire in the fireplace to take the chill out of the room. The temperature dropped steadily over the past few evenings that Miranda had been in the area, especially during the late night hours.

After the fire was burning steadily, Aimsley sat across from Miranda, who had taken a seat on the couch she had slept on earlier. Aimsley sat on the edge of a recliner, her hands once again folded together as they were earlier at the bookstore.

"Miranda. I know that you don't know me at all. But I want you to please bear with me in some of what I am going to tell you. Even to me, some of it doesn't make a bit of sense, but I promise you, I have no reason to tell you anything but the truth as I have come to know it. Please don't think I am crazy. I am not, I assure you," said Aimsley. She paused for a brief moment. "Can you keep an open mind?" asked Aimsley.

"Of course. I mean, I would guess I can. We will just have to trust each other, and keep our minds open together," responded Miranda. She was eager to see where this was going, as well as a bit apprehensive. She did not want Aimsley to feel at all like she should hold anything back. She wanted her to feel at ease.

Aimsley eased into a smile after hearing Miranda tell her this. She felt some relief at the thought of Miranda putting her trust in her.

"Where would you like me to begin?" asked Aimsley.

Miranda thought for a moment. There was so much she wanted to know, but felt it was best to start at what was the beginning of this journey for her.

"How about we start with how you found me," she said.

The smile faded from Aimsley's face just as fast as it had found its way there.

"I guess that should be the part I get out of the way first, and then you can decide for yourself whether you want to listen to anything else I tell you after that," said Aimsley, with increasing hesitancy in her voice. Miranda sat quietly, anxious to hear what she had to say.

"It's alright. Please, go on," she told her, trying to encourage Aimsley to continue without the fear of ridicule or doubt on her part.

"I found you, at least this time, because of a dream."

Rick Jurewicz

## CHAPTER SIX

"A dream?" asked Miranda.

"Yes," said Aimsley. She looked to Miranda's face for some sign to give away disbelief in Miranda's face, but to her surprise, there was none evident. "I know how that might sound..."

"No. It doesn't sound crazy at all. Please, tell me about your dream," Miranda said.

"It started about a month and a half ago. You may have noticed all of the boxes that were in my 'office' when you first walked into the house. I had been putting off for a long time going through my attic upstairs to finally get rid of things that had been lying around for such a long time. Things that I just didn't need anymore, that I felt it was time to let go of. I have lived in this house since before I had worked for the Gales. It was my aunt's house before she passed away. She left it to me, and I have lived here ever since. Anyway, it's not a very big attic, but there were a few things that I wanted to go through up there, including some old things that my aunt had stored. Mostly, it was tea kettles. She collected them, and there were only a few that were her favorites that I could never part with. The rest, however, were still very collectible and I thought I could sell a few, and maybe donate the rest to a charity auction. I had completely forgotten that I had put the box up there."

"The box with the video tape?" asked Miranda.

"Yes. It was an odd feeling finding it. In the back of my mind, I guess I knew I would come across it. I just put it out of my mind for so long. When I started going through things, there it was, like it had been there waiting for me to find it. I brought it down, and for the first time since...since I had it, I opened it to look at the tape inside. I knew you were right there on the tape, but I didn't watch it. I just couldn't. It was too hard. I left it in there, and put the box on the floor next to the fireplace. I considered throwing it into the fire, and leaving the past in the past, but I couldn't get myself to do it. I knew that you had a good life, with parents that loved you dearly, but still, something held me back from doing it..."

"How did you know who my parents were? How did you know where to find me at all?" Miranda asked her.

Aimsley looked down at the floor again and sighed.

"After the fire...after Suzanne's death, your grandmother, Victoria, was extremely distraught. She believed that there was a curse on the Gale family, and that they were all to blame for the deaths. Everyone knew within a few days that Daryl Grimes set the fire, but Victoria believed that there was something more. She wanted to protect you from it, whatever it was. I worked only a few months for the family as a housekeeper, trying to put myself through school, before Suzanne found herself pregnant. My job description changed rather quickly, at the insistence of Victoria, and I became Suzanne's personal handmaid. It's not what Suzanne wanted, but I didn't mind, and Suzanne was a very generous and caring person. Besides, the job came with a substantial raise, and Suzanne was well aware of what the Gales were paying me, so she chose to go along with it for my sake, if not for her own. We made the best of it, but it was not a real job to me. It became a labor of love. Did you want something to drink? Water? I might have a 7-Up."

"Not right now, thank you. Did you need something?" asked Miranda.

"No. I'm fine. I just know I tend to ramble on a bit, especially when I am feeling anxious," said Aimsley.

Miranda nodded her head to Aimsley with a smile. Aimsley took a deep breath, and went on.

"Anyhow, in the next three years that followed, I stayed on at the house. I had no expenses, I had no bills, and in that time I saved up enough money to pay for all of the schooling that I had already had, as well as more than enough money to finish when my time at the house would eventually come to an end. But the best part was of course not the money. Suzanne and I had become wonderful friends, and I looked at you like you were my very own daughter. In fact, just a few weeks before the fire..."

Aimsley stopped for a moment; there was a long pause like she was trying to find the words, or at least force them from herself.

"I'm sorry," Aimsley started again, softly. "Talking about this...I hadn't talked about it to anyone for years. It just brings it all back."

"It's alright," Miranda assured her. "Take your time...we have all night. You want some tea now?"

Aimsley coaxed a warm smile to her lips. "No, thank you. Suzanne - your mother - just a few weeks before the fire, made me make a promise to her. She told me that if anything ever happened to her, she wanted me to take care of you. She said that she wanted me to raise you like you were my own child. I told her she was being silly talking like that, and that nothing was going to happen to her. But she was deadly serious, more so than I had ever seen her be about anything. She made me say it to her. She wanted me to promise that not only would I take you as my own, but that I would take you as far away from the rest of the Gales as possible. I failed her on both promises."

"What happened? How did you fail?" asked Miranda.

"First, I failed by not being allowed to fulfill her first wish. After the fire, Victoria stayed out of the public eye until the trial was over. I tried to talk to her many times, but the closest I could get was to a lawyer that she had hired to be her public face during the time up until the trial, a man named Phillip Jessup. I just wanted to see you. I couldn't imagine how scared and confused you must have been. And, I wanted to tell her Suzanne's wishes. I had hoped that Suzanne had put it into a will or something, but there was never any evidence that she did. So I would stay as near as I could to you and your family. Even though I couldn't see you, I waited and I watched, until one day I saw Victoria and Jessup come out of the home where Victoria and David had been staying. She was carrying you, and I watched her hug you for the longest time. Victoria was crying..." Aimsley's emotions took hold again, and she took a moment as if to catch her breath.

"She didn't stop crying when she let the lawyer take you from her, and you were crying and reaching out for her. Jessup took you, and handed you to a woman that was waiting in an SUV nearby. Victoria looked so much older than she had ever looked before. She was always an elegant woman. Very proper. Very beautiful. Now, she looked 10 years older, and far more frail and distraught than I had ever seen her before. My heart went out to her, and I almost went to her then...but I didn't.

Instead, I followed Jessup and the woman that took you as they left town. I followed them for hours on the roads, leading all the way to the small city of Petoskey, not far from your home town of Native Springs. That was where Jessup's law office was. I watched Jessup and the woman take you into the office, and a short time later, a young couple arrived at the office and went inside. It was several minutes later that the man and woman walked out with you in their arms. I followed them as well, now that they had you with them, to what was your old home in Native Springs. Part of me wanted to get out of the car and run to them, plead with them, tell them who I was and what Suzanne wanted. If that didn't work, I thought I might just grab you and run away...but I knew that would never work. They would find me, and I would never be able to even get the chance to see you again. But as I watched them, I could tell, even from afar, how happy they were to have you in their arms. They looked like good, loving people, and somehow I just knew that with those people, you were going to be alright. So, I left you alone and returned to Arlo."

"Why do you think Victoria used Phillip Jessup? Didn't the Gales already have another lawyer? Harry Thornton?" asked Miranda.

"Yes. Harry...he has a law practice that he works for here in Arlo still, I think. He was a very shifty character, if you ask me."

"I met him. His firm takes care of the old Gale properties. He is the one that let me see the house," said Miranda.

"Really? Odd how things seem to come full circle like that," remarked Aimsley.

"Do you have any idea why Victoria didn't have Harry handle the adoption? Why she went so far out of town to have it done?" asked Miranda.

"No, not unless she was trying to protect you from the attention and the press. That would seem like the only reason I can think of, although I would have thought even Harry could've handled something like that," said Aimsley.

"You said you failed on two promises. What did you mean by that?" asked Miranda.

"The fact that you are here now, asking about the Gales, is how I failed her again. If I had not sent you that box and the tape, the Gale family would still be a part of your past, which was what Suzanne had wished for," said Aimsley.

"I don't believe it's a bad thing to want to know where you came from," said Miranda. "But you still haven't told me how the box made it to me...especially to a home that I had only arrived at and seen the very first time the day before the box arrived."

"I suppose I should tell you how I came into possession of the box and the tape in the first place, and then maybe you can understand the whole picture. After the investigation of the house was completed, myself and the family were allowed to return to the house under supervision and retrieve personal items that could be salvaged. It had been several weeks, and I was there the first day that I could go inside. An officer met me there; Victoria and David had not been back to the house yet themselves. The room that I stayed in was very close to yours, and there had been moderate damage to that area of the house, but a few things were still intact. After I got there, I saw there was really nothing for me worth salvaging. I remembered then about the day before the fire; we had been playing with the video camera, Suzanne and you and I, and I had taken the tape out of the camera. You kept on trying to play with the tape, and Suzanne finally took the tape out of your hands and placed it inside the wooden box that had been sitting on top of the piano that day. I had never seen the box before, and I am not sure Suzanne had either. She just put the tape inside of it to keep it out of your hands and sight.

"I told the officer then that I had something in the main room that belonged to me, so he escorted me to the hall outside of the main room. Just then, the officer received a call that a fight had broken out at the Buckshot Tavern in town, and he had to go, so he asked me to please hurry and get what I needed. I saw the box, still sitting atop the piano, and instead of grabbing only the video tape inside, I took the whole thing. The officer was in a hurry, so he didn't question it. That was the last time I was at the Gale house."

"What made you decide to send it to me?" asked Miranda.

"When I took it, I just wanted to take something to remember you by. There was never any intention of ever trying to do anything else with it. But very soon after I found the box in the attic, I started having these dreams - these terrible nightmares that woke me up almost every night. I thought that maybe it was the stress of the memories of that time playing havoc on my subconscious or something. I consider myself a very rational person, so it never occurred to me at first that the dreams might be...something else..."

"Something else like how?" asked Miranda. "What do you mean?"

"This is where things started to shake me up, Miranda," said Aimsley. "I would be having nightmares about that night - the night of the fire. But now, instead of finding you and bringing you safely out of the house, I could only hear you screaming. I could hear you screaming in pain, like you were burning alive." Aimsley was visibly shaken recalling the dream to Miranda. Miranda seemed to be able to feel the emotion coursing through Aimsley.

"It went on day after day - night after night - and every day I looked at the box next to the fireplace, and I would want to go and throw it into the fire, but I couldn't. Something I couldn't explain was holding me back. So I prayed for an answer as to what to do. I wasn't sleeping and I was barely eating anything. It was like nothing I had ever experienced. But the night that I prayed for an answer was the first night in over two months that I didn't remember having a dream. It was waking up the next morning though that scared me more than anything that happened before that."

"I woke up at my kitchen table with a pen in my hand and a sheet of paper on the table in front of me. On the paper, as clear as can be in handwriting that *wasn't mine*, but written by the pen in my hand, was the address to your parents new home. I didn't know it at first, but I did a search online and found your brother's Facebook page, and on his page he posted a message on his wall about the new house they had just moved into, and gave the address. I panicked, Miranda. I found the box that I shipped it to you in lying in a pile of boxes I picked up from the supermarket to clean out the attic with. I wrote the address on the box and drove all the way down to St. Ignace, just north of the Mackinaw Bridge, and sent it out. I didn't even want it postmarked from here. I was trying to get it out of my life without having it lead you back here. But apparently, you have your mother's intelligence. You found your way here anyway. I'm sorry."

"I need to tell you something as well," said Miranda. "The reason I was at my parent's home was because I had been having nightmares too. I used to have them all the time as a child, but they stopped for a long time. They only started up again, more intense than ever before, about two and a half months ago."

"Right about the time I found the box," Aimsley said, her face flushed with a deep fear. She stood up from where she had been sitting and walked towards the doorway into the kitchen, stopping short to steady herself with her hand on the doorframe.

Miranda stood up and moved in her direction. "Are you okay?"

"Yes. I'm just, I don't know what any of this means," said Aimsley, turning to face Miranda. "This all seems so impossible."

"I don't know either, but I believe for some reason I was meant to come here and find you. There's more I need to know though. I spoke to a woman in Galestone named Mary Ann. She and her husband own the Buckshot Tavern. Do you remember her?" asked Miranda.

"Yes, somewhat. It was so long ago now," said Aimsley.

"She told me things about Galestone and about the Gale family. At first everything she told me was of how great the Gales were to the community, but then she realized who I was. Her entire demeanor changed like a switch had been flipped in her. She told me I should leave the town and never come back. She even told me the town almost didn't come to help on the night when the fire broke out. Do you have any idea why the townspeople would react that way?" asked Miranda.

Aimsley walked slowly back to where she had been sitting before and took her seat again. The look on her face was that of a blank, empty stare. Miranda waited patiently for almost a full minute before she felt she had to wake Aimsley from her stare.

"Aimsley? Why would a town full of people who praised a family to the rest of the world let them burn to death in their home?" Miranda asked once more.

Aimsley finally looked at Miranda again. "The Gales had a secret world that they lived in that went back for generations upon generations. I believe it was partly why they came to Point Ridge to begin with, before it became Galestone. Point Ridge was quiet and secluded, away from the crowded, prying eyes of the rest of society. It was what your mother was trying to protect you from, and I believe your grandmother was doing the same thing by sending you away."

"What do you mean by a 'secret world'? What were they hiding from?" asked Miranda.

"I don't know the details as to what it was that they believed. I know mostly what I know from what your mother confided in me. When I first signed on to work for the Gales, before I had even met your mother, I had to sign papers that contained a confidentiality agreement. I could not discuss any activities, business, or private affairs that I may find myself privy to. At least that is how I think it was worded. At that time, it was Thornton that wrote up the legal documents," said Aimsley.

"The business activities around that time were pretty much dead, weren't they?" asked Miranda.

"I believe they still had their hands in some foreign investments. Mostly stocks and small business ventures overseas. Those were things that I picked up on through certain conversations between Thomas and Edward. But I don't believe it was these things that they were as concerned about. Not only did I have to sign those papers when I began working for the Gales, but I was also given very specific instructions as to when and where I was allowed to go on certain parts of the grounds," said Aimsley.

"What did they not want you to see?" asked Miranda, her eyes fixed on Aimsley. She was hanging on Aimsley's every word, like a child hearing a frightening ghost story, not sure if they wanted to get to the ending, but knowing they had to hear it through to its chilling conclusion. Aimsley could see the anticipation in her eyes, but only with some reluctance did she push on.

"There was a pathway behind the house that led into the woods beyond the gardens. It was the only safe passage to an area several hundred feet behind the house that was still on the Gale grounds. On Saturdays, every Saturday in fact, no house staff were allowed to go into the rear grounds of the house, and the trail into the woods was off limits at all times. Edward was the only one to maintain the trail and keep down the overgrowth of vegetation. Sometimes, he would have Suzanne's brother David help him keep trees and large branches that had fallen in storms off the trail, but it was mostly his duty to maintain access to the areas down the trail," Aimsley told Miranda.

"Do you know what was down the trail?" asked Miranda.

"There was one day when we were all in the backyard; it was you, your mother and I. You started walking towards the trail, and I told you we weren't supposed to go back there, but Suzanne said it would be alright if we took a walk down the trail. So, the three of us walked on, and the trail seemed to go on and on. I was sure that you would get tired of walking, but you just kept going along farther and farther down the path. Suzanne and I kept looking at each other, smiling and laughing about your energy and enthusiasm. Finally, we came to an open clearing. In the center of the clearing was a large, round cement slab that measured probably, oh, I'd say 30 feet across. Around the outer edge of the circle were several strange markings that looked as if they had been carved into the stone slab. I couldn't make them out as anything that I had ever seen before. They looked like they could have been writing of some kind, but nothing that made sense to me. There was a hole in the center of the slab about five feet in diameter, full of ashes, like there had been fires burned in that spot."

"When I first saw it, I was surprised that something like that had been built way back there. It looked like it had been there for a very long time, probably as long as the house itself had been there. I glanced back at Suzanne. The look on her face changed to a look of apprehensive concern. The smile that she had carried all the way down the trail had left her face. I could almost see a flash of fear in her eyes, and when she could tell that I noticed the look on her face, she forced the smile back just as fast. She was trying to cover up the feelings going on behind her false smile. I knew her well enough that I could tell what was going on in her head. She knew that fact all too well. Before I could say anything though, Victoria came rushing down the path."

"I remember Victoria saying, 'Suzanne! What do you think you are doing, bringing them down here!? Can you imagine what your father might do if he found out?'"

"Suzanne told her that she meant no harm. That Miranda wanted to explore. I don't think it was you, Miranda, that she was concerned about seeing down the trail. Victoria gave me a sharp glance, but I don't believe she was angry with me. I think the look was meant for Suzanne, more out of concern for me than anything else."

"Did you think that you might be in some sort of danger?" asked Miranda.

"No. At least I didn't believe so at the time. As long as I was important enough for Suzanne to have around to help with you, I doubt they would have let me go. As far as any other kind of danger, at the time I had no reason to think so."

"Did you ever feel threatened by anyone in the family?" asked Miranda.

"No, your family - all of them - seemed to be good people. They were all very good to me, right up until the very end," said Aimsley.

"Then why would the townspeople not want to help them?" asked Miranda.

"People have a tendency to fear what they don't understand. Even through the Gale's best efforts, it was rumored that some of the people who worked for the Gales both before and after the mines closed down saw and heard things that they weren't supposed to. It didn't even matter what the truth was. Once the whispers started through the town, there was no stopping the rumor mill. It mostly started shortly after the mines closed. It didn't matter what people chose to believe when things were going good, as long as everyone was kept fat and happy. But when things turned around in the other direction, people let their superstitious sides run wild. Some people said the family was cursed because of 'dark dealings', and that was why the mines had to be closed. Other people spoke of cults and devil worship. The rumors went on for years before I had even come to work for the family. Over time, I think a lot of people just ignored what was said. They wrote it off to people being bitter about losing jobs and such. But many long timers in the town never forgot what was said by those who had seen or heard things on the Gale estate."

"Was Daryl Grimes one of those people?" asked Miranda. She could tell that hearing the name made Aimsley uneasy.

"Grimes started working on the grounds a short time after Suzanne found out she was pregnant. I don't know much about him even now, except that he was a sick and disturbed man. Even then, when he was working for the Gales, he was quiet and kept to himself. When I did have to speak to him for anything, he was always very short tempered and not sociable in the least. But I honestly never took him for the sort that would try to murder an entire family, and me along with them," said Aimsley.

"Do you know what went on back in the woods? Do you think Grimes knew?" asked Miranda.

"I don't know what Grimes knew, or what he thought he knew. I don't believe money was the issue when he was let go. I overheard Thomas and Edward talking one night about Grimes snooping around where he shouldn't be. I walked through the kitchen to get you a snack before bed, and they stopped talking about it, but I pretended that I didn't hear anything. The next day, Grimes wasn't at work. Later, I was told by Thomas that they weren't able to keep him on any longer, and that I was welcomed to stay as long as I liked. I never even saw Grimes again until after he was arrested," said Aimsley.

"You said my mother, Suzanne, confided things in you. Did any of what she confided have to do with what went on back in the woods?" asked Miranda.

Aimsley stood up again, and walked to a window in the living room, gazing out into the trees of the vacant lot next to her home.

"Miranda, maybe I've said too much as it is. Maybe it should just be enough to know you came from a mother who loved you more than life itself. This is not a road Suzanne would have wanted you to wander down."

"I have had strange dreams and nightmares for as long as I remember. I have no memory whatsoever of my life before the parents I have now. And you having dreams, too? I have to know what was going on with that family. I know that it sounds crazy, and what about this doesn't? I am starting to think that if the Gale family was into something dark - or maybe even something supernatural - if whatever that was may have found its way to me, I need to know what that is," said Miranda, pleading for answers from Aimsley.

Aimsley turned around to face Miranda, determined to stand her ground and end this conversation for Miranda's sake. But she saw both the determination and the fear in Miranda's eyes, a look that brought to life the image of Suzanne before her once again. Even though Suzanne had wanted none of this for Miranda, it was something else that fueled the fire that brought Miranda to her.

Aimsley walked past Miranda to the bookshelf on the wall in the living room. She removed a large book from the shelf and, kneeling down on the floor, set it down on top of the coffee table. Miranda saw that it was an oversized copy of the Holy Bible, measuring twelve inches by eight, and almost three inches thick. Aimsley opened the book, revealing that it was hollowed out on the inside. She removed from the inside of the book a stack of several carefully folded and bound together sheets of old, yellowed parchment pages. Aimsley untied the strings that bound the pages. Every page was filled with writing from top to bottom, on both sides of each sheet. The writing was black but partially faded, and a few of the sheets looked as if they had been partially burned on the edges, but the writing had not been obscured as far as she could see. There were six pages in all. Aimsley held them in both her hands, looking

Miranda straight in the eyes.

"Before I sent the box to you, I did open it and look inside. I didn't realize when I took the box that there was more inside than just the tape. These were in it as well," said Aimsley, handing her the sheets of parchment.

"What are these?" asked Miranda as she looked over the strange text covering the pages. It was unfamiliar to anything that Miranda had ever seen before.

"I have no idea what they are. I had never known that they were in the box until just before I sent it to you. But I can tell you that I am pretty sure some of these symbols match the writing that I saw on the slab behind the Gale house," remarked Aimsley.

"Have you tried to find out what it was? Now that you had something to study up close?" asked Miranda.

"I did some research on it, but there were no exact matches. There were, however, some similar characters that I found that may be related to the origins of this script," said Aimsley.

"What are they?"

"What I found was a form of what some scholars refer to as angelic script."

"Angelic? Like, *angel* angelic?"

"Yes. Like the written language of the angels of Heaven. I found a website that had samplings of many different languages, both currently used languages and ancient dead ones. There was also a section of languages of unknown or unverified origin. There, I found information on what is called Enochian script. It was derived from the journals of a man in the late 1500's named John Dee. He believed that himself and a medium named Edward Kelley received messages from angels, and these angels gave them the script of the language, but there was no key as to how to decipher the language. It was believed to be the original language, the language by which God spoke when he created the Heavens and the Earth. It was also the language that was given to be used by Adam, but after the fall from grace and the expulsion from the Garden of Eden, the language was lost to him. Adam derived many aspects of the Hebrew language from what he could remember from the first language. Some Biblical scholars, who have actually taken John Dee's claims seriously, have supposedly successfully translated much of the script, but most scholars believe that Dee had made the whole thing up with Kelley. Although what is on these pages doesn't match the Enochian script that came from Dee exactly, it was the closest thing I could find that gave me any clue at all to what it might be," Aimsley told her.

"None of this makes any sense to me," said Miranda. "If the Gales were the followers of some kind of 'angel worship' cult, why would anyone think they were involved in something that might be construed as bad? And why hide? Angels are supposed to be the good guys, the servants of God, right?"

"I guess that depends upon what you read and what you choose to believe," said Aimsley. "I did some more reading on angel lore after I found out what I did about the script. Angels were the enforcers of God. And many of them, according to legends and some religious beliefs, rebelled against God. Those were the fallen legion of angels, led by Lucifer, the first angel."

"Lucifer is another name for the devil, isn't it? I have read a lot of stories, some comic books when I was younger. The name Lucifer was used as well as Satan for the name of the devil before he fell. Could the Gales have been devil worshippers of some kind?" asked Miranda.

"I don't know, Miranda. The devil has been called many names. It was in Dante's 'Divine Comedy' that the archangel Lucifer was associated with being the angel who would become the devil," said Aimsley. "It's hard to imagine that the Gale family had anything to do with devil worship, though. They were good people, to the town as well as to me for all those years. Not the type of people I'd imagine sacrificing goats and bathing in baby's blood or anything like that. They did have their secrets, though. That is for certain."

Miranda sat quietly in thought for a moment, and then an idea came to her as to how she might get some answers as to where she could find out more about the script written on the parchments given to her by Aimsley.

"Do you have a scanner for your computer?" Miranda asked Aimsley.

"Yes. Why?"

Miranda grabbed her phone and dialed Lydia's number. It rang twice, and Lydia answered.

"Hey! Is everything alright?" asked Lydia.

"Yes. Everything is fine, actually. I have a big favor to ask of you though," said Miranda.

"Anything you need, sweetie. What's up?"

"I am going to send you an e-mail with a couple of pages of scanned text. Do you think you could take it to one of your professors to have them look at it?"

"Okay, what are we talking about? Which professor?" asked Lydia.

"The one that teaches your *Modern Perspectives of Ancient Religious Practices* class. What is his name again?"

"It's Mr. Carlyle," said Lydia. "What is it that you are sending me?"

"I'm not sure, really. That is what I am hoping you can

help me with. I am going to scan and send it to you right now. If you could just take them to Mr. Carlyle and see if he can tell you what they might be, it would help a lot. Is that alright?"

"Of course I will help. Are you going to tell me what all of this is about at some point?" asked Lydia.

"As soon as I know something for sure, I will fill you in. I promise," said Miranda.

"Alright then. I should be seeing him tomorrow in his office. I can see what he says and call you to let you know," said Lydia.

"Thanks, Lyd. They should be in your e-mail in a few minutes. I will talk to you soon," Miranda told her.

"Take care of yourself, Miri. I'll talk to you soon," said Lydia, just before disconnecting the call.

Miranda and Aimsley proceeded to scan in the first two pages of the parchment pages, and sent them off to Lydia's e-mail address.

The two women sat back down in the living room. Aimsley was the first to take notice of how dark it had gotten already. The time had gone by quite rapidly during their conversation. The more serious talk was over for the time being, and from angels and ancient writing the conversation shifted to talking about Miranda's parents and what it was like growing up in Native Springs. It was mostly small talk that they found themselves wrapped up in until around 10 p.m. Aimsley got Miranda a fresh sheet and blankets for the pullout bed, and wished her goodnight. Miranda fell asleep quicker than she thought she would. There was so much going on in her head, she was sure she wouldn't get a bit of sleep. Apparently though, all that had been revealed that day had taken its toll on her.

The final thought that crossed her mind that night before slipping into unconsciousness was the final unanswered question of the day. With all that she had found out today, what now could tomorrow possibly bring?

## CHAPTER SEVEN

The smell of eggs and bacon filled the entire main level of the house the next morning. It was an inviting and delicious aroma, and Miranda realized with so little that she had eaten the night before how hungry she really was. She lifted her head to look around for her phone, and found that it had fallen off the pullout bed onto the floor beside it. She picked it up and saw the time was 9:37 a.m. She had slept for almost ten and a half hours. She felt good, and well rested. She rolled out of the bed and pulled on her jeans before walking into the kitchen where Aimsley was cooking breakfast.

"Would you like some coffee?" Aimsley asked, holding the pot in one hand and a white mug with an owl painted on the side in the other hand.

"Yes, thank you," Miranda responded as Aimsley poured her the coffee. It was a fresh ground French roast blend, and Miranda found it very satisfying. She sipped it, and set the cup down on the table as Aimsley brought her a plate with eggs over easy, three strips of bacon and white toast.

"I hope you like your eggs over easy, I guess I hoped you liked eggs at all. This is how Suzanne always liked them. I guess I just assumed."

"I do like them over easy, thanks," said Miranda. Aimsley just smiled; they continued to enjoy their breakfast, busily eating with little talking. After they finished, Miranda insisted on helping Aimsley clean up. The two sat back down at the small kitchen table when they had finished, sipping their freshly topped off cups of coffee.

"Would you mind if I take the parchment pages with me?" asked Miranda.

"As far as I am concerned, they were always yours. You are the last of the Gale family, at least around here. I never had the right to take them or anything else, really. I did it for my own selfish reasons," said Aimsley.

"Well, on behalf of the Gales, I forgive you," Miranda said in a mock diplomatic tone, grinning at Aimsley. Aimsley smiled at her when she said this, but the look of concern that Miranda had seen so many times over the last 24 hours had returned to Aimsley's face.

"Aimsley, I don't want you to feel bad about sending me the box. I know you promised my mother that you would try to protect me. But I am no ones to protect anymore. I am a grown woman, and I do have a right to know where I came from and who my family was. I know that I only really just met you yesterday, but I feel like I have known you my entire life in some way. You don't get that feeling from just anyone. I believe that is why my mother chose you over anyone else. Because if I were to need anyone, you would be there for me. I am thankful for that," Miranda told Aimsley, whose eyes glassed up once more as she looked on at Miranda.

"You are wise beyond your years, Miranda. Suzanne would be proud of the intelligent and beautiful young woman you've become," Aimsley told her.

Miranda got her things together and folded up the

couch as Aimsley put the sheets away in the laundry room. She took the parchment papers and placed them in a manila file folder that Aimsley had given to her, and tucked them safely in the case with her laptop. Aimsley walked out to her car with her, and the two of them stopped and faced each other for several seconds before Aimsley hugged Miranda tightly. Miranda hugged her back, this time she was not feeling so much like she was hugging a stranger, but a long lost friend or close relative. Aimsley loosened her grip finally and released her.

"I have something for you," Aimsley told her. She reached up her hand and gave Miranda a small crocheted decorative angel in an oval maple frame.

"I made that quite a while back, well before any of these dreams had started, and also before I found the box again. It's the only angel design I've ever done. I thought, given all that we talked about last night, it might be appropriate. Besides, Suzanne always called you her little angel."

Miranda took it and looked at it for a minute, gently running her finger across all of the fine details that Aimsley had hand stitched into the image of the angel with the soft golden halo.

"Thank you. I will be back to see you, you know. Once I get a chance to explain all of this to my parents, and get through the fact that I haven't been entirely honest with them as to what I have been doing the last few days. I just hope they will understand. I'm finding it hard to understand why they never told me I had been adopted," said Miranda.

"Maybe they weren't supposed to, Miranda. I wouldn't be too hard on them about that. You never know what conditions Victoria made for the adoption to happen," said Aimsley.

"I suppose it doesn't really matter. I think I have found what I was supposed to find, anyhow. My mother wanted me to find you. You never know - maybe that was what this was all about," said Miranda.

Aimsley really didn't believe things were all that simple and true, given all that she had known about the Gales. She forced a smile to her face, trying to hide her anxieties from Miranda.

"There is one thing that I haven't asked you about. I think it got lost in the shuffle of everything else that we talked about. My biological father. Do you know who he was? Was it the Gale's gardener, Gabe?" Miranda asked.

Aimsley gave Miranda a surprised look when Miranda mentioned Gabe's name.

"Suzanne was always so happy and cheerful around Gabe when he worked for the Gales. Anyone who saw them together could tell the fondness they had for each other. She never spoke his name after he left the Gales. She had become pregnant, and Gabe was gone. She was quite often very sad after he left, right up until you were born. But once you came into her life, the sadness went away. You became the love of her life. I always assumed Gabe was your father, but we never spoke of it," Aimsley told her.

Miranda smiled softly.

"Thank you."

There are some people in this world that weren't lucky enough to have one mother that loved them so much. But here was Miranda, having had two mothers that loved her so deeply, although one of them she had never gotten to know in life. Whatever the reasons though, her father, the gardener named Gabe, left in a hurry after Suzanne became pregnant. Was he forced to leave? Or could it have been something far more sinister?

Miranda got into her car and gave a final wave as she drove out of the driveway and away down the road. Aimsley turned and walked back up the sidewalk to her front steps. She sat down on the top step and let her head tilt back with her eyes closed as she breathed in the fresh morning air. The sun was bright that morning, and she felt warm, even sitting in the cool northern air.

It wasn't the sun she really believed that was keeping her warm. It was the feeling that she had finally fulfilled her promise to a friend long gone. She just hoped and prayed she had done the right thing. She didn't want to let Suzanne down once more.

Miranda was well on her way out of town when she saw flashing lights in the distance behind her. She checked her speed, and she was only about six miles an hour over the speed limit. She pulled herself over to the side of the road, only to have the state police car fly past her. The cop had to be going over 80 mph, and before she could pull back onto the road, two more police cars sped by, one that looked like it might have been local town police, and the other had markings that indicated it was a sheriffs department car. Following close behind were an ambulance and an unmarked car with flashing lights, all coming up behind her from the direction of Arlo.

She pulled back onto the road and continued onward. Most of the vehicles that had just past by had gone far out of her sight in their haste. Her phone started to buzz in the seat next to her. She remembered that the night before she had turned the phone to vibrate only, so if it were to ring in the middle of the night or early morning, it would not wake Aimsley. The number on the phone was not one that she recognized, so she let the call go. There had been many calls that she had been getting from solicitors. Somehow she thought that she must have gotten her number on a phone mailing list somewhere, and now her phone and her voicemail inbox had been flooded with offers from several online companies selling everything from dish washing detergent to erectile dysfunction supplements. Miranda thought that someone had played a cruel joke on her and put her on a list, and she was not amused.

She drove on, selecting her 'post punk' playlist from her iPod. Joy Division's "Transmission" was the first song randomly selected. She had her music to keep her company on the long ride home, which she thought was another thing to be thankful for on a bright and beautiful morning.

An hour and a half had passed as she traveled along the seemingly endless northern roads. By that time, she had made it back to US-2 heading east towards St. Ignace. Her phone had started vibrating again. This time though, it was Lydia's face that popped up on the caller ID screen.

"Hey Lyd," said Miranda, sounding uncharacteristically upbeat to Lydia's sharp ear.

"Hey. That stuff you sent me, Mr. Carlyle found it very interesting, but he couldn't tell me too much about it. He isn't so much an expert in languages as he is a historian and theologian. He did say it looked like it could be an early form of Hebrew, but he couldn't tell for sure," said Lydia.

"Well, thanks anyway," said Miranda, the disappointment evident in her voice.

"Don't sound so sad and sorry just yet. Carlyle has an old friend, a semi-retired professor at Sentry Tech University in Macomb that is a much bigger expert in these types of things than he is. He said the guy is obsessed with ancient religions and languages," said Lydia.

"Really? Did you get his name?" asked Miranda.

"His name's Dr. Alexey Vikhrov. I am going to text you his office info and phone number. You may have to make an appointment to meet with him, being that he isn't at the university all the time these days," said Lydia.

"Vikhrov? Is he Russian?" asked Miranda.

"Mr. Carlyle said he was born in Russia, but has lived here in the United States for almost half of his life. He's in his early sixties now. He defected from Russia in the late seventies…"

Miranda's phone began to buzz in Lydia's mid-sentence. She saw that it was the same number that called earlier in the day, which she found unusual, being that the calls she had been getting from the solicitors are rarely duplicate numbers. This was a tactic she believed was a way to try and throw people off from dodging the calls, although most of the time if it was a number that Miranda didn't recognize, she would just not answer.

"Lyd, I have a call coming through I think I should take. Tell Mr. Carlyle thank you so much for his help. I will fill you in as soon as I know more."

"Okay Miri…drive safe," said Lydia.

"I will," said Miranda, ending the call with Lydia to answer the mystery call.

"Hello?" answered Miranda.

"Is this Miranda Stratton?" asked the unfamiliar voice.

"Yes, this is, who is this?"

"Miranda, my name is Robert Rice. I'm a detective with the Michigan State Police," said the man. His voice sounded deep, but strangely calm and soothing.

Miranda thought about the state police vehicles that

passed her earlier in the day. What did they do? Tag her for speeding and decide to let her know the ticket will be in the mail?

"Um...how can I help you, Detective?" asked Miranda curiously, yet a little annoyed if in fact a ticket was what the call was all about.

"Miss Stratton, are you driving a vehicle at this moment? Am I hearing that correctly?" he asked.

"Yes, is this about earlier, because I was only going a few miles over the limit? How did you get this number so quickly?" Miranda asked, feeling a tightening in the pit of her stomach. She was beginning to sense that something was not right.

"Miss, can you please pull your vehicle to the side of the road?" asked the detective. His voice almost seemed to soften for a moment, which unnerved Miranda all the more. She pulled the car over without hesitation, gripping the wheel tighter now, although she didn't realize it at the time. Her knuckles on her left hand turned white as she held the steering wheel. The car came to a stop. She was starting to have an overwhelmingly sick feeling come over her, but had no idea why it was happening.

"I'm pulled over. What is this about?" she asked with a slight tremor in her voice.

"Miss Stratton, I'm afraid I have some bad news for you. There's been an accident," he started, pausing for what seemed like forever. Miranda stayed silent waiting for an ax to drop, not knowing where it might land.

"I'm so sorry," Detective Rice said, his voice now unsteady. "There was an accident at your parent's home, a gas leak in the basement."

"Oh my God!" Miranda said, her phone hand shaking.

"Are they...is everyone...Steven...?" She couldn't form a full sentence with her words.

"I'm sorry Miss Stratton. Your parents and your brother didn't make it. We believe they were overtaken by carbon monoxide poisoning in their sleep. They never woke up. The responders did everything they could. I'm sorry I had to tell you this over the phone. We didn't know how to find you. Your number was found in the home. Are you far? We can send someone to pick you up if you need?"

Miranda sat frozen in the seat of her car, alone on the side of US-2, still hours away from her home. She stared straight ahead, and the hand that held her phone slowly sunk to the seat below.

"Miss Stratton? Hello? Miss Stratton, are you alright?" the voice continued on the phone. She found the strength to hit the END button on the phone. She felt empty, like she was outside of her body, floating. She knew what she heard, but nothing seemed real. Tears were flowing down her face, but her hand still held its grip tight on the steering wheel.

"No!" she said with a harsh, angered tone. "*Fuck this*. Someone is fucking with me. This isn't real."

Miranda wiped the tears from her face as the phone began to buzz again, and she pressed the silencing button on the phone and threw the car back into gear. The tires spun on the gravel and then squealed as they hit the pavement. She was headed once more back in her home direction. She had to get home now, and fast. She needed to find out who was mentally terrorizing her, and why. She kept ignoring the phone's repeated buzzing, and thought about calling Aimsley to talk to her, just so she had someone to talk to, but she didn't know what she would even say. She didn't want to upset her, especially without knowing what is really going on.

*Someone was trying to scare her*, Miranda thought. She just sped onward, watching for police and traveling now a good 15-20 mph over the speed limit, which wasn't unusual on US-2. People tended to either forget it wasn't an interstate freeway, or they just didn't care. Miranda didn't care. She needed to get home to see her family.

It was roughly an hour and a half later when Miranda came to the entrance of the Sherwood Trail subdivision. She could already see the flashing lights of police cars lining the road and a road block was put up to stop traffic from coming up the road. The sick feeling came back. She pulled the car over and opened the door into the high weeds along the side of the road, and her breakfast came back up on her violently. Her face filled with tears again, but she got herself together as much as possible and approached the blockade. An officer stood waiting to turn anyone away who was trying to get past the police line.

"I'm sorry ma'am, I can't let you through at this time," said the officer, who looked younger than even Miranda was.

Miranda's eyes met the young officer's eyes straight on. "I need to get through - I need to get to my parents!"

Her voice was strong and determined, and the expression on the officer's face was almost fearful. He did not say a word in response or try to stop her, almost seeming like he had fallen into some kind of trance. After she had passed, he came back to his senses, but did not try to follow her or call her back. He picked up his radio and sent a message to someone, staying in position by his post at the blockade. Miranda could see the ambulance in the driveway, and saw the EMTs walking out of the house with a large black bag on a stretcher. Miranda realized by the size of the body bag that it might be her father. She picked up her pace and started running in the direction of the ambulance, which caught the attention of some of the other officers on the scene.

"Daddy? Daddy!" Miranda started yelling in desperation as she ran. A uniformed policeman stepped in front of her and held her as she tried to push by.

"Miss, you're not supposed to be here right now," said the officer. "You're going to have to go back behind the barricade."

"It's alright officer," said a voice from behind the policeman that was holding back Miranda. The large man came up quickly, moving much faster than it seemed someone his size should move.

"I'll take her from here," said the man, who was not wearing a police uniform, but instead a brownish-grey suit coat and dark grey slacks. His bushy, black and grey hair matched his thick salt and pepper mustache. There was a gold badge on his jacket pocket with the name 'Rice' on it. The officer released her, and she dropped to her knees on the spot in a sobbing mess of tears.

Detective Rice stood next to her for a moment, understanding the pain this poor girl was in. It was a sight he had witnessed far too many times before. He had been on the job for over 30 years, and this part never got any easier.

Rice knelt down in front of Miranda and put his hand on her shoulder. One of the other officers was walking by, and Rice motioned silently for him to find a blanket. The officer returned promptly with a thick blanket from the ambulance, and Rice draped it over Miranda's shoulders. This was not a homecoming that anyone would ever want, nor could anyone ever even imagine. He stood alongside Miranda until she was ready to come with him somewhere they could talk privately.

There were crowds of people lining the outside of the

police line. Most were locals, gawking at the excitement and trying to get a handle on what had happened in the house. Others were local newspaper and television station reporters, with cameras set up and aimed in the direction of the activity surrounding the scene.

Standing silently amongst the many onlookers watching the horrors unfold were the menacingly familiar faces of Mr. Skye and Mr. Cain. The two men keenly surveyed the media circus, making sure they were not caught on any of the many cameras at the scene, and just as intently, keeping their eyes focused on Miranda as well.

Like vile predators, they would watch and wait, ready to make a move at a moments notice when they were ordered to do so.

## CHAPTER EIGHT

"Miranda," said Detective Rice, speaking softly and kneeling in front of her after several minutes had gone by. "We should probably move down to the police station in town. There are some things that I need to go over with you. Do you think we can do that now?"

Miranda nodded her head without lifting her eyes to him, and Detective Rice offered her his hand to help her up off the ground. With everything going on around them at that moment, neither Miranda nor Detective Rice noticed the roar of the motorcycle engine that came from just beyond the police barricade near where Miranda had parked.

"Miranda!" called a voice from the other side of the barricade. "Miranda!"

Miranda looked in the direction from which the voice came and saw Jake Neilson trying to get the officer at the barricade to let him through.

"Jake!" she called to him, and started to run in his direction. The officer at the barricade looked back at Detective Rice, who gave the officer a nod to let Jake through. Jake ran up to Miranda and wrapped his arms around her tightly. She buried her head in his jacket while he held her head against him.

"They're gone, Jake," Miranda choked out, the emotions coming on strong again in his familiar arms.

"I know...I heard in town that something had happened in this neighborhood...and that people had died. I'm sorry, Miranda...I'm so sorry. When I heard the name of the family...I...I freaked out and came up here. I was so scared you were in there..."

"I'm okay...I was on my way home when I got a call. I wouldn't believe it. And then I got here...oh my God, Jake. How could something like this happen...? Mom...Dad...Steven...I don't know what to do..."

Detective Rice walked up beside the two of them.

"Miranda," said Rice. "We should head into town. Your friend can come with you if you'd like. The emergency service people and the investigators still have a lot of work to do here. We need to talk about a few things..."

"That's fine...I want Jake to come," Miranda told Rice.

"He can meet us down at the office then. I can give you a ride to the office in my car. We can have an officer bring your car to the police station," said Rice.

"I can drive," said Miranda. There was a shakiness in her voice. Rice thought she seemed too unsteady to drive.

"I don't think that is a good idea, Miss Stratton. We can..."

"I drove the whole way home. I can drive. Please..." Miranda told Rice. She needed her own hands on the wheel right now. It was one of the few things that she felt she could have control of.

"Alright, I will head down now," Detective Rice told the two of them. He nodded his head and walked away to his vehicle.

Jake walked Miranda to her car, his hand on her shoulder the whole time. At that moment, having Jake there was more comforting than she could have expected at any other time. Jake knew her parents well, although there were times when Jake and Miranda were dating that Miranda's parents weren't always happy with how things seemed to be going at times. Despite those times, they had accepted Jake as almost an extended part of the family. When Miranda broke off her relationship with Jake and left town, there was a time when Jake had stayed somewhat close to the family. After time though, he knew he had to move on and put the past behind him. But this tragic turn he felt deeply, and could only imagine the pain that Miranda had to be going through at that moment.

They spoke little as they went to her car. After she was in the car, she thanked him again for being there, started the car and pulled away down the road. As he walked to his bike, Jake felt that something seemed odd about two particular people in the crowd on the street.

The two men, one bald man in a sports coat and the other with glasses, didn't seem as focused on the attention surrounding the house as much as they seemed to be watching Miranda's car as it pulled away. Perhaps they had seen what transpired between the detective and Miranda and were wondering who she was? Jake couldn't put his finger on what is was exactly that made him feel uneasy about the two men. They started to walk to a silver sedan as Jake got on his Harley, and then pulled away down the road as Jake watched them drive off. He fired up his bike and sped on up the road.

The Native Springs Police Department was a fairly small group of six full-time officers, as well as two fill-in part timers, housed in the department headquarters in the basement section of the Native Springs Township Hall and Public Library.

It was accessed at ground level, around the backside of the building where a single entrance door could be seen beside three garage doors where the patrol cars were parked when not in use. This had been the home of the department since the old town hall and police building had been torn down several years prior, and all of the local public service resource buildings were combined into one.

It was a sad time for many of the town's youth when the day came that the old town hall had been demolished to make way for the new building's construction. The old building had not been just a place for township officials to meet and play politics for the 'good' of the town; it was also a place that local DJ Dan Benson would hold dances for the local teenagers every Friday and Saturday night almost all year round.

Because there was really nothing else like them offered anywhere in the surrounding three counties, these dances drew teens from almost all of the towns within 25 miles around Native Springs. In a small town like this, they became one of the only things that the kids could do that kept them from running the streets and causing trouble for local businesses and the public authorities. When the old town hall was demolished and replaced by the new building, the weekly dances became a thing of the past, and an era of Miranda's youth had vanished forever.

This building held no memories for Miranda whatsoever. It was, however, about to spawn some new, exceedingly unpleasant ones. Having to hear what Detective Rice had to tell her about her family's deaths was not something she wanted to do. But something felt off to Miranda. There was a strange feeling that she was having, and she knew somehow that there was something coming, like a dark and menacing storm peeking over the edge of the horizon.

Detective Rice stood waiting outside the entrance to the police station. Miranda pulled into one of the parking spots alongside the entrance and approached the detective at the door. Rice pushed the button on the wall next to the door and the secretary behind the counter, a dark haired woman wearing half-moon glasses, waved to Rice and pressed a button that made a buzzing noise that alerted the detective that he could now turn the latch to open the door. He stepped into the doorway beckoning Miranda to follow him inside.

"Can we wait for Jake first?" asked Miranda, looking over her shoulder to see if he was within sight yet.

"For right now, it's better if you and I talk alone first. Loretta can let Jake in when he gets here, and he can wait in the office with her. That alright with you, Loretta?" Rice asked the woman at the desk.

"That'll be fine," she told them, smiling at Miranda in a forced sort of half-smile.

Detective Rice led Miranda to a small conference room in the back of the department building, past all of the officer's work desks. All of the on-duty officers, as well as a few off-duty ones that were called into work that morning, were either on the scene at the Stratton home or on patrol elsewhere. Besides Loretta, they were alone in the building.

The conference room had white walls and no windows or two-way glass. It looked more like a meeting room, and less like the interrogation rooms that she had seen on TV shows and movies she had watched in the past. After they walked into the room, Rice shut the door behind him and pulled out a chair for Miranda. She sat down, and Rice took a seat in the chair directly across from her. He had no files or papers with him.

He folded his hands together atop the table and looked at Miranda wistfully. Miranda looked back at him, expressionless and seemingly lost.

"Miranda...may I call you Miranda?" asked Detective Rice.

"Yes...yes, that's fine."

"Thank you. Miranda, when I first spoke to you this morning...and I am sorry that you had to hear the news of what happened that way, over the phone...I just didn't want you stumbling into it all coming home, or finding out by some other means. I had an opportunity to head you off, and I took it, but I am still sorry you had to find out that way," Rice told her apologetically.

"I understand...thank you," she said in almost a whisper. She felt cold, her hands trembling slightly in her lap.

Rice nodded softly to her before he continued.

"We were still working on getting a clear picture of how this happened when I called you. Your brother had not arrived at school this morning, and a call was made to the home. There wasn't an answer, so the school had your father's work number, but you father's work told the school that he hadn't arrived this morning, either. This raised some concern for one of your father's co-workers, Steve Carrol. He went to the house and knocked. When no one answered, he tried a back door and entered the house. He didn't get too far into the house before he started having trouble breathing. He immediately got out and called 911. The operator suspected it could be a gas leak. The block had to be cleared because of the potential for explosion. Upon arrival, the crew for the gas company confirmed a high amount of natural gas in the home. The gas was shut off, and the house had to be cleared of gas before the emergency medical crews were cleared to enter, for obvious safety reasons. Your family had succumbed to the gas in their sleep. They probably never knew what happened."

There were tears once again in Miranda's eyes. She tried the best that she could to hold them back, but right now being the strong girl didn't seem to matter as much as it usually did with her. Nothing was making sense. Everything felt wrong.

"Miranda, there's something you need to know. We haven't released this information to the press or anyone not directly connected to the investigation, and for the time being, that is the way it will have to remain. It appears that someone tampered with the gas valve entering the home. We don't believe this was an accident," said Rice.

Miranda sat stone cold for several seconds. She looked at Rice, whose eyes stayed fixed on her.

"Are you saying...someone *killed* my parents? My brother?" asked Miranda, with shock and disbelief in her voice.

"We believe so, yes. We are pretty sure that everything about this was intentional. Upon inspection of the valve going into the house, the gas company crew found a filtering device unlike anything they had ever seen before. Natural gas has no odor to speak of. The gas company adds odor to it in case of leakage. This filter somehow blocked only the odor additive, allowing the gas to flow freely into the house steadily for several hours. It appears that everyone could have passed out in the early evening hours and not had a clue what was happening. They may have felt slightly ill, but being this is always the beginning of the flu season, they may have not thought too much of it without smelling the gas. I am just speculating at this point, of course. The investigation could turn up other possible conclusions. The only thing we are certain of is that nothing about this looks accidental. In fact, it looks professional."

"Why would someone want to hurt my family?" asked

Miranda. "Do you have any leads at all? Anything?"

"That is one of the things that we wanted to ask you. We have nothing. There are officers interviewing your father's co-workers your mother's friends and your brother's friends at school. Grief councilors have been called into the school for friends and classmates of Steven. He was a pretty popular kid, I understand."

"Yes...he was far more sociable than I ever was...he had lots of friends..." she went on, almost in a daze with all that she had been told in the last few minutes alone.

"Can you think of anything? Anyone that may have had an issue with anyone in your family?" asked Rice.

Miranda sat silently still for a moment before her emotions overtook her once more. She broke down again, sobbing with her hands holding her head above the table. Detective Rice reached across the table and placed his hand gently on her wrist, trying to offer whatever little comfort it may. Miranda looked up at him with the tears streaming down her face. She could barely form her words when she spoke to him.

"I have no idea who could have done this! I've rarely even spoken to my parents since I left home. I hardly ever came back to see them...I don't know what has been happening in their lives! What kind of a daughter am I? What kind of a sister? I don't even know if my brother had a girlfriend, or if he even cared about that sort of stuff!"

Rice feared that Miranda might start to feel survivor's guilt going through all of this. She could have just as easily been in that house last night. She could have just as easily been another body bag.

Under almost all circumstances, she would have been considered a suspect just as well as anyone else. She had an alibi though, and her phones GPS had already proved that she had been in the U.P. for the last few days. Rice had already confirmed this. Even though she had not been at the house when this happened, she was not being considered a suspect in the investigation.

"I know you are feeling guilty right now. That is a natural feeling. But I need you to try to stay strong and think. Is there anything at all you can tell me that might help us? Because frankly, right now we have nothing to go on. No suspects, no fingerprints. Nothing," said Rice, looking tired and anxious now.

Miranda sat across from the detective and tried to think of something, anything at all, that might help.

"My mother called me yesterday," she told Rice.

He pulled a notebook from his inside jacket pocket, along with an ink pen, and placed the pad on the table.

"What time was that?" asked Rice.

"It was...hold on," she said, pulling her phone from her pocket. She found the call log with Lorri's call to her. "It was 3:07 p.m."

"What did you talk about?"

"She just wanted to know how my trip was going. But we didn't talk very long. She said that someone from the gas company had just arrived at the door. Something about the meter not working right, and that they had been being overcharged. A man was there to fix it."

"We spoke to administrators at the local office for the gas company. There hadn't been any work orders for the house since the service was connected a few months back."

Rice took his cell phone from his belt and dialed it.

"Yeah, it's Rice. We need to get officers canvassing the neighborhood, asking the neighbors or anyone who might have been in the area if they saw anything going on at all at the Stratton house between 2:45 and 3:30 yesterday afternoon. Any strange vehicles, people hanging around? We have a timeframe now for possible suspects. Call me as soon as you find something. Thanks."

"That is more than we had to go on 10 minutes ago. All it takes sometimes is the smallest detail to unveil the biggest mysteries. You did well. There is something else that we need to consider here though, Miranda. I don't want to alarm you, but with the timing involved here, we have to also consider the fact that your family may not have been the target of a malicious act at all."

Miranda's facial expression revealed her confusion about Detective Rice's statement.

"What do you mean? You still think that this may have actually been some sort of an accident or mistake? You said this looked like it could have been professional. I don't understand?"

"You just arrived home from being away for months at school. You said you hardly ever come home for visits. Who knew you were back home now?" asked Rice.

Miranda began to understand the direction that Detective Rice was going with this. She felt a whole new chill run down her spine.

"You think that someone was after me? Why would someone try to hurt me?"

"I am just trying to make sure all of our angles are being covered. I want to get whoever is responsible for doing this as much as anyone else."

"I'm sorry," said Miranda. "I can't really wrap my head around this right now."

Rice placed his hand on Miranda's hand across the

table.

"I know it's been a rough day for you. It's all a lot to take in. You need to get some rest for now. Think about it. If there is anything, it will come to you. Call or come down here to the station. I imagine that I will be in the local office all night going through everything that we have so far. Sleep on it."

Rice took from his pocket a business card and jotted down a phone number on the back of it, and handed it across the table to Miranda.

"Here is my card with my contact info. My personal cell phone is on the back, in case you need anything or think of anything. Call me anytime."

Rice rose from the table and Miranda followed. He opened the door for her, and Jake was waiting in a chair beside Loretta's desk. He got up and walked towards her, but he didn't say anything as he approached her. Words didn't seem to mean very much in moments like these.

"Do you have someplace to stay tonight, Miranda?" asked Detective Rice.

"She can stay at my place tonight. I have plenty of room," said Jake.

Miranda didn't argue. She knew with how she was feeling, the familiar face close by would be comforting, even given the circumstances of their past together. Regardless of how their relationship had ended up, it was Jake that was the one who was there for her when she came to the horrific realization that this wasn't someone's bad joke; that Detective Rice had told her the truth about what had happened to her parents. And here he was now. The friendship that they had transcended their former relationship. It wasn't something that she had consciously known, merely something that she felt deep within her.

Rice looked to Miranda.

"Is that alright with you? I am sure that I can find you a place to stay if you aren't comfortable with that."

"No, it's good," she said. "Jake is an old friend. I'll figure out where I will go from there tomorrow."

Detective Rice tried not to be too expressive with the frown on his face. Right now to him, everyone was a suspect, and that included Jake Neilson. Jake had known that Miranda was in town; Rice understood this, even if she had not revealed that fact directly to him. Jake's arrival and apparent fear that he showed in thinking Miranda may have been a victim as well was enough to reveal this to Rice. Miranda reminded Rice of his own teenage daughter in many ways, and he found himself feeling protective of this girl. It was hard to find escape from the sadness that was reflected in Miranda's eyes.

Miranda walked to the door and took a quick glance back at Detective Rice before walking out. Jake followed close behind.

## CHAPTER NINE

Miranda followed Jake to his home, about five miles west of town. Jake had not told her that where he lived now was out a few miles past the subdivision that Miranda's parents had lived in. Not that the fact would have mattered. She needed someplace to stay, and really didn't feel like being alone, but it was hard not to look once more at the flashing lights and gawking crowds that lined the once quiet road that was now the scene of a police investigation. She forced herself to look away after allowing it all to capture her attention for a moment, then continued concentrating on Jake's motorcycle ahead of her. Up about another mile and a half, he turned off onto another paved road, and went on for another half-mile before he turned into a driveway of a large, blue mobile home.

As far as mobile home standards are generally concerned, this place was fairly large and new looking. It was certainly well kept, and even the yard was a nice cleared lawn with surprisingly few leaves scattered about it. Oaks and maple trees surrounded the edge of the yard, and the fallen leaves had all been pushed or blown back into the trees beyond the yard.

Jake pulled his bike underneath a covered pavilion of sorts that looked like it had probably been made just for the bike. The roof of the small structure was finished and shingled, supported by four 4-inch by 4-inch treated posts. Two sides of it had walls that were simply grey tarps to block the wind. The front and the back had tarps also, but they were rolled up tightly to the top and secured with bungee cords. It was a homemade Michigan mini-garage, but this was at least constructed with care and respectability, unlike many of the others that one might see when wandering into the backwoods communities in the surrounding area.

Miranda parked her Vibe alongside Jake's bike shelter, and grabbed her laptop case and her luggage bag from the car. Jake took the luggage bag from her without saying a word. She could tell he was trying to be as delicate as possible given the situation. He was never really at a loss for words, so his silence revealed to Miranda that he wanted to tread carefully with her, as well as the fact that he was hurting just as well. She knew some of the relationship that Jake had kept with her family after the break up. It was mostly her father that would mention Jake occasionally on the phone after Miranda had gone off to school, but Miranda rarely commented back. She thought that her father had become rather fond of Jake, despite the rocky times early on in the relationship, and that he hoped some day they would get back together. But she also knew at the same time that her father was her biggest supporter in following her own path. Now he was gone, and she was here with Jake as her friend. She believed her father would think she was in good hands.

But Miranda felt she was in no one's hands but her own. It had been stirring in her head what Detective Rice said to her just before she left the police station. Although it made no sense to her whatsoever that someone might be trying to hurt her, was it possible that this had something to do with her coming home? She wasn't the type of person to garner enemies. If nothing else, she got along just fine with most people that she came across. Although she might not be the most open and outgoing of people, those she did interact with and meet along the way she accepted for who they were, and most people respected her for that. As far as bad blood with anyone, the only person around this town that could have even come close to being in that category was Jake, and she knew that was impossible. She saw the pain in his eyes.

She followed Jake into the trailer and was probably more surprised walking in than she had been driving up to the house.

The house was clean and organized and well kept. There was a large 52" flat screen television on the wall with a couch and matching recliners in the living room. The carpet was dark blue and looked like new, and there wasn't a dirty dish anywhere in the kitchen. A thought crossed Miranda's mind at that moment that caused her some concern. Does Jake have a girlfriend that he hadn't mentioned to Miranda before she agreed to stay with him? Not that Miranda would have a problem with that, because she had no interest whatsoever in this being anything more than an old friend trying to help her out. But what would the girlfriend think? Miranda certainly didn't want to get herself in the middle of anything like that. In her experience, guys just don't live this clean and organized on their own. At least not the *straight* guys she's encountered. She couldn't hold back any more from asking the question before she would just decide to bolt out the door.

"You live here alone?" she asked, trying not to sound ungrateful or snobbish.

"Yeah," he said, as a slight grin formed on his lips. "Why? Not up to your standards?"

Jake could tell what was going through her mind. Even though they hadn't seen each other in almost four years, some things hadn't changed as far as what he could pick up from her voice and body language that revealed what was going on in her head. She would get pissed at him sometimes for doing it, and he would know when she was pissed because she would start referring to him as "Sherlock" in the most derogatory of ways.

Miranda set her laptop case down on the chair nearest the door.

"I'm sorry. I had to ask. This place looks great, really."

Jake humbly grinned to ease the momentary tension.

"It's fine. I understand where you're coming from. It actually belongs to my grandpa. At least that is what he said. I pay him rent, but not very much. He bought it after I moved out of my parent's place. He stopped over one day to see the place where I was living at the time. It was a dump, but I was alright with it. I guess he wasn't. He told me he picked up this place as an 'investment', and suggested that maybe I would want to rent it since no one else had come by to check it out. He just didn't want to have to see me living in a dump."

"He has a good heart," Miranda told him.

"Yeah. The furniture was a gift last Christmas. The TV was a housewarming gift from my parents. Ever since I started going to school they have been like that - new dishes, second hand dining room table, stuff like that."

"You're going to school? For what?"

Jake's sideways smirk came back to his face.

"Well...right now, it's for nursing," he told her.

Miranda's jaw dropped just slightly, and she caught herself letting it drop. But not before Jake caught on to it. His smile widened.

"Yeah, I thought that might be your reaction," Jake told

her.

"It's just...I'm having trouble seeing you as a nurse," Miranda said, awkwardly.

"It's a start. I plan on eventually going on to become a physician's assistant."

"That's...that's great."

Miranda slowly walked over to one of the recliners on the far side of the room and sat down. She felt exhausted from the emotional overload of the past few hours, as well as all of the other thoughts spinning around in her head about all she had discovered in the days before. Jake could see the emotional fatigue that was overcoming her.

"Hey, I'm gonna take the couch tonight. Why don't you get yourself settled into my room and get some rest," Jake told her.

"I can't take your bed, Jake."

"You can and you are," he insisted.

Jake walked over and put out his hand to Miranda. She looked at it for a moment, and reached out with her own hand and he helped her out of the chair. She hadn't realized until that moment how tired she actually was. Jake showed her to his bedroom, which was pretty much in the same orderly fashion as the rest of the house. She sat on the edge of the bed and kicked her shoes off, and pulled her legs onto the bed. Jake walked around the other side of the bed and grabbed a blue quilt off of a pile of blankets and pillows that were stacked between the wall and the nightstand, and placed it over Miranda. He closed the blinds, and began to walk out of the room. As he began to close the door behind him, Miranda wearily interrupted.

"Jake...thank you," she said.

Jake smiled at her without saying anything, and

continued on out the door. Miranda was asleep within a minute afterwards.

Miranda's eyes still felt heavy when she opened them again. She knew that she could smell food of some kind being made, but couldn't make out what it was. The clock was out of focus for the first few seconds before she could make out that the time was 5:17 p.m. Pushing herself up and out of the bed, she made her way into the bright kitchen.

Jake was at the stove, pouring a jar of spaghetti sauce into a large saucepan. There was another pot on the burner next to the sauce full of boiling water with what she assumed was spaghetti noodles cooking in it. Jake heard her approach and turned around with a smile.

"Hey...did you sleep alright?" asked Jake. "You were out cold pretty quick."

"I think so. I guess I didn't realize how tired I was," she told him.

"You've been through a lot. And you need some food. You still like spaghetti, I hope? I made it with burger, so I hope you haven't gone vegetarian on me," said Jake.

"No, it's fine. Right now I feel like I could eat almost anything," she told him, taking a sideways seat at the dining room table.

"It'll just be a few more minutes. The sauce is ready, but the noodles aren't done cooking yet."

Thoughts of Aimsley suddenly came to mind. Miranda stood up and walked over to her jacket next to her laptop. Her hurried movement caught Jake's eye.

"Everything okay?" he asked her.

"Yeah...there is just someone I have to call," she told him.

She dialed Aimsley's cell number and waited for a few rings. The call went to voicemail.

"Hello, you have reached the Book Stops Here bookstore and Aimsley Carter. I'm sorry I cannot take you call at this time. Please leave your name and number and a brief message, and I will get back to you as soon as possible."

There was a long beep, and Miranda waited to speak.

"Aimsley...it's Miranda. I really need to talk to you. Call me back as soon as you get this message. Please."

Miranda pushed END on her phone and just stood there for a moment, holding it in her hand. Jake was finishing up with the noodles while watching Miranda with concern out of the corner of his eye. Not paying full attention to what he was doing at the sink, he made a sudden noise when he burned himself with the hot water from the noodles. This snapped Miranda out of her troubling daze, and she moved quickly to Jake to help him at the counter.

"Are you alright? Let me see that," she said, grabbing his hand to analyze the burn. It was red, but not badly scalded or anything that looked serious. It more just caught Jake off guard than anything else.

"I'm fine, I'm fine," Jake told her, trying to laugh it off, although for that moment it still did hurt. "You just sit down and let me feed you already."

Miranda grabbed the two plates he had set out on the counter and put them on the table. Jake had already put out Parmesan cheese and salt and pepper, a few slices of bread with butter and two glasses. He filled Miranda's plate with spaghetti, and then took care of his own. He sat down, and the two started to have their dinner. Miranda dove in, not trying to look too eager, but she couldn't help how hungry she was. She felt like she hadn't eaten in days, even though it occurred to her that consciously, she thought, given the horrors of the day, how could she have any appetite at all?

Jake went on eating his meal, but witnessing Miranda's hunger didn't escape or surprise him. She was physically and emotionally drained, and she needed sustenance. He was afraid at some point she might bottom out, but she seemed to be dealing with things as well as could be expected, if not a little better than expected.

This worried him. He wanted to keep a close eye on her to make sure everything didn't catch up with her all at once. He was also concerned for himself as well, though. He didn't want to let his guard down in Miranda's fragile emotional state and get confused about his own feelings. Jake had a hard time getting over Miranda four years before, and even though he knew that their time together was a thing of the past, he couldn't help having the feelings stir deep inside of him that he once had, especially seeing her like he did earlier that day. The need to protect her and take care of her came on strong, and he didn't want that feeling to become confused with anything more than being there to help a friend going through a difficult time. He knew that it would not be easy.

As the pasta and sauce concoction disappeared from her plate, Miranda slowed down her pace a bit. She thought that she might be coming across like a wild animal with a fresh kill before her, like she hadn't eaten in weeks. If that was how she looked, Jake didn't let on that he had noticed. She appreciated that, knowing how sharp Jake was at picking up on things.

Jake decided to make light conversation, to try and get a handle on how she really was.

"So, who is Aimsley?" he asked. "Friend at school?"

Miranda didn't immediately know how to answer the

question. She felt she needed to tell someone what was going on, especially with the concerns she was having not yet being able to get a hold of Aimsley.

"That's not the easiest question to answer," she said, piquing Jake's interest and attention.

"Oh...sorry. It's fine. I understand," Jake told her, looking as if he was quickly trying to change the subject.

"You understand...what, exactly?" Miranda asked curiously.

Jake looked slightly embarrassed.

"Nothing. It's nothing. We don't need to go there..."

"Go *where*?"

"Well..." Jake said, looking increasingly nervous. "Is Aimsley your...girlfriend?"

Miranda stared blankly at Jake for a few seconds, letting his words sink in. Then she let out a short laugh, which startled Jake.

"No, Aimsley is not my girlfriend," Miranda said matter-of-factly. "Is that why you think I left you? Why I left town?"

Jake pushed his chair back and stood up from the table, feeling slightly embarrassed. He walked to the counter next to the kitchen sink and set the plate on the counter, staring out the window at the driveway. He said nothing at first, and Miranda stood up from her chair and stepped up a few feet behind him.

"Jake, I'm sorry," she said softly. He cocked his head slightly in her direction, looking off to the side.

"No. The truth is, I have no idea why you left," he told her, turning around the rest of the way to face her. "Listen, we can talk about this another time if you want. I've made my peace with it and moved on. Now isn't the time for this."

"I want to tell you. I want to try to explain. You deserve

an explanation. It wasn't you. It wasn't my parents. It wasn't even this town. I grew up here. It was the only home I had ever known. But I wanted more. I would have wanted you to come with me, but I never would have believed you wanted anything more than to just keep on going the way we were. Everything you said, everything you did. All the time you spent with your friends. I heard what you would always talk about. You were making big plans, but those plans back then never had you going beyond the borders of this town, and that scared the hell out of me. I needed more. I can't tell you why, or where it all came from. All I can tell you is I didn't want to hurt you, and I didn't want to get hurt. I knew the longer we drug it out together, the more it was going to hurt later on."

"Well, I did get hurt Miranda. The worst part was, I never even got to know why," Jake told her, now with a hint of bitterness in his voice.

"I'm sorry," said Miranda, her eyes glassing up once again.

"So am I. I would have gone anywhere with you. This town, my friends, aren't what mattered the most to me, Miranda. It was you. I didn't follow you because you made it clear how you felt."

Jake realized the one thing that he didn't want to happen that night was happening. He had let his feelings and emotions get the best of him, and all he wanted to do was concentrate on Miranda and the pain she was going through. She was the one who was hurting the most right now, and she needed him to be strong for her. The conversation had turned in an ugly direction, and it was up to him to fix that. There would be time for this conversation some other day if it needed to happen. Now wasn't that time.

Jake walked up to Miranda and put his hands on her

shoulders. She looked up at him dolefully.

"Miranda...I understand. Yes, I was hurt. But that was a long time ago. You are my friend, and that means more to me than anything else right now. I just want to be here for you. There's no reason to get lost in the past."

Miranda wrapped her arms around him again, and he hugged her back. It was hard for Jake to not have those old feelings rise up inside of him, especially holding her this close. She let go of him, and looked directly into his eyes. It was a deeply serious look.

"Aimsley was my nanny when I was a baby," Miranda told Jake.

"Your parents had a nanny?" he asked.

"No...not the parents that you knew," said Miranda.

"What are you talking about?"

"It's where I was the last few days. It's why I wasn't in the house when the gas leak happened. I found out that I was adopted. My parents never told me. I went up north looking for clues as to where I came from. That's how I met Aimsley."

The confusion in Jake's face was more than evident.

"You are adopted? And your parents never told you? How did you find out?"

"It's...it's a long story. Once I realized it was true, I had to know more about the family that gave me up."

"So, you just went off by yourself to a strange place to look for people that you weren't even sure wanted to be found, and you didn't even tell anyone you were doing it? I thought we were both long past reckless and stupid, Miranda." Jake was upset. He was especially sensitive to being protective of Miranda right now, and she could feel the frustration in his words.

"I know it sounds crazy. There is a lot of this that gets

even crazier. But if I had been home..." she stopped in mid-sentence. "I hated lying to my parents, but if I had told them what I was doing, they would have fought me on it."

"And we wouldn't be having this conversation right now. Because you would be dead." Jake went silent as what he had just said sunk in. He didn't want to come across harsh to Miranda, regardless of how he felt about her running off in search of her past the way that she did. It surprised him, though, that she would act that rashly. Something was driving her to be this way, but he didn't want to pry too hard. Not now.

Miranda sat down on the edge of the recliner.

"Aimsley told me about the family I came from. She knew my mother, and she knew my father. My birth mother and father. The family owned a mining company in the U.P. They had an entire town named after them. Aimsley said my mother was a very good person. Very beautiful."

"How could she not be," slipped out of Jake's mouth. He realized too late he had said it, but Miranda either didn't notice or pretended that she didn't.

"Do you trust her?" asked Jake. "Do you think she wants anything from you?"

"I trust her completely," said Miranda, without hesitation. "She wants nothing from me. I tracked her down, and she was shocked when I found her."

"How did you find her?"

"She...sent me something. It was so I could find out where I came from, if that's what I chose to do. But she's always known where I was. She is the closest thing to family that I have left."

"You just met this woman, and you think of her as family? Miranda, I am trying to understand here what is happening, and believe me, there is a lot happening. She leads you back to her after more than 20 years and she wants nothing from you?"

"I know this sounds crazy, but there are things you don't know. You just have to be patient with me and I can explain everything later. Right now, I just have to figure out what I am going to do next. I have no idea what kind of things I need to do. What kind of arrangements I need to make...Jake...I'm totally lost here. I don't know what to do..."

Miranda's voice was quivering. She was on the edge of frantic. Jake's uneasiness he had felt about her state of mind was elevating quickly. He needed to find a way to calm her and focus her.

"Miri! Miri..." Jake's eyes met hers straight on, and he pulled her full attention to him. He had not called her Miri in a long time. That seemed to trigger a break from her downward spiral. She centered her concentration on his voice.

"I will call and talk to my parents. They know what is happening. They can help. We just went through this with my grandmother a couple years back. They can help you do what you need to do. Don't worry. We will get through this together."

Miranda nodded her head and took a deep breath to help her try and relax. Her mind had started racing again, and she knew that she had to slow herself down before she started to hyperventilate.

"I'm going to go into the bedroom and make a few phone calls. Put on the TV and find something to distract yourself. I know it's hard, but try and keep things as light as you can. Put on some music if you want. Whatever it takes to stop thinking for a little while. I'll be back in a few minutes. Alright?"

"Alright," she told him. Jake handed her the TV

remote, and she clicked it on to CNN. Jake grabbed his phone and retreated to his bedroom, closing the door behind him.

Along the bottom of the television screen the constantly running ticker was predicting an unusually nasty flu season in the coming months. The top of the screen featured an upcoming story about repeated bombings and civilian deaths in Afghanistan. The two men on the screen reporting at the moment were discussing a possible connection between several murders in the New York State area that could be related to a serial killer. There was nothing "light" about watching the television news anymore.

Miranda switched the channel to a movie channel that was having a scary movie marathon, a common ritual in the weeks leading up to Halloween. Across the screen a young woman was being chased by a disfigured man wielding a chainsaw with blood spraying off of the spinning chain. *Not so light there either*, she thought. She changed the channel once more before giving up on TV, and found herself watching one of the local news broadcasts that had just started at 6 o'clock.

On the channel that she had switched to, she saw on the screen the street sign for Sherwood Trail amid the headline "Tragedy in Native Springs".

"An investigation is currently underway in the town of Native Springs after three members of a family died as the result of carbon monoxide poisoning relating to a gas leak in the home. Sources wishing to remain anonymous close to the Michigan State Police have indicated that foul play may have been involved in the deaths. The victims were Robert and Lorri Stratton, and their 17-year-old son Steven Stratton. The family had moved into the home just a few months before. We will be bringing you more on the investigation as information becomes available."

Miranda watched as the pictures of her family flashed onto the screen. The feelings of sadness and despair were present within her, but now there was something else that she had felt for the first time since she spoke to Detective Rice. It was the overwhelming anger at the thought that someone may have done this intentionally to her family. She wanted to know who could have done this, and why. She didn't notice that Jake had returned to the room and was standing behind her, his eyes also transfixed on the television screen. The news had already changed to a different story.

"Did you know about that?" Jake asked. "What did Detective Rice tell you? Miranda, what is going on?"

Miranda looked up at Jake for only a moment before the next words from the newscaster snapped her back to the attention of the television screen.

"In other news, police in the Upper Peninsula town of Arlo are investigating the shooting death of one of its longtime residents. Early this morning, the body of attorney Harold Thornton was found in a cabin owned by Thornton just a few miles south of Arlo."

Miranda shot up from her seat, her eyes widened as she stared at the picture of Harry's face on the screen before her.

"Authorities have released to the local press that Thornton was found by his wife early this morning after he had not returned home last night. He had been shot twice. Robbery is not suspected at this point, although few other details have been released."

Jake's eyes moved from Miranda to the television, and then back to her again.

"Miranda? What is it?"

What little color Miranda had left disappeared from her face as she stared at the TV. Her thoughts turned straight to Aimsley again. She grabbed her phone and dialed it, and once more, straight to voicemail. Jake stood by watching her, not sure what was happening.

"Miranda, TALK to me. What is going on? Did you know that guy they were talking about? You need to tell me what is going on! Please," Jake pleaded.

Miranda held her phone tight in her hand and felt the rush coming over her. Harry was murdered. Her parents and brother were dead. What had she done? Was she somehow responsible for this terrible chain of events? Fear and guilt were overtaking her rational thought, leading her once more back to an emotional deadfall.

Jake finally took Miranda by the shoulders, squarely bringing her face to face with him.

"Miranda, sweetie, you need to tell me what is happening."

Miranda was expressionless. She spoke slowly like she was almost in a trance.

"The man that was murdered, Harry Thornton, he was the man that I met with in Galestone. He took me to see my birth family's home. He had been their attorney years before. I was with him two days ago."

Jake stared at her in a silence. His expression was one of absence, while his own thoughts were spinning in his head. He didn't know how to put together all of what Miranda was telling him.

"Jake. I haven't told you what Detective Rice had said

to me before I left the police station with you. They found evidence at the house, they think this wasn't an accident. They suspect someone intentionally tampered with the gas valve leading into the house."

Jake felt the unpleasant feelings wash over him now....the apprehension. The fear. He slowly let go of Miranda's shoulders, but continued staring at Miranda.

"We need to tell the detective," Jake said. "He needs to know right now. If this guy is connected to what happened to your parents, you could be in danger too."

Miranda nodded her head almost indiscernibly. Jake grabbed his jacket from the hook next to the door and then picked up Miranda's leather jacket from the chair in the corner.

"We'll go straight to the police station and have Rice meet us there. He can decide what we need to do next. Grab your things. We can take your car...but I'm driving," Jake said.

Miranda still stood in a state of semi-shock. Jake recognized these signs of distress from his nurse training. She was in a fragile state of mind, and Jake had to do what he could to help get her to a safe place. She grabbed her laptop bag and her luggage bag from his bedroom. They walked out together and got into her car. Jake fired up the Vibe, quickly backing out of the driveway and started up the road.

They made the right hand turn onto the main highway when Jake glanced up into the rearview mirror. The silver sedan that had been at the scene near Miranda's parent's home was turning off of Jake's road a short distance behind them.

"Miranda," Jake said, his eyes still jumping back and forth between the mirror and the road ahead. "I don't want you to turn around. Keep your eyes forward and look into the rearview mirror on your side. Do you recognize the car behind us?"

Miranda looked at the mirror and saw the sedan.

"No...I don't think so. Why?" she asked.

"I saw that car at the scene by your parent's house. These two guys...they weren't paying as much attention to what was happening at the house as they were to you. I watched them get into a car that looked a lot like that one behind us and leave just after you did. I didn't think much about it at the time. But that was before...before I knew there was more going on. I wish you would have said something earlier."

"I'm sorry, Jake. There was just so much happening so fast. Maybe they are reporters?" said Miranda, although the tone in her voice seemed doubtful. "What should we do?"

Jake thought for a second on that last question, but the option was quickly taken out of his hands. The sedan sped up beside the Vibe as if it were going to pass them, but kept a steady speed as it drew up beside them. Mr. Cain sat in the passenger seat of the car beside the Vibe and stared without any discernable expression as the two cars were side by side. The sedan increased its speed and cut sharply in front of the Vibe, causing Jake to have to slam on the brakes and come to a sudden stop behind the sedan, throwing stones and dirt from the shoulder of the road off into the trees.

Both doors of the sedan opened, and both Mr. Cain and Mr. Skye got out of the car and started to walk quickly towards Jake and Miranda.

"Miranda, get down!" Jake threw the car into reverse and ducked down himself, driving blindly backwards several yards until he felt he was a safe enough distance away to look for a place to turn the car around. Amid the noise of the squealing tires on the pavement, Jake was sure he could hear the sound of what might have been gunfire, but there was no glass breakage from the windows, and it hadn't sounded like anything had struck the car. He looked up, and saw the two men getting back into the sedan, so he turned the wheel sharply to the left and spun the car around 180 degrees. Shifting back into drive, Jake hit the gas and headed back into the direction that they had originally come from.

"Where are we going to go, Jake?" asked Miranda, keeping her eyes behind her to watch for the sedan, which had already started back in behind them, and was catching up fast. Jake thought for a moment, and turned back onto the road that he lived on. The sedan followed suit, and Jake went on past his house by another half-mile before making a sharp left onto a two-track road heading into the woods.

Jake had to slow down when he first entered the two-track, which allowed some time for the sedan to catch up even more. He accelerated to around 45 mph, which was a fairly high speed on the rough and narrow road for a car like Miranda's. These roads were an access point to the state trail system that was used by everyone from nature hikers to snowmobilers and ORV enthusiasts. But they were also used for years and years by local youths as a place to go and party out of the watchful eyes of their parents and the local cops. They were a place that Jake and Miranda knew all too well.

Jake took a fork to the right and followed the road to another split at a "T" where he made a left hand turn, but still the sedan kept close on the trail. Suddenly the car shifted a little when the tires hit a patch of mud that remained from the hard rains that fell a few days earlier while Miranda was still up north. The jolt gave Jake an idea.

The next turn-off to the right was about 75 yards up the road, and Jake followed it.

"Miranda, hold on tight!" he said. Miranda looked at him, and then looked ahead and realized where they were heading. She braced herself as best as she could. The road ahead began to rise on an incline, and Jake increased their speed cautiously. A little distance had formed between them and their pursuers, which Jake felt would help give them the edge they would need.

As soon as they were at the top of the hill, Jake held as tight as he could to the right shoulder, pressing the gas to gain as much speed as possible for the next 60 feet ahead. The car jarred and bounced violently as they hugged the edge of the trail close to the scrub pines on the right side of the Vibe. They powered through, veering to the immediate left so that the men in the sedan following behind could see the direction that they were going as they made the rise up the hill. But unlike Jake and Miranda, instead of the cautious right hug to the shoulder, they aimed their vehicle straight on ahead up the hill.

By the time the pursuers reached the top of the hill, it was too late to do anything but brace themselves as they slammed into the giant mud bog that always settled in that spot after a hard rain.

The area was nearly impassible in the few months after the winter's snow melted, but this time of year it only took a few inches of rain to get bad enough to make it difficult to pass through. The mud and the clay mixture made for good sport for trucks and ORV's to go tearing through, but after they had had their fun, the condition of that section of the road was that much worse. Jake and Miranda missed the heart of the pit by hugging the right side of the hill, but there was not a chance in hell the sedan was moving any further.

The Vibe stopped a safe distance away for Jake and Miranda to make sure the pursuit was over. From that distance, they saw the two men in the car getting out to look at the sticky situation they had found themselves in. Jake hit the

accelerator and left the men behind, taking the shortest route back to the main roads.

Jake and Miranda drove together in silence until they reached the first dirt road off of the trails. Jake turned the wheel to head back towards town.

"Jake...wait," said Miranda. "We need to talk."

Jake pulled the car to the side of the road and turned off the engine.

"Miri, we should get to the police station. You should call Detective Rice and tell him what is going on. Those guys are going to have to call someone to get them out of there, and the police should be right out there with them when the tow truck shows up," Jake told her.

"Jake. Do you trust me?" asked Miranda.

Jake looked astonished that she would ask him such a thing.

"Of course I trust you. How can you even ask me that?"

"We can't go back to the police," she said.

"What are you talking about? Those guys might be the ones that are responsible for what happened to your family...they may have been trying to hurt you as well! We could have killed ourselves trying to get away from them. This is out of our league, Miranda," Jake told her, turning the ignition of the car. Miranda opened the door and got out of the car before he could start to pull away. Jake shut the engine back off, and got out of the car.

"What are you doing? Help me understand why we can't go to the police," demanded Jake.

"I can't expect you to believe everything that I have been going through the last several days. I am not sure what to believe myself. But some things are becoming more and more clear to me. You are right, Jake. There may be some things that are beyond us, but I have no doubt they are beyond what the police can do for us now too. If you really trust me, then you need to let me do what I need to do. You don't have to come with me. But I have to go and see someone to find out what it is these people are after. I am scared to death that everyone close to me will remain in danger unless I find out who these people are and what they want from me. I've already lost my family. I don't think I could take losing anyone else. I just don't know what I would do...do you understand? I don't believe the police can help us, Jake. You need to let me go and do this, and you need to take off somewhere for a few days, maybe longer, until I get this sorted out. I can't bear you getting hurt because of me," Miranda pleaded to him.

Jake turned around and paced back and forth as Miranda stood by and watched. He could not help but to shake his head in disbelief at what she was asking. Finally, he turned to her.

"I don't know what is really going on here, and I think you need to help me understand...but I *do* trust you, Miri. Even though I think what you are doing doesn't make sense, I trust you. But there is no way in hell I am going to let you do this alone. No argument. No pleading. If you try to cut me out of this, I'll have no choice but to tell the cops everything, for your sake. I am going with you, and that is final. Understood?"

Miranda looked at him for several seconds, and then to the ground for a moment.

"Okay. I suppose your terms are *acceptable*," she told him, secretly feeling a bit of relief that he could be so hard headed at times. Any other time in the past, it would have just angered her. But she knew, deep down, that she was scared of what lies ahead. She felt safer with Jake by her side.

Jake nodded and turned to walk back to the car. He got into the driver's seat once more. Miranda followed him to the car and got back into the passenger side door.

Jake looked to Miranda as she shut her door "So, captain," Jake asked with skeptical reluctance, "What is our heading?"

"South. We are going to Detroit," Miranda directed.

Rick Jurewicz

## CHAPTER TEN

Mr. Cain and Mr. Skye stood silently in the parking lot of the Native Springs Auto Repair Center as the company's tow truck hauled the sedan into the garage. Neither looked at the other for several minutes; they had no words for the situation they were faced with. A medium built man with long, dirty brown hair and dark framed heavy glasses wearing a grey company cap and uniform walked up to the two men holding a clipboard.

"Well, the front axle is broken and it looks like the frame might be bent as well," said the man with the clipboard in hand. "Car like that isn't the best to be two-tracking in. You musta hit that clay pit pretty fast!"

Mr. Skye looked to his side and down at the man's face, whose expression changed to a blank and fearful stare with Skye's icy gaze upon him. Mr. Cain felt it was at that point a good time to interject before the situation turned ugly.

"The car is a rental vehicle. The rental information is in the glove compartment," said Mr. Cain, reaching into his inside jacket pocket to retrieve a brown leather wallet. He removed a pair of one hundred dollar bills, folded them, and extended his hand in the direction of the man. The man instinctively reached forward to take the bills; Mr. Cain drew back his hand. The man froze for a moment with his arm half extended.

"I trust you can take care of any paperwork and arrangements that need to be handled between the company that I work for and the rental agency to make sure whatever needs to happen with this vehicle is taken care of without any further assistance from us?" said Mr. Cain, in a tone that suggested he was stating a fact rather than asking a question. The man picked up on that fact, and nodded his head as Cain put the folded bills in the man's hand.

"Tha...that shouldn't be a problem, sir," said the man.

"We would like to retrieve our personal items from the car. Would you take my associate to the car so he may do that? I need to make a telephone call."

Mr. Skye looked at Mr. Cain as he said this, and the man with the clipboard swallowed hard as he looked at Mr. Skye.

"Yeah...sure," said the man, looking to Mr. Skye now, who looked back to him. "Right this way."

The man started to walk back towards the garage, glancing over his shoulder to make sure Mr. Skye was following. Mr. Skye nodded him on.

"I will be right there," said Mr. Skye in his cold tone. The man hurried on ahead, and Mr. Skye looked to Mr. Cain.

"What are you going to tell him?" asked Mr. Skye.

"The truth," said Mr. Cain. "If I were to tell him anything else, and he found out...it wouldn't be good for either of us."

Mr. Cain reached into his left jacket pocket and removed the GPS tracking device that had been attached to Miranda's car. When the two men got out of the sedan trapped in the mud and clay, the tracking software in the phone indicated it was in the vicinity. A quick search found it in the area of the shoulder where the Vibe hit several hard bumps avoiding the clay that abruptly ended the pursuit by the two men.

"Maybe you should send a text?" asked Mr. Skye, for the first time showing a sign of concern in his face. Mr. Cain looked at Skye for a moment, and then nodded in agreement.

"Go and get our luggage. I will handle this," said Mr. Cain. Mr. Skye turned and walked to the garage as Mr. Cain pulled out his phone.

TO: ENOCH
We ran into some difficulty.

TO: CAIN
Difficulty?

TO: ENOCH
We lost the girl.

Several seconds went by before a response came. To even a hardened and deliberate man like Mr. Cain, this was unnerving.

TO: CAIN
What of the tracking device?

TO: ENOCH
It is in our possession.

Another long pause came before the message chime rang once more.

TO: CAIN

This is not ideal. There is another option however. Get to the airport in Pellston. I will have a flight plan arranged for you. We need to get ahead of her. Her resources are limited. I will send additional instructions.

    Mr. Skye approached with the bags from the car. He stood a few feet from Mr. Cain, waiting for whatever might be coming.

    "Go back and find our short and dirty little friend in the garage. Have him call us a taxi service. We have a new itinerary."

    Miranda stood in the entryway to the large room in the once beautiful home. A slight breeze blew through, causing a chill that brought goose bumps to her bare arms. Everything was dark and grey, burned and water damaged, and the smell of smoke was still lingering in the air. Besides the sound of her foot steps on the wooden floor, there was silence. The sudden squawk of a large crow that landed on the sill of a high broken window startled her.

    Far to her left, the sudden eruption of flames in the old stone fireplace shook her again, but it did not pique her feelings of apprehension as much as the silhouette of the two figures seated on the floor in front of the fireplace.

    She took one step after another, slow and cautious, towards the two figures, despite the feeling of dread she felt with every step. She then recognized the figure to the left. The white suit, now soiled with soot and dirt, and that long, blonde hair. To the man's right was the little girl, playing with blocks in front of the blazing fire in her pretty blue and white dress. Both sat with their legs crossed upon the floor. Miranda smiled to herself as she watched the little girl, happily playing, trying to put together the blocks as if she was spelling a word. Miranda saw a "C", and an "F", put together, while others were scattered about on the floor in front of the girl.

Then the voice came, like a low and silent whisper echoed through a long metal pipe.

"I AM NOT YOUR ENEMY, MIRANDA. YOU NEED NOT FEAR ME."

Miranda stepped back suddenly at the sound of the voice. The man never turned his face from the fire in front of him, but as Miranda stepped back, the little girl turned her face to Miranda's and their eyes met in a silent gaze. The little girl, Miranda now knew, was herself. But her eyes...the whites were as white as a fresh snowfall, brilliant and vivid. All else was blackness, as if there were no iris, just one large black pupil surrounded by the blinding whiteness.

Miranda felt a rush of fear through her entire body, and shuddered with a gasp that brought her to the attention that she was in the car, stopped in a parking lot, alone. She looked around her, but Jake was nowhere to be found. She was at a busy gas station, and there were cars and people filling those cars with fuel all around her. She felt a wave of anxiety come over her as she looked frantically around for something familiar. Her breath became shortened, as her fingers played at the clasp of the seat belt trying to release it.

The driver's side door opened, and Miranda let out a short scream. Jake dropped the bag he carried onto the floor of the front seat and put his arms out to Miranda's shoulders.

"Miranda...it's alright. I'm here. It's okay...it's okay," Jake said, steadying her as he drew her closer to him. He held her there for a moment, as the tears flooded her eyes again. A man from a nearby car approached upon hearing the scream from their car.

"Is everything alright here?" asked the large man, wearing khakis and a light blue Polo style shirt.

"She's fine...she just had a nightmare. She's alright," said Jake, looking up at the towering man. The man looked at Miranda and spoke directly to her.

"You sure you are alright?" he asked her. Jake felt a little put off, but understood why the man was asking. Miranda pulled gently away from Jake and nodded her head to the man, wiping the tears from her eyes.

"Yes...thank you," she said, followed by a little snort. "I'll be fine...it was only a bad dream."

The man looked at her and nodded, and went back about his business. Jake picked up the bag from the floor and pulled a turkey and provolone sandwich and a bottled water from the bag and handed them to Miranda.

"What the hell happened? Are you sure you are all right?" he asked her, finally allowing his real concern to come to the surface.

"Yeah...I'm okay. Where are we?" she asked, trying to change the subject.

"About 20 minutes past Flint. That's why the traffic is so heavy now," said Jake.

"What time is it?"

"It's past 10. The university offices are probably already closed. If this professor only takes meetings by appointment, you might not even be able to get a hold of him until tomorrow. I think we should find someplace to stay for the night. It has been a very long day, and I think we both need some rest. We can go the rest of the way early in the morning, get to the university, and try and find this guy."

"If it's after 10...have I been asleep for the past two and

a half hours?"

"Yeah. But sleeping in a car isn't like getting a good night's sleep in a bed. After what you've been through - what we've been through today - you're not only physically tired, but mentally and emotionally as well."

"We should just go there and wait for him...I know he's going to be there..."

"Miranda, please. Will you just please listen to me. You're not thinking straight. We need to stop, eat and *rest*. Both of us."

"Alright, alright. But promise me we will leave early."

"I promise you. Up, eat, and on the road."

Miranda started to eat her sandwich, and realized once again the hunger within her. Jake pulled a bag of pretzels out of the grocery bag, and opened it for the two of them.

"There's one more thing before we find a hotel. Let me see your phone?" he asked.

Miranda looked curiously at him, and pulled her phone from her jacket pocket and handed it to him. He pulled two packaged pay-as-you-go phones from the brown grocery bag as well.

"We need to get rid of our phones," Jake said, flipping her phone over and removing the battery.

"Why?" asked Miranda, sounding confused. Jake saw the look in her eyes, and realized how paranoid he might be coming across to her.

"Listen...we have no idea what is really going on. The only thing I do know is that these guys that are after you...they are very dangerous people. And with people that dangerous, they probably have good resources and know what they are doing. Just...bear with me here. I don't know if they can somehow track our cell phones. Every one of these have GPS chips in them these days. I'm not willing to take that chance. Not with your safety."

"That's very James Bond of you," said Miranda with a crooked grin. She didn't know if she was supposed to take what he was saying seriously or not, at least until the point where the window came down and he tossed her phone and the battery into the trash can near the gas pump.

"Hey!" exclaimed Miranda. She pulled the handle to open the passenger side door, and Jake grabbed her by the arm.

"Miranda, I am serious. When this is all over, I will buy you a new phone. I promise. Right now, until we know what we are dealing with, we use these new phones, and whatever we buy, we pay for in cash. No credit or debit cards. No electronic trails. Okay?"

Miranda pulled the door shut. She knew that he was right. They didn't know what they were dealing with, and this was the safer route to take.

"That's fine," she said, "but we are fairly limited on cash you realize?"

"It'll take us as far as it can. We'll try and figure out something else before it runs out completely."

Miranda had told Jake on the road to Detroit, before she had nodded off to sleep, what she had learned about the Gale family from the newspaper articles she had researched, and what she had been told in Galestone about the fire and the family's effect on Galestone. She also told him that they were going to find a professor at a university outside of the city, but as to why, she still hadn't said. For now, he was allowing her to let him in on things as they went along, but that would only go so far. Jake knew there was a lot weighing on her, and there was far more that she was not telling him. But if it came to her putting herself in any immediate danger, regardless of how she felt about the situation, he knew he would have to take control and go to the police, despite any protests from her. But for now, they would do things her way.

They drove two miles further up the road to a small motel off the main highway. The sign at the road said 'ROOMS - $39 NIGHTLY WEEKDAY RATE'.

Jake went to the office to see what was available while Miranda waited in the car. She opened the glove box and removed the leather registration wallet that her father had left the cash in a few days before. She held it tightly in her hands, remembering how many times he had done little things like that for her as long as she could remember. Beneath the wallet was a silver folding Spyderco Delica pocket knife. She removed the knife and closed the glove box. The knife was about four inches closed, with a round hole in the blade for one handed opening. She held it in her hand and smoothly moved her thumb around the edge of the thumb hole. She heard Jake come from the office on his way back to the car, and placed the knife in her right jacket pocket.

"We have the room on the end," he said, and got back into the car to pull it to the front of the room with the number '15' on the door. Miranda got out and helped Jake grab their belongings from the car, and they went inside.

The room was about as basic as you can get for a tiny roadside motel. One double bed, a small bathroom and shower, and a small table beside the bed with a single lamp on it. There wasn't even a television; only a radio alarm clock on the nightstand next to the bed, and a single wooden chair in the corner of the room next to the window.

All they needed was a place to crash for the night, and this would do just fine for that. This was the kind of place that would attract a traveling salesperson looking to stay for days on end as they pushed their wares on people and businesses in a local area. They would operate the room as their office and headquarters while they went out by day on the hunt and returned by night to fill order forms and process sales sheets. Miranda was surprised to find that even though there was no TV, there was in fact Wi-Fi available in the rooms.

Jake went back out to the car for a minute and came back with a folded blanket that Miranda had in her back seat. It was an item of convenience to carry in the car, and according to her father, an item of necessity to have at all times when traveling the roads in a northern Michigan winter.

Jake locked the door behind him, and chained it as well, before spreading the blanket on the floor next to the bed.

"What are you doing?" Miranda asked him.

"I'm giving you the bed. It's small, and I have no problem sleeping on the floor," Jake told her.

"You don't have to sleep on the floor. We can share the bed," she told him. He looked at her apprehensively.

"Jake, I think we are beyond the awkwardness of this," said Miranda, pulling back the sheets. "It's just sleep. You need your rest as well as I do, and I don't think you are going to get it down there. You stay on your side, I will stay on mine. We don't have to make it weird. Okay?"

Jake grabbed the blanket from the floor and laid it out on the bed. "We'll probably both need this anyway. It's supposed to get cold tonight."

"Shit!" exclaimed Miranda. "My phone...it was the only place that I had Aimsley's number!"

"Did she have a number for the business as well as her cell phone number?" Jake asked her.

"No. They were the same number. She only had one phone, at least as far as I know, and used it both as a personal phone and a business phone," said Miranda, angry at herself for not getting the number from the phone before she let Jake get rid of it. She wasn't blaming Jake, only herself for not keeping her head more together with all that had happened.

"Miranda, if it's her business phone number, it's probably listed. Just look it up on the laptop and put it in the new phone. But you can't call it from the new phone. If these guys are after you because of a connection to your past, and she is a part of that past, if they know that you've gone to see her, they could be watching her as well to see if you contact her," Jake said.

"I know that!" Miranda snapped, unintentionally. "I'm sorry. I have been thinking about that since I tried to call her earlier. I am terrified that they know that. That is why I want to warn her - so she can get out of town and hide somewhere. I just need to let her know."

"You need to be prepared for the possibility that they already know, Miranda. Listen, I get where you are coming from, but you aren't going to be any good to her if you get yourself caught or killed while trying to protect her. We will go to this professor so you can talk to him about whatever you need to, and then you are going to let me know everything that is going on. If we can't come up with an answer together as for what we do next, then we contact Detective Rice and tell him everything we know."

Miranda was not used to Jake being the take charge, responsible, level headed voice of reason that he was being now. He had always been tough, but more along the lines of the 'act by the seat of your pants' type of way. Throw caution to the wind, and let it ride. Either he'd become that much more focused and directed in the few years she had been away from him...or it was something more. Maybe he was truly scared, and after all that had happened that day, she couldn't blame him one bit. Whatever it was, and even though it did nothing for her fears for Aimsley, she was letting Jake be her voice of reason while she tried to get her head back on straight.

She agreed with him, and pulled her laptop from its bag while Jake started to activate and set up the new phones. As the computer slid out of the bag, it pulled the manila folder out with it and the contents of the folder fell to the floor in front of Jake. He leaned over to pick them up, and Miranda quickly knelt to the floor as well to collect them.

"What are these?" asked Jake, looking curiously at the fragile sheets as he picked them up from the floor. Miranda sighed as she gathered the rest, and returned them all to the folder, with the exception of the ones in Jake's hands.

"Miranda," he asked her again, looking at her as her eyes lowered to the bed. "What are these?"

"They are pages...old parchments that Aimsley gave to me. They belonged to the Gales," she told him. "I don't know yet what they are."

"Do you think this is what those men are after?" he asked her.

"I don't know," she said bleakly.

"Are these authentic? They look old...*very* old. If this is what they want, we should find a way to give it to them and be done with this! Hundred-year-old pieces of paper are not worth your life, my life, or anyone else's," said Jake.

"They might be even older than that. Thousands of years, maybe. And apparently to somebody out there, they are worth someone's life. Four people's lives, so far. I don't care what they are worth to anyone else, Jake. I need them so I can find out what they are. If I just give up and turn them over to these assholes, I may never know what it was that my parents and brother died for. I can't live with that! I need to know what this is all about, and why this is happening. I knew that if I went to Detective Rice with this story, these would have been taken from me and put into an evidence locker, and I may have never seen them again, and never be able to find out what any of this is all about. I'm sorry I wasn't straight with you. I didn't think you would understand."

Jake looked to the floor for a moment, and then handed Miranda back the two parchment pieces he held in his hands.

"Miranda, I am trusting you. You asked me to trust you, and I made a choice to do that, because of who I know you are. But this...this isn't the Miranda that I knew before. Even when we would do some of the crazy-ass shit that we used to do, you were always the one that could temper a wild night with a somewhat level head. You're acting without thinking things through. I know you are hurting. But you need to slow down and think about what is happening here. And, at the very least, you need to trust me as I am trusting you. Stop keeping things from me. You need to let me in," Jake pleaded with her.

Miranda put her laptop back into the case, and placed it on her side of the bed. She pulled off her jeans and slid her legs under the covers, and Jake realized when she did this that he forgot to look away, not that Miranda noticed. She reached over and turned the lamp light off next to the bed, so the only light in the room was coming from the streetlight at the corner of the parking lot. Jake said nothing as he removed his jeans as well and slipped into the bed. They laid there silent and unmoving for several minutes, tired, but so far unable to fall asleep.

"Jake," said Miranda, in the darkness.

"Yeah?"

"I'm sorry. I do trust you. There are just things that I am trying to put together. Things that make no sense right now, that I am hoping will make more sense after I talk to Dr. Vikhrov. I am just asking you to be patient with me, please. You being here with me...it means so much more than you know. Thank you."

Jake closed his eyes for a moment and just breathed.

"I would do anything you needed, Miranda."

Those were the words that came from his lips, but the feelings he had - the feelings that he swore he would not allow to come back to the surface - held a much deeper meaning as to what he would do for the girl lying beside him. Miranda's hand slid to his under the sheet, and he held it gently as she drifted into sleep. Sleep would be that much harder for him to find now, but he would give it the best effort he could. He needed real rest so that he could stay sharp. Keeping her safe was all that mattered to him now.

## CHAPTER ELEVEN

The sun shone brightly on that Wednesday morning, and vehicles of all makes and models flooded the campus of Sentry Technological University.

Started in the early 1930s, the much smaller Sentry Tech in Macomb County served as an alternative educational facility in southeastern Michigan to the larger Wayne State University in the Detroit area. Not nearly as well known as Wayne State, Sentry originally functioned as an upper class, more exclusive university catering to the suburban families north of the city. Jonathon Michael Sentry, an engineer from a well-to-do family in the Detroit area that made a fortune in the meat industry, found himself deeply involved in the quickly rising automotive boom in the early part of the 20th century. After he inherited the family fortune and business empire, of which he had no interest in continuing, he sold off all of the pieces of the business. After seeing the great potential of the growing auto empires, he invested the monies made from the sale of the meat business into the creation of an educational institution dedicated to the advancement of greater technologies in this new industry. And while the great potential of the university never peaked to the notoriety of other great state and national universities, the campus of around 25,000 students annually did flourish, and maintained itself rather well.

In its effort to have a well-rounded curriculum, the university originally offered few options for students that were not geared towards the technological professions. However, in the late 1960s and early 1970s, the university was suffering from a decrease in enrollment as students took preference to the popular University of Michigan in Ann Arbor and Wayne State in Detroit, as well as a spike in the student body of Michigan State University in East Lansing. The reaction from Sentry Tech was to expand in many areas to the curriculum, offering more course studies in the areas of psychology, philosophy and theological studies. Sentry became a more affordable school to the student body, and the enrollment numbers began to turn around in the early 1980s, and has remained strong and steady since.

It was in the later years of the 1970s that Dr. Alexey Vikhrov first defected from Russia and came to teach at Sentry Tech. The Cold War was going strong and fierce, and the United States, although accepting of Dr. Vikhrov's defection, watched defectors with great scrutiny for fear of spying, especially when it came to someone working in education and technologies. Initially, Vikhrov was hired to teach the Russian language at Sentry Tech, but it became quite clear that his true interest and passion was in languages far removed from the Russian language, as well as from technologies. Vikhrov was obsessed with the studies of religious language and documentation, and had master's degrees in theology and language studies, as well as extensive eastern cultural and historical education.

Vikhrov wasn't anything near the typical professor at a school like Sentry Tech, but to those students who took his elective classes as a diversion from the standard course of studies, he was a popular professor for his great enthusiasm and knowledge of the subjects he taught. In these days though, the classes he taught had significantly dwindled through the late 1990s and suffered even more through the early years of the 21st century. As more and more computer programming and application courses became of greater requirement, less time and interest was available for the types of classes Dr. Vikhrov could offer. He eventually went into a state of semi-retirement, only taking on one or two classes a semester and maintaining a small office space in the basement of the J.M. Sentry Administrative Building. The administrative building is the oldest and original building on campus that now serves not as a classroom building, but holds the office space for the president of the university and several other administrative offices, as well as the university registration and financial service's offices.

With tighter budgets and the increased need for computer labs and robotic technology workshops, the basement was the best that an old professor like Dr. Vikhrov could hope for. But he took it all in good humor, recognizing the changes in the world around him, he conceded there was far less interest in the old world beliefs regarding religion, even in a time when jihad was everywhere, in all directions. Religion was the driving force behind the biggest events that appeared almost daily in national and international news, but it seemed that the everyday person had little or no interest in learning about where it all came from, and why.

He cherished the classes he still got to teach, even when it was apparent that most of the students ended up in his classes to fill a required elective and not really know what they were getting themselves into. But the rest of the time he spent writing, sometimes in the quiet of his home, but most often in the solitude of his lonely basement office surrounded by the multitudes of books and documents that he had collected over the years since he first escaped to this brave new world.

Jake and Miranda pulled into the parking lot of the J.M. Sentry Building around 10:45 a.m. that morning. Both said very little after they awoke. Jake was up first, and got in and out of the shower and dressed quickly. When Miranda went to take her turn, Jake went across the street to a gas station that served hot breakfast sandwiches and grabbed a couple for both himself and Miranda, the whole time keeping an eye on the motel door to make sure no one had tracked the two of them down. No time was wasted in getting on the road after they had eaten. There was only about $230 cash left between them, and even less after they gassed up before continuing on into the more congested city.

They had no more than the names of Dr. Alexey Vikhrov and Sentry Tech University to go on in their search for the professor, so the main administrative building seemed like a good place to start. The first office inside the front entrance to the building was the student registration office. A young blonde girl, slightly younger looking than the two of them, who was no doubt a student working at the school, sat behind the first desk in the registration office. There was no one else in the office at the time, and a radio was playing low in the background "The Edge of Glory" by Lady Gaga.

Miranda was the first into the office as the girl looked up from the paperback novel she was reading, and a friendly smile came to her face, which got increasingly wider as Jake appeared in the doorway behind her. Miranda repressed the urge to roll her eyes when she noticed this; instead, she smiled back at the girl.

"Good morning," said the girl, sitting in the chair

behind the desk and sliding her book, some flashy romance rag, out of Miranda's view. "What can I assist you with today?"

"We were wondering if you could help us locate a professor on campus?" asked Miranda.

"Alright," said the girl, who turned towards the screen of the computer at her desk and started tapping the keys. "Are you a student here?"

Miranda looked the girl straight in the eyes sternly.

"Does that *matter*?" Miranda asked.

The girl looked startled for a moment by the look Miranda had given her.

"Umm...no. I was just curious if you were enrolled here," she said, again giving a slight glance at Jake, then quickly shifting her eyes back to her computer screen.

"Ah. I see," said Miranda coolly. "No, we are not students here. We are friends of a friend of Dr. Vikhrov, and we thought we would stop in and say hello."

"Okay," replied the girl, who stayed focused on the computer screen and no longer looked up at Miranda.

"Dr. Vikhrov still does have an office located on floor B-1 of this building. But he is only teaching one class this semester, and it's a Friday morning class in the McCoy Liberal Arts Building."

"Does he have office hours?" asked Miranda.

"Only by appointment, according to what it says in the notes here," said the girl. "But you are welcome to leave your name and number here, and I can make sure it goes into his mail box."

Miranda thought for a moment. "B-1...is that the basement?"

"Yes," replied the girl. "There are two sublevels, B-1 and B-2."

Miranda smiled a forced smile once more at the girl.

"Thank you. I'll just slide something under his door. Where are the stairs?"

The girl frowned and pointed down the main hall. "Just follow the hall to the end, and stairs will be on the left. There is no elevator to the basement except a freight one."

"I think we can manage a few stairs. What is the office number?"

"B121," replied the girl. The two young women held each others gaze for only a moment before the younger blonde girl looked away suddenly as if she had been distracted by something that came up on her computer screen. Miranda just turned and walked on past Jake out of the office, and Jake narrowed his eyes as she walked by. He looked to the girl behind the desk.

"Thank you for your help," he said with a smile. The girl only briefly looked up and gave him a quick, awkward smile, and went back to her screen.

Jake caught up with Miranda, who was already several strides down the hall. She seemed focused on only what she was doing, like a soldier on a mission, so Jake didn't even bother to ask what the hostility was all about back in the office.

Down two short flights of stairs and they were on B-1, looking for Dr. Vikhrov's office. The hall was quiet, and as they counted the numbers down, they noticed they were approaching one office door, the only one on the entire floor, that was wide open. They could see that the office was B121, and Jake held up his arm to Miranda and leaned into her.

"Just wait...let me check it out," he whispered to her, and Miranda nodded back to him.

Jake stepped very quietly, one foot after the other, to just before the entrance to the office door. Miranda watched from a few feet behind Jake, and gripped the Spyderco knife in her hand inside of her right jacket pocket. Jake peeked cautiously around the door frame and let out a sudden, startled scream and jumped backwards at once, losing his footing and landing on his backside in the middle of the empty hallway.

Miranda responded by pulling the knife from her pocket while jumping backwards herself. It took her a moment to realize that an equally startled sound came from inside of the office. She stood still for a moment, looking down at Jake while a man stepped out slowly from the office doorway with his hands raised in front of him. The man stood at about 5-foot-9, with thin, grey hair on the top and bushier, thicker hair on the sides with a grey mustache to match. He wore a light-grey tweed sports coat and a green sweater vest beneath, with matching grey slacks. The man looked down at Jake on the floor, who looked back in bewilderment back at him. He then turned to Miranda, who had tucked the knife back into her pocket out of the man's sight.

"Dr. Vikhrov?" asked Miranda, studying the man before her.

"Yes," said the man in his pronounced Russian accent. He took his right hand down from his 'I surrender' stance and extended it to Miranda. "And you are?"

Miranda snapped out of her embarrassed gaze and stepped forward and took Dr. Vikhrov's hand as Jake pulled himself to his feet by their side.

"I'm so sorry we startled you, Dr. Vikhrov. My name is Miranda...Gale. This is my friend, Jake Hunter."

Dr. Vikhrov smiled politely back to them. "You'll have to excuse me as well. It's not too often others venture down here. I thought I heard someone coming down the hall, and then there was silence, so I was hesitant to stick my head out and look around." He looked to Jake, who clumsily grinned back at him.

"So, what can I help you with? Please, come in. You'll have to excuse the clutter. It is rare I take meetings with students in my office any more. I don't recognize you from my class. Are you students here?"

Miranda and Jake sat down across the desk from Dr. Vikhrov, who took his seat in the tall leather chair facing them.

"No, we aren't," said Miranda. "I am a student at South Central Michigan College."

"South Central? Really? Well, what brings you all the way out here, and into the dungeons of our fine school?"

"You were recommended to me by a Dr. Carlyle at South Central."

"Richard? Richard Carlyle? Well, that is a name I haven't heard in a long time now. How is he?"

"Honestly, I have never met Dr. Carlyle. My roommate is a student in his *Modern Perspectives of Ancient Religious Practices* class."

"I see...well, you have my curiosity. You were recommended to me by a man you have never met who teaches a class you are not taking...regarding what? Richard Carlyle is a very knowledgeable and qualified educator. What could I help you with that he could not?"

Miranda unzipped her laptop case and pulled the manila folder from inside and handed it across the desk to Dr. Vikhrov. Jake sat silently by her side. This was in her court, and he was there for support in whatever way she needed. Dr. Vikhrov took the folder and opened it wide, revealing all of the pages of parchment within.

Dr. Vikhrov's first response was the narrowing of his eyes. Then, Miranda noticed his hands tremble ever so slightly as he set the folder down flat upon his desk. His eyes shot up quickly to Miranda for a brief moment before he grabbed a pair of reading glasses sitting upon the desk to his left. He put the glasses on and very carefully picked up the first page in the folder and stared at it with a look that neither Miranda nor Jake could make a proper assessment of. The several seconds that went by seemed like centuries to Miranda before Dr. Vikhrov finally spoke again.

"My God," he almost whispered, still peering down at the parchment in his hands. He looked directly at Miranda's face, and she could almost feel a chill run down the back of her neck. "Where in heaven did you get this?"

"I guess you could say that I inherited it. It was passed down in my family. I am the last in the family line, as far as I know," Miranda told him.

"Does anyone else know about this?" Dr. Vikhrov asked.

Jake and Miranda looked at each other momentarily, and then back at Vikhrov.

"My roommate, who I sent it to so she could show Dr. Carlyle, and Dr. Carlyle himself. But he didn't know what it was. That was why he referred us to you."

"So, you have no idea what this is either?" Dr. Vikhrov asked.

"We were hoping that you could enlighten us on that," said Miranda.

Dr. Vikhrov placed the parchment on the desk beside the other sheets still lying in the folder. He sat back in his chair, almost as if he was coming to grips with some uncomfortable truth, and having some difficulty trying to grasp a hold on the situation himself.

"I have, for many years, studied all manner of

documents similar to these. The textures. The smells. The overall composition of papyrus and parchments dating back thousands of years. Over time, you get a feel for it. You know it like you know the spices of your favorite recipes, and the savory, hidden subtle elements of a fine wine. Without proper scientific testing, you cannot get a truly accurate date, but to the trained researcher, certain facts are more than obvious. I would venture to guess that these documents, which are astonishingly in exceptional condition, especially given the fact that there is no indication that they have been kept in an airtight environment, are almost 2,000 years old."

Jake's jaw dropped. Miranda had no immediate reaction. She was still waiting for the real definitive answer. What is so important in these documents worth dying - or killing - for?

Dr. Vikhrov leaned forward again, his excitement starting to become more evident.

"The script," he pointed to on the top page, "It has been commonly misrepresented as a broken or erroneous form of Hebrew, but it is in fact more appropriately an altered version of a kind of writing called Enochian script, which is sometimes referred to as 'angelic' script. It was believed that this was the language that was spoken by God when he created the Heavens and the Earth, and was the language of the angels as spoken to by God."

Dr. Vikhrov looked up at Miranda, who was still expressionless. "But I am getting the feeling, Miss Gale, that I am not yet telling you anything that you haven't already figured out for yourself. Am I correct?"

Jake looked at Miranda with a questionable gaze, quickly realizing there was still more that Miranda had not shared with him. She looked at him for only a moment; he lowered his face down toward his chest, and did not look back up at her. She understood how he felt, but she couldn't concern herself with that now, as cold as that might seem. She needed to find out what she had come here for.

"Can you translate it? Can you find out what it actually is?" Miranda asked Dr. Vikhrov.

"I already have, actually," he stated.

"You haven't even looked at the entire manuscript yet," she said.

"Oh, but I have. Many years ago. I have seen these all before, rewritten and copied, many times. I believe that I myself have done the most accurate of translations, but many of them are similar."

Miranda sunk in her chair. She felt suddenly empty. If there was nothing new or unknown about the contents of these pages, how could they have been the reason her family had died?

"So, these parchments...there is nothing special about them, besides being really old? Everyone knows what's on them?" asked Jake, who saw Miranda's growing disappointment start to pull her down.

"Well, *everyone* is not quite accurate," said Dr. Vikhrov. "These particular documents, and the history that surrounds them, have been a particular interest to me. More of an obsessive hobby, actually. What is contained in these documents, and the authenticity of the text, has been the subject of scholarly debate for more than 1,000 years. The text itself has been accepted anecdotally for centuries, but not by serious scholars of biblical history. The only proof in existence to the source of the text lies on this desk in front of us now. In this moment right now, Miss Gale, you have brought me confirmation of the authenticity of that which I have been researching and seeking for the better part of my life!"

Miranda sat up straight again, and felt like her blood might start to boil. It was not in anger, but in anticipation of that which she could hold back no longer.

"Dr. Vikhrov," she said calmly, restraining the absence of her patience. "What is this document? What is written on the pages?"

"This, Miss Gale, is the Caducus Oraclum, also commonly referred to as the lost Gospel of Lucifer, The Fallen Star of the Morning."

## CHAPTER TWELVE

"The Gospel of Lucifer?" asked Jake, bewildered. "I don't know a whole lot about things in the Bible, but isn't Lucifer the Devil?"

"Well, yes and no. There have been over the centuries many different theories about this. The name Lucifer had been first mentioned, but not greatly elaborated on, in the book of Isaiah, chapter 14, verse 12. 'How art thou fallen, O' Lucifer, son of the morning! How thou art now cut down to the very ground, thou who once laid low the nations; for thou said in thine heart; I will ascend into heaven; I will exalt my throne above the stars of God; I will sit also upon the mount of the congregation, in the far side of the north'."

"Many biblical scholars believe that the name of Lucifer was translated in error, meant to be that of a 'shining star' in the most derogatory sense. A play of words, so to speak, regarding how Satan saw himself as his own bright beacon of glory. It wasn't until much later, in the 1300s A.D., that the name Lucifer became popularly synonymous with that of what we know as 'the Devil' in Dante Alighieri's *Divine Comedy*."

"So then, what is this? What is the Gospel of Lucifer?" asked Miranda.

"The Gospel of Lucifer is an ancient manuscript that supposedly tells Lucifer's side of the story regarding his fall and imprisonment in Hell. To really understand the depth of what is written in these pages, you should know the history as to why and how the original documents became lost, which may shed clues as to how they came into your possession."

"Go on, please," said Miranda, waiting intently for him to continue.

"The Holy Bible, which I am sure you are aware, is primarily in two books, the Old Testament, and the New Testament. Both testaments are made up of several smaller books, and depending upon which particular faith you follow, whether it be Jewish, Catholic, Eastern Orthodox or Protestant, the Old Testament, for instance, will be composed of different books and different numbers of books. The Jewish version of the Old Testament contains only 24 books, while the Catholic version contains 46 books. Depending upon which faith, certain books are accepted as Biblical canon, or rule of law."

"Alright. So where does this book fit into it all?" asked Jake.

"The books contained in the many different forms and versions of the Holy Bible are not the only biblical texts in existence. There are several different books that, depending upon the given source material and content, have never made the cut as one of the canonical scriptures of the Bible. You've heard of the Dead Sea Scrolls?"

"Yes," Miranda replied.

"They were 972 biblical texts discovered between 1946 and 1956 that made up much of what is known as the Hebrew Bible. This was not the first time that such a discovery was made since the birth of Jesus Christ. What I am going to tell you now is what is considered more the stuff of myth and legend in the circles of the scholarly elite in these fields.

"It was rumored that around the year 542 A.D. in the area known as Samaria in Palestine, which was also known as the burial place of John the Baptist, there was a discovery of roughly 500 documents, both of religious and secular nature in a cave deep within the mountainous region. Most of the known documents were thought to be written both during the time of Christ by witnesses other than those accepted by the Holy Church, and by several others who gave accounts in the years following His death of the state of the regions he had traveled. *This* document stood out from the others, due to the writing style used that had never been seen before, at least in this form. There were no clues as to its author, or how it came to be with the documents it had been found with. The Church was very insistent that all discovered documents of that time period, and especially anything to do with Jesus Christ, were to be immediately turned over to the Church for examination and review. Those who discovered this treasure trove of documents were greatly rewarded for their find, and equally for their silence as to the existence of the documents and the location as to where they had been found, a place which had come to be called, for reasons unknown, 'Cadere Gladii'. Translated from Latin, it means 'Fall of the Sword'.

"Now came the part of the story that came in some circles to be called the 'Tale of Two Cardinals'. The documents were analyzed and archived in the Church libraries, and remained entombed there for the better part of 30 years. The Italian Cardinal Abatescianni, acting on his own for what he felt was the good of the Church and the sanctity of Holy Scripture, proposed to the Pope that the non-canonical text be destroyed at once. Opposing this act was the French Cardinal Daviau, who believed that all documents held by the Church held significance, from both a religious and historical perspective. While the Pope decided to take the matter into consideration, Cardinal Abatescianni proceeded with a plan to destroy the documents without consent from the Holy Father. Upon discovery of the Italian cardinal's plan, Cardinal Daviau conceived of his own plan for the greater good and, with a small group of priests believing as he did, took the documents from the Church archives and fled. Cardinal Daviau and those first few priests became the first of a long line of an order of people dedicated to the protection and preservation of documents that had religious significance and historical fact that may be threatened by those who feared their existence. 'Afin de Sainteté', it came to be called by the French cardinal. The Order of Sanctity. They were the caretakers and protectors of these texts for centuries. It is rumored that the Order still exists today."

"Would members of the Order use violence to protect the documents?" Jake asked.

"I would guess it was not the preferred method they would choose, but if push came to shove, who knows? What the real talent was behind the Order was secrecy. At the height of the Order's network, there were several families throughout Europe that protected different parts of the documents, and copies were created and interjected into society at different times through the past 1,500 years. That is how the Caducus Oraclum got out, although the Church denied any authenticity of it or any other documents discovered at 'Cadere Gladii'.

"So where are the rest of the documents? Is it possible that my family was one of the caretakers of the Order of Sanctity?" Miranda asked.

"Yes...and no, Miss Gale," said Dr. Vikhrov.

"Please, call me Miranda," she stated, starting to feel

less comfortable with the name she chose for her own anonymity.

"Okay, Miranda. In the late 1660s, John Milton published "Paradise Lost", depicting the story of Lucifer's fall from the grace of Heaven after his rebellion against God. It was believed that Milton was in fact a member of the Order of Sanctity, and used some of what he learned in this Lucifer text to weave his story, although much of his tale strays from that which the text tells us. After that, the story takes a dramatic turn. It appears that not all of the original text of the Gospel of Lucifer had been copied and released into the rest of the world. A final segment in the last pages had been omitted from the released copies. The rumors that surfaced spoke of a prophecy of some sort relating to the fallen angel. In fact, that is where this document's original and true name comes from. 'Caducus Oraclum' translates from Latin to the English *'Prophecy of the Fallen'*.

"There was a fracture in the early 1700s in the Order of Sanctity, according to what few sources could be found, and none could be accurately verified. A small faction within the Order became a cult like following, basing their beliefs on what is written in the Caducus Oraclum. This faction broke off from the original group, taking with them the original documentation of the Oraclum; these papers that lay here before us now."

Miranda felt cold. Even worse than that, she felt guilty for just being alive. If it had not been for her being so hell bent on discovering her past, only to find out her past was tied to some twisted devil cult, she believed that her family would still be alive.

"So, I would imagine that it was my family that became this devil worship cult that stole the Oraclum and disappeared," she said bitterly.

"Don't be too harsh just yet, Miranda. This is not 'devil worship' like you've seen in the movies or heard of on the television news. The beliefs that are based on the Gospel of Lucifer in the Oraclum are far from that."

"I don't understand...what makes it any different?" she asked.

"The Gospel of Lucifer describes a very different story than that of Dante's, Milton's, or that of the rest of the Holy Bible, and it pre-dates all other known documentation of the fall of Lucifer."

"But Lucifer still fell from the grace of God? He is still God's enemy. Excuse me if I can't see how that could be a good, positive thing," said Miranda, with an increasing harshness in her voice, though not intended to be directed at Dr. Vikhrov himself.

"This is true," said Dr. Vikhrov, noticing the tension in Miranda voice. He glanced briefly to Jake before he continued. "But the reasons given by all other accounts make the difference more evident." Dr. Vikhrov started with the first page in front of him.

"Allow me to paraphrase a bit. The text is lengthy, and it has been a while since I have actually gone through it word for word. Lucifer was the first, and by far the most powerful of all the angels. He was glorious and beautiful, and loved God as much as God loved him. After him came the rest of the archangels. There was Michael, Gabriel, Raphael, Uriel, Azriel; all great servants of the Lord God, but none so much or as well beloved as Lucifer. It was Lucifer who first brought the light to the Heavens and the Earth, by God's command. Lucifer commanded the angels in their duties, faithfully serving the Lord and never bowing to any feelings of personal glory or desire. Through the hands of the angels, the world took form

and shape, and life was given and flourished. The ground became fertile, and the skies provided cleansing and nourishing waters from above."

Vikhrov moved from page to page slowly, and Miranda and Jake listened intently. Jake still was having trouble grasping what he had fallen into, while Miranda listened with cool conviction to absorb and make sense of all of it.

Vikhrov continued. "After the angels had done their work for the Lord, He intended to put this new world into the hands of its intended caretakers. It was to be in the hands of man. This took Lucifer and the others by surprise, but they of course obeyed without question. Lucifer, however, although obedient, watched what was happening with great scrutiny. What he found, to his great interest, was that God had granted man a freedom unlike any that had been given before. He had created mankind, and through the multitudes of angels, crafted a beautiful and lustrous world for them to be given, and all that was asked in return was for their love and devotion to Him. All else was theirs to do with as they chose, with only the Lord asking to obey laws He had set forth for them. Never before had Lucifer seen such a thing. All he had ever known was love for his Father, and servitude to Him as well. For the first time, he felt envy for something; but it was not the glory and throne of God. He envied *man*. He envied the freedom to live their lives on their own. He approached God, and asked him why His loyal servants, the angels on high, were not offered this gift of freedom for all of their service and loyalty to the Lord. God told Lucifer that it was not the duty and purpose of the angels to have such freedom, and in return they remain always in the presence of the Almighty. Lucifer bowed to the Lord and accepted this, but still chose to watch mankind with even greater scrutiny. God left mankind alone, and would only intercede in the affairs of man when prayed to through acts of prophecy and miracles. The angels were also commanded to not interfere or mingle with man. When given an order by the Lord, the only choice for an angel of the Lord was to obey.

"Lucifer watched over the centuries and witnessed through man the birth of sin and became disgusted at the way man so callously abused the gifts the Lord had given them. This made him want such freedom even more, so that he could show the Lord how truly it could be appreciated. He went to the Lord once more, proclaiming how mankind had fallen into sin and were not deserving of the gifts he had given. The Lord then proclaimed that he would live as they do, and spread the word of hope and love to all, so that all who repent shall be forgiven and can live beside the Lord forever. This angered Lucifer even more. Now these souls could live forever by His side, as the angels have done for all time, yet he felt the angels must serve as slaves while man was to receive the joys of eternal Heaven.

"In the Lord's final day on Earth as a man, Lucifer came to him once more and pleaded with him to grant him the freedom that he has granted for all of mankind. The Lord once again told his Morning Star that his place lies in the Heavens as the commander of his legions of angels. Lucifer left in anger. His heart was full and heavy, for as much as he loved his Father, a resentment had grown within him that could no longer be contained.

"When the Father returned to the throne of Heaven, Lucifer pleaded one final time with Him, and God denied him for a third and final time. In the time that the Lord walked the world of man, Lucifer prepared for the possibility that he would be denied a final time, and convinced one third of the angelic host to follow him as he left the kingdom of Heaven upon the Father's return. As Lucifer and his followers marched towards the outland borders of Heaven, they found that the rest of the angels of Heaven, remaining loyal to the Lord and led by the archangels Michael and Gabriel, blocked their way. Only then did Lucifer draw a sword from nothingness and present it against his brothers, as did all who followed behind him. In turn, Michael and the others did the same with all manner of weapons similar to the weapons of man. The first and only war ever to take place in the kingdom of Heaven raged on for seven days and seven nights. The Lord wept at the loss and destruction, but most of all he wept knowing the love and torment in the hearts of his sons, both fallen and remaining.

"It was Michael who struck the final blow that ended the war, defeating Lucifer in battle by shattering his sword with a mighty crash that echoed across both Heaven and Earth. In the end, the defeated angels were cast into a shadowy void where they could see the world of Earth through the dreams of man, but could never share in the freedoms and wonders and joys of mankind for all of eternity. Any angel that remained in Heaven held the power to open a gateway to this place called Hell, but after this day, no matter what sympathies would be felt for their fallen brothers, no angel dared to ever defy the Lord God again, knowing full well what their fate would be."

Miranda and Jake sat silent for several seconds before it had fully occurred to them that Dr. Vikhrov had stopped speaking. He looked up at them and gave them a brief smile. Miranda took a deep breath and looked down at her hands folded tightly in her lap.

"Miranda," Jake said, placing his hand on Miranda's wrist. She looked to her left at Jake, who then turned to Dr. Vikhrov. "Doctor, would you please excuse us for a moment? I need to discuss something with Miranda in private. It'll just be a minute."

"It's no problem. I have nowhere else I need to be today, and given this day's revelations, I personally cannot be happier that you have come here. Please, take your time," said Dr. Vikhrov.

Jake stood up and stepped out of the office with Miranda following closely behind, wondering all the while what Jake needed to say so suddenly. Jake stopped several feet from Dr. Vikhrov's office door, far enough where he felt they could have the privacy that they needed.

"Jake, what is it?" she asked.

"I need you to listen to me, Miranda. Those stories on those pages, as fascinating as they may be, are not worth anyone else getting hurt for. Not you. Not me. Not anyone. Now you know what they are, and I have no doubt that they are very valuable pieces of history, with a price tag that so far has at least four people's lives on it; maybe even more. We need to get these to the police and wash our hands of them," Jake said in a hushed voice.

Miranda turned from him and walked to the other side of the hallway. Despite the incredible story that they had just heard from Dr. Vikhrov's vast knowledge of the Caducus Oraclum, Miranda felt that nothing had been revealed of any deeper meaning that made any more sense of her parent's death. Someone wanted those ancient scripts because they were worth a lot of money to the right people. Either that, or someone wanted them so they could make sure that they would never be seen again. Either way, she felt cold and empty. Somewhere deep inside, she wanted to believe that if her parents and her brother had to die for this - for something that she had inadvertently set into motion - that it would mean something more than a motive drenched in simple greed or self serving idealism.

"You're right, Jake. I'm sorry I dragged you into any of this. We can do whatever you think is right," she told him, her head lowered towards the floor. Jake saw Miranda now in a way that he had never seen her before. She looked helpless and defeated, which was not a sight that gave him any sort of good feeling at all, despite the relief that he was feeling that they could be rid of the damned parchment pages.

Dr. Vikhrov stepped out of the office and looked down the hallway towards the two of them, and just stood silently staring for several seconds before Miranda noticed the almost dumbfounded look on his face. She walked towards him, concerned at first until she realized that the look in his eyes revealed something else might be going on.

"What is it, doctor?" Miranda asked, a spark in her voice revealing that some of the waning vitality she had was beginning to find new life.

At first, he said nothing, looking nervously around to verify for himself that they were well and truly alone in the vast basement hallway. He silently beckoned them back into his office with a wave of his fingers, and once inside, closed the door behind them and took his position back around his side of the desk. He sat down, and placed his fingertips gently on the two pieces of parchment that sat in front of him on the desk.

"These two final pages are not part of any of the copies that I have ever come across before. I believe you might be in possession of the *entire* Caducus Oraclum as it was originally written," said Dr. Vikhrov. There was a feverish enthusiasm in his voice, and it was evident to both Miranda and Jake.

"So, what exactly does that mean? There is more to the

story?" asked Jake.

"Not to the story as it has happened thus far. What I've told you; more precisely, what this has told us, is what has happened already. What remains here, and has been lost to time until now, is the tale of what is to come. These last two pages contain the prophecy that was rumored to exist back around the time when the Order of Sanctity was divided. I believe this it what actually divided the Order."

"What does it say?" Miranda asked anxiously.

Dr. Vikhrov placed his glasses back on the bridge of his nose, and peered down at the miniscule script on the parchment.

"Please be patient. I had translated and gone over the rest of all of this before many, many times, but this is all new, and I have to take care in translating it correctly," he told Jake and Miranda.

Miranda unconsciously reached over and grabbed Jake's hand on his lap. Jake gripped it back, all the while trying to be supportive, but fearful Miranda might find something new in all of this that could change her mind in turning the documents over to the authorities. Dr. Vikhrov commenced in translating the prophecy, while the two of them sat in silence as he began to speak.

"The Lord God, on high over all, vowed after the fall of his most beloved angel, to leave mankind to himself, along with the guidance and teachings that he had left to them, and so bequeathed all of his angels be forbidden in interfering in the world of man from that day forward. Faith would be the only guiding force now that would be in the hands and hearts of man, and their lives and their sins would be of their own making. God would hear the prayers of man, and serve them through their souls and their faith, but no force of Heaven would henceforth act upon the world of man. Any act by any angel, interfering in the world of Hell or Earth, would be punished by the Lord on high."

Dr. Vikhrov stopped momentarily, running his finger along the next few lines and then, gently tapped his finger upon the parchment.

"This," he stated, "is where it really seems to get interesting."

He continued on. "Cast into the darkness and fallen, the Lightbringer foresaw the coming of one who, not of Heaven or of the Earth, was beyond the reach of the touch of Heaven's wrath or power, as decreed by the Lord Himself, and who would hold the key to set free the Morning Star, so that he could bring forth into the world the enlightenment that was denied by God to mankind. This chosen one would hold the decision by their own free will, as granted by the Lord God, to leave Lucifer in his dark confinement, or to set him free to grant his knowledge and bestow upon mankind its true deserve."

"This, I believe, is what the past generations of your family, and all of those who followed with them, had been searching for and waiting for ever since they broke away from the Order of Sanctity. It wasn't just about worshipping a fallen adversary of God. It was waiting for the one that could set him free upon the world," said Dr. Vikhrov, the enthusiasm practically gushing from within him.

"Doctor," said Miranda. "What exactly did they think would happen if Lucifer was set free?"

"The prophecy hints that he may bring great knowledge to the world. It might be the cure for disease or the secrets of great technologies. The very intricate craftwork of the fabric of the universe itself. Even more so, the very revelation of his existence to man would cause the greatest upheaval to the religions of the world like no other thing has done since Christ himself walked the Earth."

"But what if it's all a lie?" Jake muttered, looking to Miranda. Dr. Vikhrov narrowed his eyes skeptically at what Jake might be implying.

"I'm not saying that I think you are wrong or misleading in what you've told us, doctor. I'm not even saying that I think these documents aren't truly ancient religious artifacts of enormous historical value. I can't even believe at this point I am taking this where I am going to, but what if they actually *are* a message from Lucifer? *The* Lucifer. If that was actually true, then what has everything that man has even known about him taught us? It's that he is the devil. The father of *lies*. If such a being existed that could open some magical portal and set him free, then why in the hell should we believe that anything good could come of that? It could all be his grand trick just to be set free," Jake blasted, with a steady anger rising in his voice.

"Jake..." Miranda started, and Jake held his hand up to stop her. Dr. Vikhrov abruptly leaned forward; Jake's sudden movement disturbed him, and he wasn't sure what Jake would do. Jake rose suddenly from his chair and stepped away from Miranda.

"No, Miranda. Why are we sitting here, listening to these stories? I know you, and you know that neither one of us has even cared a day about religion or the Bible. Yeah, I believe in God, because I choose to, not because of what some book tells me I should believe or how I should act. So how is this bullshit any different? Tell me!"

"Why are you doing this?" asked Miranda, standing from her chair and stepping closer to Jake. His sudden reaction was confounding her, and she didn't know what the best way was to calm him down. She had seen him angry before, and she had been the cause of it more than a few times. But this was...different.

He turned around to face her, and she could clearly see there was fear in his eyes.

"Something isn't right about this. I don't know what it is, Miranda. There is something very wrong about all of this. I have a bad feeling. I can't put a finger on where it's coming from. All I know right now is it's scaring the hell out of me," Jake said, with a tremor in his voice.

"Jake," she whispered to him, close to his face. "You do believe this, don't you?"

"I don't know what I believe," Jake whispered back. "What I do know is that I have a very bad feeling; there is some dark shit going on here. I am not scared for me. I am scared for you. And right now, we need to figure out where we are going to go, and what our next move is going to be. Because for the first time, I am starting to realize that at least for now, we have to keep moving. If there are people that know what is in that prophecy, and they believe it, I have no doubt that someone either wants it for themselves, or wants to make sure that no one else ever knows what is in it, and that includes making sure anyone who may have come across it never tells anyone what they may know."

"I think," said Dr. Vikhrov, "that perhaps there have been some things that you haven't told me?"

Miranda turned to Dr. Vikhrov, who was looking disconcerted at the young man and woman.

"My real name," Miranda started, with a hint of shame in her voice, "is Miranda Stratton, Dr. Vikhrov. I am sorry that I wasn't up front with you. Gale is my birth family's name, and it is where the parchment pages came from indirectly, but I have never met my birth family. As far as I know, they may actually be dead and gone. My adopted family...the only family I have ever known, was murdered yesterday, and I believe my having the Caducus Oraclum might have something to do with it."

Dr. Vikhrov sat in astonished disbelief at what Miranda had just told him. He closed his eyes for several seconds, and then raised them and looked at Miranda. He rose slowly from his chair, and reached out his hands toward hers. She was taken aback, but placed her hands in his, as Jake watched standing by their side.

"Child," he said to her softly. "I am sorry for your loss. I lost a family too, back in Russia, when I was a far younger man. No words can make the pain disappear completely. They can comfort you for a time, but the pain still lingers deep within. You must be wary of things that may come. There are forces on opposing sides that would both kill and die for what is in these pages. It is true that there are those that would just as soon see these burned, along with all those who know what is written upon them. I am afraid that even if you had not brought them to me to find what they reveal, they would still try and hunt you down, just to be certain you didn't know what was written in them."

"Do you know who it might be that is after them?" asked Miranda.

"No. I can only speculate. Radical factions of the Holy Church. Stray believers in the prophecy of Lucifer's keymaster. Someone either knows or believes you have them. Go with God, Miranda. May He guide you, regardless of what you choose to believe. If you keep Him with you, in your heart, He will help you on your journey."

"What about you? What happens if these people find out that we came to see you?" Miranda asked him.

"I have been thinking of making a return visit to my homeland. If they have any indication that we have talked, then perhaps now is as good a time as any to take an extended vacation. Go, now. If you have to, to keep them out of the wrong hands, burn them yourself. It is enough to know for me that they were real after all of these years researching the copies of them. I can't thank you enough for that." He looked at Jake, nodding to him. "Take her, now. Keep her safe."

Miranda hugged the aged Russian, which caught him off guard just as much as it did when he extended his hands to hers. Perhaps she felt, too, that he was a person that truly might understand her pain. Jake nodded to him in return as they left the office, and he and Miranda walked on down the hall.

Dr. Vikhrov sat down in his desk chair. He knew when he told her he would visit home that he had no intention of returning to Russia. Everything that once made the old country his home had died years before in a fire that not only consumed his family, but had scarred his very soul. He may have wished God to guide and protect Miranda in whatever trials she may face ahead, but he himself resented God for taking everything that he loved. It was part of the reason he had searched so long and hard through the multitudes of historical and theological texts that had consumed the better part of his life following his defection from Russia. He, like Miranda, had never stopped searching for some greater meaning to make sense of the losses he suffered so long ago.

Whatever was to come for him now may come. It no longer mattered to him. He was tired, and the best he could hope for any longer was to find his own sense of peace, and to hope against hope that whatever it was that Miranda sought to find her peace, that maybe in some small way, she could find a little bit for him along the way as well.

## CHAPTER THIRTEEN

When Miranda was very young, around the age of eight, the family of her best friend at the time, Jessica Kowalski, invited her to take a day trip with them to nearby Mackinaw Island, which is a popular tourist destination in northern Michigan known for its rich historical significance, as well as the trappings of a world famous fudge producing industry. Miranda didn't care so much for the historical side of things. She and Jessica were more excited about having their fill of fudge, going on a picnic, taking the hydroplane ferryboat ride to the island and seeing if they could talk Jessica's parents into going on a horse-drawn carriage tour of the island, as Jessica had overheard her father mentioning to her mother.

Mrs. Kowalski had called Miranda's mother and asked her if Miranda could go with them on that Saturday in late June. It would be a long day, and Mrs. Kowalski said it would be alright for Miranda to spend the night that night, and they would bring Miranda home after church the next morning. This would be the very first time that Miranda stayed overnight at someone's home other than that of a close relative.

Ever since she came to live with them, Lorri Stratton had been very protective of Miranda, and wasn't sure how she felt about Miranda being gone somewhere overnight. It was Miranda's father that finally convinced Lorri that she had to let go some and allow Miranda to go along with the Kowalski family to the island. Lorri finally agreed that it was alright, although she wasn't at first sure she knew how she felt about Miranda going along to church with the Kowalskis.

    Robert and Lorri Stratton had not been a church going family. In fact, the one and only time that Miranda could remember going to church was for her grandmother's funeral when she was only six years old. It wasn't that they weren't believers in God. They lived what could be considered, for the most part, a Christian based lifestyle. They tried to do right by others, and did their best to raise their children to do the same. But watching what had become of the sense of organized religion in the world around them steered them away from any particular denomination, and they felt that living a life by example rather than following the teaching of any particular religious denomination would suit the way that they raised the children best, and would leave it to both Miranda and Steven to choose their own paths as far as faith was concerned when they were ready.

    The Kowalski family was Catholic, so Lorri knew that Miranda would most likely find the whole experience odd and fascinating. She was a very perceptive and inquisitive little girl, and Lorri finally decided that it would be alright for Miranda to go along with the Kowalskis to the church service as well. She had thought maybe she would just pick Miranda up early, before the Kowalskis left for the service, but ultimately decided that maybe if she and Robert got a sitter for Steven that night as well, they could have an evening out that, for the two of them, was long overdue. Lorri called her sister, Kelly, who still lived in Native Springs at that time, and she took Steven for the night.

Early that Saturday morning, Lorri kissed Miranda in the driveway, and watched her ride away with Jessica and the rest of the Kowalski family. Miranda was so excited she could hardly contain herself. She quickly forgot about the dreams she so often had about the man at the piano. It seemed easier to push those thoughts aside when she had more to occupy her mind, which was one of the reasons that she learned to read so quickly at a young age.

Books kept her mind flush and occupied, which was helpful to keep the darker, scarier things away. Sometimes even after she went to bed and kissed her mother goodnight, Miranda would sneak a flashlight into her bed beneath the covers and read one of the many books that had found their home on her bedroom bookshelves.

The car ride on I-75 seemed to pass quickly as the two girls played and laughed with each other, looking at picture books and trying to make up funny stories along the way, always trying to top the other with their wild creativity.

Mrs. Kowalski told the girls to look on up ahead, and the girls were in awe when they saw the first glimpses of the top of the southern tower of the Mackinac Bridge as they approached the outskirts of Mackinaw City. At that age, the tower seemed enormous, reaching into the clear blue sky over the treetops that day. The bridge is indeed a spectacular sight at any age, spanning the Straits of Mackinac over five miles, and was once the world's longest suspension bridge. But to a child of eight, especially one who had never experienced seeing it before, it seemed a truly wondrous thing indeed.

Mr. Kowalski parked the car in a large parking lot owned by one of the three major ferry companies along the waterfront areas on the shores of Lake Huron. Mrs. Kowalski grabbed a day bag with the picnic lunch they had packed before they picked up Miranda, while Mr. Kowalski grabbed a small cooler with drinks, and the four of them boarded the large, double-decker hydroplane ferry that would take them to the island.

    The girls of course wanted to ride up top in the open-air deck, even though it was still cool in the morning along the shoreline, so Mr. and Mrs. Kowalski decided to let the family sit up top for the ride. As the boat took off and gained speed, the girls quickly felt how cool it actually was sitting up high in the wind, and occasionally caught some of the spray that kicked up above the top deck when the boat would slap across the waves. The waves seemed a little rougher than usual for the morning hours, and the wind was a little heavier as well, but the forecast for the day was supposed to be clear and sunny, with temperatures in the low 80s. The coming days' weather was already evidenced by the clear skies, but the wind and the waves hadn't quite caught up just yet to the soft blue that spanned the horizon.

    Once they reached the island shore, Miranda and Jessica followed along behind Mr. and Mrs. Kowalski in the mad rush of visitors to the island. The people getting off the boat scrambled to get a locker so they could store items that they didn't want to carry all day long around the island, but early in the morning there were plenty of lockers still available. The Kowalskis packed the lunch bag and the cooler into a locker for later, and the four of them emerged onto the already busy roadway that circled the entire distance around the island.

    The area around the docks was by far the busiest part of the island at any given time, where the merchants of the lucrative fudge trades set up their shops it seemed every 50 feet or so, with the divisions of shops in between selling every sort of "Mackinac Island" or "Up North, Michigan" sweatshirt or t-shirt that anyone could imagine. Visitors could also find trinkets of all sorts, from sailing vessels in a bottle to toy muskets and pistols similar to that used in the American Revolutionary War, as well as every sort of book on the history of the area back to the times when the Native American Indians were the sole residents of these lands.

Miranda found the books in these stores fascinating, which amused Mrs. Kowalski that at such a young age Miranda was such an avid reader. In one store, Miranda found a book titled "Lore of the Great Turtle", which was a collection of Ojibwa legends about the island itself, as well as other great stories about the folklore and history through Native American eyes of the upper Great Lakes region. Mrs. Kowalski thought that it might be a nice keepsake from their trip to the island, and bought it for her as a gift. For Jessica, she bought a small, hand-carved Indian princess figurine that had been made by an older Ojibwa gentleman in a small shop on one of the side streets that rose up the hillsides to the higher elevations of the island.

Miranda loved her book, and thanked Mrs. Kowalski over and over again, while Jessica found herself so lost in the intricacies of her wooden doll that she had actually forgotten to thank her mother at all.

All day long, the *clippity-clap, clippity-clap* of the horse-drawn carriages up and down Main Street filled the air, along with the not-so-fresh scent of that which the horses left behind as they traipsed up and down the paved roadways. It was the unfortunate, yet notably important job of the few who had to follow along the paths of the mighty animals to collect the leavings behind before too much overtook the streets of the wildly popular island. Although the reputation of its old-fashioned and motor vehicle free environment was one of the island's many appealing draws, this was one aspect that left much to be desired.

This fact did not change the minds of the two young girls who were determined to get Mr. and Mrs. Kowalski to take them on a carriage ride. Ultimately, Mr. Kowalski told the girls that after they had had their lunch on a grassy area along the water's edge, they would take a carriage tour that ended at Fort Mackinac, which would be the final destination of their day at the island.

Miranda and Jessica ate hurriedly through the sandwiches that Mrs. Kowalski packed for them, although it did little good to speed things along, as Mr. and Mrs. Kowalski took their time eating and enjoying the cool breeze under the now blazing sun. The temperatures were now already exceeding those that were expected, and there were people everywhere chugging drinks from water bottles in every direction.

Finally, the four of them made it back to the carriage tour stop and boarded the carriage that would take them up through some of the more historic parts of the island; they passed many old houses that were the original structures built on the island through the 1700s and 1800s. Along the way was the magnificent Grand Hotel, where the tour driver had said that a famous movie was filmed back in the late 1970s.

There was also the mysterious place called the Skull Cave, which Miranda found to be somewhat chilling by the name alone. Skull Cave was a small cave used by the Native Americans in the 18th century as a burial place; years later it was discovered to be strewn with human bones. Next along the way was the wondrous Arch Rock, a natural arch formation of limestone thought to be made in one of the glacial periods. Finally, they came to Fort Mackinac.

The Fort, as it is today, has its outer white walls built out of limestone, high atop the limestone bluffs that overlook the Straits of Mackinac. Built during the American Revolutionary War by the British, it was not relinquished to the American forces until 1796. During the War of 1812, the British easily reclaimed the Fort during the duration of the war, fighting back and killing many American soldiers during the Battle of Mackinac Island in 1814.

After the war was over, the United States took over control of the fort once more in the year 1815, and its role as an important military stronghold was greatly diminished. Eventually, the fort became a museum site and tribute to an important era in United States history, and to this day draws thousands of visitors every year.

The Kowalskis and Miranda toured the buildings of the fort, many of which had scene re-creations of British soldiers and captains that played important roles at the fort from that historical period. Archeologists were almost constantly doing new digs on the fort grounds and the areas surrounding the fort, finding new clues about the lives of the people that lived back in the colonial days and in the more recent years after the wars had ended.

It was almost 4 p.m., and many of the visitors were told that one of the final reenactment scenes of the day was going to be starting in just a few minutes. Miranda and the Kowalskis headed out into one of the open areas where a crowd had gathered, and stood along the sidelines watching many of the actors that were dressed like British colonial red-coat soldiers lined up in a battle scene. Although there were no major battles within the fort walls, the actors put on a show nevertheless, firing authentic muskets loaded with powder into the air, and finally finishing with a cannon firing harmlessly without cannonball out towards the waters of the straits.

As the costumed soldiers ran around the grassy yard of the fort, yelling and firing and feigning mortal despair, things had caught Miranda's attention that escaped the eyes of all of the others.

There were more soldiers there than just the ones that played their roles in the reenactment. But these soldiers had far more serious looks on the pale faces they wore. The clothing they were wearing was far more tattered and covered with what looked like soot and blood. Some were wet, as if they had been caught in a storm or a wrecked ship; and more than a few did not wear the familiar red coats of the British soldiers. These soldiers wore blue jackets and white, dirty trousers, with high black, once shiny boots.

As one of the men in blue walked past Miranda calmly as the red-coat actors scurried about, the man turned his head towards Miranda and revealed that his left cheek and lower left part of his jaw were completely missing, as if blown off by gunfire. Miranda gasped and drew closer to Mrs. Kowalski, who looked at Miranda with concern when she saw the terror in her eyes. The man promptly looked away and kept walking at the same pace as before, and it was then that Miranda noticed that there were more there like him, intertwined with the play actors, but some lying about missing a limb, or writhing in agony in the grass as they bled from their gunfire wounds.

That was the first time that Miranda has started to hyperventilate. The terror had overcome her, and Mr. and Mrs. Kowalski quickly noticed and took the girls away from the area and outside the walls of the fort. Mrs. Kowalski got Miranda to calm down, and gave her cold water from a vendor outside of the fort who had offered it at no charge, seeing the condition the young girl was in.

After a short time, Miranda was feeling much better. Mr. Kowalski blamed the heat of the day and the fact that the girls probably had not been drinking enough water to stay properly hydrated. When Mrs. Kowalski asked Miranda if there was anything else wrong, Miranda silently just shook her head side to side, finally telling her she was okay now.

They made their way back to the docks, and caught the 5:30 p.m. ferry back to Mackinaw City. Mrs. Kowalski considered calling Miranda's parents and letting them know what had happened, in case they thought perhaps she should come home that night. But after seeing the girls laughing and playing again on the ferry ride home, and seeing that both girls had quite an appetite for the pizza they had for dinner at a tavern-style restaurant in downtown Mackinaw City, Mrs. Kowalski had decided that it probably was the heat that had affected poor Miranda. The four of them decided to stay for the fireworks display that took place at dusk on every Saturday of the summer in Mackinaw City.

They arrived home late, and both girls had fallen asleep in the car well before they had arrived back in Native Springs. They wandered wearily into Jessica's bedroom, and both quickly fell asleep again in Jessica's bed after the long, enjoyable day at the island.

It was around 9 a.m. when Mrs. Kowalski came into the bedroom to wake the girls and tell them to start getting ready for church. The service was at 10 a.m. at the Catholic Shrine, and Miranda's mother had packed a nice, light colored dress covered with a purple floral design throughout. She got dressed in the bathroom, brushed her teeth and her hair, and was not nervous at all about going to church. She was actually quite excited, more so than Jessica was. She had never been to a church service before, and was interested to see what it was all about. This pleased Mrs. Kowalski, who came from a family line that had all been Catholic for as far back as she could trace her lineage. Not that she was trying to influence her religious beliefs on Miranda in any way. She was just glad that Miranda had the interest to be open to new ideas and experiences. Jessica was not ever interested in going to church, and Mrs. Kowalski often found herself nudging her to keep her from falling asleep during mass.

The sun was warming the air quickly that morning, and in the car ride to the church, Mr. Kowalski said that he wouldn't doubt it if they decided to have outdoor mass that day. There had not been rain for several days, so the bench pews would be dry and warm. Mr. Kowalski had arrived at the Shrine parking lot a little earlier than usual, fully expecting an outdoor mass at that time of the year to draw a huge crowd of tourists to the church, along with the local crowd.

The Shrine is the home of one of the world's largest crucifixes, with the statue of Christ on the cross being over 30 feet high upon the massive cross carved from a redwood tree. This mighty spectacle alone draws people from all over the world, flocking to gaze upon the awe inspiring bronze sculpture. On a sunny and warm day in late June, the numbers were sure to be high for those attending an actual mass before cross that morning.

Miranda and the Kowalskis hurried over the busy highway from the parking lot across from the church. There were several different walkways down to the grounds where the outdoor mass was held. Miranda looked down at the reddish-brown brick pathway that they took, reading every four feet another persons name on a brick. *Dr. and Mrs. Donald Green.* The next one read *In Loving Memory of Beatrice Warren.* It went on and on along the way, all those who had donated money to make the pathway and grounds lush and beautiful. And they were truly beautiful.

Tall maple trees and pines filled the spaces in between sidewalks and pathways that led to smaller monuments built along the way to honor saints and missionaries that once walked the lands of the north. The thick green of the trees allowed little flecks of sunlight to break through to the paved walk before them now. Up ahead, the trees parted and Miranda's eyes lit up in wonder at her first glimpse of the massive cross upon the mound beyond the two long rows of benches that faced the grey marble alter positioned down below the statue of Christ.

Miranda stopped in her tracks at the first sight of the bronze Son of God, which caused a sudden disruption to the flow of foot traffic behind them. Mrs. Kowalski ushered Miranda on so they could find a seat, and Miranda began to follow along behind Jessica just as she had been doing before. Her eyes kept on going back to the face of the Man on the cross, and as she got closer, she felt a mild sense of trepidation. Miranda was certain, at least as much as she could be, that the eyes of the statue were fixed on her, watching her every move.

The crowds grew more and more with every second gone by, and it almost seemed as if they were filing in from every path by the bus load. Jessica said something to Miranda, but she didn't hear what it was, not that Jessica even noticed. Miranda's eyes were just as much fixed on the statue as she felt the statues eyes were fixed upon her. Mrs. Kowalski noticed how Miranda stared at the cross, and smiled down at her.

"He's beautiful, isn't He?" she whispered to Miranda.

Miranda nodded her head slightly and then looked to Mrs. Kowalski.

"Who is he?"

"You don't know who that is?" asked Mrs. Kowalski, trying to dampen her sense of astonishment.

Miranda shook her head.

"That is Jesus," said Mrs. Kowalski.

"He's God's son," Jessica interjected, before getting distracted again, fiddling with a pamphlet of some kind that she found beneath her seat.

"Have you ever been to church before, Miranda?" asked Mrs. Kowalski.

"No..." Miranda said, almost inaudibly as she noticed the two iron spikes that held the man to the cross. "Who did that to Him?"

"People that were afraid of His teachings. Some of them were the religious leaders of the time. Some of them were people who didn't like the fact that people were calling Him a king. But I think most of all, it comes down to people who are just full of fear or full of greed."

"What a terrible way to die," said Miranda, looking upward sadly at the cross.

"He died for all of us, but then He rose from the dead. His Father took him up to Heaven, and He watches over all of us. That is why we are here. To praise Him and thank Him and to learn from Him through His teachings." Miranda looked at Mrs. Kowalski as she spoke, and then looked back at Jesus on the cross.

The man in the robe on the shiny marble alter began to speak, and all soon became silent throughout the crowd.

The mass lasted for just over an hour, and there was singing at times throughout the service, and there were also times when almost everyone in the crowd chanted the same things at the same times, and Miranda found it a little unsettling that everyone seemed to know what to say but her. Towards the end of the service, men and woman went out into the crowd and the people in the benches lined up to receive small, round white discs of some sort that they ate, and then they would return to their seats.

Mr. and Mrs. Kowalski had Jessica stay with Miranda on the bench while they went up to get their little discs, and when they returned, Mrs. Kowalski told Miranda that the discs were little wafers that were like bread, and they represented the body of Jesus. Miranda said nothing to this, understandably, because it made no sense to Miranda why people would be eating the body of the Son of God. She pretended to understand, and Mrs. Kowalski once again gave her a soft and reassuring smile.

"Now, we bow our heads and we pray," said Mrs. Kowalski.

"What do you pray for?" asked Miranda.

"People pray for all sorts of different reasons. It is simply just talking to God. Sometimes we pray to thank Him. Sometimes we pray for something we think that we need. Sometimes we pray for healing or forgiveness."

Mrs. Kowalski bowed her head, and Miranda did the same. She didn't know much about praying. She had only once heard talk of prayer in her own home. She was five years old, and she remembered walking past her mother and father's bedroom, and she saw her mother kneeling on the floor with her arms rested and folded on the bed. There were tears in her eyes, and Miranda walked in and put her hand on her mother's shoulder. Even at the age of five, she was a sharp and perceptive little girl.

"What's wrong, Mommy? Why are you sad?" Miranda asked her mother.

Lorri wrapped her arms around her little girl, and

sobbed even harder. Miranda hugged her back hard, and tears started to form in her own eyes, although she didn't even know why.

"I was just saying a little prayer, baby, for your grandma," said Lorri, trying to gain some composure for Miranda, and for herself as well.

"What's a prayer?" asked Miranda.

"It's when we talk to God, when we need his help. Your grandmother is very sick, and she might not be around for very much longer," said Lorri, wiping the tears from her face.

"Where is she going?" asked Miranda, looking sad and worried after hearing what Lorri said.

"To Heaven, to be with God. I am praying that she gets better though. I want her to. I don't want her to go yet," said Lorri, holding her little girl's hand.

"I don't want her to go, either, Mommy," said Miranda, hugging her mother tightly now. "I want to pray, too."

"Okay, baby," said Lorri, squeezing her daughter tightly back. "We can pray together then."

A week later, Miranda was in a church for the first and only time until that day with the Kowalskis, at her grandmother's funeral. And then, like now, as she prayed before the statue of Jesus on the cross, she wondered why it was that even after she and her mother prayed for her grandmother to get better, God didn't listen to them.

Miranda stopped praying, and looked at the statue once more, and she saw those eyes looking at her once again. But this time, she saw something that no one else from that day would claim to see.

"Why is he crying," Miranda asked, looking at the statue.

Mrs. Kowalski looked around, but saw no one crying. "Why is who crying, Miranda?" asked Mrs. Kowalski.

"Jesus. Why is he crying?"

Mrs. Kowalski looked up at the statue, for a moment hoping to be witness to some sort of miracle. But there were no tears coming from the eyes of the mighty bronze statue.

"Miranda," she whispered. "There is no one crying. Maybe you see the sunlight hitting the face of the statue, and it might be playing with your eyes."

Miranda said nothing more about it. She felt slightly embarrassed being the only person who saw what she was seeing, and she didn't understand why. But what she saw was no trick of the light. There were tears running down both sides of His face. It frightened her, and she was ready to leave.

Mrs. Kowalski asked Miranda if she wanted to get up closer to the statue after the mass, but Miranda told her she wasn't feeling very well and asked if they could take her home now. Mrs. Kowalski looked concerned, and they took her right home after the mass.

When they got to Miranda's house, she said goodbye to Jessica and very politely told Mr. and Mrs. Kowalski she had a nice time, and thanked them for taking her along. Mrs. Kowalski walked her to the front door and they met Lorri at the door. Lorri gave Miranda a hug and asked if she had a good time, and Miranda told her she did, but then quickly took her bags up to her bedroom. Mrs. Kowalski stayed for a few moments after Miranda went upstairs, and told Lorri what Miranda had said about not feeling well. She then went on to tell her how much of a delight she was to have with them, and how wonderful a little girl she was. Lorri smiled and thanked her, but was anxious to get upstairs to see that Miranda was alright.

No sooner than Mrs. Kowalski had turned and walked away did Lorri head right upstairs to Miranda's room to check on her daughter. Miranda was playing with a raven haired doll that her aunt had bought her, sitting quietly on her bed.

"Baby? Are you feeling okay? Mrs. Kowalski said you weren't feeling very well," asked Lorri.

"I feel good, Mommy. I just wanted to come home," stated Miranda, taking no attention away from the doll in her hands.

Lorri found Miranda's actions strange, but finally just thought that perhaps after the long day that she had spent with the Kowalskis, she was overtired and needed some rest. She left Miranda alone to play with her doll, took care of her laundry, and went back to reading her book that she had been reading before Miranda got home.

Miranda stayed in her room that afternoon, deep in thought. If God was there, and if He was listening, then why didn't He help her grandmother? Why did He let her and her mother suffer the way that they did? And why did He cry, up there on the cross? She had cried, and Lorri had cried, and it changed nothing.

Miranda's initial fascination that morning had turned into a child's contempt for things that are usually far too complex for a child of her age to contemplate and realize. She decided that if God was truly there, He had stopped listening to people and their prayers probably a long time ago. That was a sense of reality that she had embraced from that moment forward, and had never bothered herself with thoughts of God and religion of any sort from then on.

Until today.

## CHAPTER FOURTEEN

Jake and Miranda had been sitting in the car for several minutes in silence in the parking lot of the university's main building. Miranda had just stared out the passenger side window, seemingly lost in thought, while watching a seagull as it loitered a few feet outside the car waiting for something to be discarded out of the window. Jake was trying to be sensitive to the situation as much as possible, but staying still for too long, especially given the latest revelations to their predicament, wasn't something that he felt comfortable with.

"Miranda," he said softly. "We need to figure out what we are going to do."

Miranda knew that Jake most likely still wanted to go to the police. A few hours before, submitting to that wasn't an option for Miranda until she had figured out what it was that these people were most likely after. She knew what it was now that was written on these parchment pages, but it gave her no peace of mind at all. She felt empty and lost, and wished more than anything that she could call her dad and ask him for his advice. He was always so level headed, and always had so much confidence believing that in whatever she faced, she would make the right decisions and get through whatever came her way.

But she knew that she could never hear her father's voice again, and for the first time in a long time, whatever sense of confidence that she had in herself - that strength that he instilled in her that would carry her through all obstacles that came before her whenever she had doubts about anything - seemed far beyond her reach. It was an unusual feeling for her, and it did not sit well with her.

"What do you want to do, Miranda?" Jake asked her once more. His voice was calming in its tone, yet she could sense the uncharacteristic trepidation in it.

"I don't know, Jake. I just...I can't think. Anywhere we go, I feel like we are putting more people in danger. I can't be responsible for anyone else getting hurt."

"You are not responsible. None of this is your fault. Listen, we will do whatever you feel we need to do. But, can I make one suggestion?"

"Go ahead," she said, almost imperceptibly nodding her head while looking down at her lap.

"We need some time, and we need a plan, so let's find a place that we can lay low for a while. If we can find a way to expose these things to the public, let people know, and I mean a lot of people. TV - other media - at that point, the target will be taken off of you."

"How are we going to do that? There aren't many people that can even make out what the parchments say or what they mean. We just talked to one of the only people that probably can tell anyone what they are, and now I probably put him in danger as well."

Jake said nothing, and just stared ahead.

"Okay. Then we'll disappear. We will go where no one can ever find us."

"Jake, I can't ask you to do that," said Miranda.

"You didn't."

"You should just let me go," Miranda told him. "Get a bus ride home, go and tell the police everything, except that you came to Dr. Vikhrov with me. Tell Detective Rice I left you at a rest stop a hundred miles north. If these people think you don't know anything more than they are after me for something, then maybe they will leave you alone."

"That's not going to happen," Jake said. "People like this; these fanatics...they'll stop at almost nothing when it comes to protecting their secrets. They won't let anyone get by that might be a threat to them or their beliefs. We hear about this stuff almost every day on the news. Suicide bombings. Public executions. All in the name of whatever higher power they believe in. And even more so, I am not going to let you run away alone and not be there to help you. Never again."

"So what then? Give up your life and your dreams just to hide with me forever?"

"If that's what it takes, then yes," he said, trying not to lose himself in the moment and let his heart overpower his head.

Miranda looked at him with a strange sadness in her eyes. She could almost feel it, like a warmth running through her being, the depth of caring he had for her, and it made her feel even worse. She did not feel the love for him that he felt for her. She did care for him very deeply as well, but whatever they once had was long past. It was up to her to find another path, and not to get Jake any more caught up in it than she already had gotten him.

"Dr. Vikhrov said there were people working on both sides of this prophecy. We need to get somewhere where we can buy some time and find some resources to try and find out which side it is that is coming after us for it, and who they might be," said Miranda.

"And then we try to figure out who the other side is," said Jake, following where Miranda's thinking was going. "Do you think whoever is on the other side might help us?"

"I guess it can't get any worse than where we are now. They can either help us, or they'll try and kill us as well. Let's just hope there is such a thing as a balance between good and evil. If the *bad* ones are the ones trying to kill us for the Oraclum, then maybe the other side will help us."

"Unless one side or the other is just the lesser of two evils," said Jake. A thought came to Jake as he said this. He remembered a campfire story his favorite uncle told him as a kid when he camped with him at a lake north of Traverse City years before. It was a frightening story that he couldn't quite remember, but the "lesser of two evils" comment he had just uttered reminded him of the story, and more importantly, of his uncle.

"Do you remember my Uncle Jim? He's not a blood uncle, but I have known him since I was born. He has a vacation cabin about an hour north of Chicago on a small lake. I don't think anyone could make the connection between us if we could get there, and it would be a good place to get off the radar and start trying to find out who we need to talk to for help. I know where he keeps the key, and he told us we can use it whenever we wanted to. Our only problem is getting there. We have just over $200 left between us, and we can't use the credit cards or it will make a trail."

Miranda thought about the money problem. She didn't know what they would need when they got to where they were going. She also couldn't say how long it would take to find all the information they would need to try and track down who else might want the Oraclum that may be able to help them…if, in fact, such others were still even out there.

"There is one thing we can do. I hate doing it. I don't want anyone else close to me involved, but I think we've run out of other options. I will need to call my roommate at South Central. She can loan us whatever cash we need. I feel like shit having to ask though."

"Is she hard to get along with?" asked Jake.

"No. Lydia…she's an angel. She is…well, beside you…she's my best friend. I would do anything for her, and she would do the same for me. That's what makes this so damn hard. I don't want to put her in any danger as well."

"If we play this right, no one will ever have to know," said Jake. "How much time would she need to get the cash?"

"I wouldn't think too long. She has access to all of her family bank accounts and trusts at school," said Miranda.

"Trusts?"

"She comes from a wealthy family. She doesn't act like it though. She wants to prove herself on her own."

"I think I like her already," said Jake. "Once we get on the road, you can call her. We should be able to get to South Central in under two hours, and it's on the way to the Indiana border. I imagine that should give her enough time, and we can meet her in a public place." Jake tapped his thumb on the steering wheel for a moment, hesitating to say what was now on his mind.

"Miranda, I don't want to make you worry more, but if these people know where you go to school, you have to remember that they could possibly be watching your apartment already. That doesn't mean they are after Lydia, though. They could just be waiting to see if you try and show up there for anything."

Miranda had been so caught up in thinking about everything else that had been going on that the thought these people could already be watching the apartment or Lydia hadn't crossed her mind. She felt another wave of fear rush over her, but she knew that the choices she and Jake had were limited. If they were watching Lydia, there was nothing she could do at that point anyhow. She was far more afraid for Lydia's safety than her own. Now, she felt she needed to see her and be sure for herself that Lydia was alright.

"Okay. Let's get going then. Ten minutes on the road, I will call her and tell her what we need. I am going to ask her for $2,000. If we are only buying gas and food, it should be enough for the time being."

Jake nodded his head and reached down to turn the ignition key. The car was turning over, but it was not starting right up as it had been. There were no signs of any trouble before, and Jake tried again and again before hitting the steering wheel with his fist in frustration.

"Son of a bitch!" he exclaimed, then popped the hood latch and got out of the car to see what might be going on with the engine. Miranda sat in the car, contemplating what else might go wrong. Jake fiddled with a few different things that Miranda could not see, and had Miranda try the key a few more times before finally slamming the hood back down. He got back into the car with a look of annoyance on his face.

"Do you know what it is?" asked Miranda.

"No. These goddamn newer engines! It's not like working on my bike. I used to fix old cars with my dad all the time. There was fuel and fire. If the car wouldn't start, chances are it was one or the other. Now they pack so much shit under the hoods, and everything has electronic sensors attached to it. Nothing in this world is made simple anymore!" Jake exclaimed.

"So, now what?" she asked.

"We are going to have to get it towed. We might have to try and rent a car to meet Lydia, and once we get the cash we can pay for the repair, whatever it is."

Jake walked into a nearby convenience store and used the phone inside to call for a tow truck, which arrived within 20 minutes. The truck gave them a ride to the service station about two miles down the road. The place was called Billy K's Auto Service Central, and Miranda and Jake sat in the lobby for about an hour before one of the mechanics, a tall, thin African-American man, came out to talk to them. He approached Jake, which was just as well as far as Miranda was concerned. She knew almost nothing about car talk, with the exception of how to drive in all weather conditions, and where to put the gas and oil.

The name on the man's shirt said "Huey", and he walked up with a clipboard in his hands.

"Well, what you've got going on here is a bad sensor. The engine computer told us which one it is from a code, but your dashboard engine light was burned out, so you all probably never saw it come on," said Huey. "We replaced the bulb in the dash, but we can't get the sensor until tomorrow, early morning."

"Isn't there any way you can rush it or something?" asked Jake. "Maybe send someone to get one?"

"We have to special order it, and it won't get here until our truck delivery late tonight. Besides, we have a whole lot of customers ahead of you today that made their appointments far in advance. You're lucky we can get you in at all this week," said Huey.

"How much is it going to cost?" asked Jake, trying to

compose himself better. He didn't want to come across too urgent to this man and draw too much attention.

Huey looked down at his clipboard and did a few quick calculations.

"Parts and labor...about $235," Huey told him. "If you've got a credit card, you can charge the amount now, but if not, I'll need at least half down for the part."

"How much is the part?" asked Jake.

"The part is $185, the rest is labor. It's an easy fix. Most of the money is in the sensor."

Jake walked with Huey several feet away from Miranda, who watched as they walked away. She wondered what Jake might be up to, but decided it was best to let the men do their talking.

"Huey," he said, with his hand on Huey's shoulder. "Is there any way that I can give you a credit card, but have you charge it after the repair is finished?"

"Uh, you'll have to make arrangements with Billy if you wanna do something like that. I can't authorize that myself."

"Can you get Billy for me?" asked Jake.

Huey went into a back office behind a two-way mirror, and stepped out with an older, somewhat heavier African-American man. Huey pointed to Jake, and the man walked over to him.

"Is there a problem with something, son?" asked the man, whose name was clearly printed on his blue work shirt as well, which read "Billy K."

"No, there's no problem. It's just that...my credit card is good, but we just don't want it run until after the repair is done and we are on our way. That's all."

"And how do I know your card is good if I don't run it? How would I know it's not stolen? Listen, I've been playing this

## In the Shadows of Fate

game for a long time. If you don't like the way I do business, you can find another tow service and take your car somewhere else," said Billy K. firmly, and he turned to start walking back to his office. Jake reached out his hand and placed it on Billy K's shoulder.

"Wait. Please. Just give me one minute," he said, and looked at Huey for a moment. "Privately."

Billy K. looked at the hand on his shoulder, and then looked to Huey. He gave Huey a nod indicating everything was alright. Huey returned to the garage, periodically looking over to check up on his boss.

"Okay then. Talk. You have one minute," said Billy K., and looked at his watch. Jake hadn't known what he was going to say to try and convince Billy K. of anything - until Billy K. looked at his watch.

"Listen. I don't want any trouble any more that you do. We are in a...situation. We haven't broken any laws. We're not wanted by the police. We don't have a lot of cash," said Jake, and looked over to make sure Miranda was not paying attention to him at that moment. She was looking down at a magazine, and Jake turned back to Billy K. He slid a gold and silver colored wristwatch off from his wrist and handed it out towards Billy. The shop owner looked down at the watch, and Jake nodded to him. He took it in his hand to examine it closer.

"Just look at it. It's the real deal. Real gold with silver accents. It's a Rolex. My grandfather won this in a poker game in the early 1970s. He gave it to me for a high school graduation present. It was insured at more than $2,000. If you want it for payment, it's yours. No questions asked."

Billy K. looked at the watch with great scrutiny, and then looked back to Jake with the same scrutiny.

"You sure you wanna do this?" Billy asked.

"Yes. I'm sure. It'll more than cover everything."

Billy placed it in his pocket. "I have a guy that knows about this stuff. He'll check it out within the hour. If it looks good, you've got yourself a deal."

"Do you have a rental car available?" asked Jake.

"That," said Billy, "Would require the credit card, and no $2,000 wristwatch is gonna cover that."

"Then do you have a place nearby that we will be able to stay for the night? Someplace cheap, and can we get a ride there and back in the morning?"

"Don't want much, do you?" asked Billy K. "Once I get this checked out, Huey can give you a ride up to my cousin's motel a half-mile up the road. It's not much, but it's cheap and close, and it'll give you a bed for the night."

Jake nodded to Billy K., who returned to his office to make a phone call to his 'guy'.

Miranda stood up, and Jake walked over to her.

"Everything all right?" she asked.

"Yeah. Everything is covered. They'll run the credit card in the morning, and the owner is setting us up with a ride to a place to stay for the night. No rental cars available."

"He's doing all that?" she asked, curiously.

"I guess they felt sorry for us. Anyway, it's covered. Don't worry. First thing in the morning we can be on the road to Lydia.

Within an hour's time, Billy K. had Huey taking Miranda and Jake to the Grand Avenue Motor Court, a half-mile from the garage. Jake walked to the main office and met Billy K's cousin Matt, who on Billy's word set them up in a room. The two of them then walked down to a small family style restaurant about a block west of the motel. They chose their orders from the restaurant's 'value selections', still watching what little cash they had very closely.

The neighborhood was not the worst around, still being in the vicinity of the university, but the motel itself was kind of a dive. It was right across the street from a club called "The Westside Warehouse", which by day looked like just that - a plain, unremarkable warehouse building. But to the local college crowd, it was one of the hottest nightspots around, with dancing, live music or DJ's seven nights a week.

The marquee out near the road just across from the motel read 'Annual Halloween Bash TONIGHT - closing for renovations for one month starting tomorrow!' Halloween was still more than a week away, but the owners and management knew that it would be a travesty if they didn't have their highlight party of the year, with costume contests and cash prizes, and even a surprise trip this year. The girls always got in for free; the sexier the costume, the better. Guys paid, mostly without argument or hesitation, the $25 cover fee for the event, and the place was usually packed to capacity by 9 p.m.

The staff of the Westside Warehouse had a Mardi Gras costume theme this year, with flashy costumes of all sorts related to the New Orleans Mardi Gras parade theme, along with strings of colored beads and feathers galore. The stage area was decorated to look like one of the popular classic festive parade floats, with jesters and heads of lions with golden crowns draped in purple and green vestments.

Jake and Miranda mostly stayed in the motel room after their early dinner. Jake found a paperback novel left under the bed, which for him passed the time and helped to pull his mind away from the things that have been going on, at least for a short while. On the other hand, it concerned him how clean the rest of the room was if something as large as a book could be missed under the bed by the cleaning personnel.

He'd been in worse, though, recalling a trip he had made to Florida during one spring break two years before with a couple of other guys. After the split with Miranda, and before he decided to clean up his act and do something with his life, he had a few binges of crazy drunkenness and excessive partying. Not that he hadn't delved into this kind of behavior before, but his state of mind wasn't in the best of places after Miranda had left.

The trip to Florida was set up by Jake's cousin Randy and a couple of Randy's friends from Central Michigan University in Mt. Pleasant, Michigan. Jake had chipped in his portion of the money for the trip, paying for one-fourth of a condo for the week near the Orlando area, and so had Randy. But just two weeks before they were to leave on the trip, Randy broke his leg in a skiing accident at a resort in Harbor Springs, and decided not to go on the trip. Instead of calling off the trip entirely and losing out on their money, Jake and the two other guys decided to chip in together to pay for Randy's quarter of the condo.

Jake did not know either of the other two guys before the trip, meeting them for the first time in Mount Pleasant when they were leaving on the road to head south for the week-long stay. Jake left his car at the apartment complex that the two other guys, Keith and Coomba (which was not his real name, rather a nickname that Jake never learned the origin of) were living in at the time.

The condo in Kissimmee, Florida, was a beautiful four bedroom place on the ground floor, less than 50 feet from the pool area. The drinking had begun as soon as they walked in the door, and later in the same day, Coomba had almost gotten them into three fights due to his flirtations with several different girls at the pool who were on vacation with their boyfriends. These were the kinds of things that sometimes happened on spring break trips to almost anywhere, but these guys liked to push the envelope as far as it could go, and Jake was still in that place where he really didn't care what happened. That was, until the third night of their stay at the condo.

After the pool had closed for the evening at midnight, Jake, Keith and Coomba snuck back in for a quiet after hours swim. That idea took a bad turn when Coomba ran back to the room, only to return carrying the 32 inch flat panel television from the room. He had decided to find out how well the TV would work as a boogie board in the pool that night, and Keith egged him on to do it. That was the point when Jake began to think that these guys had taken things too far. As it was, so did the condo management, who had received complaints that there were people in the pool area after hours, and caught the three young men in the act of the TV boogie board incident.

The owner of the condo they were renting was notified, and they were promptly evicted from the unit without refund. Jake was ready to go home, but the other two were not done partying. On a week in April during college spring break time, almost everywhere to stay was booked to the max. One of the front desk receptionists at a hotel on the main strip in Kissimmee suggested that it was possible they might find a room at the Carriageway Motor Court, and was nice enough to give them directions. The route they took to the motor court led them a few miles east of the downtown area through some seedy streets until they finally found the place. It was a shoddy, run down little place with piles of trash lying out on the corner of the parking lot.

Jake and the others went in to the main office, and a man stumbled in to meet them through a doorway at the back of the office. He stood there in blue boxers and an oversized t-shirt, reeking of weed.

Fingering through his scheduling book, he told them that he had one room available for the next three nights, and it was $75 per night. Reluctantly, Jake handed over his cash to Coomba and Keith, all the while thinking about the different ways he wanted to kill Randy for hooking him up with these two losers. They walked to their room, which was a musty little hole in the wall with two twin beds and a small bathroom. Coomba volunteered to sleep on the floor, which no one argued with, being that it was his dumb-ass antics that got them into this situation in the first place. When they awoke the next morning, all three of them were covered in little red bites that they discovered later were caused by bed bugs. They left the next day to head home, but not before demanding a refund for the time remaining that they had paid for up front. Coomba, of course, gave his money right back to the guy when he bought a bag of weed from him for the trip home, which both Keith and Coomba took turns smoking on the drive back north. They offered some to Jake, who was in no way a marijuana virgin, but after everything else that had happened, he just wanted to be able to get home in one piece.

It was that trip that finally got Jake to open his eyes and start looking forward in life rather than living in the past. And now, here it was two years later, and he was in another run down little motel; but this time, she was here with him, and the circumstances couldn't be anything close to happy or normal by any means. At this point, the best he could hope for in the next 12 hours was no bed bugs. He continued to read his book, a horror novella called "Cabal" by Clive Barker, and tried not to think about anything at all, until he dozed off in the bed.

Miranda sat at a small table built into the wall near the

window of the motel room. There was no Wi-Fi signal from the motel itself, but she was picking up a more distant signal from one of the local businesses nearby. It was a slow connection, but she still managed to be able to use her laptop to try and find any more information that she could about the Caducus Oraclum or about the Enochian script.

She had found no more about the Enochian script than she already had, and had even less luck with the Oraclum. There was very little information at all online about the Oraclum, and what she did find was leading more to the belief of the existence of the Oraclum to be more of myth and legend than anything else. She was getting nowhere, and after another long and stressful day, her eyes felt heavier and heavier as she stared at the screen.

She closed out the browser and stared out the window of the motel, watching the cars drive into the Westside Warehouse. The crowds gathered outside the doors as people lined up to get inside. She couldn't make out any of the costumes from that distance, but she did see how many of them were either glowing or lit up bright in the growing darkness outside the club.

Halloween was Miranda's favorite holiday when she was growing up, and it stayed her favorite ever since she was a child. She loved to spook people whenever possible, and never took to any costume that was not scary. One time she was a witch, and another a vampire. And long before zombies became an everyday phenomenon in modern culture, she had dressed two years in a row as the scariest undead creature she could imagine.

The first year was a zombie nurse, with a bloody mouth and a large fake scalpel in her chest. The year after that, she dressed up as a living dead punk rock girl with darkened eyes and black fingernail polish. In fact, the only time that she didn't dress up for Halloween as something scary was at seven years old, when her mother made her dress up like an angel. She hated it, and from that time on, it was the scarier the better.

 Thinking back about those times tempted her, just for a moment, to look at the photo albums that she had on her computer of her and her family. She quickly closed the screen of the laptop and slid the computer back into its bag alongside the folder with the parchment pages. She looked back at Jake, who had been fast asleep for some time now, and then closed the curtains to the room. Miranda changed from her t-shirt into a lightweight black tank top, pulled off her jeans and slipped into the bed.

 She tried not to let her mind go to the place that thought of only loss and grief, and even deeper, the growing anger at the things that had happened to her in the last few days. She closed her eyes, listening to the distant pulsing of bass and beat from the club across the street, and she tried to let its rhythms carry her into a quiet and restful slumber.

 She stood under the bright full moon in a lush and beautiful garden. The air was still and silent, and her nostrils were filled with the scent of a hundred different flowers. She looked down at herself and noticed that she was wearing a long and sheer white nightgown, with her feet bare in the soft grass of the lawn. There was a large stone fountain in the middle of the garden, and surrounding the fountain every few feet was a ring of white pea stone that formed another circle about a foot wide. It took her a moment before she noticed there was water running in the fountain, springing from a statuette of a fairy and flowing down all surfaces of the fairy's body, creating the illusion that her entire body glistened in the reflected moonlight.

Miranda stood on the edge of the yard along the tall hedges, and finally came to the realization that she was in the back garden of the Gale Estate. At first, she had not recognized it because everything was lush and new; well groomed and cared for. The fountain that she had seen on her visit to the home just days before had been dry and dirty and covered with bird feces. Now it looked scrubbed clean with crystal clear waters flowing through it. The vegetation on the grounds had been overgrown and overrun with weeds. Now, it was cut and weeded and trimmed to perfection.

The front of the house faced the east, and there was a path to the north end of the back gardens that led to a much smaller house that was very plain and simple, only about 15 feet across the front by 20 feet deep, with a four by six foot porch outside the front door. There was a single candle lit in the window, but everything else in the house was dark.

Miranda heard a rustling beyond the hedges along a path that led into the woods. At first, she felt the fear that crept over her. But even greater than the fear was her compulsion to follow down the dark path through the trees to see what was hidden beyond the shadows. She moved on, slowly into the path that, with the moon high and luminescent in the sky, began to feel more and more like a tunnel with cracks of light from the outside world desperately trying to break through its stone ceiling.

She thought she had heard a voice in the distance down the path, and as she got closer, she was more certain as to what she had heard. She slowed herself even more, stepping silently and deliberately until she could see candles burning in the distance in what appeared to be a small clearing.

Initially she could see no one around, although she was

sure that she had heard voices. She came to the edge of the clearing and saw the figure of a woman with dark, long and curly hair standing beyond the candles in a gown very similar to the one she was wearing now. The candles cast a soft glow on the woman's face, revealing her gentle and serene features.

The woman was looking in a direction that was to the far right side of where Miranda was standing, and it took Miranda a few moments to realize that she somehow *knew* who this woman was that she was looking at, although she had never before seen her face...except perhaps in some small way looking into a mirror. She was looking at Suzanne Gale. She was looking at her mother.

Miranda stepped forward away from the path that had led her to the clearing.

"Hello?" said Miranda, taking cautious steps toward Suzanne. Suzanne did not respond to her.

"Suzanne? Is that you?" she said again, but still, there was no reaction from Suzanne, as if she could not hear Miranda's voice calling to her.

"You've come," Suzanne said, looking off in the direction that Miranda had seen her looking to when she first came upon her. There was someone else there; Miranda stopped and looked to see who it was.

Out of the darkness came the other person who was there; a man about six feet tall, walking barefoot in the soft grass of the clearing. He wore khaki work trousers and a white button down shirt, with hair as black as the night he stepped out of that rested just above his shoulders. He was shaved clean, and even though the moon and the candles cast little light, there was enough for Miranda to tell he had strong and handsome features, almost like she might have imagined from a romance novel, although she could never stomach reading anything like that.

"Of course I came," the man said to her mother. "There is no way that I could not come. I am giving up more than you could possibly imagine for you. But I wouldn't trade my love for you for all the treasures of eternity."

Suzanne smiled and moved in closer to embrace the man. They kissed, and Miranda stood frozen watching the two in their embrace. She quickly realized how uncomfortable she felt watching them, like she was some kind of peeping Tom.

Suzanne removed the man's white shirt, and Miranda saw something that distracted her feeling of discomfort as she fixed her eyes on the man fully now. His back was completely tattooed, from the lower part of his neck across his upper back from shoulder to shoulder, and on down to what looked like below his waistline. He turned his body and the moon's light fully illuminated his muscular back, starkly magnifying every detail of his tattoos.

Miranda could see clearly that it was the exact same style of script that was written on the parchment pages of the Caducus Oraclum. The man's back, although somewhat tanned, was like a white sheet in the moonlight detailing the intricate lettering of the script.

As the two continued their embrace, Miranda heard a noise in the distant woods beyond them that at first sounded like thunder, but quickly became the roar of a forest fire that seemed to be rushing at them with a hurricane's force.

"Suzanne!" she cried, but there was no response once more, as if everything that was happening around them went completely unnoticed by the entwined couple. "MOTHER!"

Still, there was no response, and Miranda turned and ran as fast as she could back down the path as the firestorm raged behind her. She found herself in the backyard where the fountain was at, but now the fountain itself was filling with water at an extraordinary rate, overflowing and quickly flooding the entire garden as if it were a tidal wave raging over the stone walls of the fountain.

Miranda was trapped between an inferno behind her and the flood rapidly growing in front of her. She ran headlong into the water and desperately started to swim, but it was only seconds before the massive surge of water drew her under. It pushed her back towards the flames racing up from behind, and she opened her eyes to see the collision of fire and water, with herself trapped in the middle of it all. She could feel the heat, and fiercely kicked and pulled her way to the surface, finally breaking through with a loud gasp for air.

But she was not in the garden of the Gale Estate any longer, nor was she in the tempest of fire and water. She was in a surprisingly clean bathroom stall, sitting with her legs sprawled in front of her on a closed toilet seat. The door of the stall was closed, and a female voice spoke from the other side of the door.

"Are you alright in there?" asked the girl beyond the stall door.

Miranda looked down at herself and noticed that she was only wearing what she had fallen asleep in: black, booty short style underwear with lace trim, and a black spaghetti strap tank top that was cut a bit short. It was not what she usually slept in, but means were limited the last few days, and doing laundry hadn't been a priority. She realized that she was also barefoot as well.

"Hey...should I call somebody?" asked the voice again. Miranda was disoriented and confused, but managed to get a few words out.

"No...I'm fine. Just a little fuzzy headed," she said to the girl through the door.

"Okay," said the girl. "I just wanted to make sure. You seemed kinda out of it when you walked into the club."

"Where am I?" asked Miranda. No sooner had she asked did she realize she had to be in the Westside Warehouse. The constant pulsating beats were just a slight variation of the ones she was hearing when she had fallen asleep in the motel room.

"You're at the Westside Halloween Bash. You don't remember? You must really be fucked up," said the girl.

Miranda opened the stall door and stepped out into the dimly lit restroom. The girl that stood before her was a little shorter than she was, dressed up like a girl from an insurance commercial that Miranda had seen on TV, wearing an all white shirt and pants with a blue apron, and a brown wig on her head.

"They let me in here like this?" asked Miranda, looking again at her lack of clothing.

The girl let out a brief chuckle. "Tonight, less is more, and they can actually get away with it, being it's the Halloween party. The guy at the door probably thought you were dressed like a hooker!" The insurance girl could tell that Miranda was still very out of sorts, and reached out to take Miranda's hand to lead her to the sink to splash some cold water on her face.

When Miranda's hand made contact with the girl's hand, Miranda felt a rush of raw emotion run through her like an electrical current flowing from a hot wire. She impulsively reached out to her side and grabbed the edge of the stall door to steady herself, and she felt as if a hundred moving images flashed before her eyes in an instant.

Time seemed to slow. The first thing that came into her vision was the image of the girl that was there with her in the bathroom. Her name was Kelly. Miranda suddenly knew that, although she didn't know how she could. It was as if Miranda was standing in a room with Kelly, far and away from the place where they were now on this night.

Kelly knelt down next to a bed in a small bedroom, and there was a woman lying in the bed, very silent and still. Kelly held the woman's hand in her own, and tears streamed down her face. The woman in the bed was Kelly's mother, which was another fact that Miranda could not explain how she knew. The grief Kelly felt was overwhelming, so much that Miranda could feel the grief as if it were a tangible thing, emanating a strange vibration of its own.

The next flash was a few years prior to this, when Kelly was on a date with her first real boyfriend. She was 16 years old, and she and her boyfriend Mark were alone on a back road two-track in the back seat of Mark's car. Their lips and their hands wandered with nervous tension and anxious excitement. Once again, Miranda could feel the emotions as if they created their own pulsing sensations. Kelly and Mark both felt the intensity of the moment...the fear of the darkness around them...the danger of getting caught...

The next vision was equally emotional, but sickened Miranda. Kelly was six years old, and she was staying with her grandfather. It was not an uncommon thing for Kelly to stay with her grandfather on weekends when her parents had gone away, but on this particular weekend, her grandfather wanted to teach her a new 'game'; one that Kelly was very uncomfortable with, and it frightened her. Her grandfather made sure to tell her to never tell anyone about their little game...

Miranda dug deep within her consciousness and pulled herself out of the vision, in the same moment yanking her hand hard away from Kelly's hand. The sudden motion startled

Kelly, and she stared for a moment into Miranda's wide and frightened eyes. Miranda wasn't feeling her own sense of fear though; she was still reeling from the fear that Kelly had felt in the vision. Even Kelly felt as if Miranda's wild eyes were staring into her very soul, and Kelly turned away quickly and ran out of the bathroom without saying another word.

Miranda slowly walked over to the mirror in the bathroom and leaned her hands down on the countertop, looking up at her reflection. Her pupils looked wider than they should in that light, although even at the mirror it wasn't exceptionally bright in the dingy club bathroom. She wondered perhaps through the course of the afternoon if someone had slipped something into her food or something that she had drank. She had experimented with some things in the past, mostly only pot though, with one rare instance trying a hit of acid at a party that only made her sleepy and a little lightheaded. The acid was a major let down from what she had expected from all the movies she had seen in the past. She'd expected maybe seeing bright silver peace signs and floating colors; perhaps a flying cow or even a unicorn. It hadn't been any of those things, and she never tried it again.

There was nothing that gave any kind of explanation whatsoever as to what had just happened to the poor girl that tried to help her but went running terrified out of the restroom.

Miranda knew she had to get out of the club. She had no idea how she could have gotten into the restroom, and had no memory of leaving the motel room or walking into the Westside Warehouse. A cold, frightened feeling had now come over her.

Where was Jake? Had something happened to him? She knew that if someone had found them in the motel and tried to take or harm her in any way, he would have tried to fight them off regardless of what might happen to himself. She quickly moved for the door of the restroom and pulled it open.

The club was packed so tight that it was clear the only way out was to squeeze through the crowd of monsters and gypsies and pimps and punks...and everything else you could imagine a wild, young sea of frenzied college kids could think of. The lighting inside the main dance floor was overall darker than the bathroom was, but the lights were flashing in every direction and were of every color. Miranda already felt disoriented enough as it was not knowing how the hell she got there, and the swarming flecks of color everywhere she moved her eyes, along with the strobe lights near the DJ booth, made it far more difficult to grasp which direction she needed to find to lead her out of the building.

She started forward, pressing her way between a large, hairy, science fiction creature that was laughing with a man in a gynecologist uniform with the words 'Free Breast Exams' printed across his chest. The crowd was so tight is was impossible to maneuver without making contact with people. A man in a Native American headdress accidentally bumped into Miranda as he passed by her, spilling part of his plastic cup of beer on her arm.

"Oh, Jesus, I'm so sorry," he yelled to her over the booming music, and placed his hand on her shoulder as he apologized. He was clearly drunk when he touched her, but what came next was darkly sobering.

The rush that had come over her in the bathroom with Kelly happened once again as the man's hand touched her skin. She saw the young man, whose name was Caleb, at a party with some friends a few months before. His best friend Brent, who he had known since childhood, had gone out of town, and Caleb had taken Brent's girlfriend Julie to the party, where he kept feeding her drinks all night long. She had gotten so drunk that it was easy for Caleb to make his move, and they slept together that night. Miranda could feel that had been Caleb's intention all along.

Julie was so guilt ridden after that night she couldn't allow herself to stay with Brent afterwards. She blamed herself for what happened and didn't want to be responsible for causing a lifelong friendship to fall apart. She told Caleb this, and he left her to believing that was how it all happened. He didn't care. He had always resented Brent for finding a girl as perfect as Julie, and wanted to get him back, although Brent had never done anything to deserve such punishment from his lifelong friend.

Next, Miranda saw Caleb breaking into a restaurant with some friends late one weekend night in high school. One of the guys he was with had worked at the restaurant the summer before, and knew where the extra beer and liquor was stored. Caleb was terrified, but at the same time filled with the thrill of the moment.

Miranda then witnessed Caleb's first kiss at 11 years of age, out behind the backstop of the baseball field at school where the kids would play during recess; his heart raced, and he felt funny throughout his entire being as he awkwardly puckered his lips and kissed a girl that strongly resembled a much younger Julie...but this young girl was not Julie. In fact, it was a girl that died in a car wreck with her parents a couple of years after that kiss. Her death broke Caleb's heart.

Miranda pulled away from Caleb's touch and pushed her way further through the crowd. She took one short glance over her shoulder back at him as she moved away, only to see him standing stunned and dazed over the brief moment of contact he had had with her. Caleb could not see, nor could he know what it was that Miranda had seen in those few seconds. But like Kelly, Caleb felt as if someone had just walked right through his soul.

Miranda's head was spinning. Every direction she looked the lights seemed to dizzy her even more. Across the room in every direction she looked until she could see a sign that said 'EXIT'. She started to push through in that direction but was feeling the push of the crowd back upon her. It took her a moment to realize that she was trying to push her way through the dance floor, and looked in the other direction for another way out. She saw a small hallway that looked as if a crowd of people were coming into the club from that way, and turned to head back toward that hall.

She made it about 10 feet closer to the door when she felt a blow to her back that knocked her to the floor. A fight had broken out in the area that she had just been standing, and one of the drunken idiots was thrown into her, knocking her to the ground. Hands came to her aid from almost every direction, and flashes in her head were almost too much for her to bear.

A child's first ride on a roller coaster...

A young woman raped by her brother's best friend from college...

A teenage girl being laughed at in a high school locker room by other girls because she was flat chested...

And then the vision was of Jake, just moments after she had told him she was leaving and that it was over between them. He was angry, throwing plastic lawn ornaments around in his parent's yard. He got onto his bike and tore off down the highway. He took it to 60 miles an hour. Then 70. When he reached 80 he saw a deer run out in the road far ahead. He didn't slow down. The deer stood still, frozen, and it was only at the last second that he applied the brakes enough to be able to stop the bike short, before hitting the deer.

When he was almost at a stop, the tire caught some loose asphalt that was left from when someone had filled in a pot hole, and the bike went down on its side and slid another 30 feet to a stop, just inches from the deer, throwing Jake off to the side and into the gravel shoulder of the road. The deer ran off, finally breaking free from its trance of fright, and Jake, shaken but not broken, turned and watched the animal run off. There were tears on his face...

"Miranda! Are you all right?"

Jake had her by the arms and helped her to stand. He still had contact with her, but the vision she was having was gone.

"Jake?" she said. Her voice sounded shaky and her hands were quivering slightly.

"Are you hurt?" he asked, pulling her through the crowd and walking backwards while keeping his hands firmly around hers.

"I - I don't think so," she told him. As soon as they were in a place in the club where there was a little more room around them, Jake took off his coat and wrapped it around Miranda. He put his arm around her and led her out the front door of the club.

Once outside, they walked about a hundred feet into the parking lot before Jake stopped and faced her.

"What is going on? What were you doing in there? What were you thinking?" Jake asked, visually rattled and with a tone on the edge of anger in his voice.

Miranda's eyes filled with a glassy glare that caught the light of the parking lot lamps, and Jake's heart dropped.

"I don't know, Jake, I swear I don't know!" she said, the tears now running down the sides of her face. "I was having a dream, and I woke up...and I was in the club. That's all I remember! I don't know how I got there..."

Jake took her in his arms again, and held on to her tight as she cried into his chest. He started to walk her back across the street to the motel, all the while trying to put together the strange and complicated puzzle that the last few days have been, and thinking all along how much this girl has moved his heart and soul once again. There was nothing he wouldn't do for her.

Jake did not sleep the rest of the night. He watched Miranda as she slept - when he finally did get her to fall back asleep - and made sure that nothing else would happen the rest of the night.

## CHAPTER FIFTEEN

The next morning it was quiet in the room. Miranda woke up in the bed to see Jake sitting in the armchair that he had placed near the door of the motel room. It reminded her of a movie she had seen once where an FBI agent was guarding a woman in witness protection while they were hiding out in a seedy motel in the Nevada desert. She couldn't remember the name of the movie, although it didn't really matter anyway. They were in a seedy motel, and that was the only similarity. Jake was no trained FBI Special Agent. He was a nursing student and one of Miranda's closest friends. And it wasn't drug dealers that he was trying to protect her from. They were running from mysterious individuals who had murdered her family; and now, they were seemingly coming after her.

Jake was also protecting Miranda from herself as well. She still had no recollection as to how she ended up in the club bathroom the night before. It all seemed like a dream, but she knew it was all too real. The things she saw in her head...she couldn't be sure if her mind had been playing tricks on her, at least at first. She knew what she was seeing had felt real with the others before she had touched Jake. It wasn't until she saw what she had seen when Jake touched her that she knew for certain what she was seeing was real.

"I'm glad you got *some* sleep," Jake said, looking weary from sitting in the chair all night.

Miranda felt her stomach tighten with the guilt she was feeling about the night before. She couldn't imagine what had gone through Jake's head when he woke up to find her gone. On top of that, not being able to offer any kind of sensible explanation as to why she was gone in the first place made her feel even worse. He had gotten almost no sleep making sure that she stayed safe and sound in the room the rest of the night.

She pulled herself up in the bed and pushed the long curls out of her face.

"How did you find me over there?" she asked.

"After the initial panic, the only thing I could think to do was go to the closest place with the most people to see if they had seen anything. A guy who had been in line overheard me asking someone else after I had described you. He said, 'You mean the dark haired blue eyed hottie in the tight black undies?' I had a hunch that had to be you."

Miranda's head sunk a little. She wasn't shy or overly self conscious, but being out in her underwear in public and not having any memory of it was a little unnerving.

Jake continued. "I still had to wait 20 minutes to get into the club. I offered all the cash I had to let me in, but the guy at the door wouldn't budge. You really don't remember anything before I found you?"

Miranda thought about this for a minute. She was still trying to make sense of things that sense could not in any rational way be made of. She hated keeping anything from Jake, after all she has put him through while he has tried to help her, but she wasn't ready to tell him about the things that she had seen when she came into contact with the people in the club.

"The only thing I can remember is waking up in the bathroom stall, and then trying to find my way out of the club. The last thing before any of that was falling asleep in this bed."

Jake didn't have much of a reaction to this. He was starting to almost feel numb to the strange happenings that followed along with Miranda coming back into his life. It wasn't that the things didn't occur to him as odd or just plain strange. He acknowledged them, but was learning to stay focused on the task of keeping Miranda safe regardless of whatever the obstacles were that came at them along the way. Understanding them was for another time and another place.

"Why don't you hop in the shower and get dressed? I'll clean up afterwards and run to the office to see about getting a ride back to the garage," said Jake.

"I'm sorry about everything, Jake," she told him. "You should have just left me behind to let me deal with all of this myself. You don't deserve any of this."

Jake walked over to the bed and sat down beside her.

"That was never going to happen," he told her. "I'm not about to let anything happen to you. Not if I can do anything about it. We may not be what we once were, but that doesn't mean that I don't care about you any less. You were...you are...an important part of my life. You always will be."

Miranda heard the words coming from Jake's lips, looking up into his eyes that stared at her with softness and sincerity. It was the depth of his compassion and strength that she felt behind those beautiful eyes that brought her back in her mind to better times, seemingly ages before this moment. She leaned into him and pulled him by his shirt gently closer to her until his lips met hers. For that moment, they both found themselves lost in the kiss, until Jake pulled away.

"Miranda...I don't know if this is a good idea. Maybe...I

think...things aren't so clear right now..."

Miranda stopped him short and once again pulled him to her in an even harder and more intentional kiss. When she finally let up, his lips moved just a few inches away from hers. She reached down and pulled her black spaghetti strap tank top over her head, and he began to remove his shirt as well. He slipped beneath the covers in the bed beside her, and together they became lost in a distant place, far and away from all of the thoughts and heartache of the last few days, in the intimate moments that followed. If only for a short time, they could forget the loss and the pain, rapt in the memories a time between them long gone by.

The shower was surprisingly hot, although the pressure wasn't the best, but Miranda appreciated it still. Her mind was fixed on so many different things, but now it was complicated even more by what had just happened between her and Jake. She felt like she needed to find whatever kind of release she could to break away from everything else that has happened, and she wanted to think that Jake did too. She was sure that the deeper feelings that she had had for Jake at one time were only a part of her past.

Miranda couldn't escape the feelings of guilt she was now having. She knew - in fact, she had *seen* - how much she had broken his heart the first time around. What if he hadn't come to terms with what the relationship had come to now? The fact they were only friends; friends that had been through a difficult time together and needed an escape from the harsh reality that was hounding them now.

If he still had deeper feelings for her, how could she possibly allow herself to let him stay beside her if she had to keep running? It wouldn't be fair to him, and after all he is risking for her, all she would end up doing for him is breaking his heart all over again. She leaned her head against the shower wall and let the water run over her, wishing all the while that it could wash away everything that had happened over the last few hours, and even more so, over the last few days of her life.

Jake had many of the same thoughts on his mind. While Miranda showered, he had spent time gathering their things in the room and trying to concentrate on what their next steps were going to be. But his thoughts couldn't escape what had just happened between them. He knew all too well what his feelings were for Miranda. That had never changed. But he also knew how careful he had to be with her now. Was there more to this than just a whim to try and forget everything that was happening around them?

Jake knew that wasn't what he needed to be concentrating on right now. It was thoughts like these that he feared to allow himself to believe; Miranda had just gone through a great emotional trauma, and she was fragile. His own guilt was creeping up on him now. How could he allow himself to take advantage of the situation like that? It wasn't as if he didn't love her. He knew deep within his heart that he did. But love doesn't give you the right to take what you want, even if it feels right. Real love is having the strength to sacrifice what you want the most for those you care about. He knew he had to put all of his feelings aside if he truly wanted to help Miranda through all of this. The only thing that was important to him at that point was keeping her safe.

When Miranda got out of the shower, Jake told her that he was going to get some food from the store just down the block and then see about getting a ride to the garage from someone down at the motel office. Miranda decided now might be a good time to try and call Lydia. She thought Lydia might need some more time to get the money together, if she could do it at all. If she couldn't, Miranda did not know what they would do. They were almost out of cash, and they had no way of knowing how close the people who are pursuing them might be.

"Hello?" Lydia's voice was the most refreshing thing she felt she had heard in days.

"Lyd?" she said, cautiously. She could not help the thought that every time she spoke to someone she cared about, she might be putting them in danger. She almost hung up the phone, not knowing what she might do next.

"Miranda! Oh my God, are you all right? Where are you?" Lydia almost yelled into the phone, her voice frantic.

"I'm alright, Lyd. What's wrong? Why are you so upset?"

"The police stopped by here looking for you. They asked if I had seen or heard from you."

Shit. If the police are calling to question her, then Miranda was sure that the people after her must know about Lydia as well.

Lydia went on. "A detective from Native Springs called and asked me the same questions. He couldn't tell me why he was calling, so I got on the net and...oh my God, honey...your parents...I'm so sorry. I was scared to death something had happened to you too."

"I'm okay. Jake is with me," Miranda told her.

"Jake?" she asked, puzzled. "Are we talking high school *boyfriend* Jake?"

"Listen, it's a long, long story. You don't know how good it is just to hear your voice."

"Miranda, what's going on? Where are you?"

Miranda paused for several seconds. She didn't know

where to begin or what to say. She didn't know how to tell Lydia how much she felt that this was her fault. How she felt that if she hadn't looked into the past, how none of this would have happened.

"Miranda? Are you there?" asked Lydia.

"Yes. Sorry. Lydia, if there is anyone that I want to tell what happened in the last few days, it would be you. But I'm running out of time and I need your help."

"What do you need? I will do whatever I can to help," Lydia told her without hesitation.

"Jake and I need to lie low for a while, so we can sort things out. We need to try and figure out who murdered my family."

"Isn't that the job of the police? Miranda, why do you think this is something that you need to be doing? You've just gone through something very traumatic..." Lydia went on before Miranda cut her sentence short.

"Lydia, I know this sounds crazy, but this is bigger than the police. I swear as soon as this is all over, I will tell you everything. But right now, I need to borrow some money. I hate asking, and I promise, no matter how long it takes, I will pay you back every penny. I didn't want to have to ask this. Someone is after us, Lyd...and I'm scared."

"I don't care about getting paid back, Miranda. All I care about is that you are alright. Whatever is going on...I trust you. Just please, be safe."

"Thank you, Lyd. You have no idea what that means to me."

"How much do you need?" asked Lydia.

"About $3,000. That should give us some time to figure out what we are going to do next."

"Consider it done. I should have it within an hour. Do

you want me to come to wherever you are?"

"No, we are heading to town and should be there in about two hours. I was thinking that we'd meet at *Baristas*."

"Okay, that's fine. Do you need anything else?"

"A hug, maybe..."

"You'll get the biggest one you've ever had!"

"Thanks, Lyd." Miranda paused, trying to choose her words carefully to get across the seriousness of the situation without overly alarming Lydia.

"Lydia, I want you to just...be careful. I am sure you are okay, but if you see anything out of the ordinary, I want you to get somewhere safe. Go to a crowded area. Get to the police. Don't take any chances, *please*."

Lydia snickered. "Are you trying to scare me?"

"Yes, I am," said Miranda, her voice unusually cold and direct.

Lydia felt a chill run through her like it had come right through the phone and up her arm.

"Okay. I'll be careful. I promise," Lydia said, her voice now conveying a sobering tone. "See you soon."

"See you soon, sweetie," said Miranda. She hung up the phone.

Miranda sat for a minute afterward, realizing the heaviness in her heart that she felt bringing so much grief upon those she cared about. She regretted even her own existence.

Miranda thought about the movie *It's a Wonderful Life*. If the angel in the film, Clarence, came to her to try and convince her that her life had a positive impact on anyone around her, she believed he would be hard pressed at this point to make a good argument. As things were now, she would have to break Jake's heart a second time. The parents who raised her, good and loving people as they were, would still be alive. Jake would not be in danger alongside of her. And now, Lydia could be in harm's way as well. She still hadn't heard from Aimsley, and feared she could already be dead. It seemed that everyone she came across since she found the Gale family back in her life was plagued with the touch of death and despair, and she was the unwilling agent of these foul things.

Miranda noticed that one of the side pockets of her laptop bag was only half zipped. She didn't remember leaving it like that herself. She was in the habit of making sure things were properly closed up and put away when it came to traveling, especially when it came to things like her computer case.

Miranda slipped her finger inside of the pocket and felt the edge of an envelope that she knew she had not put there herself. She pulled it from the pocket, and it had her name handwritten across the front of it in very neat and pristine handwriting.

The envelope was not sealed. The top fold had been neatly tucked into the bottom flap of the envelope. She opened it, and removed a full sized sheet of paper, crisp and folded in thirds. Within the folds of that sheet of paper was another smaller piece of paper that Miranda could tell by its overall look and texture was far older and more brittle, folded in half. She read the larger of the two first.

Miranda,

You don't really know how much it meant to me to see you again after all of these years. Your mother would be so proud of the woman that you have become. I wanted to give you something when you were here, but I thought that perhaps it might be better for you to find this once you were well on your way. You had said that you studied journalism. I take it you are becoming quite a writer. That reminded me once again of your mother, and how she, too, loved to write. So much was lost in the fire, things that were very dear to your mother and to myself. But I had managed to keep this all these years. It is a poem that your mother had written after you were born. I thought that you would like to have it. After the ones we love are gone, it is only their legacy that we have to look upon to remember them by. Your mother's legacy lies within your heart, Miranda. These are simply her words, perhaps they are a window into her very soul. Take care, Miranda.

    Aimsley

    The handwriting of the letter was as neat as the name on the envelope. Miranda took the smaller piece of paper and unfolded it. She looked upon the words written by the woman who had given her life. These were the words of Suzanne Gale. Miranda ran her fingers along the text on the page, and then finally read the words aloud.

"In the shadows of fate we are so blind,
To the wonders, the mysteries, the secrets divine,
For no greater strength was ever to be,
Than found in the heart, down deep within thee,
In darkness we strive to seek out the light,
To escape the temptations we find in the night,
In tempests the soul may be lashed by the winds,
Pure hearts filled with virtue, enticed now by sin,
And here, our fates might now be revealed,
From out of the shadows, no longer concealed,
Still within our hands 'tis our destiny held,

Once shining so bright, from grace he had fell."

There was something deeply haunting about the words of Suzanne's poem. Miranda could not put a finger on what it was, but she felt a certain darkness was hidden within their meaning. She folded both letters back up and replaced them in her laptop case.

The door to the room opened, and Jake was standing outside. He had in one hand a small paper bag, and in the other a four cup beverage carrier with two steaming hot cups of coffee.

"You all set to go? Matt has time to take us to the garage right now. I thought we could just eat in the car," he said, seeming surprisingly casual after what had gone on between them just over an hour before.

"Yeah, I'm all set," she said, grabbing the rest of their things and following him out to the main office where Matt was waiting outside.

"What is for breakfast then?" she asked.

Jake pulled out a package of powdered sugar coated donuts and a small bag of beef jerky. Miranda raised her eyebrows as a slight grin slipped onto her face. One brow was raised slightly higher than the other.

"It's all we could afford. Something filling and delicious, hence the donuts. And I figured that we could use a little protein as well, hence the beef jerky." He held the jerky bag up to her eye level.

Miranda snatched the bag of jerky, tore it open and took a piece out of the bag.

"I guess I am feeling a little more carnivorous this morning over anything else," she said. She put it between her teeth and ripped a small piece off. It probably had been the toughest piece of jerky she'd ever had, but right now it was satisfying enough. Jake watched her and smiled, until she noticed that he was watching her. She stopped in mid-chew and looked at him, and he quickly looked away and tore open the package of donuts.

Matt had been watching the two of them curiously in the rearview mirror. He thought there was something odd about them, but didn't pay much attention to it. He had seen a lot of odd over the years that he had owned the motel, not to mention the things he had to clean up after. There had been one time that he had to pay a special cleaning crew to come in and clean a room that a dead goat had been left in. There hadn't been any signs as to exactly how the goat had died. It was just dead, and the rest of the room was a total disaster, littered with beer bottles and used condoms, and a dozen pairs of dirty, booze-soaked socks.

He had absolutely no idea what any of it was about, but the renters had paid in cash, and there was an extra $600 for the mess that was left. The names given for the room were fake, but that didn't matter to Matt. He paid the cleaners $150 to clean up and get rid of the goat, and an extra $50 for them to "forget" about the whole ordeal. The rest, he pocketed for himself. *Life in the big city*, he thought.

The car pulled into Billy K's, and Miranda's Vibe was already sitting out front.

"Hey," said Matt, as Jake started to get out of the car. "Make sure you didn't get any of that powder shit all over my backseat. My old lady don't need to be thinkin' I been using coke again! Been off that shit for six months now."

Jake brushed down the backseat, all the while thinking of what else might be ground into the fabric of the seat. He made a quick job of it, and he and Miranda thanked Matt and walked over to the office to see Billy K.

Billy K walked out to them with keys in hand.

"You're all set," he said, handing Jake the keys.

"Thank you," said Jake with a short nod.

"The pleasure was all mine," said Billy K., grinning as he walked away. Miranda found the short and sweet exchange kind of peculiar, but didn't think a lot on it. She had too many other things on her mind already. As they got closer to the car, Miranda pulled the keys from Jake's hands and walked around to the driver's side.

"What are you doing?" asked Jake, reaching out for the keys from her.

She pulled her hand back away from his. "You were up all night watching to make sure I didn't misbehave any more. You need to try and get some sleep. I'll be fine driving. I promise."

He knew that she was right. He hadn't gotten any sleep after the club incident, and knew it would do neither of them any good if he veered off into the path of a semi and got them splattered along the highway. He pulled his hand away and sulked over to the passenger's side, which he was never accustomed to taking a seat in.

They placed their bags in the backseat and drove off down the road. Next stop – *Feast'n'Baristas*. Home again.

Rick Jurewicz

## CHAPTER SIXTEEN

The traffic had not been all that bad for a Thursday in the early afternoon hours. They had made good time into Preston, the home of South Central Michigan College, and the only home Miranda felt she had left. Jake had slept most of the trip into town, which was good, although Miranda had watched him stir quite a bit as she drove along the expressway. She wondered if he was dreaming, and if so, of what it might be.

Miranda wondered if anyone else had had dreams like she has had. Thinking about her own haunting dream, she was starting to feel a strange comfort in its familiarity to her. The man...his dark eyes...the sound of the rising tempo in the music from the piano...something stirred deep within her, but she couldn't put a finger on what it was.

Thoughts kept fluttering through her head as she drove along. It had started like this not long after she first noticed Jake had fallen asleep. Thoughts of Robert and Lorri, and of Steven. Miranda wondered so much about her little brother's life, and it sickened her to think about all of the things that he would not get to experience. Had he ever been kissed? Did he even care about girls? What kind of dreams did he have? So many things...so many questions, never to be answered. She didn't care about what might happen to her from that moment on. The only thing she cared about was all of the hurt she caused in the wake of what she had inadvertently set into motion.

Miranda made a decision at that point. After she and Jake got the money from Lydia, and they were far enough away from everyone else that they knew, she would leave. Slip out in the night, and far away from everyone else from her past. She would then send the cursed Oraclum to some news agency and wait until the storm blew over.

But she would not ever return. There was nothing left for her in Michigan, and the further away she could go, the lesser the chance of hurting anyone else she cared for.

She knew that Jake wouldn't understand. She knew that he would be hurt still. But eventually, he would move on as well. Miranda had to stop herself from thinking. She found her iPod and slipped one headphone into her ear so she could still hear what was going on around her, but she would not disturb Jake with the music.

Whenever Miranda didn't want to let her thoughts go to dark and disturbing places, it was the magic of random shuffle on her music player that would often divert her from such a course. Usually the iPod would select songs that she hadn't heard in a long time, and her mind would find itself trying to remember the last time she had heard the song. She found it amazing how, outside of sight, the more subtle senses triggered the most powerful memories. Whenever she smelled cedar, she could close her eyes and find herself in her grandmother's cabin on Lake Huron near Roger's City; or the smell of eucalyptus would remind her of her Aunt Laura's backyard in the summers when she would stay with her cousins for weeks at a time and swim in their enormous four-foot-deep circular pool set up in the yard.

But now, it was the sense of hearing that was sparking the deepest memories and emotions. The random shuffle's first selection was, oddly enough, "Ice Ice Baby" by Vanilla Ice. It was hardly a song that one might expect to find in any collection of Miranda's, and even she had forgotten that is was on the iPod, but it was a guilty pleasure song that took her back to her junior year of high school, hanging out at the local park where all of the town's Little League and high school baseball and softball games were played.

It had been her and Jake, and her friends Annie and Cassie, along with Jake's best friend Wes. Cassie had a mix CD that her older sister's boyfriend had made for her sister, and it was loaded with a bunch of early 90s cheesy music that Cassie became addicted to. *That* song was played over and over again. What Miranda remembered most about that time was Annie coming to her and confiding a secret in her that she had been keeping to herself for quite some time.

Annie was a very pretty girl with short brown hair, and she always wore long skirts and dresses that were usually earth tones; browns and greens mostly, often with leaf patterns and sometimes blues that looked like flowing waterfalls as she walked along. It was one of those nights in the park that Annie walked off by herself, and Miranda had followed behind her.

Miranda found her sitting alone on one of the short bleachers beside a Little League baseball diamond, and she climbed up on the bench and sat next to her. She seemed very distant, and Miranda asked her if everything was alright. Annie looked very nervous at first, but then made Miranda promise not to tell anyone what she was going to tell her. Miranda was a little shaken by the serious tone in Annie's voice, but nodded her promise to Annie, who then slowly pulled her long brown skirt up high onto her thigh. It was from just above her knee and on up her thigh that there were several cuts, not on just the one leg, but on both legs. Some looked as if they had been there only a day or two, while the others were already well scarred over. A few looked almost faded away except for faint red and white lines.

"Oh my God, Annie..." whispered Miranda. "Who did this to you?"

Annie's head dropped down, and Miranda could see a tear run down her face.

"I did it to myself," Annie told her.

Miranda sat still and silent for a long moment. She didn't understand what was happening. She had never heard of someone doing this to themselves; growing up in a little town like Native Springs, if these things happened, people never talked about it, if they ever even knew of it at all.

Miranda didn't know what to say. She just hugged Annie and told her she was there for her, for whatever she needed. Annie shed a few more tears that night with Miranda, and thanked her for listening to her. Miranda and Annie grew apart as the school year went on. Annie started hanging around with another group of friends from a neighboring town, rarely seen after school on the streets of Native Springs.

One day many months later, Jake and Miranda went to see a movie in the town that Annie spent most of her time. They saw Annie on the street as they drove by; she was holding hands with another girl in front of the ice cream parlor in the center of town. Jake raised his eyebrows and flashed a quick smile at Miranda, but Miranda remembered how she smiled for a different reason altogether. She had hoped, deep down, that Annie had faced her demons and had moved on past them. It was moments like that in which she could remember believing in something that seemed so distant from her now. She once believed in hope.

But that was a long time ago. And the demons they faced now were far darker and more dangerous. Miranda nudged Jake.

"Jake. You need to wake up. We're about five blocks away from the café."

Jake stirred groggily, and cranked the seat back into its upright position.

"How long was I asleep? We're here already?"

"Almost two hours. You needed it. Do we have a game plan?" she asked.

Jake seemed suddenly alert and focused, as if he just realized the seriousness of the situation all over again.

"Is this coffee shop close to the end of the block?" he asked.

"No. It's in the dead center. Is that bad?" she asked.

"I don't know, really. I've never had to strategically plan escape routes or anything. I guess we only have two directions on the street that we have to watch. Drive up on past the place and circle the block a couple of times. We can see if anything looks suspicious, and I can get a lay of the land, so to speak."

Miranda drove the Vibe around the block twice, as Jake suggested, and Jake surveyed the area examining as much as he could take in. Jake saw nothing that led him to believe there was anything to be concerned about...but the all too familiar Pontiac Vibe did not escape the sharp and seasoned eyes of Mr. Skye and Mr. Cain, who had been lying in wait for quite some time now. As soon as they had seen Miranda and Jake, Mr. Cain dialed his phone.

"She's here, as you said," stated Cain. "Yes. I...yes. Understood."

Mr. Skye looked to Mr. Cain as he hung up the phone.

"We are to wait for further instructions," said Mr. Cain. Mr. Skye looked less than pleased.

Miranda parked her car near the farthest corner of the block from *Feast'n'Baristas,* and she and Jake walked as briskly as they could to the entrance without attracting undue attention. As they walked inside, Miranda almost immediately caught the attention of Donatello.

"ME-RAN-DAH! Couldn't stay away, could you girl?" he said with his usual pronounced grin.

Miranda ran up to him and gave him a huge hug; Jake saw the sudden surprise in the barista's eyes when she had grabbed hold of him.

"Donny! You are a sight for sore eyes," she told him.

Donatello looked bewildered as Miranda finally released him from her grip.

"It has only been about a week now, hasn't it?" he asked her.

"It's been the longest week ever, Donny. I'll have to tell you about it some time," she said without thinking, realizing that this was probably the last time she would ever see the lanky and loveable barista. She felt a tightening in her chest when she thought this, but shook it off as best as she could. "Have you seen Lydia, Donny?"

"Yes. She's at the table in the corner," he told her, pointing off to an area out of the way near the back of the café.

Lydia sat alone, her eyes moving nervously around the café's busy dining floor. Miranda paused for a moment to look at her as she scanned the room, and when their eyes met, a wide and genuine smile came to Lydia's face.

Miranda walked quickly to her, and Jake followed

closely behind. Jake nodded to Donny on the way past him, and Donny returned a friendly nod. Lydia got up from her seat as Miranda approached her, and the two friends hugged tightly without a word being spoken.

"Are you alright?" whispered Lydia into Miranda's ear. Miranda held tight and said nothing in return. She didn't want to let go of her friend. She knew after today that she would not see her again. She would pay her back, eventually, when she could, but she would not return. Miranda finally let up on her grip.

"I'm okay."

Lydia stared at Miranda's face for a long, solemn moment, but said nothing. She knew better. She knew Miranda was lying to her, and she understood.

"Lyd, this is Jake. Jake, Lydia Snow," Miranda introduced them; Jake held his hand out, and Lydia shook it in turn. They both gave a short, polite smile, but under the circumstances, formal introductions seemed unnecessary. Lydia sat back down in her chair, and Jake and Miranda followed suit.

Lydia reached into the bag beside her chair, laid an envelope on the table and slid it to Miranda. Miranda took it, and put it into her inside jacket pocket.

"There's $4,000 there. I know it's more than you asked for, but I wanted to make sure that you had enough. It's from a stash of cash that I have been saving for a while. Not from an account, so no one will know it's missing. It's mine, anyway, but still," said Lydia.

"Thank you Lyd. I swear I will pay you back as soon as this mess gets sorted out," Miranda told her.

"Don't worry about that...I don't know what's going on, but I am always here for you...whenever you are ready to talk, I am ready to listen."

Miranda had been listening, but her focus was lost on something else now. She stared towards the front windows of the coffee shop, where the bright afternoon sun was blazing through the glass. Donatello stood in the rays of light, wiping down bistro tables that sat just inside the window beside the front door. The sunlight had taken on a strange form surrounding Donatello. It took several seconds for Miranda to fully realize that she could see the light, not as simple rays or blinding illumination, but as tiny, individual particles that formed the rays that were shining through the glass. Miranda watched with the keenest of vision as the light particles around Donatello seemed to be absorbed into the surface of his skin as they came close to his body.

Donatello could feel Miranda's eyes upon him, and he stopped what he was doing and stood straight up and looked at Miranda. Miranda stood up from her chair; in that moment, all other motion in the coffee shop ceased to an almost incomprehensible crawl.

Miranda looked around at the others in the coffee shop. All seemed frozen in time, including Jake and Lydia, whose eyes had been fixed on Miranda at the moment that time seemed to have stopped. She turned and looked back at Donatello, whose lips were pressed together in a smile much unlike the wide, toothy grin he had offered each and every day she came to the coffee shop. With this smile, he gave a nod of his head, and Miranda walked slowly towards her long-time friend, stopping short five feet away from him.

"You do not need to fear me, Miranda. I mean you no harm," said Donatello, in his familiar Jamaican accent.

"Donny - what's going on? What's happening?" asked Miranda. Her voice sounded shaky, and Donatello looked down at the floor for a second or two, then back up to

Miranda.

"You're starting to see things, aren't you Miranda? Your eyes...they are focusing on the world in a different way. We did not know when or how, or even if, this would happen. But it is now," he said, still trying to keep a calming smile on his face.

"Who...what do you mean? Please, tell me what is going on," she pleaded.

Donatello lowered his head again. "I'm sorry Miranda. To my shame, I cannot help you. It is forbidden for me to interfere."

Miranda stared at him for what seemed like forever. He raised his head to her once more, and then looked down again, and still she said nothing. Now, he felt the only right thing to do was to look her straight in the eye.

"I was sent here only to watch you. To keep an eye on you. To...monitor you, I suppose would be the best way to describe it," he said, keeping his eyes to hers.

"WHO sent you? Donny...you're my friend. Tell me, *please*...what the hell is going on?!"

Donatello's face revealed the sadness within him. His eyes held a somber weight that subsided only when his expression suddenly became cold and serious. Miranda was taken aback by its stark change.

"Miranda," he said, stepping closer to her. He gently put his large hand against her cheek. "I am your friend. This is true. I have done my duty; I have also found a true friend in you. But it is forbidden for me to help you."

Donatello cocked his head to the side for a moment, and then looked back at Miranda. He let out a short sigh.

"Look...past my shoulder, through the glass," said Donatello, with a sudden urgency in his voice. "There are two men coming to the front of the shop. Go...through the back door past the bathrooms. The door leads to the alley. Run, sweet Miranda. May God go with you."

Miranda looked and saw the two men, still in slow motion but starting to speed up, heading for the front entrance of the coffee shop. She immediately recognized the men as the ones who had chased her and Jake through the two-tracks in Native Springs.

She looked back at Donatello, whose eyes still looked sullen and sad, and gave him a fast kiss on the cheek, then turned to her friends back at the table.

"Jake! We have to go, now!" she yelled, and Jake looked and saw the two men rushing for the door.

Mr. Cain motioned for Mr. Skye to head through the front door, while he headed down the block. Miranda ran to Jake, and everyone in the coffee shop stopped what they were doing and watched the commotion being made by the two.

"Lydia," said Miranda, "Run into the kitchen and stay there. Hide! Wait until we are outside, and then go! Get out of town. Go home. *Cincinnati* home. Don't go back to the apartment, and stay out of sight. Do you understand?"

Lydia nodded nervously.

"Go!" snapped Miranda, and Lydia jumped up and headed for the kitchen. Mr. Skye was at the door when Jake pulled Miranda down the back hall to the alley door. When Mr. Skye was inside the doorway, he could see Miranda and Jake heading towards the back door, but as he stepped forward to follow, one of the bistro chairs spontaneously fell in front of him. He caught his leg in the legs of the stool and fell face down hard on the floor.

Mr. Skye lifted his head and shook off the chair. He looked to his left but saw no one near that could have shoved the chair out in front of him. Pushing himself up from the floor, he regained his bearings and limped to the back of the shop.

Donatello watched him limp through the busy café, as well did all of the other patrons in silence as Mr. Skye glanced about while feeling the eyes upon him.

"I am going to hear about this one," Donatello said quietly to himself, as he picked up the stool that 'jumped' out in front of Mr. Skye.

Jake and Miranda burst on through the green steel back door of the coffee shop into the alley. They looked both ways, seeing that they were about as close to the middle of the long alleyway between the buildings that they could get. The alley was lined with several dumpsters to accommodate all of the businesses housed in the two adjacent buildings, and there was barely enough room for a sanitation truck to make its way through.

"Which way?" Miranda asked, as Jake glanced side to side before choosing the direction to the left out the door. He grabbed Miranda by the hand and started only a few feet up the alley before they saw Mr. Cain round the corner at the end of the alley. Mr. Cain stopped for a moment as he made eye contact with the two of them, and then started to pick up his pace and moved quickly in their direction.

"Come on!" Jake yelled, and he and Miranda turned in the opposite direction and ran. Mr. Cain went into a full run as Mr. Skye burst through the coffee shop back door just seconds after Jake and Miranda had run past it. Mr. Cain caught up to Mr. Skye within seconds, and the two came running after Jake and Miranda, who were at the point halfway between their pursuers and the street at the end of the alley. Mr. Cain and Mr. Skye both drew their guns now as they ran, but before they could stop and take aim, a large black Hummer screeched to a halt at the end of the alley in the direction that Jake and Miranda were running.

The two of them froze in place as four men exited the vehicle and started to move in their direction. The one that led the group had short cropped blonde hair and wore a black sports coat with black slacks. The other three men were dressed somewhat similar in varying shades of grey. Miranda looked behind her at Mr. Skye and Mr. Cain, who had stopped as well and lowered the barrels of their weapons towards the ground. She gripped Jake's hand tighter, fearing what she was sure she knew was about to happen. In some strange way, she didn't want to fight fate any longer. She was ready for whatever was to come.

Miranda looked back at the men from the Hummer coming towards them, and then watched as all four men simultaneously drew guns from inside their jackets, almost appearing as if it was happening in slow motion. She closed her eyes while holding Jake's hand, and almost didn't hear the voice that was yelling to them now less than 50 feet in front of her.

"GET DOWN!" yelled the man with the cropped hair, and Jake yanked Miranda between two of the dumpsters in the alley for cover. Mr. Cain and Mr. Skye raised their guns and began to fire, but they barely could get a shot off before the bullets from the other men started to tear through them.

Jake held Miranda beneath him as the bullets flew through the air in both directions. One of the shots that had come from the handguns fired by Mr. Cain and Mr. Skye struck one of the dumpsters that was shielding them. The slug ricocheted, lightly grazing Jake's arm. After what seemed like several minutes gone by, there was finally silence. Jake and Miranda sat quietly still, waiting for whatever might come next.

The blonde man with the cropped hair appeared before

them now, his gun still drawn, and looked over the two of them. He put his weapon back into the holster inside his jacket. The man noticed the tear in Jake's jacket that revealed a small red stain of blood.

"Are you alright?" asked the man, who now up close looked as if he could be in his late thirties or early forties.

"Yeah...I think so. Just barely nicked me," Jake said, looking at the wound closer now that the shots had stopped ringing past them.

"We need to move out of here now, and get you two to a safe location. I expect more may be on their way, especially now," said the man.

Two of the other men that came with the blonde man moved past the dumpsters toward where Mr. Cain and Mr. Skye had been standing. Jake and Miranda stood up and came out from between the dumpsters, and looked in the direction the men who had just passed by had gone. They saw Mr. Cain and Mr. Skye, lying in pools of their own blood. One of the men in grey stood beside the bodies talking on a cell phone while the other man was ushering people away that had heard the commotion from nearby apartments and businesses.

Miranda stood frozen, gazing upon the bodies of the men lying in blood. There was a burning she felt deep within her that she had never felt before. These were the people responsible for murdering her family...and for as much hatred as she felt building from inside of her, it was also accompanied by a sense of anger and envy. This particular set of emotions wasn't directed at the two dead men. It was now an anger at the impossible to satisfy desire to have been the one to take the life from these men herself. It was like something that she had never felt before, and the only thing that she found to be unsettling about this feeling was the lack of shame she felt in her longing to destroy the two men lying dead on the ground.

"Miss Stratton? We need to go right now, ma'am," said the blonde man. Hearing him call her by her family's name snapped her back to the here and now.

"How do you know my name? Who are you people?" she asked the blonde man. Her voice was icy, teeming with bitter skepticism.

"We are here to help keep you safe, Miss Stratton. Right now, we have to move you out of here. We are not here to hurt you. I think that should be evident by now. Please, let us take you where all of your questions can be answered."

"And if we refuse?" Jake asked, eyeing the man carefully.

"You are not being taken against your will. But I highly advise that you come with us, for your benefit and safety. I assure you that many questions you might have can be answered by my employer," stated the man once more, looking in all directions as he spoke like a soldier watching for enemy snipers from nearby building windows.

"Who are you?" asked Miranda.

"You can call me Deacon," he said. "Anything else you need to know can be answered by my employer. But we have to go now, Miss Stratton."

"And who is your employer?" asked Jake.

"My employer is the person who is truly responsible for saving your lives today."

## CHAPTER SEVENTEEN

The black Hummer moved forward across the old highway in silence, with the exception of the evenly spaced tension cracks below them that pulsed like a heartbeat in Miranda's ears. Three of the men accompanied her and Jake in the vehicle; the man called Deacon sat shotgun, while another drove and the third sat in the back seat with the two of them, tending to the wound on Jake's arm. The man cleaned and bandaged it thoroughly; he was obviously trained to deal with these sorts of wounds. With the exception of a few questions the man helping Jake had asked him about the wound and the pain, no one in the Hummer uttered a word.

Miranda stared out the deeply tinted windows. All clues and signs she saw during the drive indicated that they were heading towards Grand Rapids. They had been on the road for almost an hour, and were only about 20 minutes from the downtown Grand Rapids area.

It had been some time since Miranda had been to the city, and as they approached, the skyline looked very different than it had the last time she visited. The new Stratusaint Tower building was the first thing in sight, stretching high into the sky over the city's other buildings. The last time Miranda was in the city, ground had only just been broken on the building; the construction was only in its infant stages. Now it was a massive monument of slightly tapering glass shooting upward from the ground and reaching into the sky. At its peak, the tower sharply tapered into a four sided pyramid point.

Miranda leaned forward and stared between the front seats at the high rise as they drew closer.

"That is where we are going," said Deacon, at last breaking the silence in the vehicle. "The Stratusaint Tower. My employer has an office there. That building is the newest in the city, with 75 stories of steel, concrete, and uniquely tempered and forged glass. It's able to withstand almost any impact or remote structural damage. You can trust it is one of the safest places to be, Miss Stratton."

"Should I be concerned about someone trying to crash a plane into me?" Miranda asked, her eyes fixed sharply on Deacon.

Deacon did not respond. Miranda sat back into her seat and looked at Jake, who could sense there was a fire stirring within her. She was showing no fear, and this did not make Jake feel at all at ease.

The Stratusaint Tower was built on the outskirts of the downtown area where once stood a massive condominium complex that had burned to the ground years before. The fire made national news at the time because of several violations of building codes that came to light after the fire. The violations not only contributed to the fire, but also may have prevented some of the 23 people that lost their lives that day a means of escaping the furious blaze. The developer of the project, Mason Wright, took his own life with a 9mm handgun to the temple after months of pressure and overwhelming guilt.

Now, the once somber grounds approaching the Tower

reflected only beauty in the dazzling gardens that covered the several acres surrounding the building. Several fountains and statuettes of playing children lined the way on each side of the roadway leading to the frontal area of the building.

What caught Miranda's attention the most was what she saw directly in front of the main entrance of the Tower. The entranceway itself into the Tower was a large concave glass gateway that was lined with several doors that people were continuously entering and exiting through. Directly in front of the gateway was a much larger fountain than the others that lined the roadway leading into the grounds. This one had several small spouts shooting upward that surrounded a large, 20-foot-high polished white stone statue of an angel, down upon one knee while looking upwards into the sky. The wings were only partially spread apart, and the arms of the angel were held up straight over its head grasping the handle of a large sword that pointed straight up into the sky.

Miranda found herself transfixed on the angel so much that she didn't take immediate notice to the fact that the Hummer had passed by the front of the building and followed through a gated pass that took them to a subterranean garage housed beneath the Tower. The shaft that followed beneath the building was long and narrow, with only enough clearance for the Hummer to pass through. They came to a stop in a parking area with only a half-dozen other vehicles parked in the small chamber.

Deacon and the other two men exited the vehicle. Jake and Miranda glanced at each other for only a moment before the doors closed, leaving them alone inside.

Deacon walked over to a large mirrored elevator door and removed his cell phone from the inside pocket of his jacket. He stood for a moment, saying very little into the phone, and put it away back in his pocket.

There was a smooth black panel beside the large door, and Miranda watched as he touched the panel with his index finger. There appeared a red glow where his finger met the screen. He dragged his finger in a precise pattern until finally his finger came to a stop. The red glow turned into a bright green, and the door beside the panel began to open. Miranda and Jake were startled as the Hummer door beside them opened abruptly.

"Please, follow me," said a man they had not yet seen, wearing a dark blue suit and tie. Jake and Miranda exited the Hummer through the door the man had opened, and he led them around the vehicle to Deacon standing by the open elevator door.

"We are ready to go up," said Deacon politely to the two of them, holding up his arm with a gesture that guided them to step into the elevator. Miranda was no longer feeling fear or apprehension in her actions at this point. She wanted answers, and she knew that if these people were trying to harm them, they could have easily done it by now. She stepped inside the elevator, with Jake close behind her, followed by Deacon.

There was only one button in the elevator car. Deacon pushed it, and the door in front of them immediately closed.

Miranda felt for a moment like she was in some fairy tale, trapped inside a mirrored world. Every surface in the elevator was reflective, save for the button that closed the door and set the car in motion. The elevator seemed to ascend quickly, but still took some time to reach its final destination near the pinnacle of the tower. When it stopped, there was no 'ding' as one might expect with most elevators. The doors opened swiftly to a long and wide hall with soft, leathery grey walls on both sides and a pristine white and grey marbled floor.

Although the floor was bright and almost reflective, the lighting in the hall was soft and pleasant.

Deacon stepped out of the elevator car first, then turned to look at Jake and Miranda.

"Follow me please," he beckoned once more, with the same polite tone in his voice as he had before.

Deacon started down the hall, with Jake and Miranda close behind. On the right side of the hall they passed a few other closed doors, but there were no doors on the left until they finally came to a large set of double doors that appeared to be in the direct center of the long hall. The two doors were tall, more than nine feet from the floor to the top, and built from darkly stained hardwood. Each door was carved in a beautiful design depicting celestial bodies; the centerpiece of the left door being an intricate sun sculpture while the right door had its matching lunar counterpart.

Deacon opened the door with the sun design carved into it and stepped a few feet inside. Miranda followed him in first, with Jake trailing behind her.

The room before them seemed overwhelming with all of the sights that they could see before them. They stood upon a white polished stone surface, much like the material the statue of the angel in the front of the building was sculpted from. It extended away from them another six feet and formed a half circle, stepping down two short steps to meet the main floor level of the room. Red and black floral design carpeting spanned the rest of the massive room. The ceiling was a good 12 feet from the carpeted floor; at the far right side of the room was a spiral staircase constructed of polished timbers. The steps themselves were half logs that ascended into the ceiling above.

The room was easily the entire length of the hallway that they had walked down, a good 200 feet or so, and the windows stretched across the room from end to end and floor to ceiling, sharply slanted inward towards the peak of the building. The glass was tinted and tempered so the sunlight wasn't as blinding as it well could have been.

Miranda realized that they were near the top of the pyramid point of the Stratusaint Tower, just beneath the peak of the building. Books lined shelves that rose to the tiles on the ceiling at either end of the room, and along the walls on either side of where the three of them stood at the entranceway to the room. Adding far more to the awe of the room was a large fireplace that was burning brightly in the far corner to their right, surrounded by several comfortable armchairs and a large brushed leather sofa. Not far beyond the fireplace was a wet bar with a wine cabinet with etched glass doors, and several shelves lined and fully stocked with high-end liquors.

To the left side of the room was the real mystique of the splendid chamber. Statues and carvings from all different cultures were set about the left wing of the room in a museum like arrangement. Miranda knew little about historical art, but could identify jade bowls and carved vases that looked Asian in design, most likely of Chinese origin.

There were golden objects that appeared to be tools and ceremonial knives encased in glass that had the ankh design that Miranda knew well to be Egyptian, carved into the polished stone stand that the glass case was set upon.

Medieval suits of armor, battle worn and rough looking, stood in line along one of the many lengthy aisles of ancient treasures. The artifacts went on and on, from all around the globe, and Miranda's eyes surveyed all that she could take in from what lie displayed before her.

Miranda stepped down onto the main floor and moved closer to the antiquities that filled the vast room. Deacon stood in silence as Jake moved closer to Miranda. Jake kept his focus on her, avoiding the many things that could distract his attention in the room. Neither of them paid any notice to the elevated area directly across the room from the entrance that they had just come in through from the hallway. A large mahogany desk stood before the great backdrop of sky through the colossal window wall, and behind it sat a figure who had watched them in silence from the moment they had arrived in the room.

The man sat still, his eyes fixed firmly upon Miranda as she moved across the room. He was a handsome man, somewhere in his mid-thirties with short, wavy dark-brown hair and soft, deep blue eyes that reminded many who looked into them of the ocean as the sun lowered slowly into the horizon. He wore a plain, light grey, oxford style button down shirt without a tie, and straight black slacks.

The man held his hands upon the desk, and only when he slowly began to rise from his seat did his presence finally catch Miranda's attention. She stopped moving, focusing her attention on the man now standing behind the desk.

A nervous smile came to his lips. He stepped out around the corner of the desk and down the two steps that brought him to the same level where Jake and Miranda were now standing.

Jake looked at the man with the same speculative consciousness that he looked upon everyone the last few days. Trust was not something he had an abundance of, even for those that may have saved their lives. Miranda stood still in the spot where she first saw the man, faced him directly and waited for him to approach. He stopped short of her by several feet, with his hands held down by his sides. His smile widened.

"My God...you look so much like your mother," said

the man. There was a sadness in his eyes, even as he held his nervous smile. His voice was soft, and yet strong and solid; a gentlemanly tone wrapped neatly in a pronounced British accent.

"My mother?" asked Miranda.

"Yes, Miranda. Your mother. My sweet, beautiful sister Suzanne. I'm sorry. I am being rude, Miranda," said the man, approaching closer now with his hands raised, gently placing one upon each of her shoulders.

"My name is David. David Gale. I am your uncle, Miranda. At long last, you have finally come home."

## CHAPTER EIGHTEEN

David nodded to Deacon, who was still standing silently by the door. Deacon nodded back and turned to leave, firmly shutting the large oak door behind him.

Miranda stood in cautious silence, as did Jake as well. The room suddenly seemed much smaller as an awkward tension filled the vast open spaces.

"Please, come and sit with me," said David, gesturing to the more comfortable area near the fireplace. Miranda and Jake followed David to the furnishings that were arranged in a semi-circle before the hearth, sitting beside one another on the large sofa that faced the crackling flames of the fire. David followed suit, taking his place on an adjacent chair, but appeared to take no more notice of the comforts of the luxurious seats than Miranda and Jake did.

David sat and faced them directly, his knees tightly together and his hands folded on his lap. Miranda could see flashes of her own eyes when she looked into his, and wondered if this is what it would have been like to stare into the eyes of her birth mother.

"I am not sure where the best place is to begin," David started. "I am sure that you have more than a few questions, and I can do only my best to answer them all. I want to assure you first that you are safe here. No one will be able to get to you here, and from this point on, as long as you will allow it, you will have every means at my disposal for your protection, as well as the protection of your family and your friends."

"Thank you, but we don't know a thing about you or anything else about any of this, so you'll excuse me when I say that doesn't offer me a lot of assurance," said Jake. He sounded harsh and agitated. Miranda picked up on it immediately, and placed her hand on his arm to try and put him at ease. Jake was concerned about his own family back home. It had not escaped his mind that these people that were after Miranda may also know who he is and how to get to his family like they did her family. They would obviously stop at nothing, leaving everyone that he and Miranda knew in danger.

David hurried over to his desk and retrieved a notebook from a drawer on the opposite side of the desk. He quickly returned to his seat across from where the two of them sat and thumbed through the first few pages of the notebook.

"You have a grandfather, Charles Neilson, 2230 Pembrook Way. Your parents, Dwaine and Rebecca Neilson, live on Fisher Road in Native Springs. Your father works at Erro Tool & Die, and your mother waits tables at Billie's Café, also in Native Springs. Is this information correct?" asked David, staring patiently at Jake, waiting for his response.

Jake leaned back slightly, not knowing how to respond. Miranda looked at him, and then back at David.

"Yes, that's correct," Miranda finally stated. "How did you know all of that?"

David snapped the notebook shut, and set it down on the glass end table beside the chair.

"If I know it, then those who are after what you have

## In the Shadows of Fate

know it as well. I have taken every precaution to assure the safety of your family, Mr. Neilson," David said. After he spoke these words, Miranda noticed a slump in his overall demeanor, as if he looked...defeated.

"I only wish I could have acted sooner, Miranda. I only wish I could have gotten to Robert and Lorri and Steven sooner. I'm so sorry, Miranda. I am so sorry that I failed you this."

"It's not your fault. You didn't do this," Miranda told him.

"It was my responsibility!" David's voice was raised, not in a yell, but a definitive statement of frustration. "This was something that was started far before either of us were born, and it is my responsibility to try to make up for it. None of this should have ever happened. As a Gale, I am responsible for doing everything I can to undo what has been done and make things right!"

David stood up suddenly and walked to the large fireplace, facing it with his back turned to Miranda and Jake. His head hung low, and Miranda could feel the weight of the burden he was carrying, even without knowing for certain what it was. She had been carrying a similar burden for days. It may not have been her that suffocated the life from her parents, but she felt responsible in a way as if she had done it with her own hands.

Miranda walked over to David and put her hand on his shoulder. David lifted his head, and turned slowly to look at her.

"I apologize for that. Please, forgive me. You are holding far too much of your own burdens on your shoulders. You don't need mine as well," he said.

David led Miranda back to her seat beside Jake, who

was looking off to the side, still not knowing what he should be feeling. Miranda sat down and placed her hand upon Jake's knee. He turned to look at her, and they sat in silence for several seconds until David began to speak once more.

"The men who were after you," David began, "We believe that they work for a man known only as Enoch. The name itself is a play on the ancient script style purported to be angelic in origin, but this man is far from any angel as you or I might imagine. Demon would probably be a better description of him. He believes that great power will come to those who are in control of those documents that you have in your possession. There is a prophecy..."

"We know about the prophecy," Miranda interrupted. David looked suddenly surprised, but nodded his head to Miranda's resourcefulness.

"Then you know the dangers involved if it fell into the wrong hands. Generations of my family - of our family - have been charged with protecting the documents from those who may try to use the Caducus Oraclum for corruption. I am guessing that you are also aware of the Order of Sanctity? The Tale of the Two Cardinals?"

"We know about them," Jake interjected. "We were also told that the group that broke away from the Order believed in the prophecy. If your family had those documents, wouldn't that mean that it was the Gales that were descended from that group?"

"It is true, my family were the caretakers of the original pieces of the Caducus Oraclum. It is also true that the Gale family was the last in the line of those that had believed that someday the prophecy may come to light. But by the time it came to the generation of my grandfather, Francis Gale, none of the family believed in the prophecy any longer. My father wanted to continue to fulfill his obligation to his father as the protector of the Oraclum for both historical and sacred purposes, but he wanted it to end with him. He wanted nothing more of it for his family after he was gone. He wanted to turn the documents back over to the Order of Sanctity, but too much time and distance had gone between those who broke away and the original Order. The Order was such a secretive society; there was no way my father could find them any longer, nor could they find us."

"So what was your father going to do, at the end of his life, if the Gales were no longer to be the custodians of the Oraclum?" Miranda asked.

David bowed his head for several moments.

"I don't know. He never told me, and if he told my mother, she never revealed it to me while she was alive. She died three years ago, but in all of the years since the tragedy, in her grief, she never spoke of the documents. I know only what I know from stories my father told me when I was young, and from the times when I would sneak into his study and read his journals. I know, I should be ashamed of such things, but you can only imagine the excitement I would get from hearing his stories. I only hungered for more. Now, the journals are long gone in the fire, and my beloved father along with them. How I wish I could, if nothing else, have his words and his stories back to look upon again. Words and stories. These are the only true things that can bring the dead back to life."

Miranda's eyelids sunk. David had only just realized his error, and felt ashamed. The talk of losses such as this, while distant past to him, were fresh in the heart of Miranda. He knew her pain, but far more time had passed for him to come to terms with it.

"How did you find us? Do you know how this Enoch

found out about Miranda?" asked Jake, breaking the silence of the sullen moment before David once again could speak. He wasn't going to leave any stone unturned if he could help it, and he still wasn't absolutely sure what to think about long lost Uncle David.

"Enoch, we believe, found out about Miranda through that greedy snake, Harry Thornton. Harry still worked for my mother and stayed attached to the estate and the home after mother moved us far from Galestone. When I was informed about his death, I was sure that Enoch must have been paying him for years to watch the estate and report on what activities may be going on there. I would imagine that you, being the right age and looking so much like my sister, caught his attention like nothing had before. Enoch is not one to leave loose ends. Thornton must have served all possible purposes for him. I never cared for the man myself, but I would have never wished such a fate upon him."

"So you didn't yourself find out from Thornton? Someone else from Galestone, then?" asked Miranda.

"Yes, and no. Aimsley Carter contacted me. It was soon after you left her in Arlo. She was scared after she heard on the local news about the murder of Harry Thornton. I hadn't seen or heard from her since I was a child, so I was..."

"Is she alright? Aimsley? Where is she?" The fear was evident in Miranda's voice.

"Aimsley is fine. When she told me about Harry, I sent one of my people to retrieve her and take her somewhere safe until all of this was sorted out. Gale International Holdings has real estate and properties around the globe. Lots of places to hide someone from the rest of the world. I assure you, she is safe." David said.

Miranda breathed a sigh of relief. She was so scared that

something had happened to Aimsley when she couldn't get a hold of her earlier in the day. David smiled at her sense of relief.

"After Aimsley let me know you had been to see her, I started to learn all that I could about you so I could find you. My mother, God rest her soul, did everything that she possibly could have done to protect you from the Gale legacy. She hid you well away from the world, not too far out of reach, but enough to have you blend in with the rest of the world. I resented her at first for taking you away from us, but over the years I came to understand why she had made the decision that she did. That is why I never tried to find you myself, although now, I am regretting that decision. Perhaps if I had found you years before, this all could have been avoided."

"We can't know that for sure," said Miranda. "We never will. You can't be too hard on yourself." She said the words out loud. *Don't be too hard on yourself*, yet she could not escape the weight she carried for what happened to her own family.

"Perhaps you are right, Miranda. I cannot change the past. I can only hope to change the future. I found out too late about your family, and it took more digging to find out about Jake. By that time, you had already fled, quite resourcefully I might add, from those men who were pursuing you. I had a man watching your friend Lydia Snow for the last few days. Not long before you arrived at the café, that man monitoring Ms. Snow identified the men that had come after you. He called for the backup that came to your assistance and brought you here."

"The backup seemed to have as much firepower and 'shoot first, ask questions later' mentality as the men that came after us," Jake retorted.

"The people that work for me are highly trained and

highly disciplined. I know that you don't trust me, Mr. Neilson. I respect that. If I were in your position I would trust absolutely no one. I want Miranda and everyone close to her kept safe by whatever means necessary. My men would not have used deadly force unless they felt it was the only course of action left to take. Those men were killers. They killed Harry Thornton, and they murdered the family that raised Miranda, who I will forever be indebted to. We want the same things, Mr. Neilson. I promise you this. I don't want any more unnecessary suffering."

Jake listened to David's words, then nodded his head in silence to David. David nodded in return.

Miranda held her laptop case close to her side. She had it since she left the car at the café, and had not let go of it since. She reached down, unzipped the case and pulled out the manila folder with the parchment pages inside. She stood up and walked over to David, handing the folder to him.

David took the folder and opened it, examining the contents inside. He looked up at Miranda as she sat back down beside Jake. Jake had a look of surprise on his face, and David looked at them both now as they sat side by side.

David turned, walked over to the large fireplace and threw the folder and all of its contents into the roaring flames.

Miranda could not fully grasp the feelings that were going through her in that moment. Those documents had been in her possession only a few days, yet caused so much chaos and despair in her life in that short amount of time. Now, so quickly and with absolute finality, they were nothing but ashes and painful memories.

She still wished all of this meant more somehow. Why did her family have to die for this? What of this shadowy villain, Enoch? What was his next move to be now that the things he wanted so badly had been destroyed?

"Those cursed papers," said David. "They have haunted our lives for far too long. It's only fitting Lucifer get them back through fire and flame. Now, no one ever need fear the damage they could have caused. You can rest now, Miranda. You both deserve it. I will have Mr. Deacon settle you in to one of the guest rooms on this floor. Whatever you need - anything at all - he will get for you. Tomorrow, we can discuss what to do until we know for certain that Enoch is finished pursuing you. I know of possible ways to get a message to him to let him know the Oraclum is no more. If that is still not enough, then I will hunt him until he is found and do whatever it takes to assure you, he can harm you no more. You are the only family I have left in this world, Miranda. Family is all we have in the end. We are all that is left of the Gale line, and I intend to set right all that our family has wrought and restore our family's legacy.

Deacon showed Jake and Miranda to a room just down the hall across from David's office. The room looked like a luxury suite that Jake expected he might see in a world class Las Vegas casino, just as he had seen in movies. It had a fully stocked bar, three bedrooms, and a 100 inch flat panel LED television in the main living area. The view was incredible overlooking the city, with slanted windows like those in David's office. Paintings hung on all of the walls protected behind glass, and there were two sculpted busts of oriental dragon design in the far corners of the main room.

"What would you two like to eat?" asked Deacon politely.

"What's on the menu?" asked Jake. He was starving for some real food after the convenience store cuisine they had survived on the last few days.

"There is no menu," said Deacon. "Mr. Gale said that

whatever you want, we are to find it and have it brought to you, sparing no expense."

Miranda had been staring out the window, gazing down at the city. She sometimes forgot how the days get so much shorter this time of year. The street lamps were already illuminating. She broke her gaze and turned around, walking up to where Deacon was standing.

"Does Mr. Gale own the entire floor?" asked Miranda.

"He didn't mention? Mr. Gale owns the entire building. The Stratusaint Tower is the United States headquarters for Gale International Holdings," stated Deacon.

"I thought the family was near destitute when he and his mother left for England after the fire?" asked Miranda.

"Mr. Gale has worked very hard to bring back the Gale name and the Gale business empire. The family had nearly nothing left, but he took what remained and built it back from the ground up."

"Pizza," Jake suddenly broke in. "I'd love a good pizza. What is the best pizza place in the city?"

"Primo Luigiano's. It's the best damn pizza I've ever had," replied Deacon.

"That's what I'd like to have," said Jake. He looked at Miranda. "Okay with you? We'll make it one meat lovers and one Hawaiian special, ham and pineapple and cheese only."

Deacon smiled. "I'll get right on that, if that is alright with you, Miss Stratton?"

Miranda nodded to Deacon. Deacon nodded in return, and stepped backwards out the door, shutting it firmly on the way out.

"What was the sudden pizza interjection?" Miranda asked Jake, puzzled.

"We haven't eaten anything good in days, Miranda. I

know pizza isn't exactly health and energy food, but it will give us something to start with and then we can sit down and figure out what the hell is going on here. I am not all that sure what to think about David. He seems like his intentions are good enough, and he finally did get rid of the Oraclum, but something doesn't feel right."

Miranda felt torn inside. If the things that David was saying were true, if Aimsley was out of harms way, and he was only trying to keep them safe - it was the only sense of hope that she has felt since what seemed like the span of a lifetime chaotically wrapped into the last few days. Trust was something that she was finding hard to come by. The things she had seen and heard and felt in the last few days were such that many haven't experienced in the course of a normal life, if there was such a thing.

Miranda had more questions for David, and she felt that David had more to tell her. She knew that she needed to see him alone. She was also well aware that Jake would not like or easily go along with letting her out of his sight for very long.

"Jake, it's probably going to be at least a half-hour until our dinner gets here. You look like you could use a hot shower. I'll listen for Deacon to get back, unless there is time for me to take one too before he's back," Miranda told him.

"You can just use the shower in the other room," Jake said. The thought of a shower was a good idea, and he knew he could really use one to help him relax.

"One of us should keep an eye on things and be out here when he gets back," said Miranda.

"Well you can go ahead of me, I can wait for Deacon," Jake told her.

Miranda smiled at him. "Well, I could, but..."

Jake grimaced. "Do I smell or something?" Jake asked,

lifting his arm, taking a quick sniff.

"No...I mean, maybe a *little*. Honestly, I was thinking more about you keeping your wound clean. Maybe there is a first aid kit in the bathroom. I can't imagine this place not having one," she said.

"They cleaned me up pretty good back in the car. Remember, I am a nursing student. But the shower idea sounds good anyway. I could use it to clear my head," said Jake.

"Then I'll wait for Deacon to get back with the pizza. Take your time. I'll let you know when he gets back if you're not out yet," said Miranda.

Jake walked up to Miranda and softly touched her cheek. She looked up at him and for a moment thought that he was going to try and kiss her. But no. She could see the apprehension in his eyes.

"We're gonna figure this out. I promise you, one way or another, we will get some sort of normal life back after all of this," Jake said, lowering his hand away from her face.

"Jake," Miranda said, looking him straight in the eyes. "Nothing is ever going to be normal, ever again."

Jake lowered his head, turned, and walked over to the bathroom, entering and shutting the door behind him. She waited for the water to start running in the shower before she approached the entrance door of the room, grabbing her leather jacket on her way. She put it on, not with any intention to try and leave the building; the jacket, worn and tattered as it was, always felt like a sort of armor to her. She wasn't sure who to trust or where the next twisted turn may come. She wanted to be ready, in her heart and in her mind. More than anything else, she wanted the truth.

The handle of the door was a large, gold plated lever handle, and she slowly pushed down on it until it clicked open.

Miranda looked both ways down the hall, but there was no one in sight anywhere. She quietly walked down to the large oak celestial doors once more. Miranda didn't know if she should knock, or just go on in. She decided to just pull the lever and go inside.

She stepped onto the white polished entrance floor, and didn't see David behind his desk where he had stood when they first entered the extravagant office earlier that day. Something - whether it was some subtle movement, or something else - caused Miranda to turn towards the fireplace. She saw David's silhouette standing in front of the roaring fire. His back was turned to her.

"David?" said Miranda.

David had turned suddenly as if he was unaware that she had entered.

"Miranda! I'm sorry, I was lost in my thoughts. So much has happened. So many revelations in the last few days. I'm so glad I have a chance to talk to you, one on one," he said, almost excitedly.

"Please, follow me," he said, and led Miranda up to the area where his desk stood. He walked around the desk and retrieved a file folder from the left hand top drawer, placing it upon the polished surface of the mahogany top.

"There is so much more I need to tell you. For reasons that I hope you can understand, it is only meant for you. I am sure your friend Jake is very important to you, and he truly intends the best for you, but the things that I am about to tell you are...well, they are going to be difficult for him to understand, as they would be for most others. I am hoping that is not the case so much for you," David said quizzically.

"What is it?" she asked. She felt anxious, yet there was a strange anticipation as well.

"I don't want you to be alarmed, Miranda. As I have said before, you are safe here, and every precaution has been taken to assure the safety of your friends and their families," David said, his tone suddenly more serious.

"I'm not sure how you saying that at this moment isn't supposed to alarm me," she replied.

"It may not have been the Oraclum that Enoch was after at all. It quite probably was *you* he wanted, Miranda," David said.

"Why? What would he want with me?" Miranda asked.

"You said you know what the prophecy was about. Is that correct?"

"I...yes. Somewhat...do you know? I wasn't entirely clear what it all meant," she said, not wanting to reveal any hint about how she may have known what was in the prophecy. She wanted to protect Dr. Vikhrov's anonymity at all costs.

"Yes, I do indeed. The prophecy speaks of a being, not of Heaven, not of Earth," he said, and pulled a sheet of paper from the folder on his desk. The paper was written in the same script that the parchments were written in.

"This being would be the key to releasing the fallen angel Lucifer from his eternal prison. Miranda. Can you read this?" asked David, passing Miranda the paper from his folder.

Miranda took the paper in her hand and looked down at it.

"No. I can't. It's just like the writing in the Oraclum," she said. Miranda held the paper out to David, but he did not take it back from her.

David smiled at her. "Try once more, please. Look at it, really look. Relax your thoughts. See what light your mind may bring."

Miranda looked curiously at him for a moment, and

then once more examined the paper. As she stared down at the script, she could almost hear the words forming in her head by the same voice she would hear in her mind when thinking to herself. She spoke what she heard out loud to David.

"I am of the first circle, anointed by the Lord my God, devoted on high to obey and defend in the Name, and by the Word, I am called..." she stopped and looked at David, her eyes widened. She slipped into a place in her mind, lost in that moment. She had seen this writing before. It was in her dream of the garden behind the Gale estate. The writing...those words...they were the tattoos on the back of the man Suzanne was embracing in the garden. The words inscribed on the back of her father...

"Go on, Miranda. What does it say?" said David, his voice soothing and calm.

She looked back down at the page again and read aloud.

"And by the Word, I am called Gabriel," she said, and stopped reading any further.

"Do you understand, Miranda? The prophecy never meant that the one who could set free Lucifer was not from Heaven or not from Earth. It was, in fact, foretelling the coming of a being that is the product of the two," David told her.

"You are trying to tell me that my father was the angel, Gabriel? *The* Gabriel, from the Bible? Do you really believe any of this? How crazy this all sounds?"

David smiled. "I do, Miranda. I know how this sounds, but I have my reasons to believe that it is the truth. That is what I believe Enoch was after. That is why it is essential that you be protected."

"Why do you think it's true? Is this why my family is dead? Because I got nosey about the past and walked straight into an insane asylum? The present...that was good enough. I had everything that I could have ever wanted or hoped for. I had the best parents, the best brother. My friends were good friends, and they were safe. I have destroyed everyone's lives around me!" Tears started to run down Miranda's cheeks. She turned her back to David.

David stepped up beside her and placed his hand on her shoulder. She pulled away impulsively; David drew back his hand.

"Miranda. Think about this - how could you have read what was on that paper?" asked David.

"I didn't. I just imagined what it might say in my head. That's all."

"You know that's not true. And there have been other things, haven't there? He told me that there might be, as you got older," David said.

Miranda turned around to face him.

"Who told you?" she asked.

"Your father. Gabriel. He came to me. He sought me out as your only living relative. He was sick and stripped of his power, punishment for disobeying God and partaking in his forbidden love with my sister. Of course, at first I didn't believe him. He showed me the markings on his back. They all still remained, even without his divine grace. I thought they were only tattoos at first, but the doctor that I had see to him told me something extraordinary. They were like burns, just beneath the surface of the skin and they had been made from the *inside out*. The markings came from within, Miranda. The doctor had never seen anything like it before. I knew he was telling the truth. Unfortunately, we couldn't save his life. He was too far gone, and died a few days after he came to me."

Miranda sat down on the steps leading up to the desk.

David sat down beside her. Her head was spinning, and she could see so many things from the last few days that could only possibly be explained now. The wolf in Galestone, cowering in fear. She thought almost nothing of it at the time, but she could feel its fear as if it was her own. The dreams and the visions. The tavern owner's sudden pain when he grabbed hold of her in Galestone. She was feeling all of these things now as extensions of her own self; her emotions taking shape and form, like an energy reaching out beyond her physical self.

"So what if it's true? What does it mean? Am I supposed to set the devil free into the world?" Miranda asked David.

"Things are not so clear and simple always, Miranda. Prophecies are set forth by God himself. It would not have been foretold if it were not His will. So many years our family has protected the secrets of the Oraclum. It is incredible that in my lifetime it has come to pass. But it has to be your decision, Miranda. Your will. Lucifer was the bringer of light, and enlightenment. Maybe it is time that the world saw that light. If it is what God intended, you could bring the greatest gift the world has ever known. It could be the end of war, or the dawn of an entirely new era. The possibilities, they are truly astounding."

David stood up and turned around in front of Miranda, facing her as she sat on the step before him.

"We don't know what lies ahead, Miranda. All I can say for certain is that I will do whatever I can to help you through this. We are all the family that we have left now. I have been away for far too long. I am just sorry that I could not have come back to you sooner," he said, reaching out his hand to help her up from the step.

Miranda reached out to her uncle to take his hand, but

it only took a fraction of a second to send a jolt through her that almost knocked her back down again. The moment that his skin touched hers for the very first time, a flood of visions and emotions coursed through her entire being.

She saw a boy with a cold, icy look in his eyes; his dark mop of hair, looking down at the child she knew was herself in her crib. She could feel his resent as if it were heat resonating from his soul. He was no longer the spoiled youngest of the family. It was all about Miranda now, getting all of the attention and all of the favors. His own mother favored her over him, he had felt. He hated Miranda from the very beginning.

A place far darker came now in her mind's eye. She could see a man being beaten and dragged before David. The man was bloody and dirty, and David grabbed him by the hair and pulled his face to his own.

"Ah, look what fate has brought me now, the father of that little bitch. What my whore of a sister saw in you, I'll never know. Did you miss me as well?" snarled David. "Take him down by the docks. Beat him some more, then chain him to blocks and throw him into the river!"

David took the man's chin in his hand and looked with the deepest hatred in his eyes into the man's swollen and bloodied face.

"You should have never come back," said David, and raised his hand across the man's face, striking hard with the back of his fist; the darkest satisfaction beaming from his cruel eyes.

As they began to drag the man away, Miranda could see the beaten man was her father, Gabriel. David saw the script markings through the back of his torn shirt.

"Stop!" yelled David, and the vision changed once

more.

David sat alone in a dark room, holding a telephone to his ear. Miranda could hear every word from both sides of the conversation.

*"What is her name?"* asked David, his voice a cold and contemptuous hiss.

*"Miranda Stratton. She came to Galestone telling people she is working on an article about Michigan mining history. What do you think?"*

Miranda recognized Harry Thornton's voice.

*"It's her,"* David said.
*"How can you be sure of it?"* asked Harry.
*"I KNOW it is her,"* David said.
*"What do you want me to do?"* asked Harry.

Next, Miranda saw David speaking to Deacon in the very room where she now was in front of him, touching his hand.

"So how do you want this handled?" asked Deacon.

"It is essential that she trust me entirely. Nothing can go out of plan from this point on. Cain and Skye should have never lost track of her. They should have been on her from the moment they were through eliminating her family," said David, in the same odious tone as he'd had while confronting Gabriel.

"Why exactly did her family have to die?" asked Deacon.

"I need her to feel alone. I need her to feel despair. I

need her to know that I am all she has left. The world is changing, my friend. Sacrifices *must* be made."

"And what of Cain and Skye?"

David stood silent for a moment, thinking on the question.

"Kill them. Do it in front of her. Be her hero. Let *me* be her savior. They are collateral damage for a greater cause."

Miranda gasped and fell back to the step she had been sitting on before David had reached out to her.

"Miranda! Are you all right? What is it? What's wrong?" David asked, his face full of apparent agitation and concern.

Miranda could feel that familiar rush of anxiety coming over her, and was attempting desperately to fight it. She tried not to look directly at David. She didn't want to give anything away of the emotional tempest rising inside of her. It was a rush of hate and fear and rage and sickness all at once.

"I get panic attacks," she said to him, still trying to compose herself. Her breathing was starting to get heavier.

"Let me help you," said David, reaching out to her once again, but she held up her hand to him.

"No, please, it's alright. I just have to work through these things on my own. Thank you." The last two words she had said to him were forced out, and made her feel even sicker to say them.

David backed a few feet away from her to give her space. She brought herself to her feet, and forced a smile at David.

"It there anything I can do? Should I call a doctor?" asked David. "I have the very best at my disposal."

"No. No, I'm okay. There has been just so much going on. I am surprised it hadn't caught up with me before now. I'm so embarrassed," she said, still holding her nervous smile. "I've had these things happen ever since I was a kid. I think I just need to get back to the room, take a hot shower and get to bed. Jake is probably wondering where I am. I'm sure he must be frantic."

David nodded his head to her. She started to walk past him slowly, steadily placing her foot upon the first step toward the door.

"Miranda," David said. His voice sounded different than it had sounded only moments before.

Miranda stopped, but did not turn to face David. She stood still, her arms by her sides. She could feel her hands starting to tremble slightly. She slowly put them into her jacket pockets as she stood just a few feet away from David. Her right hand felt the cool handle of her Spyderco Delica, and she wrapped her fingers tightly around it.

"Have you ever heard of sodium amytal?" asked David. Miranda could hear him moving around behind her, his steps slow and steady. She still did not turn her head, for fear that her face may give up too much too soon. She had to play along as best as she could, until she could get back to Jake and figure out what they needed to do next. Before she could respond, David continued.

"Sodium amytal is more commonly referred to as 'truth serum'. There is no real magic or mystery to truth serum, really. It's just a combination of chemicals that cause both sedative and hypnotic responses, altering some of the higher cognitive functions. At least, that is how Wikipedia describes it. But in my experience, I have found it highly effective in extracting information from people who are...resistant to sharing knowledge that I desire."

"That's very interesting," Miranda said, desperately

trying to disguise the tension in her voice. She still would not turn to face David. "I should really get back to the room. I'm feeling sick..."

"Oh, I am certain you aren't feeling all too well, Miranda," said David, his voice icier as he went on. "You see, truth serum works just as well on an angel made wholly human as it does any other man. Your father...he revealed many things before I was through with him. One of which was how great emotional disruption might cause things to progress much faster within you. To quicken your becoming. The things you could do. The things you could see! Some of it wasn't all that clear. After all, he was in and out of consciousness near the end. But something had just occurred to me. Something I hadn't thought of before. I thought that I had thought of everything. And then...I *touched* you."

Miranda swung herself around quickly, coming face to face with David. The knife was pulled out of her jacket, and with a quick flick of her thumb, the blade was open and held at her side.

"Let's not be too rash now, shall we, dear niece," said David, pointing a handgun with a long barrel at Miranda. She had recognized the extended barrel of the weapon as a silencer on the gun from many of the police dramas her father watched on television when she was very young.

"You are Enoch. Aren't you?" said Miranda, with more hatred than fear now in her voice.

"I am David Gale. I am the rightful heir to the Gale legacy, and I will be the one to make sure that the prophecy is fulfilled. You will release Lucifer, and I will be rewarded for returning the lightbringer to his freedom!" said David. Even now, after all the years away from her, Miranda could see the contempt and anger he had for her. Now, she may have been just a tool to get what he desired, but it sickened his ego still that she was the key to unlocking the rewards he felt he was entitled to.

"Why? Why would I possibly help you? You are NOTHING but a murderer! You killed my family! You may as well shoot me now. I will never help you!" Miranda fired back at him.

"Oh, you will," David said.

Miranda heard the large oak door latch click, and turned to see Jake walking in, followed by Deacon. David gave a nod to Deacon, who in turn nodded back and walked out the door, securing its lock as he exited.

"What the hell is going on?" Jake asked, eyeing the gun in David's hand that was pointed at Miranda.

"Jake, glad you could join us. Maybe you can talk some sense into your good friend Miranda. All I've asked is a little favor of her, and she seems unwilling to grant me this request. Please. Do convince her to make better choices," said David, lowering his gun to his side.

"What is he talking about? What is going on, Miranda?" asked Jake, still keeping one eye on David's gun. David kept a serious, almost pleading look on his face.

"It was him, Jake, it was all him! He had my parents killed. He murdered his own men just to try and convince me that I could trust him!"

Jake flashed his eyes to David, who could not repress the smirk that came to his lips.

"You son-of-a-bitch!" Jake exclaimed, starting towards David as David raised his gun back up from his side, stopping Jake in his tracks. Jake positioned himself between David and Miranda, just as they all heard a door open from the upper level above the office. Footsteps started down the spiral steps that led up to the apartment above.

The sound of the steps was steady and even. Miranda felt a rush of anxiety and joy simultaneously as Aimsley came into view, followed closely by Deacon. Deacon was holding a gun in his hand now, pointed from his hip at Aimsley's back. Aimsley was wearing the same slacks and blouse that she was wearing when Miranda last saw her.

"Aimsley!" said Miranda, "Are you alright? I'm so sorry, I never meant for any of this to happen."

"I know, sweetie. It's not your fault. I should have just left you alone. I'm the one who's sorry, Miranda..." said Aimsley, tears starting to run down her face.

"This is all so touching," said David, smugly.

"Just leave her alone!" growled Miranda, the anger welling more inside her now.

"Or what?" replied David. "Or you won't do what I've asked of you? You already told me that you won't, so..."

David raised the gun squarely at Aimsley and fired. The bullet flew perfectly through the center of her chest, leaving her standing for a moment, wide-eyed, and glancing towards Miranda before falling to the floor.

"NO!" screamed Miranda, pushing past Jake and lunging at David, who simply, yet quickly, re-directed the gun at Miranda's forehead, mere inches away from it where she stood now. Jake froze, looking at Miranda and David, and then back to Deacon standing with his gun still in hand. Miranda stared at David as if she were a wild animal ready to strike and tear him to pieces.

"Miranda! Don't!" pleaded Jake. "Please...I can't lose you again."

Miranda closed her eyes and breathed in deep, trying to calm the fury within her. She stepped backwards toward Jake, never taking her eyes off of David. She moved back until she could feel Jake behind her, and continued to go back, nudging Jake along. Deacon started to aim his gun in their direction, but David, with a subtle gesture, waved him off. Deacon lowered his gun.

"Jake," said Miranda, loud enough for both he and David to hear, "Stay behind me. He won't shoot me. He *needs* me. We are going to walk out of here, and then we are going to disappear." Jake continued on, following her direction, glancing back and forth between Deacon and David, finding it hard not to catch glimpses of the slain woman he watched David murder in cold blood right before his eyes moments before.

David once more lowered his gun, slightly.

"Miranda," he said, shaking his head side to side while looking down. "You are such a smart, strong girl."

He stepped forward in her direction, looking her in the eye. She stopped, and pulled the Delica to her own throat.

"Stop. Not another step," she told David. Jake stayed silent, not knowing what he should do in that moment, but it didn't matter at that point any longer. It was fate that took over from that second on.

"Miranda," David said once more. The twisted grin returned to his face. "Do you really think that if I could actually truly harm you, you would be of any use to me?"

David raised the gun in his hand and fired a shot directly through Miranda's midsection, just below her sternum.

Miranda gasped and dropped the knife from her hand. She felt a rush of hot and cold through her body all at once. There was the sudden onset of pain, but just as soon as the pain would come, so would the hot and cold, flaring through her like electrical impulses.

She looked down, and for a moment, she saw the gush

of blood flow from the hole in her body. The breath was gone from within her, but in mere seconds she found herself able to draw in air again.

Miranda was breathing. She was aware of her heart rate, rising to a rapid pace, then slowing down to almost nothing, now steady and constant again. Never in these moments did she ever lose her footing. She was standing still, looking down at the bloody hole in her shirt. The fingers that had held the knife found their way to the hole in her shirt, but there was no hole in her body. There was no pain. There was nothing.

She turned around to see Jake's eyes, wide and glassy. He dropped to his knees in front of her, and then Miranda saw the blood gushing from the right side of his abdomen. The bullet that had gone into Miranda's body had exited and lodged itself deep inside of Jake's, tearing through the area near his liver. The blood was coming fast, and the only thing Miranda could think to do was put pressure on the wound, but the blood was running fast through her fingers.

"Jake! Oh my God, Jake...please Jake...please...stay with me..." cried Miranda, desperate and feeling helpless. She tore off a piece of his shirt and pressed it into the wound.

"There's only one thing you can do now to save him, Miranda," said David, softly, standing just behind her now. "Release Lord Lucifer, and he will grant you a boon for his freedom. He can save Jake, Miranda. All you have to do is *want* him to be free. It is your destiny, Miranda. Pre-ordained by God. It is in your hands now. It is your choice."

Rage washed over Miranda like a tsunami. She could feel it like fire filling her every cell. She clenched her fists as her tears evaporated from her face, and rising to her feet she turned towards David, who took several steps back from her. Her eyelids were shut tightly as the room began to shake, first with the subtlest of vibrations, then rising into the intensity of a small earthquake. She opened her eyes and looked upon him, and for the first time since she laid eyes upon him, she could see fear in his expression. In fact, she could almost *taste it*.

Her pupils appeared to have dilated to a point that completely eclipsed the tranquil blue beauty that she had inherited from her mother. Now, there was only blackness in its place, and that blackness was staring right through the broken and dark soul of David Gale.

A hot lead round from a gunshot flew past Miranda's face, missing only by inches; but it was not a miss. Miranda could feel the bullet coming and changed its path in mid-air so it would crash through the glass encasement of a golden Egyptian cat statue. The thick glass shattered into several large shards; Miranda looked to Deacon, who had fired the shot. The broken shards all took flight at once from where they laid, darting across the room, piercing through several different places in Deacon's face and neck. One large fragment severed his carotid artery, causing him to bleed out quickly. He dropped to the floor, shuddering before going motionless in the pooling blood.

She turned her attention back towards David, who foolishly aimed his gun in her direction again. The gun snapped backwards in his hand, breaking three of his fingers before flying across the room, far from his reach.

David let out a scream of pain, grasping at his now feeble hand with his good one, which did nothing to ease his agony.

The room continued to tremble violently as Miranda walked slowly, one determined step after another, in the direction of David, who found himself tripping and stammering in his pain. The flames from the fireplace erupted into a wave of fire that engulfed the furniture that they had sat in earlier in the evening. Several books started flying from the shelves at the end of the room near the fireplace. Some of them passing through the flames and igniting into blazing projectiles hurtling across the room in David's direction, who desperately tried to dodge them as they came at him with incredible force. One struck him hard in the arm, knocking him to the floor on the steps leading up to the desk. He let out a wail from the pain before he had even realized his sleeve had caught fire, and patted it down with his opposite hand, extinguishing the flames.

Miranda turned her head to the other side of the room and looked upon the artifacts in their museum-like casings. The glass shattered simultaneously in all of the cases. A carved jade Buddha bust launched in David's direction. David threw himself to one side, the bust missing him by inches as it shattered into the windowed wall behind his desk. An Aztec wooden chest, adorned with golden plates on every side, became the next flying weapon, grazing his cheek as it shot past, smashing and bursting as it hit the mighty glass pyramid windows.

"Miranda," David pleaded. "Stop! You don't know what you are doing! You need my help...he will reward us both! You can still help Jake!" She could feel the desperation in his shaken words. It meant nothing to her.

"I've seen your soul, David. I've seen your heart. All you desire is your own glorification. You care for nothing but glory and power! You don't know what true suffering is, because nothing has even meant enough to you to feel real loss. Not until now!"

All of the individual pieces of a Mongol warrior's armor came at David, one at a time; sleeves of leather and an iron helmet and plating striking him from one side and then the other as he dragged his way to his desk. The flaming furniture propelled through the air like catapult missiles across the large room just over the top of the desk, once more causing David to drop to the marble floor. The fire spread across the room of antiquities, engulfing everything in the room that could burn.

David watched the pieces of history as they began to crumble to dust, fearing ever so much more for his own life.

"You must STOP this!" cried David. He was far past the point of the realization that he had no true idea of what he had released within her. She was rage and power. He could see the hatred in her eyes. The darker part of him was smiling, somewhere deep inside, but it was the rest of him now, almost frozen with both fear and pain, that faced the monster before him.

"We can change the world, Miranda. We can stop the pain. I'm sorry Miranda. I'm so sorry...I was scared...I didn't know any other way. Spare me, my niece. We are all the family that we have left."

Miranda stopped just feet from David. The books and other small artifacts and pieces of glass stopped swirling in the air around the room and dropped to the ground. The only sound was the crackle of the flames burning throughout the room. She crouched low on the ground in front of David, staring into his face. Her eyes were still as black as the night; she leaned in closer to her uncle. Impulsively, he lurched backwards, pressing himself against the desk.

"I have no family," she said, her tone dark and contemptuous. "You saw to that. They were good people. They loved me for who I was. They loved me unconditionally. They gave me a home and a name. A name I was never deserving of!"

The desk instantly split in two pieces as if it were no more than a toothpick, each half flying to opposite ends of the room and smashing into splinters. David fell flat on his back before pulling and pushing himself backwards toward the glass outer wall, but Miranda helped him along with that. He felt his body rise up off the floor and slam into the glass with such force that he could hear the snapping of ribs in his chest as the pain pulsed through him. David could only gasp as the strength to make sound escaped him. He was sure at least one, if not both of his lungs, had been punctured by fragments of his broken ribs.

Miranda stepped closer to him, stopping a few short feet away.

"This building can withstand any impact?" asked Miranda. David could say nothing; blood was sputtering from his mouth.

Miranda closed her eyes as a low rumbling came from outside of the building. The once clear night sky grew darker still as black clouds seemed to appear out of the darkness itself, eclipsing the moon and the stars in every direction. David tried to turn his head to the glass behind him, but the pain was too great and more blood coughed from his mouth. He dropped to the floor from the glass as lightning flashed from the sky all around. A bolt of lightning roared into the glass, creating a fracture about one hundred feet across. The sound was almost deafening. Miranda opened her eyes and watched as two more blasts from the sky struck the same spot near David, causing the great glass wall to drop to pieces all around him where he lie. A rush of wind filled the room, flaring up the fires to even greater ferocity.

David rose by an invisible force from the floor again, hovering just inches from its surface. The winds that came from the spontaneous storm subsided, and Miranda brought her face within inches of David's. She took his chin in her hand, much like he himself had done to her father, beaten and broken, as she had seen in the vision.

"If you want to meet the devil so bad, you can go to hell and meet him yourself."

David flew back from her hand and out into the night sky. He fell, story after story, plummeting silently, unable to yell or scream or even whisper, until the final twist of fate came upon him. As his back fell toward the earth, the uplifted sword of the polished stone angel in front of the main entrance to the building pierced his spine and on through his chest; the force of the fall pushed him deeper still, almost splitting him in two.

Miranda could hear the screams from the street below, although it was too far away for any human ear to hear. She hadn't noticed if she had been breathing or not, and then she could feel her chest moving and air coming in and out of her lungs. Her eyes were no longer black, taking on the blue hue she had seen in the mirror all of her life. The fires around the room had subsided some, and out of the corner of her eye she saw Aimsley, lifeless on the floor, and she felt an ache in her chest. She turned quickly toward Jake, and she could see something odd around him. There was a faint, dimming glow about his body, and Miranda somehow knew from that distance that he was still alive, if only barely.

She ran across the room to him and could still feel a pulse in his neck.

"Jake! Jake! Can you hear me? We have to get you to a doctor..." she said, but as she was looking at his face, she could see the glow dimming more and more quickly.

Somehow, Miranda knew. Somehow, she had become aware of almost all of the power inside of her. She acted on instinct, placing her hand over the spot where the bullet had entered and lodged itself within Jake's lower torso.

Miranda concentrated, closing her eyes again as the blackness returned, and a warm, white glow came from beneath the surface of her palm as she held it to Jake. Jake writhed and gasped, and Miranda reached out with her opposite hand to hold him still, calming him. She closed her hand, and the glow dissipated. For a moment, she held her hand in place, until she turned it over and opened her palm, revealing the spent bullet, still and whole.

Jake started to move, barely opening his eyes to see the shadowy silhouette of Miranda before him, only for a moment, and then all he could see was darkness.

# EPILOGUE

The days had been unseasonably hot for the middle of June in northern Michigan. Some days had already reached temperatures in the lower 90s, while others, after a cool drenching rain, had only peaked in the upper 60s.

Jake awoke early on a Sunday morning, around 7:30 a.m., and the temps were already that day in the upper 60s. It was going to be another hot June day. His radio alarm cranked out loudly the song "Tired" by Stone Sour.

Like any other morning, he rolled out of his bed, made himself a milk chocolate protein shake and wheat toast for breakfast, and then headed for the shower. And like every other morning, standing before the mirror after his shower, he would stare at the odd mark on the surface of the right side of his abdomen, and he would try and remember what happened on that night almost eight months earlier.

It would come to him, in flashes and in shadows, but whenever he tried to make any sense of it, it would seem like one of those picture puzzles where one slides the pieces from side to side and up and down until the picture was complete and whole. But this puzzle wasn't comprised of the far simpler nine or sixteen squares to move. This one appeared in his mind's eye to have dozens of pieces, and the more he tried to concentrate and remember what had happened, the more pieces appeared to form and make it even more difficult.

He remembered pain. He remembered a ringing in his ears. He remembered the warm and wet rush on his belly. But now, there was only a small scar that looked as if it had been there since his childhood. The warm rush was evident. He would later find the blood stained shirt that he had been wearing that night shoved beneath the front seat in Miranda's car.

Miranda. That was the very last thing he would remember from that night. Miranda was leaning over him, and all he could see was the twisted dance of shadows and light; bright, then fading to a deep, dark twilight. There was the heat from where she laid her hand upon him, and the final shot of pain, followed by darkness.

He awoke in Miranda's car the next morning all the way back in Preston, groggy and confused. When he had realized Miranda was nowhere to be found, he started the car and drove straight back to Grand Rapids. But once he had gotten within a quarter-mile of the Stratusaint Tower he noticed emergency crews were still blocking routes and redirecting traffic.

"What's happening?" Jake asked a middle-aged Grand Rapids police officer at one of the stops.

"There was some sort of freak accident at the top of the Tower last night. GRFD thinks it might have been a lightning strike from the storm that hit. Blew out the top floor windows and caused a major gas leak from a fireplace. The explosion knocked a guy outta the window and down to the ground. What a fuckin' mess! Crews been up there all day. Completely burned out the top two floors, and the whole damn building had to be evacuated," the chatty cop told him.

Jake sat silent for a moment, his heart had raced in his chest before he found his composure once more.

"Was there anyone else up there," he asked the officer.

"Don't know. Everything was burned so bad, it could be weeks before they know anything, if at all. So much for the indestructible building. Looks like God had a different idea. Anyway, no one's going in today. You can turn around up there to the left in the out lot."

Jake waited for weeks afterward to hear any news from the building fire, but no news of Miranda had ever come. And for those same weeks afterward, Detective Rice called and stopped by often, relentlessly asking questions about Miranda's whereabouts. Jake knew that Rice had thought of him as a possible suspect from the very beginning in the deaths of Miranda's parents and brother. If Jake had reappeared with Miranda's car and no Miranda, Rice would have him arrested on the spot. Although he hated having to do it, he left Miranda's car a quarter-mile down a two-track a few miles from Miranda's parent's home. When it was found, Rice was at Jake's the very next day asking questions about where he had been the days prior.

Jake told Detective Rice that he and Miranda had taken a trip down to her school in Preston, and she wanted to stay with her roommate a day or two longer, so he caught a bus back. Paid for the ticket in cash. Sorry, no receipt. He didn't think he'd need it for anything. Lydia confirmed the story. She had only met Jake for a moment, but she felt as if she had known him for a long time. Miranda would mention him often, and if there was one thing that Lydia could tell by all of the tales that Miranda had told of her and Jake, it was that, despite their parting of ways, Jake Neilson was a good guy. If there was a reason that this story had to be told, she was going to stand by it; if for no other reason, she would do it for Miranda.

Jake had called Lydia before he had made it all of the way back to Native Springs. *Miranda had decided to stay with her for a couple more days, and Jake headed home. Two days after Jake left, Miranda left to head back up to Native Springs as well.*

Lydia confirmed everything to Detective Rice, as well as the other local Preston detectives that came to ask questions about Miranda's disappearance and the discovery of her abandoned car in Native Springs.

Without any other evidence, and Lydia's story to back him up, Rice started to eventually back off from Jake, occasionally calling to ask if he had remembered anything else, or had perhaps heard from Miranda. Every week Jake would get a text from Lydia asking the same things.

Sometimes he would call her back, and they would talk, albeit briefly, about what might have happened or where she might be. Both always kept the fear in the back of their minds that she may have never made it out of the building the night of the fire. Jake had told Lydia everything that had happened that night, up until the point where everything had gone to black. It was the least that he could do for her after backing up his story to Detective Rice, and it is what he believed Miranda would have wanted.

But they both *knew* that there had to be far more to it all. There was no explanation whatsoever as to how Jake ended up back in Preston, and they both wanted to believe that Miranda had something to do with it. But why did she disappear? The answer had come to Jake one day, just a few months after the night at the tower.

The letter was not stamped nor postmarked, and it was not sealed in the envelope. The top flap of the envelope was tucked inside the open edge, between the wall of the envelope and the handwritten letter within. She had given him letters like this before, and when he read it, he knew for certain it was from her. There was some relief in receiving it; he knew she was alive, and that she had survived the fire that night months before. But the tone of what was written gave him an unsettling feeling deep in his gut. This letter was meant for only him, and he did not share it with Rice, Lydia, or anyone else.

Jake,

I don't have the words to express how sorry I am for everything that I have put you through, nor do I have the words to tell you how much everything that you have done for me means to me...or what you mean to me.

I wanted you to know that I am alright. Please, do not try to find me. I have made this decision with a heavy heart, but everyone is better off the further away from me as possible. There is nothing left for me in the lives of those close to me, and I fear that my presence in your life, or anyone else that I care for, will lead to nothing but heartache and unknown dangers.

You, along with Lydia, are the last parts of my previous life that mean anything to me. Everything else is gone, taken from me, by my own reckless pursuit of things better left untouched. My parents...Steven...they deserved so much more, and they gave me so much love, a gift that I can never fully repay to them.

I am not deserving myself of that love, nor was I deserving of the life and name that they had given me and welcomed me into so selflessly and freely. I destroyed their lives just by searching for a past that was filled with darkness and tragedy, and even though I may not have been aware of it at the time, it is now the only legacy I deserve to carry.

    Don't look back, Jake. Look into the future, and forget about me. This is all that I can ever ask of you again, and all that I ever will, with one exception - please look after Lydia. It is probably best if you not tell her about this letter. I don't think she would understand.

    You will not hear from me again, but I will never forget what we have shared together, both the good times and the bad.

Yours always,
*Miranda Gale*

    McAlister's Cross Street Bookseller was located in the downtown area of Petoskey, Michigan, situated conveniently next door to the Roasted Renegade Coffeehouse, which served the finest unique coffee concoctions in all of the northern Michigan area. The two businesses complimented each other nicely, and both shared a flare for finding interesting ways to stand apart from other businesses similar in purpose, embracing the culture and overall feel of northwest Michigan lifestyle with an urban twist and modern art ambiance.

    Sketched charcoal drawings lined the high ceiling walls of the coffeehouse, featuring both past and present baristas who worked there over the years, as well as the other tattooed cuisine artisans that fashioned the delectable homemade soup and sandwich selections that served customers from all around the area every day of the week.

    Like most coffee shops these days, many of the tables and booths were occupied by businessmen and hipsters alike, plugged into their laptop computers, iPad's, and other assorted electronic devices, sipping their cups and browsing the vastness of unlimited cyberspace.

On many days and nights, sitting quietly in the far back corner, alone in a small, two-person booth, unnoticed by any and all, was Miranda Gale.

She would sit, day in and day out, watching people come and go, sipping their drinks and talking amongst themselves. Some would silently read the newspaper, while others may come in with several friends and be, at times, obnoxious and intrusive to others. Miranda didn't care either way. She found a subtle pleasure that came with the distraction of watching the people live their lives, and she would think of the different lives she had had at one time or another.

Miranda had discovered many of the things that she could do now after the night at the Stratusaint Tower. Petoskey was only 20 or so miles from Native Springs, but she didn't have to hide to not be found. She could choose who saw or noticed her, and she could virtually hide in plain sight. No one would take notice of her unless she wanted them to, and if she were to ever come across someone from her past who would surely recognize her, she could, just by the sheer force of her will and her mind, have them find themselves in a blank stare when they looked in her direction. Eventually, they would look away, and forget themselves for the moment, leaving them in a state that felt much like déjà vu.

That is how she moved about in the world these days. She could go anywhere, and take anything she wanted if she chose, and no one would know any different. But she opted to actually take a part-time job at the corner specialty foods place up the street from the Renegade, O' Riley's American Palate Designs. She signed the application *Megan Gaunt*, and used a set of random numbers as a social security number, but she had convinced the manager, who was a thin, librarian looking woman with a bun in her hair who wore long plaid dresses, that she would be better off paying her cash every night after her shift. The woman agreed, although in the back of her mind she would never know why she did.

Miranda found an apartment in the top floor above McAlister's that had been abandoned and unlived in for some time. The door had been locked, but locks were not a problem for Miranda. She would touch a door knob, and the tumbling lock mechanism inside would click and pop, and the knob would easily turn for her hands. Just in the same way that she could move about in the world almost unseen, Miranda had taken residence in the apartment in the top floor overlooking Little Traverse Bay, the small portion of Lake Michigan between Petoskey and Harbor Springs, just northwest across the bay.

Over the months she had been there she brought in a couple of chairs that she rarely used (she preferred to sit on the floor); a coffee table that only ever had a few classic novels found laying upon it, such as Jack Kerouac's *On the Road* and F. Scott Fitzgerald's *The Great Gatsby*; and four televisions that connected to a cable line that ran outside of the apartment off the small wooden balcony and down from the fire escape. She found that, when she wanted, she could take in all of the information being broadcast at once, even if the four televisions were on four different stations at a time.

There were other things she found as well, although like everything else, she did not know how to feel about them. When it occurred to her to do so, she would eat. It was in those moments when the delicious aroma from the fresh soups cooking down in the Roasted Renegade would capture her attention that she may venture to have a bowl, or whatever it may be that she came across to try. But she soon realized it was only to satisfy her taste, not her *need* to eat. The same was true for sleep. She could, if she wanted to, sleep for however long she chose, but she did not need to.

Many nights in early spring she sat out on the balcony overlooking the bay, seeing if she could count the stars in the sky, and she would often wonder if her parents were out there, somewhere in the vastness of it all. Her bitterness and self loathing would overtake her in moments like these, and she found it a nice distraction to venture down into the bookstore in the late night hours, long after the store had closed.

It had been rumored for years that the building that the bookstore was located in was haunted, and that was a fact that Miranda found to be true. In the many hours she had spent sitting alone in the dimly lit basement section of the bookstore, curled up on a soft cushioned arm chair reading book after book, she had noticed the little girl peeking at her from around the shelves.

The girl had a frilly party frock dress, with a rosebud trimming on the waist and a white, poplin collar. Her hair was blonde and cut shoulder length, and she had a tiny nose and thin lips. She looked to be somewhere between 10 and 12 years old. Her grey eyes stared at Miranda cautiously that first night, and at first, Miranda did not realize she was seeing a ghost.

"Hey. It's okay...you don't have to hide from me. I'm not going to hurt you," Miranda told the shy girl, who slowly began to step out from behind the tall shelf.

It was not long before Miranda saw that even though almost her entire upper body seemed solid and alive, her feet faded in and out of transparency. With the old style dress, it became clear to Miranda that the girl had been there for quite some time.

"What is your name?" Miranda asked the girl.

"My name is Miss Daniella Flock," the girl said nervously. "What is your name?"

"My name is Miranda. How do you do?"

Daniella bobbed a slight curtsy to Miranda, and replied that she was very well.

"Are you always here?" Miranda asked her, holding a smile on her face, trying not to frighten her away.

"Yes, I am...I don't know how long I have been here. People don't see me all too often, ma'am."

Miranda thought for a moment, then asked her, "Do you know what year it is, Daniella?"

"Why, silly, it's 1923, ma'am!" Daniella said with a snicker.

Over the next couple of months, Miranda would return night after night to the bookstore. She and Daniella would talk about the books around them, and Miranda would read her a new book almost every night. Daniella was happy to have her new friend. Miranda would never tell her that she had been there for nearly a century. She had thought to ask, on several occasions, if Daniella knew how and why she was there in the bookstore instead of somewhere else, but had decided that perhaps the question was better left alone.

Then came the night in mid-June, eight months after Miranda's world as she new it violently crashed to its end.

Like any of the other nights, Miranda went into the basement to meet Daniella and find a new book to read. Miranda sat on the floor in front of Daniella, and as she started to read, she stopped, and looked at Daniella.

"Have you ever tried to read these books yourself, Daniella?" asked Miranda.

"I can read...it's just...I have trouble holding the

books," she said coyly.

"Here," said Miranda, and held out *The Ocean at the End of the Lane* by Neil Gaiman. Daniella slowly reached out for the book. Miranda softly set it upon Daniella's fingertips, and she could feel the resistance from the weight of the book resting on Daniella's hand.

Miranda let go of the book, and the book stayed in Daniella's hands, and Daniella brought her eyes up to Miranda's; they smiled together, but only seconds later the book fell through Daniella's hands and dropped to the floor.

Daniella sighed, and dropped her chin, but Miranda was determined to give it another go.

"Don't worry, sweetie. Here. We'll try it again."

Miranda picked up the book, and Daniella held out her hands again, concentrating hard on keeping herself in a solid form. As Miranda lowered the book on to her hands once more, she reached beneath the book and held her hand beneath Danielle's hands to try and help her steady the book. When she did this, for the first time in all of the weeks she had read with Daniella, Miranda could physically feel Daniella's hand. The brief moment of joy was gone in a flash.

Miranda could see the little girl, scared and crying, yelling over and over again at someone in the darkness. What light there was in the room dimly came through the dirty old window panes of that very basement. A hand came out of the darkness and struck Daniella across the face, and she cried even harder.

"No, please no! You're hurting me!" cried Daniella, screaming toward the dark, shadowy figure before her.

"You shut that mouth, girl, or I will shut it for good!" yelled the deep voice back at Daniella.

A man's hands grabbed her wrist and tore at her dress;

the same dress that Miranda had always seen her in every single night.

"Please, Daddy...don't. Not any more..." pleaded Daniella. Daniella's father took the young girl forcefully and violently on the basement floor. Both during and after the vile act, he put his hands around her neck and squeezed tighter and tighter until she could plead and scream no more...and then she lied still on the dirty basement floor.

Miranda pulled away from Daniella, but it was too late. Not only had Miranda seen what had happened to the girl, but Daniella had seen it as well - lost and deeply buried somewhere far away to protect her innocent soul, but now everything was as if it were happening right now. Daniella looked at Miranda in horror, and screamed a blood curdling scream that shattered all of the windows and anything else made of glass in the entire room.

Daniella faded in and out of sight like a flickering fluorescent bulb on the verge of burning itself out, shaking violently before running into the wall that held an old, unused fireplace, disappearing into the stonework.

"Daniella! Wait! I'm...I'm sorry! Please...don't go..." pleaded Miranda, but Daniella did not return. Nor did she return the next night, or the night after that.

Miranda did not return to the basement after the third night without Daniella. She sat alone in the apartment all night and morning, on into the afternoon; the heavy humid dampness and heat filled the still air.

There were several items that had been in the apartment before she took it and made it her own; old lamps and newspapers, a box of books that had been stored in the empty rooms, some kitchen pots and pans laying scattered about, and so on.

Miranda's heart was broken once more, and she could not get out of her head what Daniella's father had done to that poor, innocent little girl. What the world had done to that little girl. What this world had done to *her*.

Miranda sat on the floor cross-legged in the middle of the apartment. The windows on both sides of the room were open, but no breeze came through the room. Just heat and thick, humid air was all anyone in the small city was feeling on that mid-June day. She was wearing her faded blue jeans and a white tank top which revealed the tattoo that she had gotten in the days after Daniella had disappeared.

It covered her entire back; the tops of the feathered angel wings rising high on her shoulders, with the feathers stretching down the sides of her back, transforming from feathers to a scale like design, on down to the tips of the wings resting low on her back, where they now had the appearance of leathery, bat-like wings with single horned claws.

She looked up at the four televisions before her. She was thinking about Daniella, and then she thought of Lorri...standing in the kitchen, smiling at her...and Robert, carrying her bags from the car every single time she had come home...and Steven, young and full of so much more life to be had.

The first television came on. The stereo Miranda had found at a resale shop boomed Moby's cover of Joy Division's "New Dawn Fades".

"Thirty-three people were killed today in a roadside bombing in southern Afghanistan..." the TV muttered as she stared at the screen. The second television lit up.

"And the police questioned friends and neighbors of the man who held the two young women for the past six years since they were 14-year-old junior high school students from the Boston area. The man, Joseph Stone, was found hanging in his bathroom when the girls were found, an apparent suicide after police received a tip."

Miranda's heart began to beat faster and faster, and she clenched her fists tighter...the third television clicked on...

"Walked in to the elementary school and started shooting, killing four 3rd grade students and a teacher before taking his own life. Authorities can find no motive for...

She didn't even realize that she had stopped breathing. Tears were running down her face, and her hands and arms were shaking. She closed her eyes tightly and the fourth television sparked to life...

"The young girl's uncle was taken into custody. Sources from the sheriff's department had indicated that the girl, Melody Parker, age 8, had been raped repeatedly over the past several months. Her body was found buried beneath the family home's back porch after an extensive search..."

The room was hotter inside than the temperature had reached outside by several degrees. The chair, the coffee table, the pots and pans, and books, even all four televisions were floating several inches off the floor, and Miranda's body trembled as she squeezed her fists so hard now her nails cut through her skin and blood seeped from her palms. The stereo lifted up as well, and the entire room began to shake, not violently, but enough for those in the store below to notice something was not right in the rooms above. Everything had a vibration to it in the building, and the floating items around Miranda started to crash and spark, and the plastered walls cracked all around the rooms in the entire apartment.

Miranda let out a loud gasp, and then opened her eyes wide, revealing the blackness like it had come that night at the tower. The tremors stopped cold, and everything in the air around the room that was hovering seconds before came crashing to the floors around Miranda. Powerful winds that came from inside the apartment blew out every window and door around her, sending shattered glass and splintered doors flying out onto the streets and back alley around the building.

The winds whipped through the streets of the Gaslight shopping and dining district of downtown Petoskey. People stopped in the streets, looking to the skies to see what was happening all of a sudden in the town that was only humid and still just moments before.

The outdoor patios of the Roasted Renegade and the bar and restaurant a few doors down cleared quickly as the winds rose steadily more, and onlookers were pointing towards the sky over the bay. The sky was quickly darkening, and where there were blue skies a few minutes before were now billowing, black clouds that rolled across the entire skyline. The thickest of the clouds roared with a low rumbling, not like a single instance of thunder, rolling into another; this was more like a slow, steadily building eruption climbing to its climax.

The winds caught a plastic tarp that was hanging from scaffolding outside the corner building where construction work was being done. The scaffold was three stories high, and the winds were strong enough now to push the tarp against the highest scaffold section, causing the entire structure to crash down across three cars, setting off car alarms to ring loud throughout the streets.

People ran for cover and safety in every direction. One mother tucked herself and her stroller with her twin toddlers into a doorway of a locked apartment building, wrapping her arms around the children, while another man was waving people from the street into the storefront of a clothing store.

The man looked to the sky over the bay as the thicker, blacker cloud was at least as large, if not larger than, the entire bay itself, stretching for miles. A loud boom echoed through the atmosphere as the cloud erupted with fire from within, filling the thick darkness with flashes of orange, red and yellow.

The men and women on the street that saw this stopped in their tracks, staring into the vast black behemoth that roared in the sky above. Another blast came, even louder than the first, shaking the ground and causing an even greater panic as everyone who had looked at the last fiery burst went running up the street, desperately seeking somewhere to hide for some semblance of safety.

Day had become night, until the entire canopy of darkness above ignited with a barrage of lightning-like blasts the color of fire that hammered at once into a single spot in the now vacant park near the intersection of two main streets that connect the eastern and western sections of the city. The resulting force of the impact of the blazing lightning sent a shock wave outward from its center, firing power and light poles like rockets in all directions, and sending mounds of earth up from the point of impact that acted like shrapnel, cutting through road surfaces and buildings in the immediate proximity of the blast.

Dust rose high in the air after the mighty wave had subsided, and the blackness above the city dissipated within minutes, back into the hazy blueness that dominated several minutes earlier.

There was silence in all directions. Electricity was out, and no voices could be heard in the city streets. The damage and devastation was incredible surrounding the impact site; the buildings closest to the blast looked as if a bomb had taken off the entire backsides of the structures, exposing rooms and hallways from inside, and no recognizable features or items could be distinguished within.

As the dust began to settle, the scene of the destruction was slowly and painfully being taken in by the residents and tourists of the proud northern town. No one took notice of the figure that appeared down on hands and knees in the center of the massive crater that now took the place that had once been a lush green park at the core of the city of Petoskey.

The man's hands lay upon the ground, first a stark white, but filling quickly with color against the pale gravel surface.

He stood up, and started to brush the dust from his white suit jacket and pants. His movements were fluid and precise; he adjusted the collar of his black, button down shirt that he wore beneath the white jacket.

His head was bowed to the ground, and finally, he lifted his chin to the sky, eyes closed at first, then opening them to the bright sun overhead that radiantly reflected the color of his thick blonde hair. His eyes were as black as the deepest midnight black, but soon changed in a seemingly relaxing manner to a pleasant, deep blue hue that likened to the color of the sky itself that hazy, humid afternoon.

The man gazed out across the bay, seemingly unaware or uncaring of the brutal destruction that was surrounding the very spot where he now stood.

He breathed in, tasting the air, licking the moisture that formed on his lips, and then he smiled. He took his first step forward...

...and the Devil walked the Earth once more.

## About the Author

RICK JUREWICZ is an avid lover of fantasy, sci-fi, horror and dark drama, and has been writing short stories and poetry most of his adult life, some of which has been featured in print publications and online. ***In the Shadows of Fate*** is Rick's first novel.

Rick and his family are lifelong residents of Northern Michigan.

Made in the USA
Middletown, DE
23 February 2021